### THE GAULT FAMILY

Rich and powerful beyond measure, they control every facet of the small town's life—except the brazen behavior of their son...

### KATE FELLOWS

Sophisticated yet tortured by hungers she cannot quell, she becomes a scapegoat for a whole town's fears...

### BILLY GOFORTH

The deputy sheriff with a forbidden love who must ultimately choose between his future and his principles...

### REVEREND DORR SEELY

The minister with the colossal ego, he concocts The Tenth Crusade—a quest for decency—and performs unspeakable acts with a teenager in a motel room...

### DUKE VENABLE

The upstanding county sheriff who's made a fortune from bootlegging and bribes...

### INEZ MACKLIN

Honey-colored beauty, worshipped by one man, brutalized by another...

### THE RAPIST

Striking terror in the hearts of everyone in town, he could be any of many men repressed by the false morality of...

# KING OF HEAVEN

# KING
## OF
# HEAVEN

## BURT HIRSCHFELD

BALLANTINE BOOKS • NEW YORK

# KING
## OF
# HEAVEN

## BURT HIRSCHFELD

BALLANTINE BOOKS • NEW YORK

Library of Congress Catalog Card Number: 82-90915

ISBN 0-345-29864-0

Manufactured in the United States of America

First Edition: May 1983

"Otis Ambrose Gault came into this section of Florida and went down on his knees and prayed to God for guidance. 'Drive out the heathen,' God told Otis Ambrose Gault. 'Drive out Mine enemies and make this place safe and good for My people in My name for I am the One and True God, Lord of the Universe, King of Heaven, and everything above and below.'"

—*Reverend Dorr C. P. Seely*

# CHAPTER
## 1

"COME IF YOU want," Goforth's wife said over the telephone, "but it won't do any good." And then she hung up.

He examined the dead instrument at length, faulting it for
not responding to the moral seriousness of his call. All his life
people had failed him; parents, women, friends. He learned to
exist inside a hard emotional barrier, committed to his work
and freed of personal responsibility to others or to guilt.

His body, his face, the slow way he moved and in low gear,
but with the implicit promise of a quick and violent response
to anyone who posed a threat. He had reptilian eyes, alert,
still, almost without color, seeing everything. His leathery cheeks
were tanned permanently by the sun, his jaw bony and strong,
set at an angle that announced that he was a man giving nothing
away. His mouth, under a full dark mustache, was sensual and
mobile, giving him an almost roguish look, at once misleading
and mysterious. His hair was black and thick, shaped to his
long narrow head, neither too long nor too short. Most men
thought him dangerous and kept their distance; women thought
him dangerous, and longed to get past the barrier.

1

He existed; cut off from his past, all that a haze of hopes and disappointments not meant to be examined. He existed; rejecting the future, for him there was only *now*. He existed; locked into a present turned shaky and refusing to hold.

Nothing fit, everything was out of place. The telephone on the wall of the ancient train station in the east end of King of Heaven. So sleek, so modern, so technically efficient. Attached to a building out of another era, a disturbing anomaly, a mass-produced snail clinging stubbornly to a hand-made, antiquated structure.

No one cared, no one even noticed. Less and less to matter. Only the job, the way a man did his w much of himself went into it, how much meaning give it. How much satisfaction there was to be tak A real man was what he did. Simple. . . .

The doors of the train station were nailed shut, the wi boarded up. Not much different, Goforth believed, than th unseen barriers of custom and tradition and myth that kept Tokeneke County enslaved to the old ways. A place quiet and slow-moving, comparatively untouched by the social and political convulsions that took place beyond the limits of the county, isolated, wary, and often afraid.

The spur line had been run through Tokeneke and into King of Heaven itself at the turn of the century, admitted grudgingly for fear of the alterations it would cause in the domestic way of life. But sound business reasoning had prevailed, as it always did in Tokeneke, and the spur was put to good use transporting the orange crop to markets in the North. A small concession: once a week on Thursday afternoons, a passenger train used to rumble into town, load up and quickly depart. Most folks were satisfied to remain in King of Heaven, in the county, profoundly convinced there was no better place to live anywhere.

But now the tracks were overgrown, the station in disrepair, the line labeled superfluous, obsolete, unprofitable, some twenty years ago. A victim of refrigerated express trucking on the Interstate Highways. Any citizen who wanted to depart King of Heaven was served best by Trailways, which ran a bus in to town twice a week.

Goforth went back to his patrol car and drove off without urgency. Everyone in King of Heaven, everything, existed in deliberate, natural rhythms: the tides out in the Gulf of Mexico, the high hot empty sky, the slow change of seasons. An antebellum town, wide streets lined with graceful Regency houses and neat lawns, enlivened by rose bushes and azaleas. Great spreading live oaks cooled the sidewalks in dappled patterns of light and shadow.

At this time of day the air was stagnant, heavy with the salt smell of the Gulf, oppressive on the skin. But in the air-conditioned patrol car, Goforth was comfortable, oblivious to the outside. He slowly circled Soldiers' and Sailors' Park with its marble and polished steel memorial, rimmed by hedges shaped like great awkward animals and birds. In the early morning heat the benches lining the crushed oyster shell paths were empty and even the gulls clustered in the shade as if to wait for the passing of the hot sun before winging out to sea.

Out past the high school, on to Fantasia, and around the weathered monument to Jefferson Davis set in a small plot of greenery that divided the avenue into separate lanes. Exactly a mile and a fifth along, the road squeezed down to a single-lane blacktop that curved through orange groves and on up-country. Here tiny parcels of land served as family farms with modest frame houses with open porches and used-up Fords or Chevys up on cinder blocks in the front yards. Out back, chickens and cows and horses were raised and there were vegetable gardens framed in protective chicken wire.

Children paused in their games to wave and Goforth waved back, some known to him, all familiar. The same unblinking blue eyes, the snubbed noses, the strong bodies and patient expressions, as if waiting for life to unreel predictably before them. Out here expectations were in short supply, something you learned early. Out here the lucky ones got to live as their parents lived and their parents before them. In Tokeneke County folks discovered sooner than later to avoid trouble, to be suspicious of new ways, to reject new ideas.

They clung to their roots here—the hard, mean facts of their lives, as well as the glorious myths in which they had invested so much of themselves. They believed passionately in their *Southernness*, in the purity and nobility of blood and history, in the bonds that linked them inexorably to town and to each other, allied against a changing world, alien, and forever threatening. They nurtured views constructed out of generations of bias, lives lived out within the narrow security of an emotional moat, their loyalties sharply focused and immutable. They were polite but paranoid, generous and mean-spirited, gentle and loving, and always dangerous to outsiders.

Goforth knew them well. He was a product of their prejudices and their dreams, their fears and their nightmares, their honor and their deceits. He had always been one of them, yet somehow apart. He cornered hard on Tango Road, trailing a long dust cloud, going toward the river.

How long had it been? Five weeks, nearer to six. Not seeing her even once, not even by accident downtown along Main Street. Or in the five-and-dime, or Mayberry's General Store, or Francine's Diner for a cup of coffee. Hard to believe that in a place smaller than a small city and only barely larger than a town you could keep from meeting your own wife.

There was some profit to it. No longer did he have to fight through those daily wars, those constant verbal skirmishes, struggling with the pointless, endless strain of trying to please her, of trying to be the man she really wanted, and always failing. He wondered why she had married him; obviously he had never come up to her standards. Life was easier without her, but no more satisfying. Trouble was he missed her, the look and the sound of her, the familiarity of her body, the way she smelled and the way she tasted.

There was, he decided, something profoundly wrong with him. Why else could he not live contentedly with Charlene? She was better'n most to look at, smart and often amusing with a quick, barbed tongue, a good woman around the house, honest, speaking her mind when it was in order. All virtues, all good. What in hell was wrong with him?

He recognized now the reason for his call. The reason he wanted to see her. He would admit his shortcomings and make her understand that he intended to reclaim their marriage, keep it going, make it better. He would try to express his feelings in words she would comprehend and appreciate. Soft loving words that would mend old wounds and bind them closer than before. He was going to do it.

The house was set back off the road at the end of a long gravel driveway in a stand of scrub pine, looking down at the river midway through the bend where it swept down toward the Gulf with no particular urgency. Out back, a deck built board and pile by Goforth without help, creosote-treated and stained. A private place to have a brew and read and doze, reflect on the way things were or might have been.

Charlene, in green polyester slacks and a contrasting sleeveless shirt, admitted him. "You want a beer?" She headed back into the bedroom. The slacks were tight across her bottom and he could see the line of her panties and he remembered again what a fine, voluptuous body she had. "There's some cold in the fridge."

He helped himself and went after her, taking up a position in the doorway. "The Years of Our Lives" was on the television and a suitcase was on the bed.

"Goin' somewhere?" he said.

"What?"

"Think you could turn down the sound?"

"What? Oh, sure, do it."

"There," he said. "Isn't that better?"

"What? Oh, I guess so. What is it?"

"I thought we could talk."

"Go on, talk."

"Goin' somewhere?"

"You betcha."

"Care to say where?"

"That's for me to know and you not to be concerned about."

Those gelid eyes assessed her gravely, as if trying to summon back a vagrant memory. "For long?" It wasn't going according to plan. Nothing ever had. Getting married; never wanted to do that. But he had. Never intended to become a peace officer and spend his days chasing speeders and busting teenagers under the influence of too much bootleg. But here he was, deputy sheriff in Tokeneke County, his days relatively unmarked, spending the time of his life without consideration, holding on. To what?

"Forever," she answered.

The word brought him around as if to deflect a blow, fearful of what came next. "Ten years," he said.

"What?" She never stopped folding and packing. She worked swiftly, efficiently, a very neat person.

"We been married ten years."

"I saw a lawyer."

He didn't know what to say. "Old man Lockman?"

"Don't matter who. Nobody around here. A out-of-town lawyer, out of county, okay?"

That convinced him. "You really mean it?"

"It's time it ended."

Loss and failure, familiar reactions. The building blocks on which his life had been constructed. He yearned to make a major pronouncement, something searing and penetrating to turn it around, to make things right between them. He looked at the television, a mocking eye. What he said was, "Just like that?"

She snickered and faced him. "Hah! Two years fightin' an' fussin' and livin' like strangers."

"You blame me."

"No blame attached. 'Cept as it comes down on us both."

"I always meant to do right by you."

"Meant to do and doin' so is not the same thing."

"Kids, if we had kids it might've been different."

"Kids. You never wanted kids."

"I never wanted any, but I never really didn't want 'em, either. Maybe if you'd've insisted."

"All those years, Billy, I went along with you. I figured you was a god almost. I feared goin' up against you on anything. No way I could insist on anything back then."

"We could still have a kid."

"You're forty, almost forty-one. I'm thirty-nine. My time for havin' kids is over with."

"You're healthy, strong, still a fine-lookin' woman."

"Ah, Billy, all you cared about was the job. Gettin' it right, bein' a good peace officer, servin' the people. That was your life, that and playin' cards with those pals of yours and drinkin' beer, bein' a deputy. That don't cut it with me anymore. I want somethin' else."

"What? What do you want?"

"More, I reckon. Better."

"I don't understand."

"No, I suppose you don't. I don't mean to hurt you, Billy, but you were never here when I needed you."

"That's not fair."

"Where in hell you been these last few years? Where you been?"

"Makin a livin' for us, paying for this house."

"I never wanted the house. Sittin' out here on the river all by my own self. Nothin' to do, nobody to talk to, sittin' and waitin' for you to get home."

"You were always married to that hellish television," he said.

She slammed the suitcase shut, locked it. "You never were here."

"You knew who I was, what I was, when you married me. That was enough for you back then."

She straightened up and faced him. There was regret in her voice when she spoke. "I knew. I knew about you breakin' your back out at the sawmill, about workin' for Miss Ivy when she ran girls in and out of that ol' prefab buildin' of hers. You bounced drunks and kept the whores safe and you swore you never hurt anybody any more'n you had to, and you were proud of that. And I was proud of you, Billy, that you were rougher and stronger than most, but gentler inside and fair. You always were a fair man."

She breathed deeply as if seeking some reason to go on. "You used to talk about makin' something of yourself. Said you was plannin' to go to law school. . . ."

"And I did."

"And you did. Until Duke Venable talked you into becomin' a deputy sheriff. . . ."

"It got some cash income comin' our way."

"I admired it, back then. How hard you worked, studyin' and bein' a deputy. I certainly did admire you back then, Billy. You were different than any man I ever met, better'n any I met." She broke off and her lips squeezed to a flat line and she carried the suitcase into the living room. "No hard feelin's on my part," she said over her shoulder. "Just didn't wash out for us is all."

"Where'd we go wrong?"

"You got yourself all stoked up on the job, on becomin' sheriff. Never did like it here, Billy. Tokeneke's the same today as it was last year or the year before that. Never changin', folks clutchin' at yesterday for fear they might drown if they was to let go. There's another world outside and I want my share of it."

"I'm not sure I know what you're talkin' about."

"Maybe someday you will."

"You aim to get a divorce?"

"Seems like the thing to do, don't it? What brought you out here today, Billy?"

He made a gesture of dismissal, abrupt and almost defensive. "Nothin' that matters." He arranged a smile on his strongly planed face. "Take good care of yourself, Charlene, you hear me?"

"You the same."

# CHAPTER
## 2

THERE WAS NOTHING static about Kate Fellows. Even asleep she seemed poised to spring into motion, her body coiled and tense, one arm reaching as if for balance. A great fall of nearly orange hair spilled across the pillow framing her face—delicate bones and shadowed hollows, softened by a wide and lush mouth.

She woke minutes before the alarm went off, a habit of her childhood when to oversleep was considered slothful and indolent, on the edge of being a sin against Lord Jesus Himself. Still wearing the lightweight pajamas she had slept in, she did her exercises; clasped hands coming overhead then swinging down between her spread legs, alternately off to each side. Next, onto her back on the floor; fifty situps, fifty legups, twenty-five pushups. A thin film of sweat coated her tawny skin.

She stripped off the pajamas and donned panties and bra and a blue and red running suit. She was halfway to the door when the phone brought her back.

9

"I wake you?" There was that pinched, almost mocking challenge in his voice, a voice surprisingly adolescent over the phone. How odd that he should remind her of her mother; she wondered what his reaction would be if she told him?

"I'm on my way out."

"Working out." He made it into a taunt, an accusation. He laughed. "You're in better shape than I am, in more ways than one." It *was* the voice, she decided; the same chattiness as her mother, with a suggestion of real concern, yet edged with malice, sharply probing and so often hurtful.

"Why this early call, Wesley?"

"What if I come over?" Never a direct declaration of intent, of desire. Never a polite question. Never a cry for help, for succor, for warmth and safety; Wesley, like her mother, admitted to no private flaws, no human wants, no weaknesses of body or soul.

"Now?" A shiver twisted down her spine. How many men like Wesley Gault had she known? Men who made her tremble with passion and guilt, men who provoked her libido and dulled her sensitivity, left her feeble and yearning to do their bidding in all things. How many men whose domineering aura reduced her to willing victim? And always they ended it, left her alone with harsh memories and unfulfilled needs of her own.

"Shall I tell you what talkin' to you over the phone this way does to me?" he said huskily.

She didn't want to hear it, but on the screen of her mind she saw him, naked, strong, looming over her hard and quivering. She shivered again. "This way of doing things, Wesley. You know I don't like it."

"You know how it is, I need time to work out my life. I'm comin' over."

"No. No, not now. Where's your wife?"

"Mae-Mae? Sacked out as usual. Besides, sugar, I have got me an early business meetin' at the bank which leaves me a fine opportunity to spend some time with the most beautiful woman in the world. . . ."

"Time enough for a quickie."

"Now, honey, you know how I feel about you." He giggled, pleased with himself. "I'll be over in a few minutes. . . ."

"And what if someone sees you coming out of my apartment? You know King of Heaven better than I do, how long would I last?"

He spoke without embarrassment or concern. "About as long as it would take for word to reach that little ol' stuffed shirt B. J. Moody is how long. But I'll make sure nobody sees me, hon."

"Then don't blame me for saying no."

His voice grew throatier, more insinuating. "I got to tell you how much I am achin' to lay hands on that magnificent body of yours, to do you up, down and sideways...."

"Wesley, I am too old to get into an obscene telephone call with you. Especially," she added lightly, "at this ungodly hour of the day."

Encouraged, he went on. "Shall I tell you exactly what I'd like to do to you right this instant? Shall I describe in detail what is happenin' to me as I talk to you, this very minute? Shall I tell—"

"Shut up, Wesley." She was laughing. "I ought to have my head examined, letting you sweet-talk me. I'm old enough to know better."

"Meet me. I'll hire us a motel room."

"No."

"Somewhere safe."

"No place around here is safe."

"We can drive over to Alabama and—"

"There's still Mae-Mae."

"That little twit. I am goin' to get shuck of her, sure as I'm talkin' to you. She is a pain, a duly certifiable pain...."

"I've got to hang up, Wesley."

"Meet me."

"Uh-uh."

"A man in my condition, I'm liable to perform some socially unacceptable act."

"Take it out on your wife."

"Anybody ever tell you you have a filthy mind, teacher-lady? Meet me."

"No way."

"I'll get me another woman."

"You won't find it hard to do." The thought was troubling, made her again aware of her vulnerability. She was a woman out of place in King of Heaven and her relationship with Wesley Gault was oppressive, threatening, but only to her. When it ended—and certainly it would end one day—he could go on living here, she could not. "Pay a visit to Miss Ivy's, Wesley," she said, anxious to see him.

"I might just do that," he said, before he hung up.

She stared at the dead phone in her hand and decided it was time to call Hank Berger, her agent in New York. Never could tell when she might need a friend, an advisor, someone to help her find a job.

By the time Kate arrived at the college theater, the cast had begun running through the last act. She took a seat at the rear of the auditorium, once again admiring the technical advantages of the building. The acoustics were superb, each word the actors spoke carrying easily to the rear rows, and the sight lines were all excellent, with no obstructed views. The stage was flexible, thrust out into the hall for this production, with banks of seats rising steeply on three sides. Backstage, offices, rehearsal rooms and dance studios, workshops where scenery could be constructed efficiently and quickly.

But there the advantages over professional theater companies ended. No amount of makeup could transform a twenty-year-old Floridian into a neurotic New England Catholic. Nor could the magic of costume and light convincingly make one of her students into an aging matinee idol. Nor did the actors own the controlled vigor and talent and experience vital to cause the play to come alive as it deserved. The student director had done his best; it wasn't enough. Not yet, perhaps never. Still, it was a reasonably solid production and should satisfy the audience it would draw.

Broadway. Regret coursed through her body and her mind reached back. She longed to appear again on a New York stage, to perform for the most sophisticated audiences, to work with the best actors, the best directors, creators, people excited by what they did, by what they dreamed, by all the tomorrows that lay ahead. Until the other reality intruded. The extended periods out of work. The repeated rejections. The diminished sense of self that so often enveloped an actress, the swollen denial of worth and the sense of hopelessness that finally sent her off in search of some other kind of life. A life with security, with respect for her as a person, a life with continuity and conviction and reward. The search brought her to Gault Christian. And kept her in King of Heaven, Florida. But under her skin crawled the worm of discontent, never fully satisfied no matter what nourishment it was offered.

The rehearsal ended.

She and the student director exchanged comments. She offered suggestions. With the certainty of inexperience and youth, he rejected them all. She smiled, she soothed his ego, she assured him he was on the right track, and retreated across the set toward the area backstage and her office in the wing behind it.

She stopped at the electric coffee maker and filled a cup. She loathed Styrofoam and wondered how many coffees she had drunk out of how many such cups. A student stagehand smiled her way in admiration and supplication. She put a name to the pretty face.

"How's it going, Jody?"

"Just fine, Miss Fellows. I just love the play."

"It's a fine piece of work."

"I hope I get to play in something as good some day."

"Your turn will come. You're a sophomore, aren't you?"

"Freshman."

"There you are, plenty of time."

"I wonder, Miss Fellows, if you could spare me a couple of minutes? I'd sure like to talk to you."

Kate assessed the girl gravely. Pretty and blond, but not nearly as pretty as she would be when she matured. Still unformed with a slender athletic body, almost boyish in the bony set of her shoulders, and the way she held her head, tilted and curious. Kate smiled.

"About what?"

Jody was surprised. "Why, about my career in the theater, of course."

"Of course." Kate spoke soberly. "Check with my secretary and she'll set up an appointment." She turned and headed toward her office, aware of the admiring glance that followed her. When Jody Joiner grew up she wanted to be just like Kate Fellows. Confident and beautiful and smart.

Well, almost like her. More talented, naturally, and much more successful. Famous, actually. Famous and rich and an international movie star. And certainly not stuck away forever in some backwoods Florida redneck college, out of touch with all the exciting and glamorous things going on in the world. No way Jody was about to let that happen. No way at all.

# CHAPTER
## 3

WHEN HE THOUGHT back on it, Goforth damned that night.
Damned the bad luck that drew him to Silver Sands that night
that caused him to find Inez Macklin up between the dunes.
Damned hearing her feeble cries for help. Damned the grotesque impulse that led him to become a peace officer in the
first place.

Fact was Goforth would never have gone there if not for
the trouble with Charlene. 'Course, trouble with his wife was
nothing new to Goforth. Not then, not for the ten years or so
they'd been together. Trouble was a regular guest in their house,
regular but not welcome, as far as Goforth was concerned.

Thing was, Charlene was a dancer. Always had been. Woman
seemed to shimmy and shake even when sitting in place. Thing
was, dancing was forbidden by ordinance in Tokeneke County,
likewise the sale of alcoholic beverages by the drink or by the
bottle. There were no bars in Tokeneke, no nightclubs or discos,
no package stores, no beer parlors. There were, however, sixty-
eight churches in the county, and one motion picture theater.

The churches were open and active seven days a week, day and night. The motion picture theater gave a single showing each night, closed on Sundays, Christmas and Good Friday. No exceptions made.

But there were folks in Tokeneke who just had to belly up to a bar for their drinking whiskey; they could drive across the county line to indulge themselves.

Fact was anybody who solemnly craved a drink and couldn't abide all that driving could just put himself into the back room at Fred Abernathy's grocery and meat market a block back toward the beach from Courthouse Square and drink his fill in comfort and seclusion, if not luxury. Richer folks, the executives who worked at the Gault Concentrate Plant or the paper mill or the factory out on the edge of The Bottoms where women's dresses were cut and sewn according to patterns sent down from New York City, those folks went out to Tokeneke Field Club. There drinks were openly served and no money ever changed hands, chits being the accepted method of transacting business. Younger folks patronized Patsy's which always had a five-piece combo playing music along with a large sign forbidding dancing on the premises. At Patsy's you brown-bagged your bottle and danced, if that was your pleasure, and no one stopped you.

But Charlene had always said the back room at Abernathy's was grungy and Patsy's was for kids and they didn't belong to the Field Club, naturally. They didn't go out dancing or drinking very much or even to a movie. From time to time Charlene complained. Turned fierce. Yelling and calling names and saying as how they never did anything, never went anywhere, never had *fun*. That life with him was no *fun* anymore.

Maybe so. Only there was a lot more to it than just *fun*. Their marriage, that is. Butting heads more than less. Never getting enough. Of anything. Not loving, not talking, hardly ever talking, not about a single thing that mattered. And that was not all Goforth's doing, not by a long shot. The poets were wrong about love; never did conquer all. Not a single time. Just scrambled a man's brains to where most of the time he didn't know which way was up. Nor care.

On the beach this night he went over it all in his mind. Ten years of marriage, a lot of it good, the recent times bad. All of it had a value, he needed it to have a value, meaning beyond his own understanding.

He advanced along the beach hearing the slap of the small waves on the sand in counterpoint to the night noises. The waters of the Gulf stretched into shadowed mystery all the way down to the Yucatan, with no sounds of man at work or at play to intrude. The natural order of things, the way he remembered it when he was a boy. The way so much of it still was in King of Heaven, the way it was supposed to be.

He lit a cigarette and in the flare of the match spied a sand crab scuttling from one hiding place to another. As a boy, he had hunted at night, armed with a flashlight and a bucket. Run them down, trap them by hand, dump them in the bucket for safekeeping. Made good eating, and all for free. He supposed kids still hunted crabs at night. But not on Silver Sands, not so's you could see.

He went on sniffing the air. Soon the weather would change. Cool nights, cool enough to be good for the oranges, but not so cold as to freeze them. Of course, there were the cold spells. Somehow surprising to the owners of the citrus groves, no matter that they came almost every season. Out came the smoke pots, panic up and down the state, headlines shouting out the news of economic disaster, as if it were the first time. Every year the same. No one learned. No one remembered.

Except Goforth. He remembered. Boy and man, he had worked in Papa James Gault's groves. Twelve hours a day, boxing oranges, hoisting the heavy crates onto waiting trucks. Or doing stoop labor in Papa James' cotton fields. Niggerwork they called it, not fit for a white man. But plenty of whites were doing niggerwork back then, plenty had to. Or go without.

Goforth remembered. He swore to make it out of the fields and the groves, to escape the factory or the plant, or the work gangs out on the roads laying in culverts or building up bridges. And by God and by Jesus he'd done it.

Become Senior Deputy. Best man on the force, no doubt about it. With more'n a fighting chance to move on up to sheriff, when the time came.

The heat of the cigarette burned Goforth's fingers and he flicked it aside. As an afterthought, he ground the smoldering butt into the sand, covered it up. He kept on walking, an angular

man with wide shoulders and a long, measured stride, reptilian
eyes searching the night ahead.

Back of the dunes, the great houses of the managers of
Tokeneke under Papa James: the managers, the bankers, the
politicians, the executives, the rich and the powerful. But no
freer of the folks up on The Hill than Goforth was, or some
sorry colored lady doing their laundry or minding their babies.

On past the Richardson place, an alien sound brought him
up short, senses cocked, coming up on the balls of his booted
feet. Ahead, and to the rear, the hardpack was deserted. Higher
up, no movement, no hint of trouble. His muscles went slack
and he began the return trip.

This time, when it came, there was no mistaking it. A call
for help. He went up onto the dunes, sea oats going down under
each footfall, hand resting securely on the butt of his issue
.357 Magnum.

He felt no fear. Fear no longer played a part on the job.
There were things to be done, he was expected to do them. He
expected himself to do them. And he did. Committed, wholly
captured by the idea of being a peace officer and what that
implied. He was past the last house on the strand, pushing
through the rough scrub and brambles, flashlight in his left
hand. A sudden sibilance brought him around, the beam reaching ahead like a long soft finger. A ghostly shape in the dune
grass halted him, knees bent, right arm extended, the Magnum
steady in hand. He took two steps ahead and brought the light
down.

On the sand, on her stomach, a woman almost naked. Across
her shoulders, the remnants of what had once been a blouse.
She struggled to push herself up and fell back, breathing harsh,
crying weakly. He knelt, holstering the pistol, careful not to
touch her.

"I'm a deputy, miss."

She tried to crawl away, the effort forcing thick exhalations
out of her. She was young, her back tapered and strong, her
buttocks high and tightly clenched. Her legs were long and
shapely. When he touched her shoulder, she screamed and
rolled away, coming to rest along a ridge of sand on her back.
He went after her. Bruises and cuts had transformed her face
into a grotesque mask, blood oozing. Her eyes were swollen

and her lips puffed, twisted out of shape. At his approach, she recoiled, whimpering.

"Who did this to you?"

"Don't hit me again, please don't."

He played the light along her body. Where her thighs met, a glistening trickle. Semen. Goforth snapped off the light and crouched alongside her. Someone had brought her here, flown into a rage when she resisted his advances, beaten her and raped her.

He straightened up. "I'm goin' to call for some help, miss."

Her mouth fell open. "Please, please. I'm so afraid. I hurt so much. Please don't leave me."

He tried to explain that in order to radio for assistance he had to return to his squad car, thought better of it. "I'm goin' to carry you on down to my car, miss, ride you out to the hospital. Won't be easy so you just grit your teeth and hang on to me, hear?"

She was heavier than she looked. A very solidly constructed woman, her skin surprisingly velvety and warm under his hands. Halfway back to the car a heaviness came into his crotch, and he was ashamed, glad she couldn't know about him. It wasn't until much later that he learned her name was Inez.

# CHAPTER
## 4

LAVERNE MILLICENT GAULT Christian College was named after its founder, Papa James' mother. A lady of impeccable Baptist credentials, she admitted to little formal education, a lack LaVerne Millicent held to be unconscionable. Gault Christian was the result.

Originally intended to be a finishing school for the finest young ladies of North Florida and Southern Alabama, it ran upon hard times during the Great Depression. Substantial infusions of Gault money failed to remedy the problems and it became clear, even to LaVerne Millicent, that changes were in order. By matriarchal fiat Gault Christian was upgraded to a full-fledged college. Eventually. Inevitably. Thanks to certain cash payments from the Gault family to certain members of the legislature in Tallahassee.

In 1945, with World War II coming to an end, and in an effort to capitalize on the G. I. Bill of Rights, Gault Christian, by a vote of the trustees, and the concurrence of the then president, and on direct orders from Papa James, went coeducational. Urinals were installed, discreetly.

The present student population stood at three thousand, with

21

a faculty ratio of one to twenty. A current joke on campus claimed that an education at Gault Christian was equal to that provided at any good high school in the country. B. J. Moody, president of the school and a staunch advocate of decency, discipline and devotion to learning on the minds and morals of young Americans, would have taken umbrage had he heard. But such witticisms were always pronounced behind his ample back.

Gault Christian was deliberately reminiscent of the Old South, recreated ante-bellum mansions complete with columned porticos and covered walkways. Only occasionally a jarring note; a more contemporary structure thrown up to accommodate the college's growth: the science laboratory, the library—its stacks filled with books chosen for moral content and good, clean language, the new theater arts building, containing classrooms, rehearsal halls, dance and music studios and an auditorium that could seat nine hundred people. All set down on the rolling pastoral slope along the edge of Lake Ranaqua, its crushed-shell pathways lined with magnolia trees dripping Spanish moss. Year round the slow-moving air was heavy with the sweet fresh scent of the orange groves which circled the college and in which industrious students might earn spending money by picking the ripe fruit.

The administrative offices were in a building set behind the James Ira Gault Chapel—Gault Cathedral, some called it without a smile—in which all students were expected to attend daily morning services.

In his no-nonsense office overlooking the parking lot, President B. J. Moody held forth, dealing with administrative affairs, struggling to raise monies for the endowment fund, upgrading academic standards, fighting off the incessant demands of faculty and maintenance for more of this and more of that, dispensing appropriate punishment to those students who refused to follow the very fair, very reasonable Christian rules by which the school was governed:

No smoking on campus.
No student drinking at any time, anywhere.
No dancing on campus.
No loud music.

Male and female students must remain at least three feet apart at all times; no physical contact permitted.

Rules, as B. J. Moody often pointed out, were made to be observed.

Transgressors suffered swift and certain retribution. Those who would not learn did not remain long at Gault Christian.

Privately Moody was a man of lukewarm commitments. Even his religious beliefs simmered rather than boiled, though he never let on. He was a Christian, he was a Baptist, necessary prerequisites for anyone holding his job, facts the Search Committee had noticed when making its choice.

He was a careful man who displayed no arrogance toward his betters, no weakness toward his inferiors. He worked hard to get along, determined to make no waves. He permitted no one else to muddy his waters.

How well he had done. Not yet forty years old and president of a college, with more and better still to come. Another year or two in King of Heaven then on to greater glory. Perhaps a state university or even a substantial private institution. There were no limits to the strides he could yet make. Definitely would make.

It was late afternoon and the westering sun cast long, cooling shadows across the orange groves, the college, down to the edge of Lake Ranaqua. It was B. J. Moody's favorite time of day, tranquil, slow, the campus relatively still now, most students concealed in their dormitory rooms or in the Greek letter houses that ringed the school. He made his way without urgency to the second floor of the Theater Arts Building, and the studios of WLMG, the college radio station.

He savored the upcoming meeting—brief as it would necessarily be—with Kate Fellows. Three years ago he had hired her, and ever since watched with considerable pride while she created the School of Theater Arts out of an idea and a dream. It was, thanks to her fine intelligence and hard work, an outstanding department with a growing and active student body. Soon, Moody was convinced, the world of academic theater would rank Kate Fellows with Paul Baker and Robert Brustein. Her student productions were skillfully staged, artistically envisioned, a compliment to B. J. Moody's administration, to the acuity of his hiring practices.

She was also, he amended with silent glee, the best-looking female in all of Tokeneke County.

Stunning, in fact. Tall with a finely turned body, full at bosom and bottom. Her features were delicate, in contrast to the darkly sensual cast of her mouth. Sea-green eyes gazed out past finely etched cheekbones with a hint of mockery, as if she recognized the absurdity and futility of human endeavor. All framed in an electric circle of orange-colored hair that made her seem years younger than she was.

More than once Moody conjured up visions of Kate Fellows naked, caught in the throes of an unholy passion, an unruly need that imprisoned her, enslaved her, to be released only by him at his whim and his pleasure. Idle fantasy, not to be entertained seriously, not to be indulged. For B. J. Moody was very much married to Mrs. Moody and it was always when he lay straining and panting in her chubby arms that these visions came to him. And as surely as God made little green apples, B. J. Moody knew that in his heart he was a sinner of monumental proportions. But he was not about to let on.

WLMG; Christian Voice of the New South.

The slogan had been Moody's idea, and he was inordinately proud of it. Proud too of the student broadcasts, each in harmony with the philosophy and moral principles on which Gault Christian College had been established and was still administered.

Kate ran the station, directed many of its programs, created and expanded its audience until WLMG was among the most powerful and influential broadcasting voices in the Deep South.

Kate was waiting in the reception room when he appeared, coming forward to greet him, a pleasant smile spreading her delicately shaped lips. She moved gracefully in that slow, sinuous way of hers, as if every step, every motion, had been planned and rehearsed. He took her hand in both of his, fingertips stroking the smooth skin at her wrist.

"How good of you to invite me," he said.

"Under the circumstances, it seemed politic for you to be present."

He looked around inquiringly. "Always ready to help my favorite teacher."

"Reverend Seely is waiting in studio B."

"Shall we join him, then?"

"One thing," she said. He turned back to her. "Dress rehearsal coming up. All of us would be honored if you would attend, you and Mrs. Moody."

Another play. Most of them were talky, too passive for his taste, too crowded with unsettling ideas and images. This one: He could recall neither title nor author. Never mind, there were better ways to spend his time.

*"Long Day's Journey Into Night,"* she said.

He shifted uncomfortably. "Yes, I know." Was that by that Tennessee Williams fellow? Never did care for his plays, too frankly sexual with frightening undertones best left to private meanderings. Or was this one by that Brooklyn Jew, the one who divorced the movie star; God, what a piece of work she had been.

"O'Neill's best work," Kate said.

"Eugene O'Neill," he murmured. Irish-Catholic, of course. Papists were not welcomed with enthusiasm in Tokeneke County, but better a Catholic than one of those strange New York intellectual-atheist types with their destructive and dirty ideas.

"When?" he said.

"Tomorrow evening." Offered with one of her more inviting smiles.

He had to smile in return. "What a shame, Mrs. Moody's cousins from Savannah . . ."

"Family obligations. . . ."

"You understand."

"If you'd like, I can supply extra tickets."

"Not at all, no special treatment. A subsequent performance, I'll make every effort. Now, shall we see what it is the good Reverend wants of us . . . ? "

He trailed her into the studio and produced a smile of greeting for the man waiting for them. Reverend Dorr C. P. Seely was tall, lean, with the residual grace of a middle-aging athlete. His features were distinctly etched, each separate and seemingly unrelated, with a bony jawline aggressively tilted. Even at his ease, Seely appeared braced against the wind, pale eyes peering into the distance as if looking for an unwelcome visitor.

His handshake was firm, restrained, and brief.

"Good of you to see me, B. J." He issued words one at a time, determined to avoid any misunderstanding. A careful man, a watchful man. "And you, too, Miss Fellows," he added, as an afterthought. When she smiled, he jerked his eyes away as if to maintain that even this transient contact was to risk being contaminated.

"How may we help you, Dorr?" Moody said. He admired the look of the preacher, big, rawboned, powerful, a man designed by the Lord Himself to carry the good fight against His enemies. But Moody also feared him, feared the festering rage he perceived under that polite and carefully controlled facade.

"I am a man of God," Seely intoned in a voice Biblical and incantatory, the voice of someone used to speaking to large assemblages in great halls. "And it is my destiny to bring the word of our Lord Christ Jesus to as many believers and heathens as is possible." His eyes went from Moody to Kate and ended on some point in space unseen by anyone else.

Kate shivered. Seely frightened her, the hard gaze of a desert prophet, the almost palpable tension in his stance, the tightness around his wide mouth. He was, she knew, a True Believer, the most dangerous kind of man.

"Twenty years a minister," Seely said. "And I have yet to do God's work in all of its wondrous possibilities. I aim to finally rouse my auditors to the passion and glory due Our Lord Christ Jesus, Amen." The blaze went out of his eyes and his voice softened. "We are each only signposts for men to follow to Christ, those of us who preach the gospel. Is that not so, B. J.?"

"Well put, Dorr."

"Miss Fellows? You don't agree?"

She attempted a smile. "Anyone who has listened to you preach, Reverend Seely, will never forget the experience."

He nodded once, brought a clenched hand up as if to strike. "I do not like what I see around me. What I hear. What I sense. The old values are being cast aside for new and disturbing beliefs. Harmful ways. Destructive acts against man, society, and God Himself. Our very existence as Christians and as Americans is threatened. Look at our very sweet home of King of Heaven. Even as we speak our ways and our traditions are under attack."

When no one challenged the assertion, he went on. "Changes and threats of changes. We are compelled to alter our way of life to suit the insidious desires of outsiders, strangers, a different kind of folk. Foreigners."

A fugitive thought fled through Kate's brain—familiar, faint, troublesome—eluding examination. "I don't understand," she said.

He eyed her severely. "Take the black folks, the bold way they meet a white man's eyes nowadays. The rude way of talkin' the young ones have. The hostile manner in which they drive their automobiles.

"I hear talk of organizers comin' in to organize the field workers, the folks who work in the plants, on the farms. Dissatisfaction runs rampant in the nation and it is comin' down here to King of Heaven. There are plans to build subsidized low-cost housing out in the county. Who will live in those places? Strangers, welfare cases, people who refuse to do their share to keep up the high standards of our lives. The people of Tokeneke County have got to rise up against the interlopers and be as one before God and the flag."

A twinge of apprehension squeezed Moody's bowels. There was a mean and cruel presence in Dorr Seely. He was a man bent on getting close to trouble, creating conflict, sidling up to where bones got broken and blood got spilled. "There's thunder and lightnin' in you, Dorr."

"I am a man of conviction, of deep beliefs, of powerful passions. . . ."

"How may we help you?"

Seely waved one big arm. "This radio station of yours . . ."

"Just about the finest in North Central Florida . . ."

"It certainly is. Fact is, I would consider it a friendly act if a certain amount of air time were made available to me so that I might send the holy words of the Lord God Himself to the thousands, hundreds of thousands, maybe as many as two million, my research tells me, good people in our fair state, in South Alabama and Mississippi, even to those sports fishermen out in the Gulf, to all good Christians who need to hear God's unadulterated words."

Kate said, "You want us to broadcast your Sunday sermons?"

His smile was mirthless. "I am offerin' to do a full hour of air time each evenin' for which I would supply a taped broadcast. Broadcasts of such importance and vitality that folks are bound to be summoned to stand before their Maker and look to Him for guidance. Poor souls cryin' out for aid that I can surely bring to them."

"One hour a night," Moody said reflectively. "That is a great deal of time, Dorr."

Seely's mouth flattened out. "I had me a meetin' with Papa James and Mr. Nolan and they believe, as do I, that we are comin' up against a crucial moment in history when the future is waitin' to be grasped. Our time to fight for what is right is upon us. We must struggle against the anti-Christ who would take over our town, our county, our people. . . ."

"One hour a night," Moody said. "That is prime time, expensive. . . ."

Seely frowned. The cold pale eyes shifted across Moody's face. "The love and worship of God cannot be measured in dollars and cents. I am talkin' about Christ Jesus, the Holy Spirit, you are talkin' about money. . . ."

"You say you spoke to the Gaults?"

"They are behind me every step. We are goin' to enlist the righteous folk of the county in our crusade."

"Crusade?" Kate said.

"A crusade to save King of Heaven from the Philistines."

Moody cleared his throat. "May I ask one or two questions, Dorr?"

"Ask them of the people on The Hill."

Moody stepped back as if struck. "There's no need for that. I mean, if the Gault's are supportin' you . . ."

"They are."

"Then certainly I am."

"Good."

"When do you want to begin the broadcasts?"

Seely looked over at Kate. "Just as soon as we can pull it all together, with your help, kind lady. Let's say before the end of the week. . . ."

# CHAPTER
## 5

THIS WAS TOKENEKE COUNTY. Established 1847, two years after Florida was admitted to the Union. Created out of sand and scrub pine and a great deal of watery swamp land by Otis Ambrose Gault, a small hard man with grandiose ideas. Earlier in his life, Otis Gault had led a force of adventurers into Central America in an attempt to set up his own nation. Native forces turned him back with an excessive loss of blood, fortune and life, none of it his. Bitter and angry that the United States of America had failed to support him in his overseas endeavor, Gault returned to Florida and proceeded to make his dreams come true closer to home.

He led his men against the Tokeneke Indians, a small, peaceful tribe distantly related to the Seminoles. In a matter of weeks he had either killed or driven off all of the Indians, burning their villages and their crops. This done Gault staked out a claim to a trapezoidal area running north and south, bounded by the Gulf of Mexico on one side and the ambitions of other more powerful forces on the other. He named it after the tribe he had destroyed, the name pleasant to his ear.

Having waged war and imposed peace, Gault put his people to work building a house for himself on a low rise within eyeshot of the Gulf. Only when the work was completed—the house, barns, stables and fences that enclosed some ten thousand acres—did he encourage his followers to build for themselves. He deeded over sections of land he had never owned in the first place on which to settle, each to farm as he wished, reminding each of his obligations to The Hill, as his place came to be known. This done, he established a county seat, facing the Gulf and spreading out from behind the beaches in neatly squared off rows, all off a central green which in time came to be called Courthouse Square. The town was named King of Heaven, an indication of Gault's dependence on Divine guidance and benevolence. He caused a church to be erected, white and pristine with a tall steeple and a minister who spoke endlessly of sin and sensuality and obedience to authority. That minister lived long and died a contented and wealthy man.

Growth in and around King of Heaven was carefully scrutinized, minutely dissected, and usually postponed. Newcomers were discouraged from settling. Businesses were examined at length and only reluctantly admitted to trade in the town. Restrictions on housing were rigidly enforced. The black people of King of Heaven were relegated to the west side of the Tokeneke River, from where it emptied into the Gulf to a point five miles north where it bent on its meandering course up into Georgia. A bridge was constructed across the river when it was determined that without cheap black labor the oranges would remain unpicked, the cotton unplucked, the laundry and much of the housework around town left undone. At night the blacks withdrew to Northtown, as their section was called, never seen after dark. And so it remained to this day.

The years passed and Tokeneke thrived. In direct proportion to how much Gault interests thrived. Cotton was followed by oranges, and cattle ranches and farmland, paper mills and banks, clothing factories, plants to transform natural orange juice into concentrate so that it could be reconstituted into orange juice. Trucking operations were established, railroad lines were brought into the county; advertising agencies were employed.

Each division functioned independently, responsible only to the Gault then in charge up on The Hill. When discipline weakened or profits fell or productivity sagged, the executive responsible could expect a call from The Hill. Or worse, a visit from a Gault. Positive results were expected, excuses not accepted.

Life in Tokeneke proceeded through good times and bad, through peace and war, without stress or strain from outside. Here was a place virtually unchanged—or changing at an imperceptible pace, grudgingly, giving way only when absolutely necessary.

Tokeneke remained a place where folks lived out their allotted time in order and tranquility, as ordained by those up on The Hill, the way their neighbors chose to live, the way the Creator intended for them to live. As one, they resisted new ideas, alien ideas—those harebrained schemes out of Washington, D. C. Federal programs were opposed, Federal monies refused, Federal help rejected. Outsiders were met with hostility and scorned. Modernity kept at a safe distance.

Tokeneke, many folk who lived there claimed, was the Garden of Eden reincarnate. An ideal place to live, the only place. And those who felt otherwise could just pick themselves up and skedaddle. Wasn't nothin' keepin' them back. That's what they said, many folks. Mostly white folks said that, rich white folks, mostly rich white folks with a strong hold on power. They said it.

And looking over it all, the big house on The Hill. With every generation it grew bigger. Wings added, sun rooms, extra bedrooms and baths, broken down into apartments; whatever it took to keep Gaults living in place, where they belonged. Wesley Gault was an exception; he insisted on having his own house to live in, a house set right in the middle of town. Liked to walk to his job at the bank, Wesley said. Liked to be in touch with the people. Wesley was considered a maverick. Feisty. Not yet settled in. A mite full of himself. But not so much as to be banished or excluded from family concerns. After all, it was reasoned, he was a young man, only twenty-five. Time, and a tighter hand, would slow him down, bring him into line, put him on the right track.

Putting Wesley on the right track was a frequent topic of conversation up on The Hill. So it was this afternoon in the dining room of the big house. A massive chamber extending from front to back, it rose the two full floors of the house, heraldic banners descending from the vaulted ceiling, stained glass windows casting a multi-colored hue over the long dark table that ran down the center of the room. At each place, silver plate. Down at the far end, Papa James flanked by his only living child, Nolan, and Mae-Mae, Wesley's young wife.

Papa James was an incredibly tall man, stern and stiff in his chair, shoveling food into his mouth at a remarkable pace, false teeth clicking as he chewed. He whined out his displeasure with them.

"Send men to the moon, they do, and can't put dentures that fit in a man's mouth."

Mr. Nolan Gault, as big around as he was tall, it seemed, head set directly down between massive shoulders, dressed all in black to minimize his bulk, rolled his eyes in dismay. He was sick of discussing his father's teeth, his father's bursitis, his father's skin eruptions, hemorrhoids, and sleeping habits. He was tired of hearing over and over of Papa James' vagrant romantic urges which evoked memories of even more ancient conquests made all over the Western Hemisphere, Europe and much of Central America, to hear Papa James tell it. He was tired of being witness to his own father's verbose ramblings. Here he was fifty-three years old and still obliged to cater to an old man subject to fainting spells, forgetfulness, melancholy and incontinence. Mr. Nolan wished his father would die.

"What you here for, Mae-Mae?" the old man demanded to know.

"She already said it, Papa," Mr. Nolan said. He gestured to a servant who brought him a second portion of dessert, strawberry-rhubarb pie à la mode.

"No reason she can't say it again," the old man grumped.

Mae-Mae swallowed hard. Papa James terrified her, all old people terrified her. Wrinkled and ugly, smelling bad, a terrible promise of what was to come. Mae-Mae hated, just *loathed*, the idea of turning old and ugly. But Papa James Gault was still the most important and powerful Gault of them all and he found her cute and appealing, a pleasant toy to have around, now and again. She meant to do nothing to alter that relationship. She positioned her small plump mouth in what she intended to be a winning smile and batted her eyelids at him.

"Y'all look at me, Papa James. I am a good-lookin' woman, am I not? I have always been and intend to keep on bein' one, the good Lord willin' and all o' that. Men have always favored me with their attention, evah since I developed along certain lines, if y'all know what I am sayin'."

Papa James took out his teeth and picked at them meanly. "Weren't a woman I ever got on top of failed to mention how well I came inside of her. I mean, no piddlin' squeaks out of James Gault. No dribblin' my vital juice like a leaky faucet. I flopped and leaped about like a hooked bigmouth, I did. Up and down, in and out, holdin' on lest I fall off an' bust some essential bone. Whoopin' and hollerin' so's the whole damned world could tell old James Gault was a-comin'. And you know why I enjoyed it so damned much? Why I got and give so much pleasure? Well, let me tell you, natural foods is what. Lots of bran to keep the old plumbin' in first-class operating order. Vitamins. It's that what put me on to Pro-Gel and Nat-Way. Made a fortune with them, I did. And why? 'Cause folks are wise to all that artificial poison's bein' pumped into their bloodstreams is why." He jammed his teeth back in his mouth, clicking them into place. "What in hell's the matter with that whelp of your'n, Nolan? He some kind of pervert? Must have bad blood." He leered in Mae-Mae's direction.

"I'll speak to the boy. Mae-Mae, you certain you're doin' your part in this delicate matter?"

"I have tried everything I can think of, honest I have. I have purchased very extreme lingerie bought via the mails from Beverly Hills, California and places like that. Black, lacy items, Mr. Nolan. You ought to see them. Hardly a part of me is concealed. Stickin' out here and stickin' out there."

"That didn't work?"

"One time I met Wesley at the front door wearing this itty-bitty French *thing*, barely came down to here. I wiggled and I squealed and put myself real close to him."

"And?"

"Candles and champagne. Gourmet dinners and romantic music. I have even read poetry to him at bedtime. Short of turnin' myself into some kind of a perverted person, I have done everythin' there is to do, I swear."

Papa James began to choke. Mr. Nolan slammed the old

man on the back and his teeth came flying out. He popped them back in.

"What do you want me to do?" Mr. Nolan said.

Mae-Mae turned wide round eyes his way. "Somebody, somebody has got to talk to Wesley. Remind him that he is my husband and bound to fulfill his marital duties, under God."

Mr. Nolan would have leaned forward had his immense stomach not been in the way. His whisper was a bellow. "You tryin' to tell me my son is a queer?"

"Never, never, never. Just the opposite. Some nights Wesley stays out all night."

"All night!"

"Comes home smelling of bourbon and perfume and God only knows what other stuff. Puts me in a terrible state."

"Boy's a Gault after all," Papa James muttered. He teetered Mae-Mae's way and tweaked her perky breast. "Bring those up to my room, little girl, and I will show you a dirty trick or two." He cackled with pleasure.

"Where is Wesley?" Mr. Nolan said.

"I don't know." She shifted her chair away from Papa James. "I never know."

"I'll get Duke Venable on it, he'll find the boy."

Mae-Mae grew concerned. "Is that a good idea, gettin' the law involved?"

"Do it, do it!" Papa James cried happily. "Whose law is it anyway? Whose sheriff is it? Drag that boy in here kickin' and screamin', fix him good. Tie the bitch down to a table and we'll all help the boy mount up, make sure he drives it all the way home. Yessir, same as they do around the farm. Yessir, we'll get you thoroughly screwed and tatooed, little girl. Depend on it, you depend on it, you hear me?"

"Everybody hears you, Papa James," Nolan answered dryly. "Everyone this side of Tampa Bay. . . ."

The old man glared, sputtered, and clicked his teeth in disdain.

Francine's Diner was not a diner at all. No more than fifty feet into Maple Street, down from Courthouse Square, it was situated in a narrow store. Outside, usually a few ol' boys hanging out, swapping lies. Inside, tables covered with threadbare white cloths lined the walls front to back, a counter separating the dining room from the kitchen. Simple food was served: fried steaks, chips, hamburgers, ham and eggs, sometimes a stew. Choice of three kinds of potatoes along with the vegetable of the day. Grits came with everything. Coffee was twenty-five cents a thick white mug full, served with real milk, fillups free.

If the restaurant was plain, Francine Joiner was carefully adorned. Hair the color of glistening brass, flaring stiffly away from her head, eyes precisely blued and lined, lips heavily painted. Sparkling earrings jangled as she moved about and three or four gold chains of varying lengths and weights were strung around her graceful neck. Step back and Francine might have passed for twenty-eight, thirty. Up close, lines fanned out from the corners of her eyes and the tight set of her mouth signaled a woman wary and sometimes dissatisfied. The white uniform she wore set off her full, womanly figure, restrained and provocative at the same time.

On a stool at the far end of the counter, Lonnie Peden, big and glowering, watching Francine as she moved about serving customers or taking cash. When she glanced his way, he raised his mug for a refill. She came with a Silex half full of strong hot coffee.

She poured. "Anything else?"

"You ain't said yes yet."

She looked into his eyes, spooked, like a cat's, a restless, unreliable man. "Uh-uh. No way. Not ever."

"You think you can do better'n me? Not in King of Heaven you can't. Thirty, maybe forty thousand people in this town, not a better man around."

"You sure do have a bad opinion of yourself, same as always. Boy, didn't you learn nothin' out in the big world?"

He hunched forward, his strong athlete's shoulders rolling. He stirred the steam out of his coffee. "What you got against me, Francine? All's I've done is ask you to party with me."

Her eyes raked the room. Her customers seemed content. She turned her attention back to Lonnie. "I ain't gonna do it."

"Give me one good reason why not?"

"Cause you scare me is why. You scare hell out of me, Lonnie."

"Shoot, I ain't goin' to hurt you."

"But you will, you surely will. All my life I've known roughnecks like you. Swore they'd treat me kindly. You know what—they hurt me. Every last one of them hurt me. I let you, you will too."

His smile was a thing of beauty, hard to resist. Slow, almost boyish and shy. She wanted to smile back at him.

"What've you got to lose?" he said.

"I'm crowdin' up near forty," she said without rancor. "My daughter's grown and goin' to college, first one in my family ever made it that far. I got this place and a ramshackle house to show for my years. No husband, not much of anythin' else. I know I shouldn't be mad at anybody cause it's not anybody else's fault, the way things are, but I am mad. Deep down I am. I try not to hurt folks and not to let them hurt me, you understand what I'm saying' to you, Lonnie? But what I've done is I've made a life here for myself, such as it is. I work hard—too hard and too damned long and I get too little back for what I give. I ain't never gonna get rich and I ain't never gonna get famous, the way you was. But that's all right. I don't expect much anymore. Haven't for a long time. Mostly I gave up expectin' anything from any man. Just tryin' to give my child a better life for herself. For myself, I ain't expectin', just markin' time is all. Hangin' on. Mired down in yesterday like most everybody else in King of Heaven."

"Reckon I could pluck you out of yesterday and put you into tomorrow, you give me the chance."

"Big talk from a used-to-be football hero. Those times are over for you, Lonnie Peden. Okay, you did things, went places, met all kinds of people. Only it's done with, you're back with us now, stuck with the way things are *here,* a town with good weather and bad habits, beholden to the Gaults like the rest of us, stuck in time like a busted clock."

His broad thrusting face drew down in a scowl, brows shadowing those dark eyes. His voice rumbled, gravelly and laced with repressed anger.

"I ain't beholden to nobody."

"More big talk. I hear things."

"Like what?"

"About you, about what you're up to."

The anger washed out of his face, replaced by that winning smile, smug and satisfied, too damned sure of himself. He was, she confessed reluctantly, the best-looking man she'd ever known. Always had been. But not for her, never for her.

"Been talkin' about me, have you, Francine?"

"Been listening. Not many secrets kept in this place."

"Such as what?"

"Such as runnin' loads of stolen oranges out of the groves at night . . ."

"Who told you that?"

"I hear things. Big all-American football player, star in the professionals, stealing oranges at night like some trashy boy with holes in his pants."

"I ain't admittin' nothin', but what you heard ain't all there is, not by a long shot, dammit."

She grinned tauntingly. "Oranges out of the county and a case or two of illegal whiskey back in. Way to go, Lonnie. Back in the big time, ain't you?"

"Listen, lady. I took out nearly four thousand oranges in that wagon of mine the other night. And I made more'n a dozen trips since I got back. Easy pickin's and there's more to come."

"Such as?"

"Whatever, " he said. He pushed the coffee mug aside. "I am my own man and I do my own thing in my own time."

"You ain't bigger'n the folks on The Hill."

"Got nothin' to do with The Hill."

"Got to do with the sheriff, though. Don't it?"

"Back off, woman. You know where I'm comin' from, where most of us been. Folks like us, we're stuck in this town. Okay, football got me out for a while but runnin' backs with busted knees are worthless. Listen, Francine, my daddy worked the cotton fields when he was a boy, same as your daddy, I reckon. It was a step up for him when he got to rollin' logs off the flatbeds at the sawmill. He broke his back doin' it. If it wasn't for football, I'd've gone the same way."

"Football's over."

"I know that, I always knew it had to stop. And that's all right. Onliest thing is, all that money, it's gone."

"All of it?"

"In a good cause." He grinned again, charming, insinuating, ever dangerous. "I had a lot of laughs."

"Yesterday's laughs don't cut much ice today."

"Which is why I got to do what I got to do."

"Why'd you come back?"

"It's where I belong. This is home."

"How come you're not on the television the way that Don Meredith is? You're a handsomer man than he is. . . ."

He reached for her and she stepped back. "So you think I'm handsome?"

She shrugged. "Don't go on so, you been told lots of times before."

"What am I supposed to do, run errands for the Gaults? Bust my gut like my daddy did?"

"Work for your momma."

"Killin' cockroaches and termites? Not for me."

"That's a steady business, always bugs around need killin'."

"I got bigger plans. Money is what lets a man be himself in this world. Money and power. I mean to have both."

"In Tokeneke? You foolin' yourself, Lonnie."

"Hell I am. This county is dry and all those Sunday Baptists and Methodists mean to keep it that way. Okay with me. But folks who want a drink will always find some way to get it. I mean to see they get it from me."

"You're gonna get your head broke."

"All jocks ain't dumb, Francine. I ain't dumb."

"You goin' up against Duke Venable?"

"Leave it to me. There's all kinds of stuff goin' down in this county, I aim to get my cut of it. Nothin' wrong with that, is there?"

She stared at him. "There's gonna be trouble."

"Maybe, maybe not." Again that slow grin. "Point is, you goin' to go out with me or not?"

She measured him deliberately. "Not," she said, and walked down to the other end of the counter. Minutes later her daughter, Jody, appeared.

"Can I get a coffee, Momma?"

"What are you doin' here?"

"Just dropped by for a coffee. Got a free period and decided to come see you is all. Nothin' wrong with a daughter visitin' her momma, is there?"

"Guess not." She filled a mug with coffee. "You want something to eat?"

"Nothin'. Who's that down the end of the counter?"

"Somebody for you to stay clear of, hear?"

"He keeps checkin' us out, Momma. Who you think he's got eyes for, you or me?"

"Don't talk nasty to me, girl. You're still a baby."

"I'm eighteen."

"Just a child, remember. Drink your coffee and go on back to campus. Next time you have free time you open a book and study. I ain't sendin' you to college to have a good time."

Jody pushed herself erect. "Don't you worry, Momma, I ain't havin' all that good a time, except in Miss Fellows' classes. Or workin' on the play. You goin' to come and see it?"

"Maybe."

"I can't wait till I get to act in one."

"Empty dreams. You get your degree, become a teacher. You'll have a good life 'stead of feedin' roughnecks all day long. Now you git, hear!"

On her way out, she held open the screen door for the Reverend Seely. She inclined her head and smiled. "Mornin', Reverend. "

"Mornin', Jody. You're lookin' sprightly this mornin'."

"It's my momma's coffee, it perks up the dead. Bye now!" And she was gone.

He took a place at the counter, greeted Francine and asked for coffee.

"I listened to that broadcast of yours over WLMG the other night, Reverend. It certainly was somethin', the way you carry on." The pale eyes inspected her face as if hunting any suggestion of insincerity. Satisfied that she meant what she said, he smiled.

"I do thank you for listenin' in, Francine. We are reachin' out to Christians everywhere."

"This Holy Crusade of yours . . . ?"

He ducked his head. Such a high-sounding name for such a minor effort. "Just tryin' to keep things around here the way they oughta be is all. Put the fear of God into a few folks is all."

"Sounded to me like you was a mite perturbed, Reverend. Sounded like maybe you was holdin' back...."

"I have always struggled against my temper...."

Francine laughed. "Well, at those camp meetin's Momma and Daddy used to carry me to when I was a child—no holdin' back then. Plenty of hell and damnation, shoutin' and stompin'. I kind've admired it. I remember one old boy carryin' on about how he was goin' to tear the temple down so's to save the souls of the righteous."

"I'll give some thought to what you're sayin', Francine." He addressed his cup. "That Jody of yours turnin' into a fine lookin' young lady, she is."

"Nice of you to say so." She moved along the counter to the cash register and accepted Lonnie Peden's check, made change.

"One last chance," he said for her ears alone.

"Last chance to do what?"

"To move on up into the big time."

"With Lonnie Peden, a genuine American hero, you mean? Ain't that somethin'?"

"There's folks who'd put it exactly that way."

"Give them the chance."

"You're makin' a mistake."

"One more in a long line. Bye now. Come back and see us, hear...?"

He left without answering, limping slightly, a genuine American hero brought down by a busted knee. Life had a way of doing that, she thought as she headed back to the kitchen. To everyone.

Benjamin Dark located Wesley Gault. He reported in to the dispatcher who noted it in his log.

"You sure he's inside Miss Ivy's, Benjamin?"

"Anybody else in the county drivin' a green Porsche you know about?"

"That's Wesley, all right."

"Which is what I said." Dark, a compactly constructed black man with a mincing walk, was careful to keep any suggestion of annoyance out of his voice. "He's in there, all right."

"Guess you'd best go in and get him out, Benjamin. He's wanted up on The Hill."

Dark grew melancholy. Vertical creases deepened in his leathery cheeks and his yellowing eyes grew hooded and sad. He tugged at his graying mustache.

"I'd as soon not do that."

"How's that, Benjamin?"

Dark understood that the dispatcher was toying with him, mocking him, having sport at his expense. Well, all right. Not much to be done about it.

"Be a good thing you get another deputy out to Miss Ivy's soonest you can. I'll wait around till then."

It was Billy Goforth who came rolling up in his squad car fifteen minutes later. He wore a khaki rain jacket and old work boots and stared at Benjamin out of those gelid eyes, making the other man uneasy.

"Sent you, did they?" Dark said, keeping his voice light.

"Benjamin, I was just settlin' in for the night. A six-pack and a game on the television. My feet were up and my butt down. All easy and nice. Until the office called. Said I was to run right on out to Miss Ivy's and do for Benjamin Dark what Benjamin Dark gets paid at least as much I get paid to do."

"Now, Billy, that ain't exactly the whole truth. You the best paid of all the deputies. You senior to us all and if Duke had a mind to hand out stripes, you'd have 'em sewed on all up and down your sleeves."

"No regulation says you can't do your own dirty work, Benjamin."

Dark shifted from one foot to the other, weighing his answer. "I am a man who believes in tradition. The old ways being the ways I'm used to and comfortable with, the best ways. That bein' the case, ain't no power on God's earth goin' to get me to go up into the fanciest white man's cat house in all of North Florida and pull a Gault out of there. Specially not Wesley Gault."

"Seems to me you gettin' so's you can't hold your pecker and pee at the same time."

"I'm old but I ain't dumb. I am a black deputy on the white side of the river. That means somethin'."

"We got full and fair integration in King of Heaven, Benjamin."

Dark giggled and slapped his thigh. "By law, maybe. On paper, maybe. Only law and paper don't run the county. Duke Venable does according to the folks on The Hill. White's still right and black's left back, like always. Certainly wish you'd put on your uniform, Billy."

Goforth looked up at the house. Miss Ivy functioned in an old mansion done in the Federal style, carefully and skillfully refurbished. Set a couple of miles outside of town and surrounded by undeveloped land, it provided solitude and security for those who patronized it, parking around in back. It was the kind of house neither deputy would ever be able to live in, the kind of establishment neither of them had ever been able to patronize, a stately reminder of their rightful places in the order of things. Still, the night air was soft and smelled sweetly of orange blossoms and being here was pleasant. Goforth started up onto the veranda.

"You keepin' track of all the favors I do you, Benjamin?"

"Write every one of them down in my notebook, Billy."

Goforth rang the bell; inside, chimes. "You doin' any night-fishin'?"

"Been thinkin' on it. You interested?"

"Sounds good." Goforth cleared his throat. "Ain't this somethin'? Two legally sworn peace officers payin' an unofficial call on the local whorehouse. Don't that gall you, Benjamin?"

"Don't mean diddly-shit to me. Duke says do, we do. The Hill tells him, he tells us. It's the way of things."

The door opened and a pretty black girl gazed out at them. "Evenin' Mr. Goforth. Evenin' Benjamin."

"Evenin', Debra. You tell Miss Ivy we're here, come to carry Mr. Wesley home."

Her eyes rolled. "Might take a few minutes. Mr. Wesley, he's occupied right now."

"You carry the word along, Debra. We'll wait out here and

enjoy the night. Say ten minutes, that's how long we'll wait. After that—"

The girl nodded once. "I'll tell Miss Ivy. Miss Ivy, she's good at arrangin' things."

# CHAPTER
## 6
---

THE PHONE RANG and that familiar voice—pursed with asperity and righteous superiority—greeted her.

"How are you, Katherine?"

It was her mother. Once every month Kate Fellows called her mother. Once every month to report on her activities—the pleasant occurrences, the triumphs, if any, the high points. Kate's mother took a dim view of negativism. Special occasions rated an extra phone call: Christmas, Easter, the Fourth of July. Kate's father had looked upon the Fourth of July as a unique and precious holiday, marking it with prayers of gratitude for all the good things handed down to the United States of America and its fine, upstanding, Christian population. When Kate was a child, there was always a family picnic and a baseball game on the Fourth of July.

Mother's Day, too, was always special in the Fellows family. A private and exceedingly personal celebration of Mrs. Fellows' elevated position in the cosmic scheme. To forget Mother's Day was to deliver a profound insult to Kate's mother, a deep and lasting hurt. It would result in a cool, biting reminder of a mother's contribution to Western civilization, that Mary mother of Jesus was a woman even as Mrs. Fellows was, and that without mothers the cherished Free World would certainly perish. All delivered with reason and condescension, all very civilized and controlled. The result: extended periods of guilt and depression for Kate. She resented being treated like a child and grew angry at herself for failing once again to measure up to her mother's unbending and lofty moral standards.

"Oh, mother," Kate said, setting herself against a rising apprehension. "I wasn't expecting you to call."

"How are you, dear?"

"I'm fine. Is everything all right with you?"

"At my age, as good as can be expected." Mrs. Fellows, in her middle seventies, was healthy, active and energetic. She was a memeber of the local school board, a Trustee of her church, she belonged to a garden club, a chorale, and she played nine holes of golf three mornings a week. She possessed all her own teeth, her heart was sound and she wore glasses only for reading. She would, Kate was convinced, live to be a hundred. "It does get lonely," Mrs. Fellows was saying. "Living alone after all those years . . . I visited your father yesterday. . . ."

Kate's father was dead, dead for nearly five years. Her mother attended the grave every Sunday, on the Fourth of July, and on her own birthday. Her *birthday!* A spasm of despair twisted Kate's body; her stomach began to ache and her brain tipped and yawed in waves of self-loathing; she'd forgotten her mother's birthday.

"Oh, mother, I'm so sorry."

"These things happen, dear." Her mother's voice was honeyed, a sweet enticement to personal disaster.

"I meant to call. . . ."

"It doesn't really matter."

"Of course it does."

"We parents, we expect to be overlooked."

"Oh, mother. . . . It's just that I've been so busy."

"Of course you have, it's only natural that you forgot. I understand. Even as a child, you were always self-involved. Your interests took precedence over everything else." She laughed, a soft, threatening, reminiscent laugh. "You always had to be reminded of your obligations—first things first, your father used to say. Dear, blessed man. What a marvelous person he was. Everybody admired him, praised him. He was very widely liked, you know. As a man, as a concerned and considerate citizen, as a preacher. You don't see his like nowadays. No, indeed, we're living in a time of selfishness and greed and rampant immorality. Men like your father were the foundation on which this nation was built. If only there were more of his ilk today."

"Yes." Kate spoke flatly, passively, waiting for her mother to go on.

"He was a unique man. Oh, I confess that perhaps he might have done better as a provider, I don't know. But your father was a man of God first and always. Money was never primary with your father. If it weren't for his military pension and the Social Security and a few stocks and bonds and income property he left I don't know what I'd do...."

"Maybe I can send you something extra this month, mother." She vowed to put an additional hundred dollars in her monthly check to her mother, a sop to her own conscience, a material reminder that Kate was a dutiful and generous child. But she was no longer a child, no longer beholden to the past, no longer dependent on *them* for food and shelter and permission to go out with boys. "I'll put the check in the mail today, mother," she added.

"Do whatever you think best, dear. After all, you have your own life to lead. To a certain extent, I admire what you've done. We've all had dreams, you know. Yes, even I have. Oh, I don't go on about them much, unfulfilled dreams are such a bore to other people, I always say. Who cares if I sacrificed my ambitions to be your father's wife and your mother? No one, I always say. No regrets, no regrets at all. You learn to live with adversity and with disappointment." She produced a harsh, flinty laugh, fading rapidly. "Oh, well, we mustn't talk too long. The long-distance rates are so outrageous these days, the price of everything going up. This inflation, all those welfare frauds ... oh, dear, I do go on at times. You call if you like, next time, dear...."

"Mother, I do have a gift for you, I simply forgot to—"

"That's all right, dear. I'll be just fine."

"Is there anything in particular you need?"

"I'll be all right. You look to your own self, it's what folks do best nowadays."

"Goodbye, mother."

The following morning Kate bought an expensive perfume and sent it along to her mother with a note of apology. But it failed to lessen the guilt she felt, the sense of again being in the wrong, of being inadequate, ungiving, a failure as a daughter. Kate wondered if she would ever truly measure up.

Three generations of Gaults confronted each other as if at different points of a triangle. Papa James, clicking his teeth, wallowing in memories. Mr. Nolan, chins shimmering, tiny eyes blazing as he stared at his son. Wesley, wiry and defiant, yet poised as if ready for flight.

"I have always suspected there was something wrong with you!" Mr. Nolan trumpeted and stamped a heavy foot. They were in the library of the big house, books overflowing the shelves, piled on tables and on the floor, a room for collecting rather than contemplation. "Actin' the way you do, you can't be right in the head."

"Sendin' the law after me," Wesley said cheerfully. "Shame on you, Daddy."

"Spendin' your time in a whorehouse, bespoilin' your body with harlots when you ought to be home with your darlin' wife."

"Mae-Mae is an idiot."

"And that's not all," Mr. Nolan went on. "There's your job at the bank—you been neglectin' your responsibilities, your duties to the bank and to your family."

"I do my job."

"Hah!" Mr. Nolan said in a thin, penetrating voice. "Call it doin' your job when you approve a loan for a housin' project out in Wing Farms? I call that committin' financial and social suicide is what I call it."

Papa James broke in. "Onliest way to run a bank is to take in cash hand over fist and give out no more'n is absolutely necessary. Ever tell you how granddaddy and daddy operated? Wrote up every mortgage the bank put out so's they could call in the loan after three years, they had a mind to. Half them redneck farmers couldn't read back then, never knew what they was puttin' their names to. Cost 'em, too. Everything they had. Them little farmers, they didn't have any cash, never did have, so's when the time came to call in the loans they was up the creek without a paddle. Nothin' they could do, by God. Built up their holdin's thataway, daddy and granddaddy did, easy as pie. Sharp they was, the kind of folks made America what it is today."

"Yes, Daddy," Mr. Nolan said patiently, eyes holding on Wesley. "That Henderson loan was a bad move."

Wesley shook his head. "I don't agree." He wasn't sure he could defend his business actions successfully. His father was a big man in every way, strong, smart and tough, like his forebears, a relentless wheeler and dealer. Much tougher than Wesley ever hoped to be. "Yes, sir, that was a sound deal. Those apartments . . ."

"Apartments!" The word broke out of Papa James with a spray of spittle. His voice was reedy, placed too high in the sinuses. "Not in Tokeneke County, you don't. Ain't gonna have apartments in my county. Ain't gonna have trashy niggers movin' in from all over the state, livin' off welfare and using dope and cuttin' good clean white Christian folks up. Got laws against it. Rules, regulations, ordinances. Who says apartments?"

"P and Z approved the submission," Wesley said.

"I'll take care of the Planning Board," Mr. Nolan said. "That loan is canceled, hear me, Wesley? Canceled. Terminated. Ain't gonna be forthcomin'. And that is that."

"They'll go elsewhere for their money. Outside the county. They bought Wing Farms fair and square and—"

"Maybe yes, maybe no. I'll tend to that. You start usin' the pitiful amount of brains the good Lord gave you. No loans for outside construction, no apartments, no condos, no supermarkets, no cloverleaf highways, no soot, no muggers. . . . Ain't gonna turn King of Heaven into Disneyworld. No high-rise office buildings. No airports and no parking garages. No traffic jams and no public transportation system. No criminals and no crime. . . ."

"You can't stop progress, Daddy."

"Progress, hell, it's a disaster. I ain't havin' none of it. This is our town. Our county. It's made as much of space as of stuff. Just ain't gonna have it changed."

Papa James smacked his lips together, teetered in Wesley's direction. "You sure look awful, boy. What you been up to?"

Wesley slumped down into a great red leather chair. He had refused to leave Miss Ivy's of his own free will, had put up a fight when the deputies appeared. Landed one or two good right hands, not that it did much good. They held him down, two of them cuffed him and dragged him kicking and screaming out of the place. At first he thought they hadn't landed a punch. But his ribs had begun to ache and there was a swelling on the underside of his jaw. He grinned up at his grandfather. "Just havin' a good old time, Papa James."

"Get it from that perky little wife of your'n."

"Mae-Mae! Damn woman doesn't know first thing about havin' fun. Tight as they come she is, in every hole of her body."

"Watch your mouth, boy!" Mr. Nolan bellowed.

"What? What's that he said?" Papa James staggered and almost fell. He snuffled and coughed and spit into the palm of one hand and rubbed it dry on his trouser leg.

"I'm worried about you, Wesley," Mr. Nolan said. "Actin' the way you do. Not fit for a Gault. There's work to be done, problems to solve. One day all of this will be yours."

"Then turn me loose to do my job the way I see fit."

"You're just a boy. . . ."

"I'm twenty-five!"

"There you are. Just a child."

"When I was twenty-five," Papa James murmured reminiscently, "I was a married man with responsibilities, a wife and a child. What was that boy's name? John, yes John. John Alexander after Alexander the Great. His mother was a great reader of history, she was. They passed away, both of them. Yes, within two days of each other. Some kind of epidemic . . . I can't remember what it was exactly. I was twenty-five, leasin' mineral rights on Indian lands in Oklahoma for oil rights. Forty-eight hours and both of them was gone. I loved that woman something fierce and that boy, what was his name? John Alexander. He was a feisty little fellow. I was only twenty-five and seven months later I struck it rich on those leases, but I surely do miss that boy. I miss him sorely."

Wesley pulled his eyes back to his father. "Let me do the job my way."

"You do as I say!" Mr. Nolan yelled.

Papa James sputtered. "Listen hear to me, both of you listen. Wesley—" His manner grew gentler and his eyes blinked and became moist. "I ever tell you, Wesley, you look like him, like that little boy. . . . You got to do somethin' for me, boy."

"What's that, Papa James?"

"First, you go directly home and crawl into that wife of yours. Plow her every which way but up. She needs some plain and fancy lovin', and you give it to her. Some of that cathouse howlin' you been doin'. Put a bun in her oven, boy. Make a passle of kids. One or two ain't good enough. Some die on you, some turn out not so good, others go away. So you make a whole mess of 'em, hear. Keep that wife of yours—what's her name?"

"Mae-Mae."

"Mae-Mae. Keep Mae-Mae barefoot and pregnant, the way they used to say. You hear me, son?"

"I hear you, Papa James."

"And get your head straight about business. I was your age, I was a full-fledged businessman. Wheelin' 'n' dealin', makin' my fortune, one way or the other. Onliest thing let me keep this county the way it is was gettin' rich enough and strong enough to be able to buy what I wanted and who I wanted. People and things, that's what money's for, to buy 'em both. You hear what I'm sayin' to you?"

"Papa James made a fortune by the time he was twenty-five," Mr. Nolan said.

The old man nodded. "Money and power, a man can't have too much of either. I went out into the oil fields breakin' my back roustaboutin'. Twenty-four cents a barrel it was back then. Great Depression was over the land. My daddy could barely keep this place goin'. Learned to find the edge and take it, make it mine, get my own way. It's dog eat dog and the meanest, shrewdest, hungriest dog is the dog that gets. You got to rut around in the mud, boy, scratch and bite and tear until you get what you are after. Rules is made to break and laws to bend, unless they are your rules and your laws. Onliest thing that counts is family, boy, family. And the land. My own daddy told me that. Protect it, he told me, with your life's blood, and find a way to get more, always more. Thataway you protect what you already got. A man can't own too much land, daddy always said, and he was a hundred and ten percent correct. You listenin' to me?

"Those days way back—Herbert Hoover, FDR, WPA, NRA, those old days. Daddy said for me to make my own way then come back and make over the county, turn it into my own place. I doubled the land the family held back then, near to tripled it finally. Don't think I didn't know what folks was sayin', that I cheated 'em and flummoxed 'em and took what wasn't rightly mine. Don't you believe it, not for a minute. All weaklin's, them folks, cowards, folks without nerve or darin' or the will to win. A man has to stand up for what he wants, fight for it, win for it. I tell you, boy, us Gaults know how to win and that's all there is to that—winnin'."

Breathing hard, Papa James brought his eyes around to Mr. Nolan, then back to Wesley. He clicked his teeth and abruptly the familiar action became harsh and ominous. "Learned how to win out in Oklahoma, I did. All that land and under it oceans of oil. Only nobody knew exactly where the oil was. So I nosed around, playin' like I was dumb, watchin', teachin' myself all the sharp angles of the oil business, bein' smart while playin' dumb. I found out about oil leases. Man don't have to buy even a single acre to get hisself rights to what's under it. Them Okies, dumbest people in the world they was, never did find out what was goin' on till it was too late for 'em to do anything about it.

"In Oklahoma and in Louisiana and Texas. Bought up mineral rights on land already drilled by the major companies. All those dry wells. Folks said I was crazy. Sold shares in the leases and got together some capital. Once in a while I'd drill a well, just to keep it legal, keep folks off'n my back. And they always come up dry leavin' me to walk away with a tidy sum in my pocketbook.

"Then one day a terrible thing happened. You listenin' to me, boy? One of the wells came in, a real honest-to-God gusher. Made me a millionaire overnight. Had to share all that oil money with all them shareholders. Like to have ruined me. Sold out to one of the majors and moved on back to King of Heaven and ain't left the county since. Aim to die and be buried right here."

"You're a long way from dyin', Papa James," Mr. Nolan said automatically.

The old man, breathing hard, clicking his teeth, snorted as he sucked air into his withered lungs. "Need you boy, the family needs you. Youth, energy, strength. Got to get meaner is all. Mean and unforgivin', ready to fight or fuck, whichever's best. Time's runnin' out for me. Runnin' out...." He raised his eyes slowly, damp and blurred. "Do you wife good, Wesley, hear me? Stay away from those whores of Miss Ivy's."

"They say you used to be out there every Friday night doin' those whores one right after another."

The teeth slipped halfway out of the old man's mouth. He sought to secure them. "Don't smart talk me, young fella. I'll whip your butt from asshole to Ash Wednesday, and that ain't no bull." He pressed the heel of his hand against one eye to ease the throbbing pain. "All your fault, Nolan. Ought to have taught him right, this boy of yours."

Papa James staggered to the door, waved a trembling forefinger at Wesley. "Go home, boy, do your wife. Be a man, be a Gault. Go on now, get out of here and do like I told you...."

When he and Mr. Nolan were alone, Papa James clicked his teeth vigorously. "You stay on top of that boy, hear me? He's a Gault, so he's got the right stuff in him. Only he needs a dollop or two of seasonin', you follow my drift? Needs to find out what's he made out of and where he's goin'."

"Yes sir."

"One more thing—you been listenin' in on Reverend Seely the way I told you?"

"I tuned in to one program, part of it anyways."

"Part of it." Papa James snorted in disgust. "Now listen here to me, boy. Seely, he is on to somethin'."

"Like what?"

"Ain't entirely certain. Fact is, Seely ain't either. Not yet. But it's comin', I can feel it in my bones. That crusade he

keeps talkin' about, we can use it. Somehow. So you listen in
to the man. Pay attention to what he's sayin' and what he ain't
smart enough to say. Figure out how we can use him, use his
crusade. King of Heaven, this is our town. Our county. That's
our college out there at the lake. Our radio station. Seely is
our preacher, you hear what I'm sayin' to you?"

"I hear you, Papa James."

"Why'n't you have yourself a small talk with that Moody
fella, see what he can dream up. Must be good for a little more
brainwork than just ridin' herd on a bunch of college boys and
girls. See to it."

"I'll do that, Papa."

# CHAPTER
## 7

IT WAS CALLED The Convent. A three-story imitation plantation house painted white and housing nearly half the female students at Gault Christian. The first floor contained the public rooms where students could entertain their parents or other visitors. In the small reception area, off the main foyer, tea was served or punch for special functions. Meetings of various student groups were conducted in the large sitting room midway along the building. The two floors above were student quarters and as such were off-limits to guests of the opposite sex. All girls had to be in their room by ten-thirty on school nights, eleven-thirty on weekends, unless special provisions and passes were supplied.

At the rear of The Convent, the lawn fell gently down on the stand of pine and willow trees lining Lake Ranaqua. On this night, there was no moon and the campus was shrouded in darkness. Curfew past, there was no movement except for the slow rounds of the security guard on a moped. He passed the front of The Convent at 10:47 and would not return, Warren having timed him many times, until nearly an hour later. Plenty of time.

Keeping to the shadows, he made his way to the rear of The Convent and reached into the thick growth of ivy masking off the wall. He located the call button he had installed, with Barbara's help, and rang it twice. Before long, the creak of metal, Barbara descending the black iron fire escape that clung to the wall of The Convent.

Barbara Cromartie. Taller than Warren, with thick black hair that spread across her back in a luxurious fall. Even in the dark her voluptuous beauty was apparent. Warren reached for her as soon as she appeared. She avoided his hands.

"I told you not to come," she said waspishly.

"Let's go down to the lake. I want to talk to you."

"Forget it. It is over between us, Warren."

"I love you. . . ."

She giggled. "Call it anything you want, it don't cut it. I have got myself a new boyfriend. A real man this time. Not a kid like you. Somebody knows how to treat a girl, no more of that bang-bang and it's all over stuff. You would just shrivel up and die if you was to hear the kind of things he does for me. Oh, wow, turns me on just thinkin' about it."

"Whatever it is, I can do it."

"No way."

"You can teach me, I'll learn."

"Forget it." She sniffed. "Oh, damn, Warren, you are sorely in need of a bath, you know that?"

"It's the chemicals."

"Yuch. Go on home to your momma and kill all those creepy crawly things. And take a bath, you certainly do smell awful."

He reached, she slapped his hand. "Be nice to me, Barbara."

"I'm goin' back upstairs and you needn't come scratchin' 'round here anymore, hear. You forget you ever knew about that signal bell o' mine, hear. Now you just git, Warren. Git. . . ."

"You can't treat me this way, you can't. I been real nice to you, I bought you things, I did things for you. I ain't ready to give you up."

"Not your choice, is it?"

The rage lodged behind his eyes and he blinked. His limbs

tensed and his fingers balled up into fists. He took one long stride forward, face contorted, swearing at her.

She retreated quickly, back against the ivy. "Don't you hit me, Warren Peden. Come any closer and I am goin' to scream, so help me God, I will. They find you here you'll be in trouble. I'll tell 'em you tried to force me. Yes, that's it, you tried to rape me. Now you better just take off right quick, hear...."

"This ain't over," he said. "You think I don't know, you been doin' it with half the boys in the county. Everybody knows you're no good."

"Get away from me you smelly little wimp." She started back up the fire escape. "You try this one more time, I'm tellin' my boyfriend. He'll take care of you good."

He watched her climb, flashes of pale thigh under her skirt. He wasn't ready to give it up, not yet, not ever. No way he was going to do without, not anymore. Somehow he'd find a way. He'd done it before, he would again. Over and over again.

A night like most other nights. Wesley got home late, smelling of bourbon. Mae-Mae, to his surprise, was propped up in bed popping little chocolates into her little mouth and laughing up a storm every time Don Rickles insulted Johnny Carson. She washed it all down with a long pull on a Dr. Pepper.

"Hi, there, honey."

He told her "hi" and began undressing himself. "Figured you'd be asleep by now."

"I waited up for you, sugar." She crawled across the length of the bed and switched off the television, looking deceptively good in a black lacy nightgown that came to her hips; and no panties, he saw with surprise.

He kicked off his shoes and got his trousers off, unsteady work. He sat down to finish the job.

She placed one last chocolate on her tongue, maneuvered it back, chewing noisily. One last swallow of Dr. Pepper and she smiled coquettishly at him, came up on her knees.

Something was out of synch, he told himself. She often feigned sleep when he came home after a night of drinking, afraid of what he might demand of her. Forget it, sweetie. Outside was all the tail in the world, wet and wild pussy willing to do all manner of weird and wonderful exercises on his body.

"How come?" he said, heading for the bathroom.

"How come what, sweetheart?"

"You're still up. How come?"

"Like I said. I have been waitin' for your arrival with impatience and mountin' desire."

"Jesus, Mae-Mae, you know how much I despise that chintzy Scarlett O'Hara impression you do. Cut it out." He began to urinate, directing his stream into the water at the bottom of the bowl.

She put her fingers in her ears. "It is simply my natural manner of talkin', darlin'. No impression at all, just the real thing. Will you never learn to close the door while you do your duty, Wesley?"

When he came back out she was studying herself in the full-length mirror on her closet door. "What do you think, sugar?"

He looked at her, desire mingling with distaste. He wished her gone, divorced or annulled, sent away. How about killed? If only he had the nerve for it; put a pistol to that vapid head and pow! Maybe hire somebody to do it. The idea delighted him and he slid between the sheets, intending to lull himself to sleep with images of her slow, bloody murder.

"Well?" she said. She faced him, hands on hips and her chin tucked down, supplying her version of a provocative smile. In the bedroom, Mae-Mae was a practiced incompetent. At her best, a Playboy centerfold; slick and artificial. At her worst, a sexual disaster area.

"Would you repeat the question, please?"

"Look at me. I do not weigh even one single solitary ounce more today than I did when you first met me in high school. When I was captain of the pep squad. Not many men can say that about their wives."

"Fair enough."

She took a quick sideways step and another, dipping as she went, face in profile, one arm pumping in rhythm to a drumbeat she alone could hear.

"K. O. H.

"K. O. H.

"Raiders, Raiders, at the gate.

"Boom-biddy-wah-wah, boom-biddy-wah-wah,

"K. O. H."

Her movements were quicker now, the dips more pronounced, the short black skirt of her nightgown bouncing high as her pert backside jerked left and right in hard punctuation. Her smile widened, her eyes shone, her gestures grew broader, ending in a high leap, legs wide apart, landing in a perfect split. Then up again, bouncing, clapping her hands.

"And that's without pom-poms."

"Nerd," he muttered.

"What?"

"Fantastic." Bourbon fumes dulled his brain, his eyes grew heavy, he craved insensate darkness, a soft drift into oblivion, a quick removal from the real to the peaceful void. He dozed.

"Wesley!"

He grunted.

"Look at me. . . ."

An alien urgency in her voice stirred him, rendered the steady flow toward sleep inoperative. He forced his eyes open.

She stood over him on the bed, legs astraddle his supine body. She began to sway, to twitch, to dance, the shorty nightgown flipping. For a moment he saw but failed to comprehend; he came gradually back to full wakefulness. She was displaying her wares, front and back, for his approval, her movements still those of the girlish cheerleader but with plain intent to incite.

"Too little, too late," he told her.

"What? Oh, Oh, Wesley. Be nice to me and I'll be nice to you."

"I'm asleep."

"All those kinky things you say you like. I'll learn, if you want, do good for you. And all you have to do . . ."

His eyes were closed again, his mind drifting away.

". . . is give me a baby."

He rolled on his side, then onto his stomach. A contented sigh announced that he was gone for the night. All her efforts were futile, gone to waste.

"What am I supposed to do?" she said aloud. When no answer came she worked her way down between the sheets next to him and imagined she had just been declared the winner of the National Baton-Twirling Contest. And the crowd was

stomping and hollering and the television cameras were pointed
at her and Hollywood producers were begging her, just begging
for her to sign a long-term contract with them. That'd show
Wesley Francis Gault, that'd truly show him. She ran it all by
one more time. In slow motion. And faded into a contented
sleep.

Goforth couldn't keep her out of his head. She kept drifting
back, a ghostly vision, featureless, but warm and vital, so very
much alive. Stirring up old fears and emotions he had hoped
were deeply buried and forgotten.

He dressed carefully. A freshly cleaned and pressed uniform, boots highly polished, the wide-brimmed hat set squarely
on his head. A last look in the mirror told him that nobody he
knew looked better in the uniform, a man taut and tough, a
strong man, a man who was what he seemed to be. He went
to the hospital.

He took off the hat before advancing quietly into the darkened room. The girl stared up at him from the bed. A bandage
covered her forehead and her face was bruised and still swollen.
Her features were delicate, a short nose to flared nostrils and
a full, wide mouth. Her eyes were set apart, unblinking black
orbs that kept him at a distance as she inspected him with bold
curiosity.

In a vase next to the bed, some flowers. And an unopened
candy box, a book. Who had brought these things? A boyfriend? A husband? Family?

"I'm Billy Goforth," he said.

"The one who found me?"

He nodded. "How you doin'?"

Her expression never changed. "Doin' okay, considerin'."

"Thought I'd come visitin', see how you are doin'."

"I'm doin' all right, deputy."

"I thought, if you're up to it, I'd ask you some questions."

"Another deputy already asked me stuff."

"I understand. They goin' to keep you here for long?"

"Not for long. I ought to be gettin' out in a day or so."

"Got any idea who might've done this to you?"

"Never saw him."

"But how . . . ?"

"He grabbed me from behind."

"If you don't mind my askin', that time of night. What were you doin' out on the beach that time of night?"

She almost smiled. "We all got things on our minds, I reckon. I had some heavy thinkin' to take care of. It's nice out there, quiet, lonely. Sometimes I need to be off by myself that-away."

"Never gave you time to scream or call out, did he?"

"No time at all. Slapped his hand over my mouth."

"Then what?"

"Tried to fight him off but he was too much for me. I think I kicked him once, caught his shin, but he knocked me down and kept on punchin' till I was near unconscious. When he stopped, all my strength was gone."

"Black or white?"

"Huh?"

"The fella that jumped you, black man?"

Her chin lowered and she gazed up at him out of those quiet black eyes. "He was white."

"It was dark, how'd you know?"

"When he grabbed me, I caught sight of his wrist. He was white, all right."

"Right."

She shuddered as if cold and tugged at the sheet and Goforth's eyes went to her shoulders, softly rounded, the color of poured honey. She was, he decided, the most beautiful woman he'd ever seen, with an exotic cast to her as if created in some alien land. "I hope you'll be out of here soon, Inez." Her name felt awkward as he spoke it for the first time. "All right if I call you Inez?"

"It's all right."

He stepped away from the bed. "If I have anymore questions..."

"I'll be around."

At the door, he said, "You work in town?"

She nodded. "I teach school."

"That right? What grade?"

"Middle school."

"Guess I can always find you, then."

"Guess you can, deputy."

"Take care of yourself."

"Thanks for comin', deputy."

Outside he put the hat back on his head and marched back
to his car. He had, he told himself severely, conducted himself
like a silly schoolboy. Not knowing what to say in the face of
a pretty girl. She must've thought him a complete idiot and
with cause. All those dumb questions. He promised to make
up for his failure next time. If there was a next time.

Goforth went up on the dunes where he had found Inez
Macklin. Under a low moon, the sand was smooth and silvery,
giving no indication of what had taken place. No evidence that
might indicate who had raped her had been found. What kind
of a man enjoyed forcing himself on a woman? What sinister
yearning drove him out in search of a stranger to violate and
damage? Goforth had never been entirely at ease making love,
tentative and anxious to please and be pleased, but reluctant
to make demands. Casual sex always left him brooding with
residual guilt and dissatisfaction.

When he was young, he had tried to emulate his friends.
To boast of his conquests, to strut his masculinity, to brag
about his competence in bed. Mostly lies, as he remembered
it. Contorted gropings in back seats and alongside dark country
roads. Marrying Charlene had been the smartest thing he'd
done, settling in to the security of a private and sanctified
relationship.

Now he was alone again. Cast out into a world that was
threatening and often downright hostile. Months had passed
since he and Charlene had last made love, a shattering experience that ended in angry accusations. After that night, neither
of them had spoken of it again, but a gritty discomfort filtered
through their relationship, until it was agreed that Goforth would
find a place to live in town. To give them both time to reflect,
to restore damaged egos, to decide what to do.

Charlene had certainly decided. On her own, without con-
sulting him, without considering what he wanted. Not that he
blamed her, he didn't blame her.

Charlene had said it many times; she didn't understand him.
The way he distanced himself from her, withdrawing into sol-

itary fits of repressed rage and pervasive despair. She didn't know what he wanted. Or who he was.

Neither did he.

He crouched to examine the cradle of sand where Inez Macklin had been assaulted. How had she felt when the stranger forced his way inside of her? They said most women enjoyed being roughed up, craved a strong and determined man, a man who refused to take no for an answer. They said rape was a physical impossibility. *"Ever try to thread a moving needle?"* They said all women were whores in their hearts.

No way. Nobody wanted to be beaten. Forced to accept a rough stranger. Pounded and hurt in order to provide pleasure for someone else. He didn't believe it, not for a minute. Just some ol' boys blowing smoke.

Rape, battery, robbery. Whoever it was had stolen her purse, the little money she'd possessed. It galled Goforth to know that the assailant was wandering around free as air, free to commit his onerous crime again. He took it as a professional affront. He was a policeman, trained and sworn to uphold the law, to catch criminals, to prevent crime. It occurred to him that over the years he had done very little crime fighting. Mostly chasing and cleaning up the mess folks sometimes left behind.

He drove out to the hospital. Inez was alone in her room and asleep. In the soft light she looked childlike, innocent, untouched by the crueler aspects of the world. Her breasts rose and fell as she breathed, nipples in bold relief. He caught himself staring and stepped back in shame. He wanted to assure her that she was going to be all right, that he would prevent such a terrible fate from touching her again.

Back in the car, he switched on the radio, craving company, or at least the illusion of company, unable to be alone and without comfort. A familiar voice blasted out at him—Reverend Dorr C. P. Seely delivering one of his radio sermons, the heavy voice angrier than usual, with a tight focus as if taking dead aim on a vulnerable target. With unsteady hands, Goforth lit a cigarette and smoked and listened.

*"And Jesus said, 'Without me you can do nothin'. Yessir, without Jesus you are doomed. DOOMED! Without Him disaster will follow as night follows day. Get on His team—the*

*winnin' team. You listen to me! Whosoever is not of the true
faith is sin. Sin! S-I-N. Sin! Go against God's Eternal Truth
and you shall be penalized...."*

Goforth drove up county and parked near the picnic area at
the south end of The Bottoms. He lit another cigarette and
listened to the crickets and the occasional honking of a bullfrog.
To his right, unseen in the darkness, a broken red brick path
led into the marshland under cover of a formation of great
gnarled live oaks, planted two hundred years before.

*"No preacher teaches you. Only God teaches. Stick to God's
word. Shut your ears to temptation, turn your back to evil.
Don't let the Devil tease you and tempt you onto the easy road.
Watch out for bodily longings. Watch out for those dark desires
that we are tested against. Stay with the Divine Truth of Christ
Jesus who lived and died and was born again so that you might
be saved. Enlist in our Holy Crusade and praise God.*

*"Praise God."*

In The Bottoms—more than thirty thousand acres of marsh
and wetland—palmetto and shrouds of Spanish moss, alligator
and egrets, and once in a while an eagle. Here the remnants
of the Tokeneke Indians had fled for refuge against the bloody
assault of Otis Ambrose Gault and his followers, and here they
were meticulously hunted down and put to death, men, women
and children.

*"Walk in the Lord's path as our ancestors did and there is
nothin' that cannot be done, for God by Himself can accomplish
wonders. Go to Matthew Fourteen in which our Lord fed five
thousand people. Let me tell you, there were no fast-food res-
taurants in those days. No Burger King, no McDonald's, no
Wendy's. Just one little boy with five loaves and two fishes
which he had bought at market. But that boy was special because he was willin' to give Jesus everythin' he had.*

*"Praise God."*

As a boy, Goforth and his friends had claimed The Bottoms
as their own. Exploring endlessly, they had constructed tree
houses to serve as lookouts against intruding adults, had marked
safe places in which to hide themselves lest an oppressive and
demanding adult world find them. As a young man, he had
hunted white-tailed deer in the marsh, and feral pigs, and wild

turkeys. And brought compliant girls to the high, dry ground to drink beer and bootleg whiskey, and try to make out. So long ago, in another time, a simpler, better time; or was it? Had it all been about the same, his memory a sump of idle imaginings with little connection to what really went on back then? So much had happened since, so little accomplished. Made him sad to put his mind to it thataway, and full of regrets.

*"This town of ours is a good town to live in. A good town in a good county. Let's keep it that way. Only constant vigil is required to make sure it stays good and pure and clean. But skulkin' everywhere among us, seekin' ways and means to damage good people are the cunnin' representatives of the anti-Christ. They walk among us doin' their evil deeds, unloosin' devious schemes to injure you and your beloved children.*

*"Praise God."*

He struggled to find some purpose and orderliness in his life. And not to think too much about Charlene, not to remember the good feelings when first they had been married, the dreams shared, the good times. Halfway through his second cigarette, a Buick wagon went cruising past, heading toward town, but riding much too low over the rough road. He ground out the cigarette and went after it.

*"All right, people! I am goin' to tell you this—better turn away from sin and do it right now. I mean now. Put your backs to iniquity. Put your backs to greed. Put your backs to corruption in all its devilish forms. Stand back from ungodliness in everything you do and everything you are. Live right. Pray hard. Do good.*

*"And Praise God."*

Oranges stolen by a couple of smart boys who aimed to load it onto a waiting boat at the marina and over to New Orleans for a quick and tidy profit. He switched on his flasher and pressed down on the accelerator, closed in on the wagon. He hit the siren twice and a third time when the driver of the wagon failed to slow down. That did it, the wagon rolled to a stop on the shoulder. Hand on his Magnum, Goforth came up alongside, looking very mean, very tough, up to the job.

"Climb on out," he said. "Very slow, very carefully, hands where I can see them. "

"That you, Billy?"

The voice was familiar, pitched down to the diaphragm, edged with taunt. "Who are you?"

"Lonnie Peden, Billy. You know me."

"Who's that with you?"

"My baby brother, Warren. Warren, this here is Deputy Goforth."

Goforth shone his flashlight into the wagon. A soiled tarpaulin was stretched over the back, a lumpy mound. "What's that you haulin', Lonnie?"

"Ah, Billy, it ain't no concern of yours."

"Open the back, Lonnie."

"Back off, Billy, leave me be."

"Open up."

Lonnie hesitated, then spread his hands helplessly. "Do it, Warren."

Goforth lifted the edge of the tarpaulin. "Since when you in the orange business, Lonnie?"

"A man does what he can to get along."

"You got a bill of sale?"

"Billy, if'n you was to forget all about this, it might just be worth your while."

"Close it up, Warren." He backed off a stride or two. "You drive this wagon of yours downtown, Lonnie, to the sheriff's office."

"Ah, you gonna make a fuss about this?"

"Do like I say and do it now. I'll be right behind you all the way."


"Didn't mean to harm, Momma."

Joelle Peden pressed her lips together. Behind steel-rimmed glasses her eyes were harsh and unforgiving. A parched look to her skin made her seem older than her years, locked in at the joints, each movement restricted under a plain dress that hung loosely on her bony frame.

"Stealin'," she said in a flat, dry voice. "Not the way I raised you boys."

"A load of oranges, Momma," Warren protested.

She turned his way in abrupt, slow stages. "You! Not even dry behind the ears. Too smart to stay in high school. Too rich to hold a steady job. Too good to put in an honest day's work in the family business."

"The boy doesn't want to spend his life killin' bugs, Momma."

She came back around to Lonnie, perched uneasily on the bunk against the cell wall. "Just like you, Lord save us. What a hero to have. A banged up footballer without a nickel to show for it. Where'd it get you, the touchdowns, the cheers, your picture in the newspapers? No money, no business, no decent job."

"I'll take care of myself, Momma, I always have."

"Stealin' oranges at night and runnin' them across the Gulf. They goin' to put you away, boy, you understand that? Put you away for a long time. Those were Gault oranges you took. *Gault,* God save us!"

"Just bad luck, that deputy comin' up on us that way."

"You the older, Lonnie. You supposed to know better, doin' your baby brother thataway. You supposed to protect him, keep him outa harm's way."

"They goin' to send me away, Momma?" There was fear in Warren's eyes.

She shook her head. "No thanks to your brother, no. Sheriff Venable says I can take you outa here, says he's lettin' you off. This time. Only he says you better not get caught pluckin' even one little juice orange off'n a tree anywhere in the county, you understand what I'm sayin' to you?"

"Okay, Momma."

"What about me?" Lonnie said.

Mrs. Peden walked out of the unlocked cell, motioned for Warren to join her. "You stay. Sheriff says he'll tend to your case by his ownself. Brought you up to be law-abidin' and God-fearin'. You've shamed me, son, is what you've done. Disgraced me in front of the whole town and in the eyes of our Lord. . . ."

Lonnie watched them leave without speaking. He sat on the bunk staring at the open cell door wondering what would happen if he were to go after them. He supposed a squad of deputies were waiting outside, hoping he'd try something. He swung his feet up and decided to wait it out.

He didn't have long to wait. Duke Venable came trundling

down the length of the cellblock. He indicated Lonnie was to make room for him on the bunk and he sat down heavily. He lit one of the thin black cigars he was addicted to. He smoked and sucked air into his lungs as if the effort was too great for his massive bulk.

"Lonnie, you got to be one of the dumbest dudes in all of north Florida."

Lonnie clamped his mouth shut.

"How many loads you run before this one?"

Lonnie refused to give him the satisfaction of an answer.

Venable rolled his large head from side to side and examined the cigar. "Nothin'," he muttered. "Nothin' goes on in Tokeneke without I say so. You been away so long you forgot that? Must be all that tacklin' scrambled what brains you had."

They sat in silence. Until Lonnie could tolerate it no more. "What happens now?"

"To you?" Venable seemed pleasantly surprised. "Now that is good, considerin' your own good and welfare in what I take to be a conciliatory manner, boy. Maybe you ain't so dumb at that. What happens to you? You stand trial, get found guilty, and do time."

"How much time?"

"Least a year under local ordinances, maybe as much as three. Depends on the judge, who happens to be a Gault, second cousin removed from The Hill."

"Damn."

"I don't think you'd take to hard time much, Lonnie. Just ain't the same as trainin' camp."

"What do I have to do to get out of it, Sheriff?"

"Well, now, you certainly do show some promise, after all. Haulin' nightfruit is for folks past their prime, Lonnie, and kids lookin' to pick up some quick dollars. A man of your credentials and experience ought to be able to do much better for himself."

Lonnie grew more alert. "Such as?"

"Such as comin' to work for me is what."

"You mean become a deputy?"

"Shoot, no! You drive good and drivin' at night don't seem to bother you none. You know Clyde Tatum?" Lonnie shook his head negatively. "Clyde used to work for me only he got hisself shot up a week or so back. Some bad place over the county line. Seems Clyde tried to lift a load of fine Scotch and bourbon from some really hard-nosed ol' boys and they did him permanent. You follow me?"

"I'm not sure that I do."

"Here it is—Clyde was haulin' liquor into the county, distributin' it to certain approved parties . . . Clyde belonged to me."

"Belonged?"

"Every dollar he made half belonged to me. Do you follow me?"

"I do now."

"Well, good. Point is, I sorely need another good driver, somebody I can depend on and trust. Somebody who understands how business is done in the county and is willin' to go along."

"Where would I get the liquor?"

"All the arrangements, the buyin', the sellin', are made by me. You'd be a middle man, a distributor. Minimum risk, maximum gain."

"Seems to me the risk was pretty substantial for ol' Clyde."

"Life ain't much different than playin' football, Lonnie. You want the big rewards you got to play with wild abandon. You interested?"

"And these charges?"

"Dropped for lack of evidence."

"What about Goforth?"

"My deputies do like they're told."

"How do you know I won't take more'n my share?"

A narrow grin snaked across the sheriff's face. His tiny eyes disappeared in the folds of flesh above his cheekbones. "Boy, I know you are not goin' to do anythin' foolish. Else what overtook Clyde could happen again some dark and lonely night, you follow my meanin'?"

Lonnie filled his lungs with air. "You can trust me, sheriff. You can depend on me." He extended his hand.

Venable worked himself back onto his feet, left without a backward glance. "Come with me, boy. There's paperwork needs doin'. . . ."

# CHAPTER
## 8

WITH TAKE-OUT BURGERS and fries and double-rich shakes from Andy's Bar-B-Q on Shore Road near the marina, they headed out to Silver Sands. Back up against the dunes, Kate kicked off her shoes and raised her face to the warming sun. Soon the tension began to drain out of her limbs.

"Signs of autumn everywhere," she said. "The breezes are shifting, getting cooler."

"I hate winters," Jody Joiner said.

"Then stay away from New York. Cold and snow and slush all winter long."

"Oh, I can't do that! It won't matter anyway. All the excitement, Broadway, my career in theater—I'll be warm all the time."

Not the *work*, Kate said to herself. Never the work, never the *acting*, the doing, the act of building a role. A career, the glamor and excitement, the rewards; money, fame, glory. She bit into the burger, spicy sauce dribbling onto her chin. She wiped it dry with a napkin.

"Twenty years ago I was very much like you, Jody. Talking about a career even before I'd set foot on a stage."

Jody shifted around to face the older woman. "I want it so much. Someday I'll be a star."

An old-fashioned fantasy. A dim, unsettling memory floated to life in some darkened portion of Kate's brain. She looked out at the Gulf, glistening in the high sun. Diving gulls seldom came up without a fish. Eat and be eaten; what creatures feasted off the gulls?

"What do your parents think of the idea, of you becoming an actress?"

"There's only momma." The girl made a face. "She says I should finish college, become a teacher, take a steady job. Momma doesn't understand."

"She's giving you good advice."

"She doesn't see things the same way. She's frightened, worried about the future. But where's it got her, nothin' in her life but that rickety ol' diner. I want more. I want better."

Kate's parents had disapproved of her theatrical ambitions. With scorn, and the mocking taunts of her mother—"Who are you to think of being an actress?" Her father had described the theater as a place of corruption and evil, a moral charnal house.

"You believe I can?" Jody's insistent voice brought Kate back to Silver Sands. She stared at the girl. "You believe I have the looks and the talent to become a star? You do, don't you?"

Kate took Jody's hand. "It's a very difficult way to go. Actors, we're all so vulnerable. On display all the time, auditions, photo sessions, being told you're not tall enough or too tall, not pretty enough or too pretty. That your breasts are too big or too small. Always set up for rejection and believe me rejection comes in large and small ways and it always hurts."

If Jody understood, she gave no sign. "I can't believe you were never pretty enough. You're the most beautiful woman I've ever seen."

Kate turned away. "New ones get off the bus every day in New York. Younger, prettier, some of them more talented than you are. The way you look counts, but there's so much more."

"I'm a good actress, I'll get better,"

"It's so hard, hard work. You need experience, time to allow yourself to grow, develop as a human being."

"Then you think I'm beautiful enough?"

"You have to want it more than anybody else wants it, and even then there are no guarantees."

"I want it."

"Yes, I suppose you do."

"Oh, you have no idea. . . ."

Kate's head swung around, her perfect face abruptly flushed, the sea-green eyes glinting with resentment. Quickly it faded, replaced by compassion, by understanding. "Oh, but I do. It nags at you all the time, never far from your consciousness, a persistent itch that won't be scratched, a constant dissatisfaction with the way things are. All those fools who keep you from doing what you want so much to do, the invisible walls that hold you off from what you know is rightly yours. Oh, I have a very good idea. Nobody wanted it more than I did. I still want it."

"Then why are you here, stuck away in this piddlin' little town with all these awful people when you could be in New York City or in Hollywood? If it was me—"

More than once during her time in King of Heaven Kate had asked herself the same question. And the answer was always the same: she hurt too much. Too many hopes raised and predictably dashed. Too much residual pain. So much still had to be dealt with. . . .

Michael, for example. Michael had been much older than she was. A handsome man, clever and fun to be with. He'd led her skillfully from virginity to unshackled passion in his service until she came to the terrifying conviction that she was unable to survive without him. Until she discovered differently.

Always dependent on men, she thought with some bitterness. First her father, of course. Next, Michael. Then Henry Gail, her first director, and later her lover; her husbands—there had been two of them; and other lovers, almost too many to remember, more than she wanted to remember; and now Wesley. Seldom had she been without a man in her life, never totally free of a man, never independent and strong, never capable and wholly on her own. Except in failure and defeat. Her own opinions had been suspect for a long time, her abilities

doubted, her judgment, her work, her friends, her life. Men
had always caused her to feel feeble, disoriented, childish.

"What I'd really like to do," Kate, as much to herself as to
Jody, said, "is to write a play."

"How exciting!"

"About the difficulties of growing up, of surviving your
family, your background, of becoming yourself finally."

"It would be wonderful, I know."

Kate brought her attention back to the girl, as if seeing her
for the first time. Which of them, she asked silently of herself,
was teacher and which the pupil? "Some day," she said aloud.
"But not yet."

"Why?" There was a disingenuous quality about Jody, less
innocent than ignorant, made harsh by a worldliness that exceeded her years, her eyes shining and brittle, as if her search
for answers and information was all designed to advance her
toward that marvelous and inevitable end: *stardom.*

Kate spoke without thinking. "Not while my mother is alive,
it would hurt her too much." A nervous laugh trickled out of
her. "Are we ever free of our past? Always daughters, always
children, energized by a lingering guilt and those early failures."

"I don't understand."

"Nor should you. Being an actress, I'm trying to say, it's
a very hard way to go."

"I'm not afraid to work, I know I can do it. A person can
do anythin', if'n she puts her mind to it and tends to business."

"You've got time, almost four years of college in front of
you."

"I don't want to wait that long."

"If I were your mother, I'd insist you finish school. Time
changes everything. You might decide on another career."

"Never. No way."

"Or some handsome boy may sweep you off your feet."

"Boys," Jody drawled in disdain. "No hotshot campus hero's
goin' to turn me into his houseslave. It's men I'm interested
in."

That caused Kate to look at Jody with renewed concern.
Had she underestimated the girl? There was the sound of steel

in that voice, steel and cruelty. "Men do have a way of getting in the way," Kate said.

"Not in my way. Nobody's goin' to get in my way. Nobody."

Kate, staring out at the shining flat waters of the Gulf, remembered a time when she had spoken almost the same words. Where, she wondered, had it all gone wrong?

Mae-Mae came to Reverend Seely with considerable apprehension. She recognized in him an unyielding ferocity, a righteous fury, the wrath and Divine judgment of the Lord. His face reminded her of the cutting edge of a woodsman's axe, his stance rooted in certainty and Godliness, his jaw an inflexible thrust. His presence filled up his rectory office to overflowing and made her uneasy, squirming under his steady gaze. His eyes reached out to her across his desk as if able to plumb the most secret crannies of her impure soul, condemning what he saw, causing her sphincter to clench defensively, making her wonder why she had come here.

"I had no one else to turn to," she said.

Experience had taught him; give the young ones time to be afraid, and show no weakness else they would exploit it, see the easy way out. But he could offer no easy way to sinners, no simple solutions to the consequences of ungodly actions. It was the times, he assured himself; permissive, liberal, the ways of God replaced by the ways of mortals, to the detriment of all.

"What have you done?" There was no allowance for denial in his stern manner, no room to dissemble or evade.

She shivered. "It's about Wesley."

"The Gaults are fine people. With roots deep in Tokeneke County. Good Christian folk who never transgress and give freely to just causes."

"Oh, I would never say anything bad about any member of the family."

He formed a steeple with his long, strong fingers. "About your husband?"

She could not tear her eyes away from his. He seemed to grow larger, more imposing, a great angular creature with the hard bony face of a desert warrior. Waves of uncertainty and terror gripped her. She attempted a smile and failed to make it.

"Wesley, yes."

"Marriage is the keystone of a Christian existence," he intoned. Pitched for effect, his voice echoed in the hollows of his skull with the force of Divine thunder. How often he had longed for such a voice to reverberate throughout the Church, to stir the people, to move mountains in the name of Christ Jesus, Lord of the universe and all that lay beyond it. Instead he performed mostly as a marriage counselor. A social worker. A playground director. He cracked his knuckles. All that was going to change.

The sound made her twitch in place.

He noted the reaction and moved to exploit it. One finger curled her way, straightened out, joints locking, forming a probe of fearful intent. The finger held her eyes. An unexpected, swift jab caused her to recoil. Put the fear of the Lord into them, he told himself, the fear of that old terrible God of Abraham and Joseph and the ancient Israelites, a God demanding and jealous and angry when crossed. Put the fear of Dorr C. P. Seely into them.

"What about your husband?"

"I spoke to Wesley's dad, and to Papa James. . . ."

"I have always respected Papa James."

"He's very old."

"Blessed by the Lord."

"Not exactly right in the head."

"God readies each of us to cross over in His own way. Your husband?"

She sat up straight, knees clasped, hands folded in her lap, prim, pure, looking scrubbed and brushed and proper. "Wesley simply won't pay suitable attention to me." There, she'd said it. A pulse throbbed in her throat and her mouth went dry. She braced herself for criticism and condemnation, the worse, and Seely was just the man to deliver it unadorned.

He leaned her way, mighty finger jabbing. "More to the point is whether or not you pay suitable attention to your true mate in Christian wedlock. Have you been entertainin' impure thoughts, Mae-Mae? Have weird ideas infested your spirit? Have you forgotten your wifely vow of obedience, of love, of honor? Have you forgotten your place in the home, Mae-Mae? The place of every good woman in a Christian society?"

"I am at fault," she spoke without thinking. "I have failed my husband."

"At last we come to the crux of the matter. 'Look to thine own self,' Shakespeare wrote, and I say as much to you. Blame not lest ye be blamed. Cleanse your own soul, purify your own heart, empty your own mind of deceit and lies and transform yourself into a true Christian wife and as the night follows day so shall the infinite rewards of marriage be yours."

She nodded vigorously. "Oh, I believe that I've been lax, allowin' my wifely responsibilities slide by. I shall do better, I promise. But still—"

The girl was incredibly persistent. He wanted to pound his desk, send her away. Bore someone else with your picayune troubles, he wanted to say. But she was a Gault, if only by marriage, and always would be. He put his head back against the tall back of his leather chair and allowed his eyes to flutter shut.

"Talk to me, girl. Talk to me as you would to your Maker. Speak freely and tell me how I may help you." A vision of her came onto the screen of his mind, only now she was without clothes, naked and beckoning sensuously. Her hips swayed and her tight little breasts bobbled. Young women; so vital and strong, so amenable to experimentation, and without blemish. No offending rolls of excess flesh, no scars, no explosions of blue to signify the bursting of veins used for too long, no stretch marks. Reverend Seely loathed stretch marks.

"I am not so dumb as to deceive myself," Mae-Mae was saying. "Been married six years and it has not always been awful. In the good times we did things together, Wesley and me. Sailin' in the Gulf and fishin' for broadbill. He has always been such a beautiful man, Reverend, tall and finely constructed and with the face of a Greek god. Mostly Wesley did the fishin'. I cannot abide the stench of fish, you see. And the salt air does terrible things to the skin and so I spent a great deal of my time in the cabin, tryin' not to upchuck and stayin' out of the sun. Was that wrong of me, Reverend?"

"The Bible speaks of fisher*men* and makes no mention of women doin' man's work."

"Exactly my thinkin', Reverend," she said gratefully.

"Continue." If only she would get it over with, leave him alone. He resented the time wasted on such inanities, attention so easily put to better purposes, to his true mission.

"Momma raised me to be a proper Christian girl."

"I knew your mother, happier now in the lap of our Lord, I'm sure."

"Amen."

"Go on, Mae-Mae."

"Imagine how Wesley would feel if I went tomcattin' around takin' lovers and spendin' my time at Miss Ivy's and such as that."

Out at last. Thought she'd never get to it. Trouble was the girls of Tokeneke were raised to keep their thoughts pure and their thighs locked. The marriage ceremony seldom served as an effective key to the kingdom. To make matters worse, their husbands possessed scant interest in rousing their wives, or in pleasing them. The sexual revolution, so called, had made little impact on the daughters of the best families in the county.

"I," she announced with misplaced pride, he thought wryly, "am not a slut in a brothel."

No way he was going to give her an inch. He bore forward, eyes blazing, a parental finger jabbing, words filling the room. "I married you myself. You understand the duties of a wife, the responsibilities, the obligations. Six years and you are not yet a mother...."

"That's just it!" she bleated triumphantly. "Wesley won't make me pregnant."

"Are you sayin' to me that that fine young man out of that fine old family refuses to produce an heir? That is impossible for me to believe." He had no wish to raise the issue with Wesley, no desire to embroil himself in matters of concern only to a Gault. A girl like this one could create problems.

"He insists I do—" She blushed and turned away. "Unclean acts."

He tried to imagine Mae-Mae doing oral sex; the picture

was out of focus. Not the sort, that was clear. "I will not hear you speak against your husband. I've known that boy since the day he was born. I've known his daddy, his granddaddy. His people found this town. Gaults, from the very beginning . . .

"Yes sir. Otis Ambrose Gault came into this part of Florida and went down on his knees and prayed to God for guidance. 'Drive out the heathen,' God told Otis Ambrose Gault. 'Drive out Mine enemies and make this place safe and good for My people in My name, for I am the One and True God, Lord of the Universe, King of Heaven and everything above and everything below.'

"Well, I tell you—Otis Ambrose slew the savages and drove them out and gave this place its holy name and it has been a fine place to live and raise children and worship God in ever since. And nobody can say anything bad about a Gault, not to me."

"Oh, I would never say a bad word about the family, may God strike me dead."

"Praise God. Now you go on home and do right by that husband of yours and by yourself."

"You mean I should perform as he wishes?"

"I am sayin' to you to use the gifts God provided to make him happy. To make your marriage function properly in the eyes of the Lord. You get that boy to give you a baby." There. That ought to do it.

She blinked and for an extended moment he was afraid she was going to cry. If there was anything he hated worse than a complaining woman it was a crying woman.

"We certainly are livin' in a changin' world," she said finally. "I try not to judge folks but I can hardly approve some of the stuff people are doin' or sayin', now can I?"

"Certainly not." He was about to claim the press of time, another appointment, usher her out of his office. Anything to be rid of this twit of a girl, this pathetic and perpetual adolescent. And then she switched gears on him and he began to wonder exactly why she had come.

"Now you take that play the other night. . . ."

"The play?"

"By Mr. Eugene O'Neill, out at the college."

Seely took a hitch in his thoughts; where was she headed now?

"All that bad language," she said.

Lord save me, he thought. One of those offended by even a damn or a hell. It was a mistake to get mired down by the occasional use of a swear word; only way some folks had of letting off steam.

"Goddam whore." She offered the words in a whisper, as if reluctant to utter them. "Takin' the Lord's name in vain in public. I have to tell you, Reverend, I was truly startled that Dr. Moody would allow such goin's on on campus thataway. Such a blasphemy was never spoken in my presence in all the years I was a student at Christian."

It came slowly to Seely. "I was present openin' night. I heard all that unacceptable language and intend to bring up the matter with Dr. Moody. Forcefully." There, he thought with some satisfaction, that should do it, end this interview. Send her on her way.

"Well, that is up to you. I do not care to get involved." A chilly note crept into her voice, the cutting edge of a stubbornness and determination he had failed to recognize earlier. "That is not what I came for."

"Why did you come?" He wearied of her meanderings. Get on with it, he commanded silently, get it over with. He glanced at his watch, turning the gesture into an elaborate ceremony.

"I want to have a baby, I have to."

"Have to?"

"It's what all Gaults want."

And what Gaults want Gaults got. Seely longed to shout imprecations at this silly little child. "If it be God's will . . ."

"Wesley says he's goin' west if I get in a family way."

"West?"

"To Venice, California, where the girls all smoke dope and give sex away and roller skate. I know I could make Wesley happy, if he'd only give her up. . . ."

Seely almost missed it. His attention came spinning back down to Mae-Mae. She mistook his interest for disapproval, set herself for a scolding.

"Her?" he said, eyes fixed.

She nodded. "And so old."

"An older woman?"

"She must be at least forty."

Seely's age exactly; he felt youthful, vigorous, unfulfilled, the future stretching out into infinity, waiting to be discovered, explored, exploited. But how?

"Who?" he said, as if on the verge of a great discovery.

The question surprised her. "Why, Miss Kate Fellows, of course," she said, as if he should have known.

Dinner was over. Chicken croquettes and mashed potatoes with thick brown flour gravy, mixed peas and overcooked carrots. Biscuits and butter and deep-dish apple pie. He told Martha that it was a marvelous meal and said he had a few evening calls to make.

"Some poor unfortunates need my presence."

"You work so hard, that Crusade of yours, sometimes I worry about you."

"I'm strong as a bull. . . ."

"Thank the Lord."

"Amen."

"I'll wait up for you."

"I may be late."

He went into his office and dialed her number. He let it ring once and hung up, dialed again. She answered at once.

"The usual place?" he said.

"The way you've ignored me, I don't know if you deserve . . ."

"I'm leavin' right now."

"I don't know. . . ."

"Do you expect me to beg? I don't beg. Not for anybody."

"My, you do get all fired up. I'll be there."

"Same room as the last time."

"Okay."

He hung up and discovered his hands were shaking. He went back into the house and located the red leatherbound Bible he used on his calls. Martha saw him to the door. She smiled at him.

"You're a good man, Dorr Seely."

"Have a nice evening," he said to her and left. It took him nearly an hour to reach the Triple X Motel and Inn, located off Route 4, a dozen or so miles outside the county line. A glaring neon sign announced the fact that Adult Movies were shown on closed-circuit television in each room, twenty-four hours a day, short-term rates available.

A scrawny woman registered Seely and shoved a key his way, collected his money. He went down to the end of the long low building to room 128 and admitted himself. He took off his clothes and went into the bathroom, showered, toweling himself off briskly. His body tingled and his brain leapfrogged around in anticipation. It reminded him of his days at Baylor University, his football-playing days. The same heightened awareness of his own physicality, of his vulnerability and the upcoming battle, the opportunity to deliver punishment and pain within an accepted social framework. He wrapped a towel around his middle and went back into the room, checked his watch. She was late; had she changed her mind? Was this her way of hurting him, of paying him back? In answer, there was a knock at the door. He opened it and she walked in.

She faced him grinning. "All ready, ain't you?"

"What took you so long?"

"I wasn't sure about comin', still not sure I'm stayin'."

He reached for her and she skipped backward, laughing, tossing that pretty head of hers. "Not so fast, Preacher. You just call whenever it suits you and I'm supposed to jump and run and make you happy. What about my rights?"

He produced a tight, ominous display of large gleaming teeth. An impulse to summon down the wrath of Heaven, to send her trembling and contrite to her knees, to beg for his forgiveness, took hold.

"Have I treated you badly?" he said.

"I'm not a kid any more." She grew sullen, watchful, the pretty face closed up and not at all to his liking. "That's what I was, when we first got together. That first time in the rectory. You did me on the floor behind your desk. . . . I was a virgin."

Was she? Was she in fact pure when he first entered her body, giving herself to him as a reward for the kindly, Godly existence he had lived for so long?

"But no longer," he answered, eyes fixed and glazed. "What do you do when I'm not around?"

She taunted him. "Think I get it on with every boy in King

of Heaven? Maybe so. Maybe I do 'em same as I do you, only sneakin' aroun' in the dark on campus. Maybe I do Dr. Moody from time to time, same as you. How's that sit with you?"

"You and Moody . . . ?"

The expression on his face frightened her, the bones locked toughly in place, his size and strength suddenly blatant, threatening. "I'm just funnin' with you, Dorr, that's all. There ain't nobody but you, and I ain't told anybody about us, not even my best friend."

The words touched a sensitive spot in him. His fingers curled up into big fists. "If I thought you were talkin' about these meetin's of ours . . ."

She giggled and he was reminded of how truly young she still was, how relatively inexperienced. "That'd really do you in in these parts, wouldn't it? Put an end to that Tenth Crusade of your'n. Up on The Hill, they'd come down on you like a ton of bricks. Don't care what folks do, they don't, as long as it looks right."

He raised one immense fist. "I catch you runnin' off at the mouth . . ."

She glided toward him. "You can trust me, Dorr. Honest."

"What about your momma?"

"You think I'd tell her? Never."

He relaxed. "Well, all right, just keep it that way, hear?"

"Yes, sir."

"I only care about us, " he said, voice softened and intimate. "You believe that?"

"I believe you, Dorr."

"Then come on over here."

She just looked him over. "Boy, you are in bad shape. Look at the way you're stickin' out. Doesn't Martha ever take care of you, Preacher?"

"Take off your clothes." He spoke in a still, flat voice.

"I'm not so sure."

"Be nice to me."

She stepped out of her skirt, drew off her panties. "Beg," she said. For a long moment, she believed he was going to strike her, the veins in his neck standing out in bold relief, his shoulders flexed and tense. Then he slumped and she watched him sink to his knees.

"Please . . ."

"Crawl over here."

"Whatever you want, anything, anything."

"Closer, as close as you can get. Look, but no touching. Not yet. Maybe not ever." Her laughter was thick and brief. "Is that how you pray at church, Preacher? Is this what you pray for? Boy, if they could see you now, all those good Christian folks, see you thisaway. Go on, Preacher, pray for it. Pray and beg and might be I'll take pity on you. . . ."

His head inclined and the faint scent of sweat and urine filled up the cavities of his skull and he wavered dizzily. And understood that it was no accident that she had come to him stained and soiled. Had she been with another man before coming here? Was that the stench of man's body on her, his sweat, his semen . . . ?

A hoarse muffled cry broke out of him. "Goddam whore . . ." His face went between her young thighs which opened to admit him and through the mingled scents, through the roiled emotion, the blind holy passion, he knew that he had crossed over the line into the most vital part of his life.

At breakfast, the call came. A detached, crisply officious voice delivered the message, leaving no room for dispute or for delay.

"Mr. Nolan will see you in his office on The Hill at ten o'clock this morning, Reverend Seely. Be on time, please. Mr. Nolan does not tolerate tardiness." Click.

Resentment formed a tight moist knot in Seely's chest, unloosing searing droplets of anger along his nervous system. His eyes blazed and his big hands clenched and he longed to reject the summons with force and disdain. But he needed the people who lived on The Hill, needed their encouragement, their moral support, their unlimited material resources. He made ready to go.

At five minutes before the appointed hour he presented himself at the big house where a middle-aged secretary got him seated in a small anteroom.

"Mr. Nolan will see you soon."

Forty-five intolerably slow minutes passed before he was ushered into the presence of the chief operating officer of all the Gault Enterprises. Mr. Nolan examined Seely out of tiny eyes across his desk.

"More," he muttered with some irritation. "I expected more."

"I don't understand." A familiar sense of inadequacy swept over Seely, a feeling that he never quite measured up, never quite delivered on the promise of his mind and ambition and energy, never came in first. Always the near success, always the partial failure. "I'm doin' my best, sir. . . ."

"A crusade, you said. Christian warriors, you said."

"God's word . . ."

"Spare me the holier than thou babble. I want my town kept just the way it is. You were goin' to close the pass to outsiders. To do-gooders, to unionists, to the developers. You wanted the air time, I provided it. . . ."

"Dr. Moody . . ."

"Dr. Moody belongs to me. That college of his belongs to me. The radio station belongs to me. Just about everythin' in Tokeneke County belongs to us Gaults, or we control it, or it works for us. Am I makin' myself clear to you, Reverend? What I want, I get. What I say, is done."

"I understand."

"Figured you would. Now this radio show of yours, it needs jazzin' up."

Seely drew himself up. "I am not an actor, sir. I am a minister of God. I carry Christ's word to the populace."

"There, you're doin' it again. Let me say straight out—this crusade of yours ain't cuttin' it by a long shot."

"I've come up with a name for it—The Tenth Crusade."

Mr. Nolan blinked and said nothing.

Seely's uneasiness increased. "There were originally nine, you see. Actually more'n that. Only the others were just minor efforts, not truly in the cause of Christianity."

Mr. Nolan shifted around in his chair, a slow, ponderous effort that caused him to grunt and wheeze. "What I'm after is results. You have to drop a word in here and there about Jesus, salvation, sin, heaven and hell, well, all right. As long as you get down on the people who I am against."

"Against?"

"My enemies, man. Those sleazy politicians up in Talla-hassee and Washington, D. C. Those social activists I'm always readin' about in *Time* magazine. Those big-mouth movie stars like Jane Fonda and Ed Asner, always pokin' in their noses where it ain't wanted. I am talkin' about Ralph Nader and his kind, *The New York Times* and *The Washington Post*. The ones always tryin' to sabotage our way of life, destroy what's good and right in Tokeneke, in Florida, in the U. S. of America."

Seely firmed up his jaw, put resoluteness in his voice. "I am a man of God, not a politician."

Mr. Nolan swore softly. "Try thinkin' 'stead of talkin', Reverend. Wasn't it Jesus Himself went after the moneylenders, after the high priests of the temple? You do the same."

"The moneylenders . . . ?"

Mr. Nolan swore again. "The communists, there's always the communists."

"But—"

"The soft-headed judges who turn muggers and murderers and rapists loose. The wastrels in the government, the welfare cheats. The big brains in New York and Yale and the government. The ones who gave us defeat in Vietnam and degradation in Iran, the ones who gave us inflation and unemployment and high taxes and high interest rates. Throw enough of your anger against the wall and some of it's bound to stick. Fight the fight the ordinary man on the block can't fight by his own self."

"I have always believed," Seely said in a deliberate manner, "that the country was being led down the primrose path."

"'Course you did," Mr. Nolan said drily. "So lay into them. . . ."

"Yes. Somebody must bring the wrath of God down on the disbelievers and the destroyers who would ruin our great nation and its perfect systems."

"Now you're cookin', Reverend."

"The traitors among us, the dissemblers, the conspirators, the liars and the cheats."

"Amen."

"The evil ones who have forced God out of the classroom. The race-mixers, those who would despoil our people by equalizin' everythin'. The abortionists, the homosexuals, the adulterers."

"You got a quick mind, Reverend. Stay on it. Do a job for me, I'll do a job for you."

"For me?"

"You'll be famous, Reverend. Another Billy Graham, another Jerry Falwell. Folks all over will say your name with respect. We'll put you on the television, on the networks, the cables. The faithful will flock to enlist in your crusade."

"I want to reach out to human hearts all over the globe. I will make the folks cry out and holler and stomp their feet in righteous fury. I will fill up the Superdome and set the place to rockin'...."

"Right on, Reverend."

"Marchin' bands by the dozen. Pretty girls in star-spangled tights swingin' their purty little butts for Jesus and throwin' their batons to Heaven and a chorus singin' hymns. 'Stand up, Stand Up for Jesus'... listen to 'em!" Fist beating time, Seely came up on his feet, began to sing:

> "Stand up, stand up for Je-sus, Ye soldiers of
> the cross!
> "Lift high His roy-al ban-ner, It must not suffer
> loss:
> "From vic-tory un-to vic-tory, His ar-my shall
> He lead,
> "Till ev-ery foe is van-quished and Christ is
> Lord in-deed."

"Beautiful, Reverend."

"Red, white and blue buntin'. The national anthem. A single spotlight hits the pulpit and there I am, gussied up in white and holdin' up a big *golden* Bible over my head, and...I...am...prayin'.... The band stops, the girls stand still, the crowd grows hushed. It is silent. Not even a single cough. I begin to preach, to lead them into... *battle*. To enlist them in the... *cause*."

"I can see it, Reverend."

"Oh, yes, *yes!* I can see it, I see my future at last. I am on the road to glory and the end is not in sight...."

"As long as you've got the heart for it."

"My heart is strong. My will undaunted. My courage infinite. I'd face down the lion in his den, I'd fight a wild gorilla, I'd battle a thousand gallopin' Red Chinamen and never bat an eye."

"I believe you would at that," Mr. Nolan said. "There's just one small problem."

Seely's eyes rolled down from on high. "What problem is that?"

"You need some little item to launch this crusade of yours, to get it off the ground. Some stunt. Some gimmick. Some super show-business spectacular to get folks to pay attention. Some miraculous happenin'. Something really special . . ."

"Like what?"

"I don't rightly know, Reverend. But I have faith. I have confidence, in you. I'm sure you'll come up with somethin'. And soon. . . ."

Looking at Mr. Nolan, Seely's limbs went cold and he felt the ancient fears returning, making him afraid as he'd never before been afraid. This was the chance he'd been waiting for; he couldn't stand to lose it all now. He just couldn't. . . .

On the broad veranda of the Field Club, looking over the first tee of the golf course, Dorr Seely and B. J. Moody were finishing a leisurely and pleasant lunch. The food at the Field Club, if not excellent, was certainly the best available in King of Heaven. French by inclination, it was prepared in thick sauces—that would have been scorned in Paris—at inflated prices. Off to the right, in the neatly sculpted artificial lake created for that express purpose, a flock of flamingos formed graceful images on attenuated legs. Rimming the veranda, beds of flowering plants: gladiolus, amazon-lily, gloriosa. Farther out on the course, the fairway was lined with magnolia trees and dogwood, all under a warming sun. It all served to calm Seely, to remind him of the satisfying continuity of life in Tokeneke County, the rewards of a slow and satisfying life in an unchanging, God-fearing, golf-playing, truly American community.

"Let's do this more often," Moody said. Something about Seely put him off. He viewed in the minister someone on the

verge of a cataclysmic explosion, charged by repressed rage
and violence. "I admit I was surprised when you called me. . . ."

"There is somethin' on my mind, B. J."

Moody's attention came to bear. "Oh!"

"That play . . ."

"The O'Neill?" Moody was pleased that he had remembered
the author's name, if not the title of the play. "A Yankee Doodle
classic, you know."

"I am sure O'Neill is highly regarded in those pseudoso-
phisticated intellectual circles in New York City. . . ."

"A shade too talky for me. Personally I prefer singing and
dancing girls."

Seely frowned. "Vulgar," he said with majestic disapproval.

Moody sobered swiftly. "Ah."

"Vulgar and obscene."

"Obscene." Dismay rushed through Moody's nervous system. His chubby fingers bent and stretched and bent again. He
was not a man ever to make a fist. "I'm afraid I don't follow
you, Dorr."

"There you have it. I was out to the college bookstore today
and found a copy of the play. Three copies, in fact. *Long Day's
Journey Into Night*. Published by Yale University Press. Yale,
established as a Christian institution but long lapsed into sec-
ularity and liberalism."

"I suppose you're right." Moody reflected on what it would
take to get hired by Yale. Or preferably Columbia; New York
was so exciting, so much to do and see. Ah Columbia. Not as
President, of course, perhaps Dean of a graduate school. Or
advisor to incoming freshmen. He suspected he had overstayed
his welcome in King of Heaven. But no other offers were
coming his way. He cautioned himself, tread carefully. "God
has taken a beating on the campuses of the nation. . . ."

"And that calls for a remedy, don't you agree? I knew you
would. And no better place to begin than close to home."

"I don't understand."

"Have you examined the text? I have."

"The text?"

"The O'Neill play."

"Ah."

"Managed as far as page thirty-nine and was forced to cease and desist. I could tolerate no more. My mind spun at the coarse and careless language." He extracted a sheet of unlined yellow paper from his pocket. "In the first act alone, twenty-five times, the word 'damn' was used, the word 'whore' twice, there are three sacriligious uses of our Lord's name, one 'God damn it' and one 'bastard'."

"Too much."

"If you think so, why have you failed to put an end to this blasphemy? Explain that to me, B. J.? I had a trusted associate read on in the play and was informed that the phrase 'Goddam whore' is used farther along." Breathing hard, Seely paused, glaring at the other man.

Moody picked at his peach cobbler, his appetite spoiled, the fun gone out of his day. He sipped some coffee; it was cold. "Oh Dorr, you know these show business people."

"Indeed I do not. Nor are you in show business, B. J. Am I mistaken, or is that a Christian college you're runnin' out there."

"Oh. Exactly right, on every count." Running it, he reminded himself, at the tolerance of the Board of Trustees, the parents of the students, and the whim and cash flow of the Gault family. Not to mention the constant attention of most of the ministers in town. "What is it you want of me, Dorr?"

"Change the text."

"Censor the play?"

"The exercise of good taste is not censorship."

"What about freedom of expression?"

"What about decency, morality, the ethical standards of a Godly community? Our people do not want their children exposed to vile and profane language and were they informed they would take steps to stop it. I cannot abide, will not abide the Lord's name spoken in an obscene manner."

"Academic freedom. Yes, what about academic freedom?"

"The question does not apply in this case."

"Are you sure?"

"We are discussing morality, Christian fundamentals. Remember, first there was the *Word*."

Moody sighed. Avoid trouble and conflict; that was a rule

to survive by. Live life on a tranquil path, steady, uninterrupted, and present a cheerful face to the world. He set himself against the sharp pain in his chest; heartburn. "I'm not so sure," he said.

"I am," came the harsh answer. "And on Sunday I intend to address the matter in my sermon. The people of our community have a right to know what their children are being taught. And not taught."

Moody was afraid he was going to be sick.

# CHAPTER
## 9

DUKE VENABLE LOOKED the part of a sheriff. He was
over six feet tall with immense shoulders and long, heavy arms,
hands lumpy and large. Great floppy ears hung like badly
attached appendages to his big head, pointing the way to a jaw
thick and heavy with bone. Bright nervous eyes glinted out
from under lowering brows, across pink round cheeks. His
voice was a rumble, word drawled out after word as if each
was precious and reluctantly allowed to go.

"Take a seat, Billy."

Goforth admired the sheriff, but had never much liked him.
Venable was not one to inspire affection in other people. An
aura of violence and danger surrounded him and rumor had it
that in his youth he had killed three men in a bar fight with
his bare hands.

Not a verifiable story, but no one had ever questioned it.
Certainly it was the kind of thing could have happened. Venable
was that sort of a man.

"How things goin'?" He pronounced it "thangs" and drew
it out until like distant thunder it faded into silence.

"Gettin' on all right, Duke."

"Heard about you and Charlene, Billy, made me sad for
you, Billy. Sorry thing a bad marriage."

"Yes, sir."

"It's the times, boy. Me and Sarah, married more'n forty-seven years. Been up and down the line with that woman. Good times and bad times, I've seen 'em all. Can't say as how I was always an ideal husband, but I gave it my number-one best shot. A good woman, a stable family life, it's what makes for a contented man, in my opinion. Drinkin' and fornicatin' and generally cuttin' up just ain't what life's all about. I know, I been there. You find yourself a good lady, son, put a rope on her, carry her on home. Onliest thing to be, I swear it, married."

"I'll keep that in mind, Duke."

"You do that. Been goin' over the Macklin file this mornin'. Anything new come in?"

A vision of Inez lying asleep in that hospital bed drifted into Goforth's mind. "I been thinkin' I'd go 'round and go over it one more time."

Venable drummed the fingers of one hand on his old oak desk. "Seems peculiar to me that gal don't have any idea who jumped her. Ain't never yet seen a nigger gal wasn't spry enough on her feet to come or go as she liked, you catch my meanin'? Ain't never known one a man had to *force* . . ."

Goforth stared sightlessly into space. Inez Macklin was *black*. He'd held her naked in his arms, felt her warmth, the pulsations of her battered flesh, talked to her, examined her as she slept. And never known, never suspected, never saw a sign . . . a black woman.

"You listenin' to me, Billy?"

He snapped back. "Yes, sir, Duke."

"You want to ask that gal some questions, okay. Then close it up. Forget the whole thing. County can't have its number one senior deputy wastin' time 'cause some dude or other got hisself some colored poontang out on the beach." He shifted his great bulk around in his chair, grunting and huffing, settling back in. "There's somethin' I been meanin' to talk to you about, son. You know I am plannin' to retire end of the year. . . ."

"There's been some talk."

"Guess so. A man's been sheriff for thirty years, he leaves his track on a town. You know me, Billy, nothin' goes on in Tokeneke less'n I say it should, nothin' goes on for long without I find out about it. Nothin' good, nothin' bad.

"I did one fine job on this county, if 'n I say so myself. No county in the entire state of Florida has got a lower rate of crime per capita than we have here in Tokeneke County. Ain't no sheriff works on a tighter budget, neither. Built up the department from two raggedy-assed deputies plus a few part-timers to a couple of dozen. You remember how it was, Billy, back a ways, it's how you came on to the force."

"I remember."

"You just come out of the military, two years in Nam, you did."

"You got a good memory, Duke."

"But there was no jobs to be had and Miss Ivy took you on to keep the peace, make the whores feel safe."

"That was in the old house, out beyond The Bottoms. I was goin' to law school durin' the week and workin' Miss Ivy's nights and weekends."

"You had the stuff, Billy. Used your brains all of the time and your fists only when nothin' else would do. Early on I figured you had a talent for law enforcement. I was right. You been a good man ever since, best I ever had. Played it smart, played it cozy, did what you was told to do, what you was supposed to do. Deputying got you through law school."

"Six months shy of gettin' my degree."

"Always figured you'd hang out your own shingle and I'm downright pleased you never did. You been a good deputy, a good man."

"Thank you, Duke."

"You know who it was put .357 Magnums on the boys' hips, don't you?"

"It was you, Duke."

"Better believe it. And it was me got them outfitted in those snappy silver and blue uniforms. And me that brought in cars with two-way radios. And got us moved into these fine air-conditioned offices 'stead of that beat-up old trailer we had to use back when. Damn thing was a *mess*. Hot as purgatory in the summer and in winter the wind came howlin' in so fast a man couldn't keep paper on his desk. Man had to take a pee, he went on back in the piney woods. No way to fight crime, if you understand what I'm sayin'."

"I understand you, Duke."

He smacked his lips and squinted slightly. "Maybe I'm takin' the long road home, but I'll get where I'm goin', give me time. Point is, this desk—" He pounded it. "This badge—" He flashed it from under his rain jacket. "All of this—" He waved one massive arm to take it all in. "What you have here is one superior job to have and to hold, you listenin' to what I am sayin' to you, Billy?"

"Yes, sir."

"I got me a nice house up-county, I got me a powerboat and two station wagons and a powerful pickup. I got me a place down in the Keys and a piece of a shoppin' center over in New Orleans and a half share in a retirement home in Lakeland and some rental apartments in Miami itself. Point is, nobody's goin' to have to give Duke Venable any benefit dinners, no sirree. I took good care of this county, the county's took good care of the Duke.

"I gave folks what they wanted, law and order, peace and tranquility. Anybody come into the county causin' trouble, he got rode out quick enough. Anybody kept gettin' out of line, he got his head smacked. I gave the folks what they wanted, kept out the troublemakers, the integrationists, the unionists, the communists. And the by-God tourists," he ended, laughing raucously. "Damn county's no different than it was thirty, forty years ago, only better, thanks to Duke Venable."

"People owe you a vote of thanks, Duke."

"Folks on The Hill sure do. That's where the power's been and always will be, don't you forget it. Find out what they want up there and get it done yesterday, keep on their good side. Thing I'm sayin' is this, a man can't get too greedy, can't get careless. You got to protect your back, and build a good life and a good bank balance, so to speak."

The sheriff looked at Goforth with a somber, searching expression, as if they had known each other at some other time, in some other place.

"Whoever it is steps into my shoes ain't goin' to have to plot new furrows. The ground's been broken, the heavy work's been done. Just go along and get along. I been puttin' my mind to my successor and I come up with only one name entirely satisfactory to me, and the folks on The Hill. The job is yours, Billy, if you want it."

Goforth hesitated.

Venable's eyes spread and his voice climbed into his sinuses. "You do want it, don't you?"

"Oh, yes, sir. Just overtaken by surprise."

"At a loss for words, are you?"

"Just about."

"Man'd have to be out of his head not to want this job, no doubt about it. Well, all right. We're all set then. By 'n' by, I'll announce my retirement plans, officially. You raise up some kind of a suitable celebration party. Maybe get the boys to chip in for a proper goin' away present, let's say a set of solid silver tableware. The wife'd appreciate that—

" 'Course, you goin' to have to stand for election. But no sweat. Between me and the folks on The Hill it is a lock. The job is yours, son, the job and all the good things go with it."

Goforth stood up and offered his hand, the sheriff took it. "Can't think of how to thank you, Duke."

Venable smiled a fleeting smile. "Well, you put your head on it, boy. I'm as certain as I can be that you'll come up with something nice and right... don't doubt it for a minute...."

He went directly to the hospital. At the nurse's station, he announced his intention. "I'm here to talk to Inez Macklin."

The nurse on duty barely glanced at him. "Gone," she said laconically.

A momentary sense of loss bit into him. So many fragments of his life were breaking away, spinning off into deep space. "What do you mean, gone?"

"Checked out yesterday. Doctor said there was no need for her to stay on."

"Good," he made himself say. "Glad she's better. She say where she was goin'?"

"Home, I guess. Somewhere over in Northtown, they can help you better down in Administration."

He thanked her and left. Back behind the wheel of his car, his anxiety rose steeply. Anxiety and anger. Resentment over her betrayal. She should have waited for him, *he* would have carried her home, tended her gently, made sure everything was all right. She should have stayed in that hospital bed, helpless, dependent, needing *him*.

Man, his head was screwed on all wrong. What in God's name was he thinking? Black girl, white deputy in Tokeneke County and there went the sheriff's badge, lost before it even got pinned to his chest. She should've told him she was black. Keeping a thing like that to herself wasn't right. He checked himself and a grim smile drifted on and off his lips. A little beauty like that one, most likely every stud in Northtown was after her, and plenty getting what they were after. Most likely that's what her story was—just a story. Maybe there'd been no rape at all. Just some rough loving that went too far. Probably into that kind of action.

Angered, and baffled by feelings he did not quite comprehend, he headed home, trying to calm himself, to think only of the good and rich days that lay ahead. Sheriff of Tokeneke County; everything he had ever longed for was coming his way. Why then lingering doubt and uncertainty, even fear? Why not a sense of accomplishment and triumph? Why didn't he feel good?

Once back in his house the sense of loss intensified. Emptiness and desolation, no sign that this was a human habitat. No dirty dishes in the sink, no empty bottles or cans, no clothes strewn about. Even the bed appeared unslept in, the covers thrown back and smoothed down. He excoriated himself for being too orderly, too concerned with the appearances, compulsively neat. Even in this house which had become so important to him, even here he felt apart and without roots. He, who wanted so much to belong, belonged nowhere. To no one.

He shaved and showered and put on a clean uniform, checked in at the sheriff's station and went out on night patrol. Looked like a quiet night, according to the man on the desk. Why not? Duke Venable ran a quiet county, tolerated no deviations from his rules, the rules and laws he chose to enforce. Kept it a good place to live in, in Tokeneke. Quiet, peaceful, obedient; the same way Goforth would be expected to run it.

*He was a happy man, dammit.* Content at last. Going to get every last thing he ever wanted. Every last thing. . . .

Just past midnight he was cruising north of The Bottoms trying to ignore the dank, stagnant smell of the wetlands. He was on Black Rock Turnpike, which wasn't a turnpike at all, but a winding country road that went past the clothing factory along the southern end of the Lazy G. Ranch, one of three Gault ranches, when the call came over the radio. A peeping tom in Northtown. He heard Benjamin respond, say he'd cover it. Goforth hesitated for only a second, switched on his flasher, and sped to join him.

It was her house, all right. Benjamin's car was parked outside in the dirt street. A handful of people were standing around, talking and laughing, waiting for something to happen. They grew silent when Goforth appeared. A burst of derisive laughter followed him into the house; he didn't look back.

Inez wore a long robe and terrycloth slippers. She sat on a kitchen chair and plucked at her fingers. Her eyes were downcast, her stance defensive. Behind her, a sinewy black man, a twelve-gauge shotgun cradled in his left arm. He eyed Goforth with considerable hostility, his presence clearly unwelcome. Benjamin broke off in the middle of a sentence as if to say something to the late-comer, thought better of it, turned back to Inez. The girl looked at Goforth steadily as if trying to penetrate the official persona he presented.

"Just go on with whatever y'all are doin'." Goforth said, with more confidence than he felt. He took up a position against the far wall.

"So you came into this room?" Benjamin said.

"Yes," she said, still looking at Goforth. "To fetch a book. I couldn't sleep."

"You were goin' to read in bed."

"Black folks do read," the sinewy man behind her bit off.

"That a fact?" Benjamin said mildly, not looking at the man.

Goforth saw the hate in the black man's eyes, the easy way he held the shotgun. Guns were as much a part of a man's life in that part of the country as the tools in his garage or the pots in his kitchen. But he doubted the twelve-gauge was used for anything as sporting as hunting. Too much rage in this man, too much hate, and therefore extremely dangerous.

"Got a name?" Goforth said in his coldest voice.

The sinewy man gave no reply. His eyes were hard, unblinking, the hand holding the shotgun growing pale at the knuckles.

"His name's Harlan," Inez said quickly. "Harlan's my friend. . . ."

"Pleased to meet you, Harlan," Goforth said in a warning voice. "You don't mind if Deputy Dark conducts his official investigation in his own way, do you now?"

Harlan's gaze never wavered.

"Be still now, Harlan," Inez said. "Please." She turned back to Benjamin. "I figured a warm bath would help put me to sleep, reading in the bath makes me sleepy."

"So you came after a book?"

"Yes."

"And switched on the lights?"

"The corner lamp."

"What were you wearing?"

She sucked in her lip. "Nothing."

"You were naked."

"Yes."

Goforth saw her then as she had been that night on Silver Sands. Bruised, damaged, helpless and naked, warm in his hands. He felt his body respond to the memory and he shifted uneasily, clearing his mind of such thoughts.

"Where was he?" Benjamin said.

She pointed. "At that window."

Goforth followed the gesture. The shade was drawn down to the sill. He started to speak.

"The shade was up?" Benjamin said.

"Halfway. I hadn't intended to come back in here, see."

"And you saw his face."

"Yes."

"Describe it, please."

"Just a face. A blob in the light from the lamp."

"You'd recognize him?"

"I don't think so. He was standin' back from the glass, just a blob. Oh, yes, he had his hand over the lower part of his face, like a mask."

"Black?" Benjamin said.

"White," Harlan shot out. "White, dammit. He was a white man." He looked at Goforth as if expecting to be challenged. Goforth put his attention back on Benjamin and the girl.

"What did you do then?"

"I screamed."

"And?"

"And?"

"And what did the dude do? The face at the window?"

"He left."

"He ran away?"

"I reckon he ran."

"You hear a car?"

"No, but he might've been parked down the street."

"Then what?"

"I put on this robe and called Harlan."

"You live nearby, Harlan?"

"Couple of houses over is all. Took me less'n a minute to get over."

"You were dressed and ready to go?"

"I was up, watchin' the television. Didn't even stop to put my shoes on."

"Just snatched up the shotgun and ran," Goforth said. "That how it happened?"

"You got it right, Deputy."

"You looked for the perpetrator?" Benjamin said.

"I looked. He was long gone."

"Okay," Benjamin said. "Thanks for your cooperation."

"That's all?" Harlan said in challenge.

"We'll take a look around in the morning. Maybe some tire tracks, like that. But I doubt we'll find anything."

"And if he comes back?" Harlan said.

"Not likely. Man's got a yen to look is all, you scared him off. All that screamin' and a twelve-gauge, put the fear of the Lord into him."

"I don't think so, " Harlan said, making no effort to conceal his antagonism.

"What do you think, Harlan?" Goforth said, straightening up to his full height.

"I think the same one hit Inez on the beach was here tonight, come back for more of the same."

"Not the way it works," Benjamin said. "Not usually."

"That sucker shows up one more time," Harlan said, "I am gonna blow him away."

Benjamin led the way outside, Goforth following. At the side of the small house, Benjamin flashed his light along the ground. "There. Here's where it was, down on one knee. Look here, this indentation, the toe of his shoe."

"See those ridges?" Goforth said. "He was wearing basketball shoes, most likely. You know the way they're made, with a protective strip of rubber running around the front of the shoe. That's the way they are with those ridges."

"Could be you're right, Billy." Benjamin walked back to his car. "I'll call in and report."

"It's your squeal."

"That's right, it is. No need for you to have come all the way out here."

"No harm intended, Benjamin."

"I'll call it in," he said again tonelessly.

Harlan came out of the house and walked rapidly down the street, without a glance their way.

"That is one uptight boy," Goforth said.

"He ain't alone here in Northtown. There's lots of 'em. They keep it to themselves when they cross over the bridge is all."

"If you say so." He left Benjamin standing there and went back to his car, drove around for a while. Slowly, aimlessly, mind drifting and settling nowhere. He parked in front of the Gem Cinema, now dark and empty, the night's showing having ended nearly two hours earlier. The younger patrons would have had their sodas and ice cream at the Hill-Bartlett Pharmacy by now and headed out-county to park and neck; the older ones would be home in bed, having arrived in time for the eleven o'clock news on the television. The fragrance of hibiscus and azaleas drifted on the slow night air, with only the chirping of crickets to break the silence. A good place to be, Goforth assured himself, to live out your life. People were friendly enough without being too nosy, reliable, predictable. A man knew what was expected of him, knew how he would be treated and what his position was in the social order. A place to die among friends, appreciated, treasured, with kind words spoken over his grave. And that was important to Goforth, more important than anything else. What he had always wanted. Without thinking, he started up the car and drove back out to her house. He knocked, and she opened the door almost at once, as if expecting him, as if waiting for him.

"All right if I talk to you?"

She hesitated. "You better come inside." She put herself beyond the frayed sofa that divided the room from the kitchen area. "Anything you'd like, Deputy?"

"My name's Billy."

"I don't want to hear your name, nor nothin' else about you, hear."

"I don't mean you harm."

"But only harm can come of it, ain't that right?"

"I thought I'd ask some more questions."

She shook her head and lowered her eyes. "Go ahead and ask, and then go." But there was no harshness in her manner.

"I went to the hospital, you checked out."

"I'm okay now."

The bruises and swelling had diminished and the clean lines of her triangular face were unbroken. Her tawny skin was stretched taut and gleaming over high cheekbones and a firm long jawline. Her mouth was voluptuous and slightly wider than it needed to be, her eyes great luminous ovals. "You're a very beautiful woman," Goforth said.

"I don't want to hear that. From you."

"What about Harlan? He tell you you're beautiful?"

"He's my friend."

"He carry you home from the hospital?"

"You jealous?" she taunted.

He began to protest, broke it off. "I would have done it."

"White deputy, black girl," she said mockingly. "How's that gonna look?"

"Nobody has to know."

"I ain't passin'. No matter what you think, I ain't passin'."

"I never knew you weren't white."

"I never said I was."

"Or that you wasn't."

"It's not something on my mind all of the time." A mischievous grin turned up the corners of her mouth. "'Sides, Deputy, I'm on the inside lookin' out, the view is different, you see."

"Guess so. Anyway—"

"Yes?"

"Anyway, anything I can do to help?"

"I'm all right now. I'll be all right."

"You mean Harlan will protect you?"

"From now on, I'll take care of myself."

"Keep away from the beaches."

"I don't think I want to live that careful."

"It's your life."

"Yes."

"Well. Guess I'll leave you get to bed. It's been a busy night."

"That's a fact."

"Anything come up, don't be afraid to give us a call."

"I'll remember you said so."

"Didn't mean to trouble you."

"No trouble."

He opened the door and stepped outside. "About Harlan," she called in a soft voice. "It ain't at all serious . . ." Then she went back inside and closed the door.

"Wife trouble, " Benjamin said, voice edged with irony. "Tell me about it." He worked without haste attaching the jig to his fishing line.

"You ever been married?" Goforth said. "Most times I fished for crappies, I used minnows."

"Most folks fishin' at night don't use jigs. I just get weary baitin' hooks and payin' for minnows. All's I know is jigs catch me more fish and bigger ones." He lifted his eyes to Goforth at the front end of the small rowboat, face shadowed in the light of the old Coleman lantern hanging over the dark waters of Lake Oweonoke. "Three legal wives, three or four more for convenience."

Goforth grinned. "You're a lover, Benjamin."

"Man lives long enough, most things come around."

"Charlene, she's called it quits." He brought a can of beer out of the ice chest and drank. "Claims I spent more time on the job and playin' poker than with her. Reckon she's right."

"Women always keep after a man to do somethin', be somethin' other'n what he is."

"Reckon I gave her cause enough to up and go." He dropped his line over the side. "I ain't so sure about this spinner, Benjamin."

"Just stay with it, man. The way you'd use a pork chunk

and spinnerbait to take a bass, well, you got to give the same flash to the crappies. Just keep the jig movin' up and down alongside the boat, all the while the wind's goin' to move us in an arc around the anchor. Crappies keep findin' it in different locations. We can fish all night that way."

"I ain't so sure about this, Benjamin."

"Trust me, man. See the way the lantern's drawin' bugs. Well, the bugs'll draw the shad and the shad concentrate the crappies. Just keep the tip of your rod in the light. Those fish are smart. They'll lift your bait and you'll never know they've done it, less'n you stay alert."

"This is your show, Benjamin. I sure do enjoy night fishin'."

"Me the same. Water ain't so crowded and you can keep your secret fishin' places secret."

"You always go up channel thisaway?"

"Sometimes. Bigger fish hang out where the cover's thickest, stumps and snags and whatever in the water, that's the secret of it."

Back in the woods an owl hooted, the sound echoing off the water. Benjamin reeled up a crappie and cackled happily, deposited him in the ice chest and helped himself to a beer in return. "Number one, forty-nine more to go."

"You figure we'll hit the limit?"

"Got to be optimistic." He dropped his line back in. Neither of them spoke for a long time, reeling fish in from time to time until Goforth broke the silence. "You ever get lonely, Benjamin?"

"Always. Sometimes when I'm with somebody. Worst feelin' is to be lonely when you're livin' tight to another human person."

"I used to feel that way with Charlene, sometimes. But I didn't want the marriage to break up."

"I been there."

"Husbandin' is not what I do best."

"You fish pretty good."

"Being a peace officer, that's what I was meant to be."

"You're a good cop, Billy."

"Both of us are."

"Not the same. Oh, I can handle trouble okay when it comes my way, black trouble. White trouble I leave to hard rocks like you and Duke Venable."

"Never saw you back down from anything, Benjamin."

"Maybe so. But it don't mean I ain't scared. Just too old and too dumb to let on anymore." Benjamin busied himself with his fishing line. When he spoke, he chose his words carefully.

"I lived a long time, seen a lot of stuff, but it always brings me up short when a smart man does a dumb thing. Goin' over to Northtown is dumb, goin' back to see that gal later like you done was dumb. You ain't a fool, Billy, you know what you're cuttin' yourself in for."

Goforth exhaled. "I can't put her out of my head."

"She's black, you're white."

"Dammit, Benjamin, you're like everybody else around here."

"Reckon I am at that."

They fished in silence again. Presently Benjamin beat the water with one of the oars. "Stirs the crappies up," he explained. "Helps get 'em concentrated. Ought to come on strong now."

He was right and for nearly an hour they pulled in fish in rapid succession. Then abruptly nothing happened.

"Are we finished here?"

"Maybe, maybe not. Sometimes you leave too soon, miss the best fishin' of the night. We'll just hang on. Pass me a beer, you don't mind."

They drank and talked about fishing, about tracking deer, about guns. And again the silence, uneasy silence this time as if each of them wanted to speak of something and neither knew how to begin. Goforth cleared his throat.

"Had me a little talk with Duke the other day."

"So they say."

"They say what about?"

"That he's puttin' you up to take over when he steps down is what."

"I always wanted that job."

"Ambition's a reasonable thing in a young man."

"It just seemed sensible, bein' a deputy to get on as best I could, as far as I could."

"You'll make a good sheriff, Billy."

"Funny, but I never intended to be a deputy for always. Went to law school, meant to practice law."

"But you didn't?"

"Started working part time for Duke and got to like it. He made me a deputy and that was it. Seemed like a fine idea at the time."

"And now?"

"Now I ain't so sure. Fact is, I ain't so sure of very much anymore. You ever feel that way, Benjamin?"

"On and off." He gulped the rest of his beer, dropped the can into the bottom of the boat. "Never meant to be a deputy myself, you see."

"That a fact?"

"Betcha. Started out to be a ballplayer."

"Baseball?"

"Played in the old Negro leagues. Nobody uses that word anymore, but that's what we were then—Negroes. Sure way to rile a man up was to call him black. Nothin' stays the same, does it? Guess you are too young to know about the Negro leagues?"

"We're of an age."

"Shoot. I passed sixty a long time ago, a long time. Next to me, you're a child."

"You don't look even forty. I thought you were forty, Benjamin."

"Left off playin' baseball when I was forty. Could've squeezed out a couple more years, but it was time to go. Felt like it, too. They wanted to send me to the minor leagues and I couldn't tolerate that. Pride and all that. So I packed it in."

"You played in the big leagues?"

"Three years with the New York Giants when they were up at the old Polo Grounds on the edge of the Harlem River. Man, I was there when Willie Mays came up. One look at that body of his, those big hands of his, and you just knew he was somethin' special. Ol' Durocher, he like to have wet his pants watchin' that boy play. Didn't blame him none either."

"You quit playin' after the Giants?"

"Nope, went back into the Negro league. I was an infielder. Good glove, good speed, a soft bat. I sure did love to play baseball."

"You must've been somethin', Benjamin."

"I could've been, I could've been. But my timin' was all wrong. I dreamed of greatness. And maybe I would've been great if my chance had come early. I wore myself out on rocky fields and in the back of rickety buses until most of my speed was gone an' my hands not so quick anymore. Oh, but I sorely wanted greatness." He took another beer. "Still have dreams about baseball," he went on in a slow, low voice, full of regret. "Same old dream every time. I'm in the World Series, y' understand. Me, in the Yankee Stadium. Me, playin' with all those big name stars in front of all those folks cheerin' and stompin' and carryin' on.

"See, it's the last of the ninth in the seventh game and the winnin' run is on second base and the tyin' run is at third and I come up to bat. Man, the television cameras are pointed at me, and the people are yellin' out my name and my teammates are cheerin' for me to get a hit. It's like that.

"The pitch comes at me and I swing, my best swing, eye on the ball, and hit it square and that ball zips past the pitcher and is goin' over second base and I am runnin' just as fast as I can go. Onliest thing is I can't get to first base. I just can't make it there and the throw comes in and I see it comin' and I keep runnin' only there is no way I can get there. I am thrown out. The game is over. We lose. Just can't make it to first base. Boy, that is tough."

"That is tough," Goforth said softly.

"Yeah. Well. What you goin' to do? Had enough fishin' for one night?"

Benjamin looked out into the dead-still night. He was humming—a flat line of sound, not knowing he was making it. Part of him was somewhere else.

"Well, " Benjamin muttered as if responding to another, earlier conversation, "bein' old ain't great but when all of your friends is dead it ain't so bad, either." He snapped back to the present with a rueful grin. "Had enough fishin' for one night? What say we head on back, if'n that's all right with you?"

"Whatever you say, Benjamin."

"Yeah. Let's head on back."

# CHAPTER
## 10

THE MORNING BEGAN badly for Kate. She woke feeling
She checked her schedule. The show was a hit and requests
for additional tickets were coming from all over the county and
North Central Florida. A reporter from *The Tampa Times* was
coming up to interview her at noon and there were requests for
additional interviews to sift through and consider. And reviews
to read and collate, paste into the production scrapbook, and
people kept dropping into her office to offer congratulations,
to reminisce about productions of the play they had seen in
New York, or on tour, or at other schools. And casting for the
next play was to begin. That, plus three classes to teach that
morning. It was a heavy load, hectic, stressful; she loved every
second of it.

"Will four this afternoon be all right?" she said over the
telephone to Dr. Moody's secretary, a smile in her voice. There
had been no immediacy in the summons, no suggestion of crisis
in the call.

"Now," the secretary said.

"Now?" She started to protest, to make some other arrangement, but decided against it. "I'm on my way," she said, with forced brightness.

She went through the empty theater, the old sense of mystery and magic suspended. Halfway up the aisle she glanced back. The set was struck, only a worklight standing center stage. So much had happened in her three years at Gault, so much that was positive and rewarding. But the longing to perform was as strong as ever; only when she was on stage acting did she feel complete, fulfilled, all that she was meant to be.

Moody, smoking a pipe, was waiting for her, a placid expression on his pudding face. Greetings taken care of, he sucked on the stem; it had gone out. He relit it and blew smoke toward the ceiling. A gentle reminder that smoking was forbidden on campus; rules were made to be broken, she thought ruefully, especially by those in power.

He made a broad, encircling gesture with the pipe. He put a small, regretful smile on his soft mouth. He avoided looking at her. "What we have here is a college supported in large measure by the church and our alumni and the parents of our students, mainly conservative, traditional people, if you follow my intent?"

She did not, but a faint cloud of apprehension cast a shadow over her. She tugged at her skirt and was immediately sorry; the gesture had drawn Moody's eyes to her legs. She sat straighter and made an attempt to appear attentive and conservative, certain it would never work.

"Rules exist," he said, with an emphatic thrust of the pipe. "Traditional ways and moral considerations. You can understand that, Miss Fellows?"

He usually addressed her by her first name; the apprehension deepened.

"You've been at Gault Christian for three years, if I remember correctly." He remembered precisely, his brain a carefully arranged system of dates, names, academic biographies. He had studied Kate's file minutes before she appeared. "And you've done reasonably well. . . ."

Reasonably well! She had built a drama department where there'd been none. Put together a student company of high competence and increasing skill. Enlarged the curriculum, the staff, and drawn more students each year. She had attracted positive attention to Gault Christian within the academic community and beyond. She had done better-than-reasonable work. Much better.

"Our purpose here is to give our young people the kind of education their mothers and fathers want them to have. A Christian education in a Christian environment. We inculcate in them the traditional values, love of God, the church, the family, an abiding respect for our nation and our American way of life. There. I believe I have made myself clear." He sat back satisfied and convinced that no more need be said. His message had been delivered and received.

"I don't understand," she said.

He was displeased. The woman was being difficult and obtuse. "I hoped not to have to dwell on details. Very well. We'll address the problem directly. I have received complaints about your play."

*Your play.* What had she done wrong? The old doubts and questions rose up out of their hiding places in the shadowed pockets of her brain. She had never given much value to herself as a person. Nor as a woman. Her center teetered on an unstable foundation and she was afraid to put her courage and strength to a real test. Passivity took hold of her, as it had so often done in the past. She felt submissive, unwilling to trust her intelligence or her instincts, unable to fight back; unwanted and unloved, and most of all ugly. Never good in a crisis. Never able to deal well with conflict. Or rejection. Never fully grown up. Never free.

"Complaints?" she said, voice trailing off.

"Objections. Objections of considerable substance." He looked past her, pipe tracing the outline of his lips, waiting. When she said nothing, he went on. "The language, dear girl."

"The language?"

"All those 'damns,' all those 'hells.'"

She'd never given them a thought. "It's the way those people talk."

"Of course. But not the way people in Tokeneke County talk."

"But, Dr. Moody . . ."

He cut her off with a gesture. "We will not debate the

question. If you're going to suggest there's a gap between what people say and what they do, you'll get no argument. But that is not the issue."

"What is the issue?"

"Dirty words."

"Mr. O'Neill may be the greatest of all American playwrights."

"Perhaps, it changes nothing."

"Who made the complaints?"

"Not relevant. Only one thing: what are we going to do about it?"

"Must we do something?"

"Oh, indeed, yes. Haven't I made that clear? We must take steps."

"What steps exactly?"

"To eliminate the offending words and phrases."

"Censor Eugene O'Neill?"

"Call it bowdlerizing, a traditional practice. Let's not permit a petty obstruction to grow into a major roadblock."

"'Damns' and 'hells,'" she said, aware of a systolic thump behind her eyes. "It does seem so petty."

"There's more." The pipe was aimed at her breasts; she wished she were flat-chested, hipless, mousy and plain. She wished she could be ordinary and unobtrusive. She wished she were pounding on producers' doors in Manhattan pleading for an acting job, being what she was meant to be in a world that accepted her as she was. "What else?" she said.

"'Goddam whore,'" he said, looking at her this time. "'Goddam whore.'"

She blushed, and guilt constricted her middle. She uncrossed her legs and sat primly with her knees tightly clamped.

"Images of brothels, of indecent acts, of sin and sexuality rampant everywhere around us. And using the Lord's name in vain."

"You want me to cut those words?"

"I expect you to exercise your best judgment. I'm here only to inform, Miss Fellows, to suggest, to advise. All my chairmen have full authority over their departments. In your place, I'd do the deed, get it over with, and move on to better things." He smiled and quickly frowned; the pipe had gone out again.

Her impulse was to agree, give in, not struggle. But a small part of her resisted, some residual stubbornness that demanded she fight back. At least for a little while.

"May I sleep on it?"

"Of course. And when you've thought it over, I know you'll make the right decision. I know you will. . . ."

A rolling fog enveloped the beach and she shivered and clutched herself, as much against the inexplicable chilling fear she felt as the damp itself. Out in the Gulf a boat horn sounded, eerie and plaintive, and she wondered if someone was in trouble. But her own problems loomed larger and more immediate. An unmarked trail had brought her to King of Heaven, to Gault Christian, and until now she had felt protected, removed from the constant buffeting and defeats she had for so long suffered. Her meeting with B. J. Moody had changed all that. There was no safe place.

She went along the beach at the water's edge. Lights from the big houses behind the dunes marked her way, each in a flickering nimbus. A gull cawed in the distance and the boat horn blared again, farther away this time. Behind her, the crunch of footfalls coming closer. She paused.

He took up a position at her right shoulder, arms circling her waist. He held her close and licked her throat. She shivered again.

"Salty. . . ."

"No complaints. I've heard complaints enough for one day."

"You're in a feisty mood."

She freed herself from his grasp. "You're late, Wesley."

"Almost didn't make it at all."

She walked back in the direction from which she had come. "What was it this time?" she said in a flat voice. "Your job at the bank? Family obligations?"

"Mae-Mae," he said, as if that explained it all.

"Oh, yes, the child bride."

"Somethin' on your mind, Kate?"

"As a matter of fact, there is. . . ."

"Well, let's go back to my car. I've got a bottle and we'll have a drink and you unload on me."

She shook off his hand. "Let me tell you, Wesley, I hate

sneaking drinks, I hate making love in cars, I stopped playing kids' games years ago. I hate this town and I'm beginning to hate my job and I don't care for you very much, either, at this minute, Wesley."

"My, lady. You sure have got a wild hair under your skin. Whatever it is you're carryin' on about, it's okay with me. I love you, lady."

"Love? Need is what you mean. What we have is a relationship of intense dependency, full of passion and ambivalence. Is that love? Maybe, I don't know."

"Call it whatever you like, sugar, but I sure do have a pretty good idea about what I need."

"Forget it."

"I can't."

"No more back-seat screwing, Wesley. I told you. When I have sex with a man, I want to do it in a bed."

"Then let's go. To your apartment."

In the night he seemed so much younger than he was, boyishly handsome in that golden way of his, a smooth-cheeked child with eyes soft and luminous, features gently flowing one into another, the shining hair falling artfully over his ears. But his expression was at the same time sad and cruel, as if he were enjoying her distress.

She spoke harshly. "And announce to my landlady that I'm having an affair with young Mr. Gault? That pillar of local society. A married man. A man fifteen years younger than I am."

"I don't care."

"But I do."

"Let's go to a motel."

"That smacks too much of one-night stands."

"Which brings us back to the back seat of my car. Or yours."

She gave a mirthless laugh and said nothing. She shivered and kept walking.

"Cold?"

"Yes."

"A drink would help. We don't even have to set foot in the car, unless you insist on it. I could use a drink myself."

He owned two cars; the Porsche, and this one, a white

Mercedes sedan. The sedan was roomier, better to have sex in. She watched him retrieve a bottle and pour bourbon into a paper cup. She gulped some down and coughed and her eyes teared.

He drank and examined her through the fog and emptied his cup. "You're the most beautiful woman in the world, Kate."

"I feel used up, empty and ugly."

"You're special. Smart, independent. You should be the heroine of a modern novel."

"A negative heroine. Someone like Anna Karenina, declining into self-doubt, nagging, hysterical. Giving up whatever strength and intelligence and potential I have to other people's ideas of how and what I should be. Women in today's fiction, they isolate their problems, and solve them. They find themselves. Me, I'm losing ground. I can't keep up."

"That's nonsense. No one I know is more involved in her life. I know what you need." He tried to embrace her.

She held him off. "You keep telling me that. Sex may give shape to your life, not to mine."

"I don't get it. You called, said you missed me, had to see me. Well, here I am. Is it wrong for me to want to make love to you? What's buggin' you tonight?"

She finished off her drink and held out the cup for more. "What I want is to take care of myself."

"I'll take care of you."

She examined him steadily; a boy-man is what she saw, still nursing at the tit. Any tit that was handy. "I have this small problem," she answered wryly.

"Small problems have always been easy for me."

She told him about her talk with Moody, omitting nothing.

"That's it?" he said, when she finished.

"As far as I can remember, all of it."

"You're right, it's a small problem."

She just looked at him without speaking.

"Make the changes," he said, "and that's the end of it. A word here and a word there, nothing major. Keep that hypocritical old reprobate happy."

"It's that simple?"

"It's that simple."

"I simply surrender, give in?"

He shrugged and looked out into the fog. "Do whatever you want to do, Kate."

"That's just it, I don't know what I want. I'm frightened...."

"What of?"

"I don't know. Lots of things. What I am. What you are. Our being together. My job, my future, so many things."

He kissed her, and, encouraged, kissed her again. After a moment she sighed and the tension drained out of her body. He stroked her back and she curved up against him and gave herself to the flow of good feelings that came over her.

He began to fumble with her blouse.

"Not here," she said.

He slid his hand onto her bare breast and circles of desire rippled under her skin. She made small gritty noises in the back of her throat and dug her fingernails into his biceps.

"Let's get in the car," he said.

"It makes me feel bad."

"The last time, I promise."

"You mean it?"

"I swear...."

"Ah," she said presently, lying on the soft leather seat, "this is crazy. You're trouble for me, Wesley, big trouble."

"I love you," he said, working his way between her thighs.

"No," she said softly, helping him, "oh, no. But it doesn't matter now, does it, baby?"

He had stopped listening.

# CHAPTER
## 11
---

FRIDAY NIGHT. The air thick and heavy with the lingering heat of day making it more like swimming weather than football. But autumn had come and that meant the start of the high school football season in King of Heaven, the focus of the town's attention. And the word was out; this year's team was something special, loaded, good enough to win the state championship. Maybe.

Located behind the high school, the stadium was situated on lowlands that sometimes flooded when the winter rains grew heavy or when a hurricane came sweeping in off the Gulf. King of Heaven teams were expected to win and coaches who failed in this purpose were swiftly replaced by men who understood the value of victory and the traditional ways, and how to maintain them.

On the field, at the fifty-yard line, flanked by a squad of perky cheerleaders, backed by the entire, uniformed marching band, Reverend Dorr C. P. Seely. He peered up at the banked rows chock full of people. More people than ever gathered in the Independent Baptist Church to hear him preach. Football, not theology, certainly did drag 'em away from those TVs of theirs.

So be it, if that's how it had to be. He was here to deliver a prayer in the Lord's name, invited to bless the players, the coaches, the trainers, the alumni association and the booster club. Ask the Lord to keep 'em all from harm, make 'em brave and fierce and able to play smart football. And win. Winning would be best of all, he knew from experience.

Fact was, Seely hadn't exactly been *invited*. Truth of the matter, he had *arranged* to be here. Arranged to make a splash before all these good folks. He certainly intended to give it his number one best shot. He cleared his throat, raised his right arm, the big hand clutching a white leather bible, and bellowed into the microphone.

"And Jesus said, 'Without me you can do nothin'.' That's what Jesus said, all right. 'Without me, you can do nothin'.' That means that without Him you just ain't goin' to win no football games, not ever. It means, without Him, mankind is doomed. DOOMED!

"Let me tell you, there are those people in the world workin' and strainin' and plyin' their nasty ways to makin' certain that we are doomed. We, we hundred-and-ten-percent Americans. We lovers of the truth and of freedom and liberty. Those are the evil ones, the secret enemies of our nation, of our state, of our special little town. They would destroy all that we hold dear, yes they would.

"They attack our precious heritage and our way of life. These dangerous and venomous elements who in their perverted ways have turned against God, against liberty and justice for all.

"I am talkin' about our ENEMIES! Yours and mine. The outsiders who tunnel away at our grand and delicate institutions in a vicious attempt to bring down all that we and our ancestors have constructed.

"You folks up in the grandstands, you young men on the field waitin' to play this great and glorious game of football, you must be the defenders of the faith, the soldiers of Christ, true Christian warriors in this ultimate struggle against God-lessness and atheism and communism. You must stand fast against the Evil One. You must fight to the death against the terrible forces aligned against us.

"'Without me, you can do nothin'.' Jesus spoke those words on earth. Without Jesus, your struggle is doomed. Without Him you cannot enlist in the crusade against wickedness and perversion and alien influences. Without Jesus you can do nothin'. Join Jesus in this holy war. Throw in with Him and He will be with you to the end and beyond. When you are on Jesus' team, you are on the winnin' team.

"Stand fast against the enemy. Onward Christian soldiers. The call is goin' out and I know you hear it and will respond.

"So you hear me good—stick to God's way in your life every day and here on the football field. Join God's team and he will be your teammate for life. When God plays He plays to win, Win, WIN! Praise God.

"Now everybody pray for a good game . . . and a good victory for King of Heaven High. . . ."

The crowd cheered and quickly fell silent as Seely led them in prayer. This done, he climbed up into the grandstand where his wife, Martha, waited.

"What do you think?" he said to her.

"You did good."

"But not great?"

"It lacks something."

"What's that?"

"You got to let it all hang out."

"Meanin' what?"

"Meaning rant and rail, shout and holler, stomp your feet and swing your fists; the way we talked about it. Rage. Ferocity. You are offended at the way of the world, Dorr, and it's up to you to let the folks know it."

Seely made no response, his eyes on the field where King of Heaven received the kickoff and ran it back for sixty-eight yards. The band blared out the school fight song and the cheerleaders jumped and jiggled and did cartwheels.

"Juicy-looking little pieces, ain't they?" Seely said to himself. They made him think of Jody Joiner and the outrageous acts she performed on his body, and he on hers. He shivered in guilt and in pleasure.

"What I need is a unique and special target to haul off and let fly at," he said.

King of Heaven's quarterback heaved a pass over the middle. Caught, it was carried down to the fourteen-yard line. The crowd went wild. The cheerleaders hugged each other. The substitues exhorted the players on the field.

"Got to focus on something people can understand, identify with, be made fearful of," said Seely. "Got to raise up the monster-corruption, the devil-decadence, and beat the life out of both."

"How . . . ?"

Seely closed his eyes and put his head back, closed off his mind, and it came floating up out of the darkness. "There is somethin' . . . but it don't actually amount to very much."

"Well, tell me, dear. . . ."

"Well. Over to Gault Christian, they're doin' a play full of obscenities, takin' the Lord's name in vain," said Seely.

A handoff sent King of Heaven's halfback scooting around the left side. He put a move on the linebacker, broke the cornerback's attempt to make an arm tackle, and went in for a touchdown. Seely came to his feet, punching the air with one big fist.

He sat back down and glanced at Martha. Her lips were pursed. "It don't amount to very much," she said. "Raises the specter of censorship, academic freedom, like that. Wouldn't mind you goin' at it, Dorr, in some other context. Somethin' stronger, with the play in the background."

"I spoke to B. J. about the foul language in the play."

"And?"

"I reckon he's talked to the Fellows woman, made her stop usin' those dirty words."

"I hope not."

"What do you mean?"

"If she turns him down, makes a fight of it on principle, we can make a real ruckus out of this."

"That's very good, my dear."

"What's she like, this Fellows woman?"

"A very fine-lookin' woman. About forty, and looks younger. Tall, red-headed, with a full figure."

King of Heaven kicked off, a long, erratically bouncing ball. The opposing halfback headed up field. The crowd rose again.

"Used to be an actress in New York City."

"Sounds better'n better. What else?"

"There is somethin'. . . ." He hesitated. "Said to me in confidence and might best be kept that way."

The ballcarrier was hit at the seventeen yard-line, and fumbled. A King of Heaven player retrieved the ball, broke away.

"Run, sucker!" Seely shouted.

Another touchdown for King of Heaven. The band trumpeted out its joy, the cheerleaders did high kicks that showed their fannies and made their breasts bounce. The coaches went wild.

Seely sat back down.

"The lady is engaged in an illicit relationship," said Seely.

"Illicit?"

"He's married."

"Who is he?"

"Wesley Gault," said Seely.

"Oh, that's good, Dorr. That's very good. This is manna from Heaven. Divine intervention. Exactly what you need."

"I don't understand."

"How do you know about Fellows and young Gault?"

"His wife, Mae-Mae."

"She told you?"

"She wants a baby."

"And he's too busy with this actress."

The quarter ended. King of Heaven had scored twenty-eight points. Their opponents were scoreless. Seely stood up, Martha at his side. "That's good, Dorr. Very good. An older woman, a loose, evil woman from New York, the very lair of Satan himself. Seduces an innocent lad away from his loving wife, prevents her from having a child. It's all there. Attack on the bedrock of our civilization, the family. Subverting Christian morals. Stepping on the most cherished values of the community. Beautiful, just beautiful. What's that poor, deprived child aim to do? Get a divorce, or what?"

"Just wants her husband to stop tomcattin' around is all. Wants him home nights. Wants to have a baby, I told you."

"So what we have is a harlot actress, a blasphemer, an adulteress, a profaner of God's sacred joining of man and woman in holy matrimony, someone dead-set on breaking up a good Christian household. A destroyer of marriages and lives.

"And on the other side, what have we got? A victim. A poor, pathetic creature, innocent, unworldly. Yearning after the traditional things in life: house, husband, family. Very fine, very good."

"Might make a pretty good sermon."

"Better'n that. What we have here is the launching pad for an intercontinental moral missile against evil and sexuality and the liberalism foisted on us by Satan and his handmaidens in sin. Why, Dorr, can't you see it? This woman is undermining the entire fabric of American life. Christianity is under siege here. Free enterprise is being cut down. The fundamental and proper application of capitalism is being ravaged. The great white middle class is going to be corrupted.

"All by Kate Fellows?"

"Unless she is stopped. She and her kind."

Seely thought it over; he didn't have to think very long. "I'm not so sure about this, dear."

"Put your trust in the Lord, Dorr. And in me. Between us we'll see you get everything you ever craved. Everything."

At half time they left, Seely accepting congratulations as they went. His prayers had worked; King of Heaven was a clear winner.

# CHAPTER
## 12

"THIS IS THE last time. . . ."

Jody, blouse unbuttoned, her upstanding young breasts exposed, looked at Dorr C. P. Seely without comprehension. She laughed that soft, taunting laugh of hers, certain he had invented a new game to spice up their lovemaking, a mysterious addition to the changing repertory they had assumed during these periodic meetings at the Triple X Motel. She enjoyed assuming different parts, took pleasure in subordinating herself to his desires, confident that in the end she too would receive pleasure as he grew wilder and stronger and more physical in his attentions to her flesh. She drew her skirt down over her hips. "What am I supposed to do, sugar?"

"I am in earnest," he said. There was an emptiness in his far-seeing eyes, as if he saw some enticing future that he alone was witness to.

"What are you sayin' to me, Dorr?" She displayed herself in only brief, sheer panties, aware of how good she looked, how provocative, how much seeing her this way stimulated him. "Let's play the daddy and daughter game, Dorr. I'll con-

fess some evil deed and you can punish me and get all worked
up and then you—"

"Be quiet, girl!" The words came from between gritted teeth,
the aging athlete's face frozen and unyielding.

"Why'd you call if you didn't aim to get it on, then? I came
just like always, just like always. Why'd you have to call?"

"I felt it only fair." His expression softened but the eyes
remained hard and shining. "Only fair to say it face to face.
There is a movement afoot, a movement that will forever alter
my life and yours."

"I don't know what you are talkin' about. Come on, Dorr,
let's play. . . ."

"The Tenth Crusade. Surely you've heard of it."

"Uh-uh. Some kind of religious thing you got goin'? Well,
all right, but what's it got to do with us here and now? Here,
let me undo your pants and—"

"Take your hands away!"

She leaped back as if struck, frightened now by the harshness
in his voice, the raw hatred in his face.

"This is the beginnin' of something, something big, Jody.
More than you can understand. It's been simmerin' for a long
time. On the back burner, so to speak. A movement of committed folks, Christians all, folks of excellent moral persuasion.
Good Americans. We are tired of the way things are goin' in
this country, tired of bein' treated like we belong in the back
of the bus. We aim to get rid of those Liberals and bleedin'
hearts and Reds who have been subvertin' the good and true
that is America. We are spreadin' our wings and about to take
off."

"What's it got to do with us?" she said plaintively.

"What we've done is wrong. What you want to continue
doing is wrong. I have sinned mortally. I have transgressed. I
have blasphemed and betrayed my beliefs and my faith and my
God. But no more. No longer will I risk my reputation in a
relationship such as ours. I have a greater debt, a larger obli-
gation, a responsibility that goes far beyond either of us, Jody."

Confusion gripped her and she struggled to sort out his
words, the meaning of what he had said. It was too difficult,
too alarming. So she put it aside and thrust out a provocative
hip.

"Come on," she drawled. "Just say what you want me to do."

"It's over."

He meant it. Her knees went weak and her brain refused to function efficiently. This wasn't what she wanted, wasn't what she was ready for, and she told him so.

"It isn't up to you," he said.

"Two years," she said in disbelief. "I was less'n sixteen when you turned me on, all that kinky stuff. I went along and now you're kickin' me out."

He went to the door, anxious to be away from here, to sever this unholy connection. "I will always remember the good times we had, and think of you, and miss all this with regret. . . ."

"No," she muttered after he was gone. "It ain't finished yet. Not nearly. . . ."

She drove aimlessly, caught up in the roil of emotions that frightened and confused her. She went out to the campus looking for a boy she knew, a boy who had tried more than once to get her into bed. She couldn't find him. She drove down to the beach and walked along Silver Sands.

Shoes in hand, she let the small waves wash over her feet, kicking furiously at the foam. She took off her skirt and blouse, her panties, dropped them in a heap on the sand and walked into the Gulf. She swam straight out until her arms grew tired. She rolled onto her back and floated, eyes shut, emptying her mind, giving herself to the rise and fall of the water.

Time and place were meaningless. Until she swallowed some water, began to cough and turn afraid. She struck out for shore. The looming shadows of the houses on Silver Sands seemed too far to reach.

She made it, stumbling up the beach, tripped and fell flat on the sand. She came up into a sitting position, hugging her knees, setting herself against the air. She wished a man would come along, any man, a man handsome and powerful and vigorous, a man who would see how beautiful she was and desire her. A rising excitement took hold of her and she came up on her feet, twirling, dipping, dancing, at one with the air and the sand, the soft and gentle sea. She fled up the beach, long blond hair streaming behind her. Up the dunes she went

and down again. Up into the saddle between them, a pale blur
in the stillness and the dark. Until he brought her down hard
with a long low tackle.

All breath was forced out of her and she gasped and was
unable to cry out. Or protest when he hit her for the first time.
The excitement she had felt turned to fear as pain stabbed into
her. She rolled up into a defensive ball, but it did no good.
She heard his hoarse oaths and threats as if they were intended
for somebody else.

Then he was between her legs, forcing himself into her,
slapping aside her feeble attempts to hold him off. How long
it went on, she never knew. Until he was back on his feet,
kicking her, calling her names, hurting her worse than before.
So much pain, so much fear. She made ready to die.

Goforth went to the hospital willing her not to be in the
same room Inez had occupied, in the same bed. A romantic
notion for a hard-headed cop, he told himself with grim irony;
he was reassured to find her in the opposite wing of the hospital.
Francine stood alongside her daughter, her face empty and pale,
eyes flat. Beyond the bed, nearer to the window, a woman
faintly familiar to Goforth. Tall, willowy, with a thick fall of
nearly orange hair and steady green eyes.

"Evenin', Mrs. Joiner."

"Jody, this is Deputy Goforth. And this—" She gestured.
"This is Miss Kate Fellows."

Now he remembered. "Believe we met before. You're out
to Gault Christian."

"Miss Fellows is Jody's actin' teacher," Francine said.

Kate, her gaze level, acknowledged the introduction with a
slight incline of her soft round chin, but made no reply.

He looked at her as if trying to match her against some
preconceived notion, trying to make some intuitive assessment
of her character, of her position in the legal spectrum. "Duke
Venable introduced us one night at one of your shows, Miss
Fellows. 'Midsummer's Night Dream,' it was."

"You like Shakespeare?"

He shrugged. "Not sure I got it all, but that was me and
not the play. I go to the plays when I can. People who can
act, do things, talented people give me lots of pleasure."

"I'm glad to hear you say so," Kate said.

He started to answer, thought better of it, and turned to Jody. Her face was swollen and bruised, battered far worse than Inez's had been.

"You got any idea who did this to you?" Goforth wondered what it would be like to be a big-city detective. Sharp, experienced, well trained. Would they be better at this than he was? Would they be more comfortable confronting the victim? How would they go about finding the perpetrator, stop him before he did it again?

Jody moaned. "I want to forget this ever happened."

"He's done it before."

"Here in town?" Francine said.

"Girl over in Northtown. Happened at Silver Sands, also. Any help you can give, Jody, it sure would be appreciated."

"Nothin's gonna help me, it's done already to me." She turned her face away and without warning shrieked, "I hate this place! I hate it! I hate it!"

Her mother bent over her, stood over her, uncertain, as if waiting to be told what to do.

Goforth watched for a while. "I'll come back another time," he said.

"I never saw him," the girl said. "Even when he was—oh, my God!—inside me, I didn't see him. His face was pressed up against me, against my face, and close as he was . . . He kissed . . . me. . . . My God! How could anybody kiss a girl he's hurtin' thataway? And afterwards—I didn't do something to *him*. I didn't hurt *him*. He beat me, he beat me something awful, and kicked me. All that hate and orneriness. Just plain ornery . . ."

"A black man?" Goforth said. "Or was he white?"

Her eyes fluttered shut. "He was white. Oh, he was white, all right."

"You said you couldn't see him?"

"His cheek, I saw his cheek. And his jaw. He was white. And young."

"How do you know that?"

A bitter sound escaped her swollen mouth. "He had pimples, I remember remarkin' on it to myself. Thing is, I never could tolerate a boy with a bad complexion. . . ."

* * *

When Goforth left, Kate left with him. He offered to buy
her a cup of coffee; she refused quickly, and just as quickly
changed her mind. In the hospital coffee shop in the basement,
they settled in at a corner table.

"Bother you if I smoke?" He extended the pack. It was as
if she hadn't heard, didn't see. At once she appeared worn,
weary, the green eyes saddened and remote.

"What sort of man would do such a thing?" she said.

He stirred his coffee. "Things like this happen." He swore
at the inadequacy of his response, the poverty of his emotions;
empty sounds without meaning.

"She's only a child."

"We'll catch him."

"And if you don't?"

He shrugged. "We will."

"Did he have to beat her? Damn, damn. There was no way
she could prevent him from—no way to stop him."

"There's a meanness in some people."

Kate stared at him, then pulled her eyes away. "What a
pretty girl she is. You wouldn't know it the way she is now,
what a pretty girl she is."

Goforth, not knowing what to say, said nothing.

After a while, Kate spoke again. Voice softer now, the anger
diminished, reflective, almost nostalgic. "She wants to be an
actress."

"Her momma told me so one time, I believe."

"She might have been killed."

"Yes, ma'am. She surely might've been killed."

Kate shivered and embraced herself.

"You all right?" he said.

"Just trying to keep up with my own problems, too."

He nodded. He understood that. Only the dead had no problems.

She managed a small smile. "Sorry to burden you with my
demons."

His smile was slow, an invitation more than a display of
mirth or of charm. "You feel like talkin' about your demons,
I've got nowhere to go for a while."

"Sometimes I think I'm just a silly woman—never grown up."

"Seems like it takes a long time to grow up, for the best of us."

She thought it over. "Luke is the name of one of my demons."

"Luke?"

"My first love, my young love. We found love together. We discovered our bodies with each other. Am I shocking you, Deputy?"

"You do police work long enough, not much shocks you or surprises you."

She nodded. "Luke and I shared our dreams. I was seventeen when Luke and I got married and he was nineteen. The next day we ran off together. From White Deer, Texas, which is flat farming country, to New York City. Light years apart. We were going to become great actors, famous and rich and be happy forevermore. New York was beautiful, full of vitality, day and night, so much to do and see, so many opportunities. What a wonderful life we had planned to have."

"What happened?"

"Luke died of leukemia nine months later. The day before his twentieth birthday. He never got to see the sweater I had knitted for him. He never got to be a star. He never even got to act on a stage."

"I'm sorry."

"I stayed on. I was going to fulfill both our dreams by becoming a successful actress, a great actress. I waited tables, I sold Bibles over the telephone, I did some modeling and once in a while I even got to act. In classes with Uta Hagen and Herbert Berghof. Sometimes a week in stock or a few months in a road tour. I worked hard learning to dance and to sing a little and to stop sounding like a girl from West Texas. And—" she broke it off.

"And?" he prompted.

She came back into focus. "And I hung on by my fingernails, making rounds, sending out pictures, going to interviews and auditions. It wears you down, subverts the spirit, breaks up your resolve. I was very lonely."

"You should've gone home."

"I couldn't do that. My father was a ridge-runner, you know. A high-sounding, thigh-slapping, Bible-thumping country preacher. His camp meetings were something to see. He talked a hell of a good game about God, Heaven and love for your fellow man. But I can't remember him ever holding me when I needed it or soothing my fears or telling me everything was going to be all right."

"And your mother?"

"She followed him until the day he died and if she'd known a way to go into the grave with him without committing a mortal sin I do believe she'd have done so. I don't remember ever being treated as a child, only as a small grownup full of sin and idle dreams. No, I didn't go home. What I did was fall in love again. His name was Robert, a businessman, older than I was, and very sure of himself. He was kind, and gentle, and made no demands on me. He wanted to marry me and I wanted someone to take care of me.

"It lasted less than a year. Robert, you see, had a lover. He had had this lover all along. One evening I came home to find them in bed together, Robert and his lover. His lover's name was Henry, Robert's best friend. Being reasonable men, they found it difficult to comprehend my hysterical reaction. I threw Robert's favorite antique Chinese vase at him and ran out screaming. . . ."

She looked away and began to talk again. "I used to imagine my father was a yo-yo, coming and going to all those camp meetings, my mother at his side. They left me behind for a neighbor to look after. She hated me and shouted at me and I used to hide in a clothes closet in the dark and press my hands over my ears so I wouldn't hear if she called. I hated her and I hated my mother for leaving me with her and afterwards I felt guilty because I was angry. I was certain there was something wrong with me."

She blinked. "Whenever I speak to my mother, the guilt comes back. A word, a phrase, a change in tone, and it all comes flooding back, the sense of being wrong. Inadequate, always wrong, always bad. My mother has a deft feel for which button to push to make me feel bad, she knows where every one of my weak spots is located.

"I used to make up adventures for myself. Put myself into exotic settings and transform myself into a beautiful princess and cause wonderful things to happen to me. Dreams, all dreams. I never have been able to take control over my life. Even when something good occurs, I know it will all be taken away from me." She smiled sheepishly, almost girlishly, shy in front of this quiet man who seemed to belong wherever he happened to be. "And you?"

"What about me?"

"Have all your dreams come true?"

His face seemed to turn solid, unchanging, unchangeable. Where there had been warmth and vulnerability, there was only hardness, the defensive hardness of a turtle's shell.

"I've been a peace officer for a long time. It's what I do, it's what I am. It's enough."

"I didn't mean to pry."

He rose and fitted the Smokey-bear hat to his head, squared and proper. "I've got my runs to make."

She offered her hand. "Thanks for the coffee, and the sympathetic ear."

"My pleasure."

"I suppose we'll see each other around."

"I suppose we will at that."

She watched him leave, straight and sinewy, positioned to repel intruders. He was, she told herself, like no other man she'd ever known.


The house was set halfway along Firefly Lane in a section of King of Heaven known as Harmony Hills. There were no hills in Harmony Hills, only a gentle undulating terrain on which workers' houses had been built under Papa James' close watch forty years before. He had made a substantial profit on each house and the bank—his bank—held the mortgages on each one. Time, plus the frequent resale of the properties, had driven up the value of the houses. And since each new buyer was forced to take out a new mortgage at higher interest rates, Papa James continued to profit.

Lonnie Peden brought a bottle of Jack Daniels with him when he came and he and Francine drank steadily, water on the side. "I don't know what to do," Francine said for the third time. The usually precisely arranged brassy-blond hair was in disarray and hollows cupped her eyes and her mouth was drawn down in despair.

"Damned place is gettin' more like New York City every day," Lonnie complained.

"She's only a baby."

Lonnie had known many such babies. Full-grown girls ready to party day or night, crawling into one bed and out of the next. How many men had Jody serviced up to now? Each of them had a mother, too, a mother who never wanted to know what her baby was up to.

"It's done with," he said. He looped an arm across her shoulder. "Ain't nothin' now to do 'cept gentle her down."

She shrugged his arm away. "I'd like to—cut his balls off is what. Cut 'em off all of you."

"Ah, Francine, we ain't all thataway."

"Is that a fact! Never met a man yet wasn't tryin' to get his hand between my legs whilst he was sweet-talkin' into my ear. Promise a girl champagne and the world till you get your way and afterwards she's hard-pressed to get a beer and a movie out of you."

"That ain't my way."

Lonnie shifted closer, taking in the sweet, thick, penetrating scent of her. He couldn't remember when he'd yearned for anyone as much. Damn, but just bein' close to her got him up.

"Listen," he said in a low, husky voice.

"That child's been damaged, maybe ruined for the rest of her life."

"You are one fine-lookin' woman, I want you to know."

"Back off, Lonnie."

"It's not what you think, I hold some honest-to-God feelin's for you."

"Talk is cheap and I've listened to some champion talkers in my day."

"Fact is I own some serious intentions about you."

"Don't say anythin' you'll be sorry about later on. 'Sides, you got a quick tongue and a shifty mind. Can't put much trust in anythin' you say to me."

"What if I asked you to marry me?"

She looked at him steadily. "Is that what you're up to?"

He sat back. "I been thinkin' on it."

"Well. You ask when you're ready. I'll come up with some kind of an answer at the time, okay?"

"You sure are a hard lady, Francine."

"If so, there's reason. Ah, Lonnie. You are a fine-lookin' man and I appreciate fine-lookin' men. And you're no worse than some I've known and most likely better'n most. Only your timin' is just about the most awful I've ever seen. . . ."

"Just want you to know how I feel. Just tryin' to say to you that I'm levelin', you can depend on me. You can trust me."

"Trust you." She thought it over. "My first husband, Jody's daddy, went out for a six-pack one evenin' and never came back. My second went off with my closest girlfriend. . . ."

"That was Queenie Newton?"

"The one and the same."

"Always thought she was kind've cute."

"Real cute." Her voice had a bite in it. "Trust you, Lonnie? I ain't the smartest lady in the whole of Tokeneke County, but I ain't close to bein' the dumbest."

"You goin' to live the rest of your life wrapped up in all that meanness and hate, Francine?"

"I'm goin' to do whatever it is I have to do to get along. Whatever it takes to make a life for me and Jody, so there it is."

"What about me?"

"What about you?"

"I told you how I felt. I told you you could trust me."

"Lonnie," she said quietly. "You ever ask yourself how come it is always the woman gets the short end?"

"Is that a fact?"

"Better believe it."

"Maybe I just better be gettin' along."

"If it suits you."

"You want me to come around and see you at the restaurant?"

"Your choice."

"You don't give an inch, do you?"

She shrugged. "Not tonight I don't. Not a goddamned inch. . . ."

# CHAPTER
## 13

THE GIRL WAS angry, the boy afraid. They perched on the edge of the plastic and chrome chairs Duke Venable kept in his office, eyes going from the big sheriff to his deputy, skittering around the room without stop. He wanted out, an avenue of escape. She ached for a suitable target for all the hatred and accumulated venom built up in her for so long.

"Goddam," she said. "Goddamit to hell and back."

Duke Venable watched her with the equanimity of a man with a lifetime of physical prowess behind him. A man never troubled by threats to his well-being, never truly hurt.

"Girl, you watch your mouth." No words offended him. He had heard it all, the rough insults and oaths of the muscular male society in which he had functioned so well for so long. There was no word or combination of words he had not used.

But on the job, in this office, he found it politic to establish swiftly his authority. No more effective way existed than censoring the way people talked, cutting of their access to language and expression and ultimately to thought itself. Thus, a minimum of effort produced a maximum amount of control. Venable enjoyed wielding power.

The girl glared and for an extended chip of time looked as though she might defy him. What a beauty she was; dark eyes blazing out of that pale, perfect face, all framed by shining dark hair. And so very young; he had almost forgotten how beautiful a young girl could be.

He brought her name back to mind and said it aloud. "Barbara Cromartie?" He made a query out of it, as if he expected some response. But she was tougher than most of them and gave no indication that she cared what he wanted, and no sign of fear.

"Tell it to me again, Barbara."

"It isn't going to change."

"Tell it anyways."

She looked at Goforth, and at Arthur, the boy she came with. No help in either quarter.

"I was on Riverwalk," she said.

"Both of you?" Goforth inserted.

She gave him a scornful look. She had told the story before and they seemed to remember nothing; how stupid could they be? "Both of us."

"Why?" Venable asked.

"Why?"

"Why were you there?"

"We were jogging. Running actually."

"After dark?"

"I run to stay in shape."

Venable gave a single slow nod as if to acknowledge the fine shape she was in. "And you, Arthur, why do you run?"

"I'm a wrestler. On the college squad."

"A wrestler. But couldn't handle the dude that jumped you?" Venable said.

Arthur lowered his eyes. "I never saw him. He came up from behind."

Barbara Cromartie broke in. "He knocked Arthur down, stunned him. Don't blame Arthur."

"Nobody's blamin' anybody," Goforth said. "What happened after that?"

"He came after me. I was up ahead so I didn't know what happened. . . ."

"He caught up with you?"

"I heard him coming, his footsteps, and I swung back. I thought it was Arthur."

"And you were pleased to see him," Venable said in a thin, insinuating voice.

Goforth knew better. No way these two were jogging. They were out there to neck, in under one of the shadowed arches along Riverwalk. Out of sight of passersby, beyond the glare of the lamplights that marked the winding walk. College students both, they chose not to risk discovery on campus where expulsion would result from any sexual activity. Neither would admit the truth, of course; not such a harsh penalty at risk. Let the story stand, Goforth decided, and go on past it.

"Okay, miss, you turned back and saw that it wasn't Arthur. It was this other man. . . ."

"That's right."

"Describe him, please." In the brief silence that followed, Goforth stopped breathing. "Some kind of identification, some kind of description."

The girl sagged. "I couldn't see him."

"The lights on the walk—"

"The nearest light was behind him, shining in my eyes."

"How far was he from you when you first saw him?"

"A few yards. No more than six feet."

"You must have caught a glimpse of his face?"

"Not really."

"You thought it was Arthur, you said. If you didn't see the perpetrator's face, how did you know it wasn't Arthur?"

She was amused at the simplicity of his approach.

"He was much slighter than Arthur, a slender man, but strong. . . ."

"As strong as Arthur?"

She stared at Goforth. "Not as strong," she said finally.

"White or black?" He spoke with mounting impatience.

"White, I think."

"You think?"

"All right, white. I'm sure of it."

"So it was a slightly built white man grabbed you?"

"Near as I can say. He forced me over against the retaining wall, began tearing at my clothes. He hit me, cursed me. . . ."

"What was his voice like?" Venable said.

"Hoarse. Very angry."

"What did he say?"

"The usual words."

"No," Goforth said. "Any particular thing that seemed unusual?"

"I don't think so. Well, maybe. Something about getting even. Something about women being no good, that kind of thing. A misogynist." Her eyes glittered triumphantly at the vacant expression in Venable's eyes.

"What?" he said, in a mumble. "What's that?"

"A man who hates women," Goforth said, watching the girl.

She turned her attention to him with renewed interest.

"He didn't go through with it," Goforth reminded her. She was good to look at. Put together nicely, the right amounts in all the right places. But nasty. Not the kind you wanted to be around for very long. But still, a victim. "What prevented him from goin' through with it?"

"Arthur," she said.

"I regained my senses," Arthur said. "I let out a yell and ran toward them."

"Punched him out?" Venable said.

"Well, no. He spied me coming and just took off down the walk. I couldn't catch him."

"And that's the end of it?"

"What do you mean?"

"I mean, you just hustled on over here to the courthouse and filed a complaint?"

"Yes. That was the end of it. We were both very upset, frightened, angry. What are you going to do about it, about catching him?"

"Oh, we'll give it our best shot. Now I reckon you can both go on back out to the school. You need a ride?"

"There's just one thing," she said, examining Goforth with mounting interest.

"What's that, miss?"

"I'd just as soon nobody knew we were down by the river, the way folks talk, and all."

Goforth glanced over at Venable who shrugged his great round shoulders and jerked his head slightly in assent. "No harm, no foul. We'll just say you two were out playin' miniature golf and somebody tried to rob you, which is why you're out past curfew." Goforth checked the boy, then the girl, for agreement. "That suit you?"

"That'll be just fine, Sheriff," she drawled.

"Oh," Goforth answered mildly. "This here is the sheriff, I'm only a deputy...."

He drove aimlessly. Out on Mill Pond Road to where it crossed Raindrop and all the way to the trotting track. He parked and got out and leaned on the high white rail fence, staring into the dark at the horse barns, smoking and remembering. Except for the strong smell of the horses and the hay there was no way to recognize this place for what it was. Not a public trotting track, it was another possession of the Gaults. Here horses were bred for profit, trained, and every Saturday races were run to get the animals used to competing, to discover what future they had. Admission was free and gambling forbidden, though no one objected to private bets being made. When he was seventeen, Goforth had worked here cleaning up horse droppings, doing odd jobs, working with the blacksmiths, even helping to groom the horses. But after six months or so he'd quit and found work stacking boards in the sawmill; it was truly hard labor and paid only a little more, but it caused him to break sweat and become aware of his body and at the end of each day he felt satisfied that he'd earned his keep. The cigarette burned down to a nub, he stubbed it out on the ground and got back in the car and drove off, no particular destination in mind, going over it all.

Venable kept insisting it was the work of an outsider, someone who didn't live in the county. Goforth didn't agree. Whoever it was knew his way around, knew where he was likely to come across women alone, knew where he could act without fear of being discovered. And knew how to get away unseen. Somebody local. Somebody with a big mad on toward women. Somebody who wanted to get even. Somebody local.

But who? And why the abrupt change in M.O.? Why move his base from the beach to the river? Why attact a girl accompanied by a young, husky boyfriend? He'd put the question to Venable and the sheriff provided a stock answer: the assailant had become obsessive in his needs, unable to wait for an easier victim, willing to take the chance when he saw Barbara separated from Arthur.

Goforth hadn't argued the point but he didn't accept it, either. His mind raced from point to point, exploring other possibilities. Barbara and Arthur were an isolated incident, a behavioral aberration, brought about by—by what? What if—?

What if Barbara was known to the rapist and the attack came out of personal resentment, a desire for singular revenge? A rejected boyfriend, perhaps? But she insisted she hadn't recognized him, couldn't see him. He sighed and pulled the car over to the side of the road.

He lit a cigarette. What was the rapist doing now, this exact minute? Having paid the price for his extraordinary attempt tonight, would he turn back to his old and proven ways? Somewhere out in the night he was plotting his next move, fixing on his next victim, some way of compensating for tonight's defeat and humiliation. His anger, his resentment, his frustration would be blown up out of proportion and he would be forced to react. Goforth struggled to place himself inside that warped mind, to anticipate his next move. And he failed.

So much he tried to do ended in failure. Not heroic failure, not dramatic but feeble and ineffective. A sense of emptiness caused him to feel uprooted and solitary, without purpose or competence.

For a long time, work had sustained him, provided direction, made life worthwhile. Now, even that had lost its cutting edge. Being a cop had cost him dearly. His marriage had fallen apart, he had no children, no accumulated wealth to show for his time on the job. Only that house out at the river, and that had come to seem shabby and tawdry and without real value.

It would all change when he became sheriff. Or so he hoped. If not, how would he go on? He had always perceived himself as clever and strong, his personal defenses unbreachable by the daily onslaughts that brought lesser men down. Now he wasn't so sure. These days there were repeated reminders of his vulnerability, his mortality; his joints ached and there was a heaviness in his thighs, a worrisome tingling in his extremities.

His body was reminding him that his youth was gone. No longer able to withstand all the hammering of time. Once he had pissed in a straight strong stream. These days he voided in brief spurts that ended in pathetic dribbles. Some essential part of himself no longer functioned with the easy efficiency of his youth. But he feared discovering what was wrong more than he feared the indications of the flaw.

The bits and pieces of his life were forming patterns and designs he preferred not to look at. Yet he wanted desperately to make sense out of what he was and had been, to bring the daily anguish into harmony with his cleverness and his fear and the courage he had so admired in himself. He needed to make sense out of all that had been and would be, to perceive an acceptable plan within which he could again function satisfactorily, to stop hanging on to the far edge of an accident about to take place.

The long white beams of an approaching vehicle lit up the road. He watched it come on in his rearview mirror and for one frozen moment believed he was about to be wiped out by the onrushing brightness. Then the beams went past with a rush of air that rocked the squad car, the red tail lights mocking him as they grew smaller.

He sped after it, and brought it back into view. He switched on his flasher and pressed down on the gas pedal. The car leaped ahead. It took nearly two miles to catch up. He drifted alongside. Lonnie Peden was behind the wheel of his station wagon. Goforth waved him over.

Lonnie stayed behind the wheel, waiting for Goforth to approach.

"Evenin', Deputy."

"Oranges again, Lonnie?"

Lonnie grinned. "Arrestin' me don't do much good, Deputy."

"So's I noticed. Sheriff dropped the charges, I reckon."

"Sheriff did that."

"You a lucky boy, Lonnie. But how long's your luck goin'

to hold out if I pull you in with another load of Gault fruit. Open up the back, Lonnie."

"You're makin' a mistake."

"Open, please."

Lonnie obeyed.

Goforth pulled the heavy tarpaulin aside. Stacked up crates containing brand name Scotch and bourbon. He stepped back. "You are smart, Lonnie."

Lonnie tugged the tarpaulin back in place. "All right if I go about my business now?"

"Your business? You in this alone, Lonnie?"

"I have got me a silent partner, like they say, Deputy. I am well connected, if you understand my meanin'. I got a friend in high places."

"I'll bet you have."

"Want me to lay a name on you?"

Goforth just looked at Lonnie and said nothing.

Lonnie gave a quick, nervous laugh. He'd known men like the deputy all his life, men who seemed almost diffident at times, remote and doubly dangerous for being so. It occurred to him that tangling with Billy Goforth would be a full-time job, painful and damaging. "Well," he said. "Both of us know the score, ain't that right, Deputy?"

"On your way," Goforth said

"Nice talkin' to you, Deputy. Any time you want some first-class drinkin' whiskey, you think of me." He hurried back to the wagon and drove off into the night.

Goforth, jaw clamped shut, watched him go. Seemed people and events were ganging up, preventing him from doing what he was hired to do. The job he had done for so long and intended to keep doing. Seemed like not many folks wanted the job done right anymore. No so's you could notice, anyway.

He set himself against going. Providing all the reasons for keeping away. Reasons that convinced him it could only bring trouble down on them both. But good sense and logic failed hold and he went anyway, drawn to her more than he had ever been drawn to a woman before.

He stared at her house. More of a cottage. A bungalow. Or

was he giving it greater value and attractiveness than it deserved?—set up on cinderblocks, rickety, lacking paint—no different than most others in Northtown.

He saw her. Behind the living room shade, moving past in that strong proud way she had. Buttocks and breasts in clear silhouette. Then she was gone.

He smoked and he watched and he waited. But for what? There was no movement along the silent dirt street, nothing to give alarm. He enjoyed the private moments.

"Freeze! Keep your hands on the wheel!"

Goforth jerked around and looked into the muzzle of a .357 Magnum. His eyes followed the line of the barrel and the stiff, extended arms encased in a pale blue uniform shirt.

"Benjamin," he said quietly.

"Billy! Damn you, man, out here in the middle of the night." He holstered the Magnum and swore, kicked dirt.

Goforth got out of the car. "Why're you here?"

"A call came in. Dammit, man, a white man staring at a black girl's house, somebody's bound to take notice, make a complaint. Damn, you are bound'n determined to make a whole bunch of trouble for yourself."

"Just doin' my job. Figured maybe he'd come around again."

"Hand that jive to Duke and anybody else cares to listen, but not to me. You got a twitch for Inez and you got it bad."

"No point in denyin' it, is there?"

"Hell, no!"

"You're my friend, Benjamin, you understand."

"Is that a fact? Deputy carryin' on with a nigger gal, I'll tell you what I understand—that you are goin' to spoil every damned thing for yourself. . . ."

"I sure do hope you're wrong."

"Man, I ain't never forgot what you done for me. The time you kept them redneck bikers from stompin' my head in outside Bobby Roy's that night. And when the bad times come and they was cuttin' troopers from the force, it was your doin' kept me on the job. Man don't forget things like that."

"You give as good as you get, Benjamin."

"Not the same. I am in your debt, man, and I know it. But that don't change my way of thinkin'. What you're up to is wrong. Flat out wrong and dumb. Goin' the way you are is like askin' for trouble. Now, you listen to me now. Best thing is to haul your pale ass out of here and don't ever come back."

"No way I can do that."

"Fool," Benjamin said without force.

"I appreciate your concern."

"Fool," Benjamin said again. He took a few steps away. "Fool. Damn fool white man. . . ."

Goforth ground his cigarette into the dirt and crossed the street and knocked on her door. After a while, she answered.

"Who is it?"

"Billy Goforth," he said, then added quickly. "Deputy Goforth, ma'am."

She opened the door and eyed him speculatively, then stepped back.

"Somebody called the sheriff's station," he said.

"Not me. I figured it was you."

"You did?"

"Figured you'd get around to comin' over when you was up to it. You want to come inside?"

"We could go someplace. Have a drink, somethin' to eat."

"You better come inside."

She closed the door behind him. "I mean it," he said, "about goin' out somewhere."

"That wouldn't be smart."

He insisted. "I want to take you somewhere."

"I ain't goin' anywhere with you, not now, not ever. You are goin' to hurt me, hurt both of us."

He felt relief and was immediately disappointed; to be strong, resolute, that was everything, the only thing. "I can't stop thinkin' about you."

"You better stop. You and me. Boy, that ain't nothin' but trouble."

He moved closer to her and she held her ground. Her eyes were immense, luminous, and he felt himself drawn softly down into the mysterious center of this girl-woman. Floating in warmth and moisture, coming to a slow stop, cradled at last in a place he had for so long longed to be.

He kissed her.

She made no move to hold him off. Nor to accept him.

He took hold of her, drew her close. Her body was pliant but unyielding, as if unable either to resist or surrender. He kissed her again.

"You want me to stop, say so."

"Stop." There was no force in it.

"I can't do that."

"You expect me to fight you? No way I can do that. You expect me to yell, bring folks chargin' in here? What good's that gonna do?"

He smiled grimly. "You yell and that Harlan, he'd be number one through that door."

"Never mind Harlan."

"You and him you got a thing goin'?"

She made a slow, gentle attempt to free herself; he tightened his grip. She spoke quietly, but with surprising intensity. "This is got nothin' to do with Harlan, or anybody else. This is just you and me, here and now, and nobody else in my life or in yours. Oh, damn—" Her anger drained away and she began to sob. "Damn you, Deputy...."

"I ain't goin' to hurt you." He kissed her tears.

She clung to him. "Oh, yes, you are."

"I don't want to."

"Oh. It is gonna be a mess, one godawful mess."

"I'll take care of you."

"You're crazy."

He kissed her voluptuous mouth and her lips were warm, soft, quivering slightly. His arms tightened around her waist. "I'll take care of us both," he murmured.

"I don't think so. But it don't matter much anymore." Her arms circled his neck and she gazed up into his face. "I been thinkin' a lot about you, Deputy."

"Can you find it in your heart to use my given name?"

"Billy..."

"That's better."

He kissed her gently. "I'll look after you, Inez. I will. Ain't nobody goin' to hurt you again, I'll see to it."

She drew his face, gave herself to his mouth, surprised at how hard his lips were, how uncertain and unskilled he was. And pleased, when she understood that here was a man desperately in need of love and she vowed to comfort, to give him everything he had ever craved, to make up for all the hurts he had ever known.

They lay side by side in her bed, not touching. He smoked and stared at the glowing ash in the darkness. She went over every detail of what had transpired, every sensation he had evoked in her body, every emotion he had stirred.

"It's been a long time," she said.

"And for me."

"Since I felt so much, I mean."

"Me the same," he said. His hand found hers and held on.

"I got to tell you. I'm more afraid now than before. So much feelings, it feels like we began at the top of the mountain and there's no place left to climb to."

"We're goin' to be all right."

"You keep sayin' so, only I ain't so sure."

"Even with my wife, it was never like this."

"Please," she said. "You want to say anything about how you feel or what you want. Say it straight out. But leave the rest of them out of it."

"The rest of them?"

"Other women. Wives, girlfriends, chicks you balled, whatever. This bed ain't big enough for anybody else, okay?"

"The bed's just right, fits us together pretty good."

"Don't get all puffed up over one good time, hear. Next time I might turn rotten on you."

That made him laugh. He squeezed her hand.

"No guarantees," he said.

"Whatever you say."

"No promises. Take what you get and so will I."

"Fair enough."

"Now you reckon we can try that again? Practice makes perfect, they say."

"I've always wanted to be perfect."

"Then you got to keep tryin'...."

# CHAPTER
## 14

HERE ON FRONTAGE street the old men sat on folding metal chairs on the wide sidewalk outside Earl's Pool Parlor and Sandwich Bar and sipped hot coffee out of paper cups and nibbled Earl's homemade doughnuts and talked about hunting and fishing, while warming themselves in the morning sun. Like a castle guard, they measured each visitor who entered the single short block, guessing at why he was here, what his business might be, eyeing strangers with distrust, distaste.

When Dorr C. P. Seely appeared they greeted him with respect, affable, friendly with one of their own. And nodded silently in B. J. Moody's direction, the college president not entirely one of them though not entirely an outsider either.

Without speaking, they watched the two men advance down the street past the Ford Agency with the shining new pickups in neat formation in front of the big show windows, past International Harvester, and the J. C. Penney Store. At the end of the street, the pink stucco Gault Building done in the Spanish style with a red tile roof that glistened luminously in the late afternoon sun. Set down strategically in woods that ran all the way back to the river, the Gault Building drew no unwanted attention, a quiet unobtrusive place, the true seat of power in Tokeneke County. A pileated woodpecker, its red crest flaming in among the dappled greens and browns of pine and cedar and moss-draped oak, darted about, making its presence known.

A handsome middle-aged woman greeted them in the marble and mirrored reception room, saw them seated on leather-and-polished-steel chairs, and left them alone. Dorr Seely and B. J. Moody, waiting in anticipatory quiet, uneasy, and not without apprehension. Until they could remain silent no more.

Seely forced a smile. He was not a man to smile easily or laugh freely. There was more resentment in him than joy, more suspicion than acceptance, more hesitancy than trust. "I will make a confession to you, B. J. Men like Mr. Nolan have always made me uneasy and anxious to leave them. It's as if they possess secret and ominous characteristics that are inaccessible to me and incomprehensible. That entire family, in all the years I've been in King of Heaven they've treated me casually, almost as if I didn't exist, coming to church on Sunday but never dealin' with me as an equal."

Moody laughed without being amused. "Well, face it. You're not their equal. You know it and they know it."

An angry answer came onto Seely's tongue and he swallowed it. He looked at his companion with the cold, flat eyes of a man who took no prisoners. He spoke in a thin, cutting voice. "All that money up on The Hill. All that power for all those years. As if they own this town, the county . . ."

"And they do. Point is to let them think as they like. For now. You are creating something, my friend, something special, something that can go way past any powers the Gaults have ever known."

Seely saw the goal, blurred and distant, he had to travel. It was steep and hard, pitted, booby-trapped. Perhaps he would never make it, but it was worth going after. Dorr C. P. Seely had his dreams of glory, of riches, of rewards unimagined and still unnamed, as extravagant as any other man's dreams.

What precisely did he want? Exactly what was he in search of? No more dissembling, he chided himself. No more avoiding the truth, no more rhetorical trick plays, no more fancy footwork.

The answer came fully formed onto the screen of his mind, an answer that dismayed and delighted him at the same time, an answer that sent spasms of apprehension along his spine. He ached with a visceral craving for attention. To be in the public eye on a scale seldom achieved by small-town preachers, to be *famous*. He longed to challenge Billy Graham's place in the evangelical sun. He hungered to usurp Jerry Falwell's position of national attention. He wanted to bask in God's favor and in the favor of the multitudes, to be their *leader*, to take them down the road to salvation and eternal life. He wanted the accolades of his followers and the fear of his enemies.

He wanted power.

The deference of great men, the attention and love of beautiful women—women like Kate Fellows; women lush and sexual, overflowing with the promise of great and mysterious pleasures. He wanted all the rewards that were possible for his ego, his fortune, his flesh. Every last ounce squeezed out of a world that had neglected him for too long. This then was his sin, a kind of peculiarly American original sin.

"The Tenth Crusade," he said in a low, gravelly voice. "It does have a fine resonance. Dedicated, holy, a collection of Christian warriors on the march."

B. J. Moody nodded soberly.

"Can I depend on your support, B. J.?"

"Absolutely. I stand at your shoulder in this affair. And the school—Gault Christian—will lend whatever assistance and authority it can to your crusade."

"*Our* crusade."

"Ours," Moody said. What had drawn him into Seely's ambitions? They had so little in common, they moved in different directions, marched to different drummers, aimed at different goals. Moody viewed himself as a simple man with a vested interest in maintaining the status quo. Don't rock the boat; a good motto to live by. Advance yourself from level to level while upsetting no one, disturbing nothing, allowing only small changes to take place, and then reluctantly.

Make no enemies; another rule of his life. Claim every man a friend. Take no risks and all the time enhance and solidify his reputation as an educator, an administrator, always a good company man. Careful, he warned himself. God forbid that he should commit some colossal blunder that might transform Mr. Nolan from a silent benefactor into a terrifying and unconquerable enemy.

A secretary appeared and escorted them into Mr. Nolan's office. He had planted himself behind an old English dining table which he used as a desk, long, wide, sleekly polished, resembling nothing so much as some medieval king confronting unwelcome envoys. His huge bulk blocked out the window behind him, making him appear even bigger than he was.

"All right, Reverend, what's this all about?"

Seely felt his nerve waver. Ever since he began playing football in the Pee Wee League, he had deferred to authority, obeyed orders, sacrificed his individuality for the good of the team. But this was no football game and Mr. Nolan was not a coach. He braced himself, drew up straight and tall, his muscular body taut, voice coming from down low, easy and strong.

"We have a project to present to you, Mr. Nolan."

Mr. Nolan rumbled and lowered himself into his chair carefully. "We? Why you here, Moody? Don't that college of yours keep you busy enough?"

Seely answered for Moody. "Dr. Moody is part of the project, Mr. Nolan. That is to say, as president of Gault Christian he is a vital element of my support structure, lending stature and status to my crusade and—"

"Cut out the horse feathers, Reverend! You're usin' up valuable time. Got businesses to run, decisions to make, responsibilities to be met. Now get to it, man."

Seely deliberately took a seat though no invitation had been forthcoming. He crossed his legs, carefully adjusting his trouser creases, placed his big hands on the arms of the chair and presented a stern, determined mask to Gault. "Mr. Nolan, the very salvation of our America is at stake."

Mr. Nolan shifted and looked away, peered back out of narrow slits. His jaw worked, his lips quivered, his tongue pushed at his cheek. "Hell with that. America don't do much for me, I return the favor."

"The Tenth Crusade," Seely said. "It's for us, Mr. Nolan, and it's for you. For all the Gaults, all the folks who believe in Jesus Christ and in the American way. I am talkin' about the future well-being of our nation, of our world."

"Get on with it," Mr. Nolan snarled.

"I have been doin' a great deal of soul-searchin' since last we spoke, Mr. Nolan, about our crusade. About the awful changes goin' on all over the country. What I am gettin' at is this—we got to organize an army. . . ."

"An army?"

"Our crusaders."

"Not actually an *army*?"

"Oh, yes, sir. An army without guns or bullets. An army equipped with Christ's truth for a weapon. We got to root out the enemy, stomp him down, grind him to dust. Wipe out the anti-Christ."

Mr. Nolan folded his pudgy hands across his belly. "I do believe you are comin' around to discussin' money. . . ."

Seely grinned. "Now, sir, good Christian Americans never let a few dollars stand between them and what was right."

"How much?"

"Last time we met, sir, we agreed that a specific target was required. . . ."

"You've located such a target?"

"B. J. and I have discussed it."

"B. J. and you." The tiny eyes swung over to Moody, who shivered.

"I am merely a follower in all this, Mr. Nolan. A man who takes orders. . . ."

Mr. Nolan grew impatient. "Let's hear it about this target, Reverend."

"You have a problem, sir." Seely felt his heart begin to pound. He had put himself smack up against the far edge of things. There was nowhere to go but straight ahead. "With your kin."

"How's that?"

"Your boy, Wesley."

Mr. Nolan's face stiffened. "Tell me about my boy."

Seely plunged ahead. "The boy is buckin' hard, Mr. Nolan. He aims to throw off saddle and halter both. He aims to break new ground for himself. Like not doin' right by his wife."

Mr. Nolan began to wheeze. His round face turned crimson. "You come in here tellin' me *that!* Just pick yourself up and get on—"

"He's out to Miss Ivy's now and then."

Mr. Nolan slumped in his seat. His massive chest heaved. "You're takin' an awful chance, Reverend."

"He's havin' a romance with another woman."

"What? Who says so?"

"Mae-Mae, his wife. Seems like she's trailed after him from time to time."

"That a honest-to-God-true fact?"

"Yes, sir."

"Damn that boy! I warned him. 'Keep dippin' into Mae-Mae's honey-pot,' I told him. 'Do your homework and make me a grandchild.' Boy just won't listen." He quieted down. "How serious is it?"

"Beautiful woman. Glamorous, sophisticated. Good at what she does, surely."

"She got a name?"

"Kate Fellows."

"Who the hell is Kate Fellows?"

Seely told him. Told him more than Mr. Nolan wanted to hear, but enough to engage his attention and stoke his rising anger. Enough to enlist him heavily in The Tenth Crusade.

# CHAPTER
## 15

HIS BRAIN WAS a horror-house of swiftly changing images and emotions. A searing rage made him tremble and he ached to lash out, to cause pain and damage, to destroy. He opened his mouth to scream but no sound came out.

He had watched it all from the secure hiding place he'd earlier staked out. It was crazy, he knew, allowing himself to be worked up over nigger pussy the way he was, but there it was. He could find no way to evict her from his thoughts, the musty scent of her lingering in the cavities of his skull, the sweet dark feel of her that night on the dunes. Her protests had been feeble in the end, her body gone limp, her passivity exciting him even more. And when it happened, it was as if it had never happened before. An explosion beyond relief. Beyond tension bursting out of his limbs. Beyond anything he had ever experienced before. Or since.

He had warned himself to stop thinking about her. And couldn't. He swore not to permit the memory of her on the sand to come back to him. And failed. He promised to fulfill his plan, a different woman each time. And was drawn back to her again and again.

The deputy was the problem. Returning the way he did to stare at Inez's house. Yes, Inez. Inez Macklin. It had been easy to discover her name, to find out that she taught at the middle school in Northtown, to clock her comings and goings. To mark her friend, Harlan, down as a threat. To mark him for death.

But the deputy. Old enough to be his father—and the very word triggered a flood of fury and hatred in him. Memories of his father were dim and only bad, stories told him by his mother with scorn and loathing directed at the man who'd created him in her belly and deserted him all, never to be heard from again.

The deputy had gone in to Inez's house, stayed on. More than two hours had passed and he could no longer deceive himself that it was police business. Taunting images of them locked together. Naked bodies pressed together. The deputy putting himself into that dark and dangerous place where *he*— the most private part of himself—had been.

He willed the deputy to come back out, determined to attack and destroy the man. To crush his skull, break his face, shatter his bones. Wipe . . . him . . . out.

It hadn't happened that way. His rage was so great he could no longer stay in the hiding place. Only by leaving would he save himself from his own murderous intentions. He forced Inez and the deputy from his mind. Elsewhere he would find a surrogate, someone equally unacceptable and inaccessible and therefore equally desirable. Necessary to nourish the insatiable angry appetite that permitted him no rest.

It was the same appetite, the same anger that had caused him to let caution fall the other night on Riverwalk, to launch himself blindly at Barbara Cromartie, caught up in a crimson passion, and the desire for revenge. But it had all come apart and he had fled in panic. Losing control, wetting his pants like some wet-nosed brat. Sooner or later he would even the score.

But carefully. Choosing his own ground. His own time. Out in the night there were only enemies, hateful persons intent on destroying him, shattering his plans, his future. But he was too smart. Never the same way twice. Never the same mistake.

Few human beings possessed his cunning or his inner strength or his surging passion.

He started toward Silver Sands and checked himself. Break the pattern, muddy up the picture in the deputy's head; as Riverwalk must surely have done. Keep them off balance. He went to Shell Beach instead.

Shell Beach faced Central America across the barrier islands and the Gulf beyond. No more than half a mile of fine white sand running in a deep arc toward Heaven's Point, the low dunes covered with a tangle of prickly simlax and Florida rosemary, and the waxy leaves of pennywort, ivy and seawort. Tracks of skunks and lizards, snakes and raccoons crisscrossed the dunes and disappeared into the undergrowth.

On weekends Shell Beach was the almost exclusive province of students from Gault Christian, and their guests. During the week, it was infrequently used, by single bathers or sun worshippers. Or an occasional couple seeking privacy. Weathered wooden walls brought visitors across the dunes from a parking lot a hundred yards away. During the hot days, a deputy paid periodic visits to Shell Beach, keeping outsiders away. The beaches of Tokeneke were intended only for the residents of the county. But at night the sands were free for all.

Squatting in the sea oats in the deeper shadows cast by the small laurel oaks, their growth slowed by sea spray and salt water, he followed the running lights of a vessel heading deeper into the Gulf. A shrimper going after a catch? Or a free-lancer seeking a load of Colombian grass off a mother ship anchored somewhere out there?

What a way to go! He imagined himself powerful and well established, a hundred tough men in his employ. Running dope, aliens, guns. A man of his time, of a changing, violent world. Making people high, making them rich, making revolutions. Profiting greatly in all the exciting ways he yearned to profit. Doing what he wanted when he wanted.

Bored with his own imaginings, he went down to the water. In faded jeans and a clean white T-shirt, he was tightly constructed, muscular, strung tautly at the joints as if ready to spring into action. He stripped off his clothing and walked into the water. He was a good swimmer and perceived himself competing in the Olympics, winning every race he entered.

After twenty minutes he came back to shore. He had some trouble locating his clothes and he became tense; he was not a person who dealt easily with the unexpected; he preferred events go according to plan. His plan. He started searching the beach when the man called out.

"Looking for these?"

He pivoted around, hands automatically shielding his genitals. The man was seated at the base of the dunes, the clothes were on the sand in front of him. Neatly folded and stacked. He smiled.

"I was concerned."

"Toss my things over."

"I was afraid you'd gone too far, that something had happened."

"Throw 'em over."

"I've been watching you."

"Why? What're you watchin' me for? Hand over my clothes."

The man spread his hands. A fugitive smile came onto his oval face as he extended one hand, a pair of Jockey shorts dangling between thumb and forefinger.

"Here you are."

"Throw 'em over."

"I thought you might get into trouble."

"I can take care of myself."

"Oh, I'm sure you can. You have an air of competence around you. I'll bet you can do anything you want to do, and do it well."

"I do all right."

"I offend you, don't I? Being here, I mean? Intruding on your privacy. I understand, I truly do understand. Privacy is so vital to one's psychic welfare, a chance to contemplate past and present, to let time wash over you unmarked, to recharge one's spiritual batteries, so to speak."

"Look. I wanna get dressed."

"Didn't mean to intrude. Just out nightwalking, exorcising my personal demons, you might say. Oh, dear, you are so young."

"You gonna let me have my things?" He was getting anxious, the familiar tension seeping back into his limbs, the hard knot of rage forming up in his gut. His hands folded up into tight hard balls.

The middling man tossed the shorts and he caught them and quickly turned away, pulled them on.

"I don't bite." A giggle sputtered and expired on the night air. "Unless asked, that is. Oh dear, I've shocked you, haven't I? So sorry. Shall I shut up?"

"The beach is free, do what you like."

He retrieved his jeans and climbed into them, pulled on the T-shirt. Running shoes in hand, he started up the sand. The middling man pushed himself erect and went after him.

"It is lovely here at night, don't you agree? Beaches are terribly special to me. Exotic, I mean." Again the giggle. "Erotic, actually, if you know what I mean. I collect shells, but of course, most beaches are pretty well picked over. Most of life is, I suppose. Do I sound cynical? I don't mean to. It's vital to keep one's self open to new experiences, new people, new ways of doing things. You really should visit Greece. Those island beaches—well, they are magnificent. How old are you?"

He came around slowly and the middling man pulled up two strides away. "Sixteen years old," he said deliberately, watching the man closely.

"I'm old enough to be your father." Giggle, giggle. "I'm awfully glad I'm not."

"My father's a bastard, wherever he is."

"Oh, I see. Life can be hard. My father was an alcoholic, a failed physician, a suicide. However, one makes the best of things. So young, so very young. You're in high school?"

"You ask a lot of questions."

"Just trying to be friendly."

"I don't want to be friendly with you."

The middling man flinched. "I understand. I'm too ancient and decrepit for you and rightly so. Look at you, handsome, virile, with a superb body." He made a gesture.

"Keep you hands off, faggot."

"A kinder, softer word is gay. I much prefer it."

"Fuck you, queer."

"Turning nasty, are we? Well, I'm used to it. Men of my persuasion usually are, you see."

"You're not from around here?"

A winsome smile. "Never shit where you eat, they say. I live in Tampa."

"What are you doin' up this away?"

"New vistas, new beaches, new people."

"New boys, you mean."

"That, too."

"Just keep your hands off me."

"Be nice. You can't blame a person for living according to his nature."

"Do what you want, just let me alone."

"If you're not in a hurry, why don't we sit down somewhere? I'm so enjoying our little talk."

"Makes no never-mind to me."

"Up on the dunes? Sand is a sensual cushion, don't you think? Always that undercurrent of movement, a world in constant flux, the promise of altered future."

"Suit yourself."

He followed the middling man up the dune and sat down an arm's length away. The sand settled under him.

"How much is it going to cost me?" the middling man said after a while.

"What?"

"How much money do you want?"

He chose not to understand. "Are you rich?"

"I've earned my share."

"Doin' what?"

"I run some nursing homes."

"Run them?"

"I own them."

"You are rich."

"I do all right." Then: "Fifty dollars . . ."

"What?"

"Don't be angry. If it's not enough . . ."

"Get your hand off."

"All right, will a hundred do?"

"To let you touch my leg?"

The middling man made an effort to clear his throat. "I want to see you the way you were when you came out of the water. With nothing on."

"I'm no fag."

"A boy your age can always use extra money. A hundred dollars. Imagine what you could do with it, what you could buy."

"Maybe you haven't got that kind of money on you."

"Oh, I've got it, and more. But it isn't the money, it never is. I am truly attracted to you, fond of you, the way you conduct yourself. Stand up, will you? Oh, yes, you are a lovely beautiful young animal. Now the jeans. Take them off. Oh, my God, the hardness of you, the size of you ... let me take down your shorts ... oh, my God ..."

The middling man's head came forward in time to receive the full force of a swinging fist on the bridge of his nose. The cartilage crumpled and blood began to run. The middling man cried out and rolled away. The boy cut off his escape, both fists pounding down in relentless fury.

A rising panic gripped the middling man and he pleaded with the boy. "Stop! Please, stop. You're hurting me badly. You're going to kill me."

The boy kept throwing punches. Until all strength abruptly drained away. He slumped to the sand next to the middling man, breathing hard. After a while, he searched the man's pockets and located a roll of bills. He removed his gold watch and the heavy gold ring on his hand.

He put on his shoes and laced them up. He rose and looked down at the middling man, then delivered a hard kick to the head. Then he hurried away, never looking back.

# CHAPTER
## 16

UNABLE TO FACE the cramped and dubious pleasures of the back seat of her 1975 Ford one more time, Kate brought Wesley back to her apartment. They made love and soon after Wesley went to sleep. She watched him and wondered how she had allowed herself to drift into this relationship. It was the same question she had asked about every relationship she'd ever had. Each one seemed to have come about by accident; a woman adrift on uncharted social waters, transported by some subterranean stream from one man to another, no longer in charge of her destiny. More than anything, she assured herself, she longed for a tight, strong, controlling hand on her existence, preferably her own. Yet, no matter how hard she tried, that result always eluded her.

Wesley was wrong for her. Much too young, and very much married. His background so different from her own, his experience at variance with hers, his hopes and dreams light years away from hers. Asleep, his unlined cheeks gave him the cast of innocence, a placid, unfettered expression. Hardly an in-

nocent, she knew. Caught up in an adulterous affair, and not
for the first time, as he had so quickly let her know. Nor did
he restrain his bedroom antics to her and his wife alone; she
knew of his visits to Miss Ivy's and wondered what other beds
he graced, not troubling himself to mention them. Brought up
amid great wealth, he'd been to the best schools, traveled
widely in the United States and Europe, experienced different
societies and cultures. None of it made much of an impression
on him; like his face, his mind and spirit were unlined, an
appealing mass still unformed, giving no indication of what he
really thought or wanted or felt. It troubled her; was that tranquil
expression only a vapid mask? Was there nothing behind it?
Was cleverness all there was to Wesley, cleverness and hand-
someness and an amusing facile way with words?

Be fair, she admonished herself. To Wesley and to herself.
He was intelligent, sensitive, caring.

Yes, he was too young. But more, he gave off an aura of
whining infantilism as he nourished himself off her maturity,
her womanly strength, her growing self-confidence. Even their
lovemaking—less gratifying and less exciting than it might
be—took on a mother-child cast, Kate nurturing, soothing,
hovering over his flesh and his psyche until he attained some
kind of incomplete passion that left him in solitary gratitude,
vowing feebly to be a better man from that moment on.

Oh, yes, he loved her. At least he said so. Over and over
again, swearing to it, waxing lyrical about it, vowing eternal
fidelity of body and mind, of undying attention and affection,
of everlasting support and commitment. He cared, he said,
about her well-being. His efforts to involve himself in her life
were genuine. And when she needed help, he was always there
to offer it. She had rejected his attempts to press money upon
her, to pay her rent; but he bought her expensive gifts and
twice took her on long weekends that were exciting and fun
and very romantic.

And more, she loved him, as much as she had ever loved
a man. And recognized that theirs was a finite affair that inevitably would come crashing down one day. But not yet. Not
yet.

Without warning, he reached for her, eyes still closed. It
was something he did, something that unleashed warring im-

pulses in her, pleased and repulsed at the same time. She gave up thinking and surrendered to his passion, flattered that this handsome young man wanted her and her middle-aged face and body.

They made love slowly and silently and when it was over they smoked and drank white wine and listened to Mozart on the tape deck he had bought her. He rested one hand on her damp vagina and she flexed her thighs automatically.

He laughed and closed his fingers on her pubic hair, applying slow firm pressure. "You are a sexual miracle," he told her. He had used the same words before.

"Cursed with an active libido and sensitive nerve endings."

"Why cursed?"

"Why not? Oh, all right, make that blessed."

"I love being with you."

"I love being with you."

"I love you, Kate."

"I love you." She sipped some wine and considered the words. "Have you ever tried to define it, love, I mean?"

"Just enjoy it."

"Either you are the most superficial man I've ever met or one of the most intuitively profound. I can't decide which."

"Let me know when you find out. Until then, I like the way things are."

"They could be better."

He came up on one elbow. "Meaning what?"

"Meaning your wife. Meaning I wish you were ten years older and I were ten years younger."

"I can't do anything about our ages, but I have done something about Mae-Mae."

Her heart began to beat more rapidly, but she said nothing.

"I asked her for a divorce. I told her I loved you and intended to marry you."

There was a thickening in her throat and it became impossible to swallow. She moved away from him, fumbling for another cigarette. Her hand was trembling when she lit it. She couldn't speak.

"I mean it, Kate. I want us to get married."

"Why can't things stay the way they are?"

"Because I want to be able to go places with you, do things

with you, not sneak around and be ashamed that we love each other."

It all sounded perfect, exactly what she'd always wanted.

"I'll tell my father," he said. "And Papa James. We'll get married as soon as the divorce comes through. You can quit your job, give up working for the rest of your life. We'll travel, any place you want to go. We'll live part of the year in New York and part of it in Sardinia or Corfu, part of it here. We'll have a wonderful life, just the two of us."

She spoke carefully, the words delicately spaced. "I don't want to stop working, Wesley. I want to work more, act more, to make the career I've never really had. I—"

"Whatever you say, it's all right with me."

"And if I say no?"

"I won't accept it. I intend to pressure you, crowd you, influence you until I get the answer I want."

She looked at him steadily out of those sea-green eyes. A smug, secretive smile faded onto his mouth. He bent over her. His breath was warm on her skin, his tongue moist and gently insistent. Her joints unlocked and her head went back and her thighs separated, the pleasure intensifying and spreading. But her mind never stopped clicking away.

The next morning Dr. Moody ushered her into his office with his customary charm and graciousness, seeing her seated. Turning his most disarming smile in her direction. "There." He rubbed one hand against the other. "You have something to tell me?" he said cheerfully.

"About our last conversation . . ."

"Yes?"

"I can't do it, Dr. Moody. I'm sorry, I can't bring myself to censor Eugene O'Neill."

His brows made the long journey to a scowl without interruption. "You disappoint me."

"I'm sorry."

"Have you considered your decision carefully?"

Would he have put that same question to a man, she wondered. Would he have doubted a man's capacity for reflection and intellectual examination? She wanted him to understand. "I'm an actress," she said. "An artist, I like to think. All art, any art, is a personal and intensely meaningful formulation. There is no way to separate the artist from his art. I can't bring myself to tinker with the carefully chosen words of a great playwright in what may be his greatest play."

"I am sympathetic to your point of view, but art for art's sake is not the ultimate consideration in these matters," said Dr. Moody.

"This is not a whim on my part. I've given it a great deal of careful thought."

"I'm sure you have! I suppose we will simply have to accept your decision."

She couldn't conceal her surprise. "Then that's it?"

"That's it. But from now on please choose your projects with a little more discrimination and concern for the sensitivity of the community."

She felt almost happy. "You can depend on me." But something was lacking, some unnamed irritant nibbling at her, causing an unnamed fear to come alive in her again. She shrugged it away. She was glad it was resolved to everyone's satisfaction, without pain caused or professional blood spilled. Over, with no known casualties.

There was no way she could enter a classroom. She canceled Speech 101 and the seminar on Theater History and walked the mile or so from the campus into King of Heaven. She wandered about, postponing the inevitable, at ease under the tall shade trees lining the streets, admiring the old white mansions and townhouses, the sun-dappled slow tempo of the place. Her mind leaped crazily about as she walked, image crashing into image, memory colliding with shattered memory, disconnected thoughts dissolving before she could examine and file them away.

Weary and irritable suddenly, she wandered down the still, almost deserted streets, past Courthouse Square to Francine's Diner. Established in an empty booth, she examined a menu while Francine wiped the plastic table top with a damp cloth.

"How you, Miss Fellows?"

"Just fine, I guess. Can I get some iced tea?"

"Anything you like. That was real nice of you, comin' to visit Jody like you did."

"She's a good girl, I like her."

"She surely does admire you."

"How is she doing?"

Francine lifted her shoulders, let them fall. "Mostly she's sore, like a trapped wild cat, just scratchin' and spittin' and hopin' to get hold of whoever done it to her."

"They don't know who?"

"Not yet. I'll get your tea." She went and returned, placed the glass in front of Kate. "Anythin' else I can get you?"

"Keep me company, if you can."

Francine slid into the seat opposite. "No sense ownin' a place if you can't put your backside on a chair once in a while. Jody talks a lot about you, Miss Fellows, wants to be like you, she says."

"That's very flattering."

"You're just as beautiful as she says you are."

"She's the one that's beautiful, a natural, still unspoiled beauty. I can see where it comes from."

"Me! Shoot, no. Some women are truly fine to see and others do the best they can with what they been handed out. Me, I slid past my best time of my life long ago. I get along on memory and the fact that most men are damned fools with their brains between their legs, pardon my sayin' so."

"You may be right."

Francine hunched forward. "Man looks at you he has ideas about love and marriage and raisin' a family in a nice house. He looks at me and gets all lumpy and itchin' to roll me onto my back and grunt and sweat over me. Believe me, I know."

Kate thought of Wesley. "Maybe that's the nature of us all, men and women alike."

"Maybe, only it would be better for everybody if it were different, I think. If maybe we got on as friends and then the other after, instead of the other way 'round." She pulled back and grew embarrassed. "I'm runnin' off at the mouth, I guess."

"Oh, no. This is the first real conversation I've had with a woman since I've been in King of Heaven."

"That a fact? Don't know why I'm surprised, don't have a single close friend myself and I was born and raised in this town. No friends, no future, not much of a present. Doesn't seem enough, somehow. There ought to be more."

"There is, there has to be."

"Such as?"

"Aren't there places you want to visit, things you'd like to do?" said Kate. "Wouldn't you like to get married again?"

"Is that what you want?"

Kate sucked some tea through a straw. It was weak, and too sweet. She smiled at Francine. "I'm beginning to believe I've never known what I wanted. Once, acting was all of it for me, with an occasional man. Now I'm forty years old—almost—and there have been too many men and not enough acting."

"You ain't content out at the school?"

"I keep telling myself I am. That I couldn't do better. The best of all possible worlds, I keep telling myself. I was never much of an actress, I'm afraid. I got by on my appearance. Flashy, flamboyant, part of the stage dressing."

"Oh, you look very much like a lady to me."

"It all comes out of a jar. The makeup, the hair color, carefully selected clothing, a lot of exercise and stay away from anything fattening, which includes just about everything you enjoy eating."

Francine laughed; Kate smiled. Neither of them spoke for a while.

"From where I sit, Miss Fellows, you got just about everything a woman could ask for. Good work, good pay, folks respect you. You got the special look of a movie star, finely made. Folks like to see you, it makes them feel real good seein' you. From where I sit, you got to be a happy person."

Kate blinked. "Call me Kate, please."

Francine reached for her hand. "But you ain't, are you? Happy, I mean?"

"I don't think I've ever been, not for long."

"Me neither, come to think of it. Not nearly so much as I'd like. Never done as much or as good as I wanted to. Guess I fell short as a wife and I got the feelin' I am fallin' short as a mother. . . ."

"I'm sure Jody wouldn't agree."

"I ain't. We ain't close, her and me. We don't hardly talk to each other, not about anything important. Not about what matters in her life or in mine, not about how we feel about

each other, or anybody else. No, I ain't never measured up."
She rolled her eyes and grinned and brought her hands together
in a prayerful position. "Ain't it a shame, two fine ladies like
us sittin' in this town bein' lonely and miserable...."

"Is there a man in your life, Francine?"

"Always comes down to that, don't it? There is somebody.
Big handsome stud of a guy. Used to be a football player and
he ain't got over it yet. Head's all swollen out of shape. Forgot
how to do a day's honest work, if he ever knew. Just has to
get on with it, he does, make it big, lots of quick money, like
that. Can't see anythin' good comin' out of him, not for me,
that is."

"I know what you mean."

"You? You got somebody?"

"He's married."

"I been there more'n once. No way you can feel good about
yourself, thataway. Least I can't. Always three folks got cheated
that way, you, your friend, and his wife. What you goin' to
do about it?"

"Shame, isn't it?"

"Sure is."

"Doesn't seem fair, does it?"

"Nope. Well. Life's never been fair. Not for one solitary
day. So there you are." Francine arranged a flat smile on her
face. She stood up. "Been nice talkin' to you."

"Nice talking to you, Francine. I hope Jody will be back at
school soon."

"I'll say you said so. Come back see us, hear."

"I will, I definitely will."

Neither of them believed it, not for a second.


Back in her apartment, Kate studied the telephone as if
expecting it to ring. A familiar caller with a desired message.
But the phone sat in silent testimony to how few people recognized her existence, to her growing discontent and loneliness,
to how few cared whether she lived or died.

She decided to make the call herself, punching out the number without hesitation, not at all surprised that she remembered
it still. She had known men who could recall their Army serial

numbers, all the way back to World War II. In a way, Hank Berger's phone owned the same singular importance in her life.

A female voice came on the line. "Theatrical Agents, Inc. May I help you?"

"I'd like to talk to Hank Berger, please. Kate Fellows calling."

"I'm putting you on hold."

Nothing had changed. The same uninterested secretary, the same wait to be put through; but would she be rejected as she had been so often in the past? Then Hank answered.

"Kate, baby! Where are you?"

"Still in King of Heaven, Hank. It's so good to talk to you again."

"Why are you wasting yourself in the boondocks? Come on back to the big time. Let me make you a star."

She laughed, pleased and hopeful, but remembering clearly the long succession of daily disappointments. The underpaid jobs in stock, the split weeks and one-nighters in Western Pennsylvania and the Midwest in ancient theaters chilly and only half filled, the insignificant roles off-Broadway and even smaller roles on Broadway. How often had she been told she was star material? That she possessed a star quality? That her future was bright and certain? But how long was she supposed to wait for theatrical glory to strike? She had been growing older, no longer an ingenue, and still lightning avoided her. Roles she coveted—and was so right for, she believed—went to other actresses. None of them were more beautiful, none of them were more experienced, none of them more talented. Or was she kidding herself? It was then she began to doubt—her talent, her judgment, her ability to succeed. And it was then that she began to teach in local acting schools, developing a small reputation that brought her to the attention of an obscure college in Florida and of its president, B. J. Moody. At the time, it had not been a difficult decision to make; after all, she had made her peace with the theater, she was never going to be a star.

"It's good to hear your voice, Hank."

"Still as beautiful as ever, I'll bet. Come on back, kid. Broadway needs leading women like you. You should see the material I'm forced to work with nowadays. Cinderella's wicked sisters, every one of them."

"I'm not Cinderella."

"Let me be the judge. I know talent, I know beauty."

"I'm not sure I can ever go back, Hank. The tension, the rejection. All those empty auditions, the readings, the interviews that lead to nothing."

"Trust me. My hunch is your time has come. It was a mistake trying to peddle you as an ingenue. You were always too sophisticated, always a leading woman. You'll knock 'em dead, believe me. Say the word, send me some photos, I'll pass the word. Merrick has a new play coming along. I'll give him a call."

She hesitated. "I'm not ready for that. It's just that—well, I had to talk to you, find out if I was still welcome."

"You must be joking! You'll always be welcome with Hank Berger. Always. Come back to New York and be my number one client. And if you don't want that anymore—" His voice softened, the harsh edges fading. "—If you don't want that, you can always become Mrs. Hank Berger. That's a standing offer, a lifetime contract, written to your own specifications."

"Oh, Hank, you're so sweet. . . ."

"Sweet," he growled in mock ferocity. "Which means thanks, but no thanks. Okay, you're the boss. Just remember, both offers hold. So! Tell me. What's happening in orange-land? I never turned on to Miami Beach. All vanilla, pre-packaged, pre-frozen."

"This isn't Miami and things are okay."

"Just okay?"

"Terrific," she said without enthusiasm.

"If you say so."

"I'm going to hang up now, Hank."

"So soon."

"Talking to you, I feel like crying."

"So cry. Whatever, it's all right with me. You take care of yourself. Stay out of drafts and don't go out alone at night. It's dangerous everywhere."

"I'll be careful."

"And next time don't take so long between calls."

"Hank . . . "

"Yeah? What?"

"I love you, Hank."

"Yeah. The way a sister loves a brother."

"That's not bad, Hank."

"No," he said before he hung up. "That's not bad."

Afterwards she did cry. For what she had given up and for what she had gained. For what was and for what she wanted to become. For all the people she had disappointed and hurt and for all the times she had been disappointed and hurt. There were still tears in her eyes when she fell asleep on the couch in her living room, wondering what was going to become of her. . . .

# CHAPTER
## 17

"POISONS IN THE BLOOD!"

"Papa James, I am tryin' to talk with Mae-Mae here, we got to get to the bottom of things."

"That's it," the old man screeched, eyes gleaming with dimly remembered triumphs of a long-ago time. "The bottom. Purify the blood and the plumbin' works proper. Diet's the thing. What you put in's what you get out. Corruption's goin' into folks these days, fake food, poisoned water, strange notions." The elongated frame teetered forward, swayed, a wily expression distorting the lean features. "It's the Bolsheviks, you see, plantin' their spies everywhere, the Bolsheviks, the Papists, the liberals, the Jews. . . ."

"Papa James, please." Mr. Nolan, torn between resentment and sorrow, between unreasoning rage and residual affection for this pitiful old creature who had once been his father, kept a discreet veneer.

Papa James gestured with a bony finger. "Decimatin' a man's God-given power, it is. When I was that boy's age, I was perpetually horny, never gettin' enough. Did my Elizabeth three, four times a day. It's all a matter of intake. If your innards work smooth all the other parts do good. Got to stop all of that pushin' and strainin'. Empty calories, polluted water, unnatural laxatives. Man's insides are rotten. Mae-Mae, you come along into the privy next time I got to go, you'll see. No sweat, no strain, no stink. Clean is what I am, inside and out."

He glared at Mae-Mae. "Ask me why?"

"Why, Papa James?"

"Nat-way," he cackled and stamped his feet in a jig. "Nat-way, Nat-way. Natural physic. Natural bran keeps the pipes in workin' order. No fatty meats, no artificial anythin', and 'specially regular doses of Pro-Gel . . ."

Mr. Nolan tried again. "Papa James."

The old man sputtered and fell back in his chair, breathing hard. Sweat stood out on his upper lip and his eyes rolled back in his head. "Lord Almighty save us from the Bolsheviks, the Jews and processed foods . . ."

Mr. Nolan examined his father briefly. "He'll be quiet now, he wore himself out."

"Are you sure?"

"Now you tell me again what Wesley said to you?"

"Wesley told me."

"Straight out!"

"In so many words."

"That he was doin' this Kate Fellows, he said that?"

"In coarse and vulgar language, Mr. Nolan. Covered up my ears with my hands, I did. My Momma didn't raise me to listen to bad language like that."

"I am goin' to have a man-to-man with that boy."

"Just spoiled the rest of that day for me. Damaged me immensely. Imagine the revolting pictures my mind perceives of Wesley's precious body enterin' some other female same way as he's done me. I have had fits of deep depression and bouts of profound despair. Fact is, I have not been able to sleep nights. I was not raised to deal with such careless and brutal treatment. My Momma . . ."

She would have gone on but Nolan cut her off. "Sweet Jesus, Mae-Mae! Keep shut! Just close your snivelin' mouth!"

She sniffed indignantly and clamped her lips together.

"You beginnin' to sound like a character out of that damned Tennessee Williams. Okay, we've established it—Wesley's gettin' it on with this redheaded woman. Ain't the first time a Southern gentleman strayed and won't be the last. What else did he tell you?"

"Said he was goin' to divorce me."

*"Divorce!"* Papa James lurched out of his chair, almost falling. His nostrils flared, his cheeks puffed, his eyes spun on their stems. "Gaults don't get divorced. None has, none's goin' to. Run out on a wife or two in the last hundred years or so. Killed one one time, but no divorces. Divorce is evil, a corruption of the communal system. Can't have it. Won't have it. Won't, you hear. Won't . . ." He sagged and Nolan eased him back in his chair.

"Papa James is right," Mr. Nolan said. "Nobody gets a divorce in this family."

"Wesley aims to." A maliciously cheerful expression drifted across Mae-Mae's face, a look of pleasure. It had been too long since this much attention had come her way and she was a woman who welcomed attention in all forms.

"Talk is cheap," Mr. Nolan said.

"What are you goin' to do about it?"

"I don't know," Mr. Nolan said.

Papa James supplied the answer, struggling unsuccessfully to stand up. "Destroy the bitch! Slut! Tramp! Whore! Give her over to the niggers, they'll do her once and for all. Divorce . . . disgrace . . . protect the family . . . got to . . ." He made a last effort to stand up, and failed, toppling over to one side, bouncing off the arm of the chair and landing on the floor with a great final thump.

Mae-Mae yelped.

Mr. Nolan spoke his father's name. Afraid the end had come, afraid the end hadn't come. The old man's leg jerked and one baleful eye rolled open. An accusing glare. His lips moved. Spittle flowed. The eye blinked. Nolan worked his great bulk down on one knee. "What's that, again, Papa James?"

"Fetch a doctor, damn it. Ain't ready to die . . ."


"It's all your fault!"

"What have I done?"

"You're diddlin' that redheaded chippy."

"Who told you that?"

"Never you mind who told me, you are. Don't deny it."

"What I do is my own private affair."

"The hell you say. You have killed your granddaddy."

"He's an old man, he's bound to die soon. Anyway don't blame me."

"You did that poor old man just fine, you did."

"Back off, Daddy. You been waitin' for Papa James to die all of your life so's you could take over the family holdings, you gotta admit that."

"Don't talk to me that way, boy! Don't you dare. By all that's holy, I am your daddy. I spawned you, hear. I love Papa James somethin' fierce, I surely do love that pathetic old man. Your unchristian ways are murderin' *my* daddy."

"He's ninety-four years old. He's been senile for years and losin' strength. I had nothin' to do with it."

"Boy, you listen to me. You are goin' to give her up. What's her name?"

"Kate Fellows, and I will do no such thing. I love her."

"Love's nothin' but a hard cock on target is all. Don't talk love to me. I loved your momma, I respected your momma. If I wanted to diddle some ole gal or other I made sure your momma never got wind of it. Not that I ever did a nasty thing like that, you listenin' to me?"

"I'm listenin'."

"You upsettin' this whole family with your cattin' around. Killin' your granddaddy and tellin' your dirty stories to that cute little wife of yours. You got to stop all that, Wesley, it just ain't right."

"Mae-Mae is a bore."

"Got nothin' to do with it."

"She's an idiot child, never grown up."

"She's got a sweet little behind and you ought to be squeezin' it 'stead of carryin' on with that bitch-woman."

"I am goin' to get rid of Mae-Mae and marry Kate."

"The hell you will! No divorce, not in this family. Ain't goin' to have folks from here to the Keys laughin' at us. Never a Gault got a divorce, never a Gault goin' to either."

"I've had Mae-Mae up to here."

"Trouble is you haven't had near enough of her. You want to diddle somebody, you diddle Mae-Mae. You got the gallopin' insomnia, you roll over and do her. You wake up mornin' with a pisshard, you fill up her belly. Am I makin' myself clear?"

"I hear every word. It's just that I can't stand the little twit."

"Stand her! Boy, you deaf or somethin'? I am speakin' my plainest to you. You get on top of Mae-Mae and you bump and hump till you are all humped out. You make her beg for a rest. You give her more than she wants. Knock her up, boy. Give me a grandchild. A boy child would be to my taste. You miss out first time around, you keep goin' till you get it right."

"I don't want any children with Mae-Mae."

"We are discussin' my wants, not yours. You come up here with your granddaddy paralyzed on his entire left side from the top of his poor old head to the tip of his littlest toe goin' on about divorce. Well, I won't have it, just won't have any of it."

"It's my life."

"You divorce Mae-Mae and I'll make your life so miserable you'll come crawlin' up here beggin' for relief. You divorce that gal and I'll kick your butt from here to Louisiana without one red cent of Gault money to pay your way."

"I don't care about the money."

Mr. Nolan stared at his son in disbelief. "Not care about money! Boy, you are fartin' in a locked room and smellin' up the place. 'Course you care about the money, you are a Gault." His great head rolled forward, squinting at his son. "That woman puttin' these strange ideas into your head, Wesley?"

Wesley grinned. "I paid Papa James a visit, got me to thinkin'. That old man is scared. . . ."

"Well, sure he is. Old as he is, nobody *wants* to die."

"That's not it. He feels he's wasted so much of his life, could've done other things. Better things. Know what he said to me? Said he wanted to be moved to another room over on the east side of the house. Said he doesn't enjoy watchin' the sun set anymore. No more endin's, he told me. I want to watch the new days start,' he said. Said all that mattered was new days startin.'"

Mr. Nolan made a face. "Man is ninety-four years old. Had

a stroke, he's three-quarters out of his head. Don't care what he says."

"Well, Daddy, I surely do admire him."

"Do you? For what he says now or for what he truly did?" He waved a fleshy hand. "All of this is his doin'. He put it all back together again, made it happen, kept it this way and delivered it over to me. No way I'm goin' to see it all go down the drain. You're my son, boy. You're a Gault, and you are goin' to make sure that the name don't die when I die."

"I told you, I don't care about the money."

"You are deceivin' yourself, boy. Those clothes on your back, so fine and fashionable, they come from Neiman's and that costs money. That green Porsche you run around in, that costs money. The house you live in, the food you eat, the pleasures you *buy*. Boy, stop playin' with yourself. All of your life you spent money like it was goin' out of style. You need it, you crave it, you ain't about to do without."

"I can make my own way."

"Hah. Try it and see. No job at the bank, no family behind you, no income of your own. In Tokeneke, you're a Gault and that means somethin'. Break out of here and see how far that takes you. Tell that redheaded woman you're givin' up the name, the money, the power that goes with it all and see how quick she puts the boot to you."

"She's not that way."

"Maybe, maybe not. Don't matter none. What does matter is that you drop her quick and permanent."

"We're goin' to get married."

"I am warnin' you . . ."

"You can't stop me."

"In this county, I do whatever I want and you better remember it. All my life I been wheelin' and dealin', inside the law and out. I got my people in the State capital and in the District of Columbia. I buy and I sell politicians, I make the laws I need to have and I break those that get in my way. I do like my daddy did and his daddy before him. Word comes down from The Hill that Mr. Nolan wants somethin' done, it gets done. One way or the other and you can make plenty bettin' on that. I am in charge of this family now and what I decide has to be done will be done and you'd best understand that.

Now you go on home and make your wife happy. Make her pregnant, which will make me happy. And leave the redheaded woman to me."

Wesley felt compelled to oppose his father to the end. "I intend to marry her."

Mr. Nolan was on his feet, trundling with strange, mincing steps around the desk. "Get straight with me, boy. I'm all you've got or likely to have that's worth spit. Me and Almighty God. Do like I've told you. Show respect to your daddy and your granddaddy who is dyin' in this house. Death is entitled to respect, a little respect for the dyin', that you killed. . . ."

A servant was waiting when Dorr C. P. Seely came out of Papa James' room. "If you'll come with me, sir, Mr. Nolan is expectin' you in his study.

Seely trailed the man down the wide, curved staircase to the first floor. They went along a corridor on a narrow Oriental carpet that failed to keep the old, polished floorboards from creaking underfoot.

Here the air was clear, absent the stink of rot that permeated Papa James' presence. What a mess the old man was, hooked up by wires and tubes and electrodes to machines that kept his heart beating, his kidneys functioning, his blood moving. None of it would do him any good; give up the ghost, Seely had silently ordered. No point in the living being in thrall to a man too mean and stubborn to step forward gratefully into the Province of the Lord.

"Through here, sir," the servant said, opening a portal and standing aside.

Seely stepped into Mr. Nolan's study. Once a sun porch, it was a long chamber with light spilling in through windows on three sides. Everywhere greenery, in great pots on the floor and spidery plants hanging from the ceiling. At the far end, Mr. Nolan was in place behind a great, hand-carved desk bought from an Irish nobleman on hard times years before and transported, with other items of the Irish lord's heritage, to the big house on The Hill. He beckoned Seely forward and indicated he was to sit in such a way that the sunlight would be in the preacher's eyes rather than his own.

"You saw my father?" he began brusquely.

It occurred to Seely that Mr. Nolan impatiently awaited his father's demise, anxious to become senior in the family, and the family's business affairs. The old man, selfish and ruthless though he was, had maintained an intimate relationship with the land, with the county and its people, and if he had used them for his own ends, he also made certain none of them suffered needlessly. Poverty was a constant in the county, especially among the blacks, but no one ever went hungry and in season there was always work for any man, woman or child who wanted it. Mr. Nolan struck Seely as a man desperate to exercise power for his own profit and pleasure only.

"I prayed for him."

"Man's too stubborn to let go and die."

"Won't be long before he stands in the golden light of Christ Jesus, Amen."

"Amen. How much time you figure he's got?"

"That's for the Lord to decide, not any mortal."

Mr. Nolan growled back of his teeth. His eyes were bright blue hard marbles. There was something different and unwelcome about Seely, as if some inner alteration had occurred, something private and potentially unsettling.

"Tell you why I sent for you, Reverend."

Seely looked away. Outside, the lawns were almost too smooth and too green to be natural. A strand of willow broke the horizon as if in defensive stance against unseen enemies, pointing the way toward the bend in the river. All this, and so much more, Gault country. Tokeneke County had always belonged to the Gaults, always would, he supposed. But changes were taking place, he felt them in himself, and he was no longer willing to suppress his own ambitions to theirs. Yet he sensed—at some almost unconscious level—that his chance had come. His future, *his* future, was within reach, now, his for the taking. Taking was the key. Even as those early Gaults had taken Tokeneke away from the Indians. Seely's turn had come and he was ready for the battle; God had armed him with weapons suitable for his time and his place; he possessed the face and the form of a prophet, the voice and the experience to draw people to him, to cause them to listen and go forth and do his bidding. He had the brains—not so smart as to be crippled by qualification and doubt, so as to put off the straight,

simple people he had to enlist in the crusade; not clever and
quick in a way that would make ordinary folk uneasy and
resentful. He had worked with his body, he talked plain, he
was an angry man.

He was, he assured himself, on the verge of greatness. No
one could stop him. No one, that is, except Dorr C. P. Seely
himself. Time had come to suck up his guts and get on with
the business at hand.

"It was the Lord Jesus who brought _me_," he said, letting
the words roll out.

"My secretary called you." Mr. Nolan didn't enjoy being
contradicted.

"God summoned me to help a great and good man on his
last journey." He slid off the chair onto his knees. His hands
came together and his head lowered. "Let us pray for Papa
James. . . ."

Mr. Nolan hawked his throat clear. "Pray for us both, Reverend. My father was a pirate and a thief. He lied and stole
and grubbed his way to a fortune. He tricked his friends and
picked the pockets of his enemies. Trusted nobody and nobody
with a brain in his head ever trusted him. And you might as
well know it."

Seely turned blazing eyes toward the fat man. "Honor thy
father, sayeth the Commandment. Get down on your knees and
pray for his easy passage. His kind made this country what it
is today. He was a great man. Kneel, sinner. Kneel and pray."

Mr. Nolan looked at him with wonder and didn't move.
And in that awful interval Seely was afraid he had gone too
far, pressing his luck. Until the big man, grunting softly, managed to make it to the floor, his immense bulk looming up
alongside the Irish desk.

"Pray," Seely commanded, holding back a visceral howl of
triumph. After a while, he rose and resumed his seat. "That's
enough," he said brusquely. "No point in burdening the Lord
with too much prayin', I'm sure He's got the message by now."

He watched Mr. Nolan struggle back into his seat, chest
heaving, huffing and puffing. The man was grotesque, an over-
sized caricature of a human being. Soon enough he'd pay the
price for his self-indulgence; the Lord would see to it. And
when that happened, it would be the young who took over in

this room. Seely warned himself to tread carefully between father and son; he could afford to antagonize neither.

"I want to discuss the Tenth Crusade with you," Seely said.

"I sent my check."

"Your father, his father before him, and those who came before them, all fought to keep this town, this county unchanged and untouched, no matter what was goin' on in the outside world."

"Damn right, and I mean to do likewise," said Nolan. "All those 'isms,' all those do-gooders, all those aimin' to bring our kind down to their level. I ain't goin' to have it."

"No way to stop it, the way the world's goin'. Businessmen formin' foundations to *give away* their profits. Social programs to *give away* your tax money. Foreign aid to *give away* our money to our enemies. Wheat to the Communists and guns to the Arabs and just about everythin' to the Jews in Palestine. No sir, it is just a matter of time before all them foreigners and their foreign ideas take over here in Florida, crowd in on Tokeneke County, turn King of Heaven into a string of fast-food shops and supermarkets and used-car lots."

"I ain't goin' to permit that, no way," said Nolan. "Not for a minute. I'll fight 'em on the sea and in the air and on the beaches."

Seely slammed his fist down on the Irish desk. Mr. Nolan flinched. "And go under anyways."

"What're you gettin' at?"

"I'm gettin' at makin' a holy war is what," said Seely. "Hittin' your enemies and mine and the enemies of every right-thinkin' American before they hit us. I'm gettin' at changin' the direction our great country's been goin' in for the last fifty years or so."

"It's that damned Franklin Delano Roosevelt who did this to us, him and all those liberals out of New York City," said Nolan. "Man thinks too much he disturbs the natural order of life, the way the good Lord intended for us to live."

"Amen to that," said Seely.

"What's this about a holy war?"

"Man won't fight for his life ain't worth a spit in the ocean. That's where the Tenth Crusade comes in."

"This crusade of yours, I figured it for an evangelical movement, Reverend. Tend the flocks, bring the lost sheep in."

"True enough, only there's more. I been thinkin' and plannin' and readin' the portents."

"Do tell . . ."

"I say unless somebody puts a stop to the way things are goin' won't do a bit of good tryin' to keep Tokeneke pure and sweet the way it is. All them outsiders, they'll come crashin' down on us here and in every other truly patriotic American town and village, you get my meanin'?"

"Couldn't agree more. What's to be done about it?"

"The Tenth Crusade," Seely intoned.

"Yes. Of course. What about it?"

"It can be the strikin' arm of the future. The army of the Lord, Christian warriors out to perform God's Divine Mission."

"I don't get it."

"It is my intention to put myself and the Tenth Crusade firmly on the battlefield, to oppose the enemies of our Christian majority. To *attack* those who have been for so long attackin' *us*. I am talkin' about those infidels who declared God to be dead. I am talkin' about dopers and boozers and political hypocrites and liars who confiscate our tax money in order to pay people *not* to work, to pay for the murder of little unborn children, to keep Christian students to pray to the One True God in the classroom. I am talkin' about those who put human secularism above love of God. I am talkin' about heretics and subversives, the boondogglers, communists and socialists, social workers and psychiatrists, the free-lovers, and the pornographers, the ones who put violence and sex and dirty words on the television in order to corrupt our young people. I am talkin' about the writers who infest our bookstores and libraries with their filth and corruption, I am talkin' about the enemies of God and the enemies of mankind. I am talkin' about puttin' sanity back in America."

Mr. Nolan fought for breath. "How?"

"Whichever way the Lord tells us to go. Each does what he can."

Mr. Nolan got the message. "Money?"

"All contributions are welcome and will be in the future. We have great plans."

"You can depend on me. And on my son, Wesley."

"A fine boy."

"But easily led into wrong thinkin'."

"He's exceedingly young."

"And inexperienced."

"He is the future, Mr. Nolan. Tokeneke's future."

"And the future of my family. All livin' creatures try to maintain the harmony of the community and the family which is the building block on which God has built the human race."

"Amen to that."

"All creatures want to extend their line, improve society, make life more beneficial according to God's eternal laws."

"Amen to that."

"How much you goin' to need for the first year, Reverend?"

Seely had been about to ask for two hundred and fifty thousand dollars, a sum that appeared monumental to him, beyond reach, a cause for disdain and rejection. He hesitated, and hesitating knew that it would indeed be a mistake to ask for that amount. He filled his lungs with air. "One million dollars," he said, with a confidence he did not feel.

Mr. Nolan showed no change of expression. "You have a large appetite, Reverend."

Seely didn't smile. "For starters," he added.

"On one condition. . . ."

Seely, anticipating an argument, camouflaged his surprise. "What condition?"

"Kate Fellows."

"Ah . . ."

"Get her for me."

Seely never hesitated. "I will."

"Brand her a whore."

"Yes."

"An evil woman."

"I'll do it."

"Shut down that filthy play of hers."

"Yes."

"Stomp her into the ground."

"I'll grind her flat."

"Hurt her."

"Oh, yes."

"Paint her scarlet. Stain her forever."

"Wickedness must be dealt with harshly."

"Ruin her."

"I'll destroy her."

"Get rid of the bitch."

"She's gone."

"In pain, disgraced, finished."

"Wrongdoin' must be punished. It's God's way."

"Beat hell out of her," said Nolan.

"She'll beg for mercy. About the money?"

"Scratch my back, I'll scratch yours."

"It's God's will."

"I'll say Amen to that."

"Amen."

# CHAPTER
## 18

"I DON'T LIKE it, Billy."

"No more'n I do, Benjamin."

"Let's call it off."

"Inez, what do you say?"

Benjamin looked at the girl. In the darkness she seemed younger than her years. Her tawny skin blended into the soft darkness, her wide eyes dominating, without guile or guilt. Conflicting reactions occupied her attention; the desire to help, the anticipatory excitement, and always the fear.

"I want him caught," she said. She spoke in a slow, reflective way, her mind leap-frogging ahead.

"He must be punished for what he did. To me."

"And others," Goforth added. He was afraid she might change her mind.

"I don't care about the others, not the same way. But nobody's got the right to invade somebody else's body, to take his pleasure at the expense of a stranger. Nobody ought to be treated like that."

"Then you want to go through with it?" Benjamin said.

Goforth was annoyed at Benjamin's persistence; she'd agreed it, and agreed again. "Don't push it, Benjamin."

"You could get hurt," Benjamin said.

"Nobody's goin' to get hurt," Goforth said, with more conviction than he felt. "You and me, Benjamin, we're on top of this."

Benjamin snorted. "Girl, where's your brains? Trustin' a white deputy in crackerland and a used-up black man? Somethin' messed up your head?"

Inez looked at one and then the other. "I thought you two were friends," she said to Goforth.

He made himself laugh. "Don't have no truck with Benjamin, he's a old man ready to collect his pension."

"May be old but I ain't stupid," said Benjamin. "Settin' her up as bait is just askin' for trouble."

"It's good police procedure."

"She ain't no policewoman, she ain't trained and she ain't fit for such work. None of us is, you want to tell the truth. Admit it, Billy. You and me, we're mostly chasers, handin' down citations for illegal parkin' and speedin' and like that. Breakin' up family fights now and again. Nearly thirty years on the job, I ain't hardly ever put my hand to this weapon in hot blood."

"You forget the times I seen you in action, Benjamin. Ain't nobody steadier, man. Ain't nobody so cool, so dependable."

"Thank you for sayin' so but those were the ol' days."

"Ain't nobody I'd rather have at my back, Benjamin."

"I say likewise for you, Billy. When I needed you you was there and I tried to do the same for you. That was then, this is now. Whoever's been doin' this stuff, he ain't about to give it up without he makes a fight of it. I don't want this girl to get herself damaged."

"Dammit, man, neither do I."

"Then let it go."

Goforth set himself against an angry response. He was trapped in an emotional swamp, imprisoned by his feelings for Inez and in some unclear way diminished by them. As if some essential part of himself had been given over, surrendered without a proper fight, leaving him flawed and defeated. Man, born in blood and pain, lived out his days only to discover his own shortcomings and failures. He braced himself. For a good cop, there was only one way to go.

"I say we try for it," he said to Inez. "But it is up to you, Inez. Yes or no?"

She sucked air into her lungs and kept her eyes averted. "Let's get it on, then. No sense hangin' around."

"Then we go."

"I still don't like it."

They climbed into the front seat of Goforth's car and drove out to Gault Christian, taking Citrus Lane through the orange groves down to the lake. He parked in the shadow of the gym building and they walked the rest of the way.

"Still don't like it," Benjamin said. "You're guessin' is all."

"It figures. He hit on two women at Silver Sands, then a couple along Riverwalk, then that dude on Shell Beach."

"You're the onliest one believes one and the same fella did all those people."

"He's movin' around."

"From women to men? Don't make any sense."

"Unless you accept the notion that rape isn't sexual at all. I do. It's anger in action, Benjamin. An exercise in power. The way I see it, the man on Shell Beach was an accident, just happened to be there, put himself in the way of our man, an unlucky bit of timin'. No different than any of the women. This guy is a loaded gun waitin' to go off."

"And I'm the target?" Inez said.

"You can still change your mind."

"Uh-uh. Just tryin' to make sense of it all. Why here in campus? Why not one of the beaches? Or the river? Some place where he's been before."

"He's changin' his M.O., movin' around, gettin' cautious. And there's plenty of girls out here at the college, and the lake. Our man has a fix on water."

"It's past curfew," Benjamin observed. "If this dude's so smart, he'll know no girls'll be out this late."

"Maybe. I ain't sayin' he's a student. I ain't sayin' he's so smart as to have all the answers. If I'm wrong, okay. If I'm right, we'll take him."

Inez turned to Goforth. "I'm scared."

"So am I."

"I don't want to get hurt again."

"We'll be close by. You see anythin', let out a yell. We'll come runnin'."

She took a deep breath. "Okay."

"Damn!" Benjamin said thickly. "We gonna do it or we gonna stand aroun' rappin'? Let's get it on."

Inez nodded and turned around and walked out of the woods down to the patch circling the lake, advancing without haste, swinging her purse in a gentle arc, a young girl out for a late night walk. To Goforth she seemed very small and very slight, defenseless. If anything went wrong, he was going to have a great deal to answer for to a great many people. Himself most of all.


The path bent to the right and Inez disappeared from view. Overhead the sky was speckled and infinite. An owl hooted in the distance and in the lake a fish leaped and splashed; the air was warm and sweet with the dizzying scent of honeysuckle. Everything was as it should be, tranquil, lovely, romantic; she longed for brightness and noise and crowds of people.

She shivered and embraced herself as she went on. Braced against attack, she could not accept yet her part in this. No way Inez Macklin would be participating in a policeman's craziness.

She longed for her mother. A mother barely recalled as a ghostly figure long gone and nearly forgotten, a mother who split when she was four years old. A father killed in a bar fight less than a year later. Raised by an aunt who married when she was eight and whose husband didn't want somebody else's kid hanging around. After that, foster homes, one after another, trying to go to school, study and do the jobs around the house nobody else wanted. Running away became a way of life for her, running and being brought back, whipped more than once and once locked in a closet for twenty-four hours without food or water or access to a bathroom.

No more. Inez Macklin was her own woman. Earning her way teaching school. School for coloreds, as it was referred to locally. Half-educated teacher teaching the ineducable. Integrated on paper to conform to federal requirements, it was all black in practice, teachers and students alike. Excepting Inez; too tan to please her colleagues and too black in her heart to pass.

To continue the myth of local integration, some of her students went on to Tokeneke High School each year. Always the best athletes, plus three or four girls, neat, clean types, straight "A" students. The rest stayed behind, fodder for the cotton fields or the citrus groves or the low-level jobs in the factories.

Maybe her life missed the mark. Maybe she was less than she wanted to be. But she was proud of the Inez Macklin she'd created. Proud of what she was doing. The kids liked her, she liked herself. And life in King of Heaven was acceptable if less than perfect. Comfortable and without stress and with the promise of more of the same to come. No reason to spoil it, was there? Then out of what insane impulse had she allowed this red-necked damned white deputy into her bed? Nothing but trouble came with him.

Girl, you are weird. Inez Macklin, sitting duck for a mad man. Asking to be jumped, beaten, raped again. No way she wanted that to happen. Stop it now. Call it off. Mark it finished. The end. No more.

She went on. Damn Billy Goforth. Sneaking into her place at night, crawling in between her legs, doing her until he was empty and able to sleep. Saying all the right words, words to bring her guard down, make her easy and weak with his wily ways, conjuring up wild dreams that could never come to pass, dreams of living out her days with him in some green and white suburb with clean kids and neat lawns. White man's suburbs, white woman's dreams.

Not for her. Not with him. Some proper loving was what it amounted to, and all that sweet nighttime talk. Made her feel so fine and full until light came and he had to run out lest somebody see him. That always gave her bad feelings about herself and about him and about how she was letting her life get away from her.

He said he loved her. She couldn't bring herself to say the same to him. The words lodged in her throat, blocked her emotions, made her angry and resentful at all that kept them from having an easier time, a life together. Talk and loving wouldn't change a thing; never work, the two of them. Not in any world she knew about.

Love, hell. Love was the excitement and relief he found between her legs. Love was the circles of joy that flushed her spirit when he took her breast into his mouth. Love was the strong, hard feel of him, the need he had of her and she of him, the way their bodies *fit*—the flights of spasmodic fancy.

Love. Inez didn't know much about love. But Goforth made her feel good. A straight and honest man. More so than most she'd come across. More so than any she'd loved. Trying to do his best in all things. Not always making it. But always trying. He had said: "I'll never hurt you."

He had said: "I'll take care of you."

Well. Look at her now. Targeted for assault. Staked out for trouble.

Life, she told herself, very definitely sucks.


Warren stood back in the trees and looked out at the lake as if it were his enemy. Pain reached up into his head from a blow he'd taken during the attempted hijacking. His arms were stiff from loading and unloading all that whiskey. He remembered how afraid he had been and wished he had been able to take out his anger on Lonnie, been able to hurt *him*.

An older brother was supposed to watch out for a younger one. It was implicit in the relationship. Let Lonnie do his own dirty work. *He* could have been killed. His life ended out there on some back country road, blood spilling into the dirt, life seeping away while his brother went on to make a fortune running illegal drinking whiskey. Death was a terrifying prospect, empty and *final*. Yet more and more it was in Warren's thoughts, dark, mysterious, revolting, insistently drawing him on.

He had always admired Lonnie, his strength and good looks, his smarts, envied him his fame and the money he made playing football, the girls that flocked his way.

All gone now. Lonnie's day in the sun was ended. His heroics were over, his rewards spent. Okay. But he had no right to put Warren's life on the line. Warren had no such possibilities of glory, not even in his craziest dreams. Only girl

ever came after him was Barbara Cromartie and she'd cut him
off too soon. Turned on to somebody else. He imagined her
pliant body writhing and squirming under that wrestler, those
fine round thighs spread in invitation. Bitch! He'd get her yet.

It angered him. The way things went wrong in his life.
Defeat after defeat leaving him always with the short end of
the stick. His eyes teared and his brain so tipped and tilted,
his fingers balled up into clenched fists. He had nothing, not
much of a past, certainly no future. Except to keep working
for his mother, killing roaches and termites and carpenter ants.
Stinking of that awful poison, stuck in the same groove for the
rest of his life. That's how it was for a family like the Pedens,
straining to break loose and knowing all of the time there was
no way out. Trapped by the layers of success above them. Held
in place under the giant heel of the folks on The Hill. Born to
kill bugs, he'd die killing them.

The pain was too great to bear.

No. Not Warren. No way he was going to stay stuck in a
backwater town pushed suffocating into someone else's notion
of how his life should be lived. He had places to go, things to
do and nobody was going to stand in his way.

Through the mist that softened the night, through the shifting
anger that blurred his focus, he watched the girl. An almost
musical grace, the way leg followed leg, giving flare to her
pale skirt, an almost mythic beauty. Wraithlike, she came on,
a creature of his imagination, born out of the force of his will
into beauty and magical interludes, charged by love and good
feelings, an insistent need for him. So much goodness. Softness. Unstained by the evil of the world.

He took off his clothes without rush, preparing himself for
the joys that lay ahead. The gentle air caressed his naked flesh
and he stretched up to bring the stars and the water and the
girl closer.

He fondled himself, all the love he felt for her was centered
in that quivering shaft of flesh and blood. Throbbing as if
sensing its moment of destiny. She was only yards away, only
a few strides.

He leaped into her path with a triumphant cry.

She gasped and stumbled backwards. Unable to flee. Unable
to make a sound. He went toward her, touching her, hands

running over her hips and onto her breasts, squeezing, giving pain. His breathing was harsh and his words were weapons.

"Cunt, filthy cunt..."

"Please..."

He reached for the collar of her blouse and ripped. It came away in his hand. She screamed and ran back down the path. He went after her.

A dozen strides and Goforth broke out of the woods and brought him down with a hard tackle. His fists pounded at Warren, who cried out in boyish alarm. It took all of Benjamin's strength to save Warren from Goforth's blind fury.

# CHAPTER
## 19

**THE MORNING BEGAN** badly for Kate. She woke feeling irritable and fragmented, leaving behind some vital aspect of persona. There was a throbbing behind her eyes, a warning of worse to come; she wondered if she were premenstrual.

The orange juice, made from concentrate, had an acidic bite to it and the coffee tasted of metal. She tried to remember when she'd last drunk a cup of good coffee or tasted freshly squeezed orange juice. Not since she'd come to Florida, certainly. No one in the state squeezed oranges.

Putting it all down to a bad dream lost in the night, she left for the campus. The department secretary greeted her with an empty show of teeth and bad news; she was expected in Dr. Moody's office in ten minutes.

Hurrying across the campus, she struggled to rid herself of the feeling that she was the object of curious and disapproving scrutiny from passing students and faculty alike.

Dr. Moody rose automatically at her entrance and looked her into an empty chair. The pink pudding face was flat, lips pursed, eyes moist and still. He brought his soft hands together in a circular movement, rubbing as if for warmth. He reminded Kate of a plump white rabbit, too hungry to run and too timid to eat.

"I shall not," he started out, "mince words."

She vowed not to provide him with an easy victory. "I have been receiving phone calls," she said.

"Phone calls?" He tried to digest the information.

"Anonymous calls."

"I see," he said. She detected a thin note of satisfaction in his voice.

"Threatening calls."

"A deranged man." He said it quickly, anxious to get on to more substantive matters.

"More than one, one a woman."

"I wouldn't have thought . . ."

"The woman, the worst of the lot. Terrible things were said. I had to leave the phone off the hook."

"I'm sorry," he said. He was not an unkind man, he assured himself. Perhaps not as sensible or as strong as he might like, but nevertheless concerned about other people, never giving hurt where it could be avoided. Kindness, personal warmth, generosity of spirit; these were the character elements he'd tried to kindle and nurture. And he believed he'd succeeded, for the most part. But these were parlous times, replete with unforeseen hazards and threats. A man of stature and ambition had to be cautious, responsive to the pressures of the world around him. He would have liked to allay her fears. "Things have gotten out of hand, my dear."

"What have I done that's wrong?"

"Pride."

"Pride? I don't understand."

"You've put yourself outside our little family here at Gault Christian, lived according to your own rules. Chosen to ignore the ways of our local community."

"Are you talking about the play?"

"Yes, of course, the play. You see, people are worked up about the drift of thought and events in the country. They are alarmed and determined to stop what is seen as a threat to them and their children, to their beliefs. Events have a life of their own. Things happen. You might have used better judgment, exorcised those offending words and phrases, and that would have been the end of it."

"I don't think so."

His expression shifted almost imperceptibly, pudding becoming a blanched muffin. "Of course it would."

"There's more."

"All I am concerned with is the play."

She pressed her case, wishing she could hold back, wishing it would all disappear. "You know, don't you, Dr. Moody?"

"I know nothing."

"About Wesley and me?"

"Please." He protested. He chose not to hear. He sought to keep the conversation securely on track. "Don't tell me anything."

"We're lovers," she said. What malevolent power caused her to go on this way, rushing forward toward imminent disaster? "Wesley and I have been lovers for some time." So ordinary to hear. Said so matter-of-fact. But hers was a forbidden involvement, a dangerous connection.

"My sole function is to protect the sensibilities of our students. To deliver to our young people the kind and quality of education their parents wish them to have. God, church and country, there you have it. Without these, the academics are nothing."

"They intend to drive me out."

"Nonsense."

"To damage me."

He stared. He saw her differently, for the first time. She alarmed him. "You must learn to bend with the prevailing breezes. There's still time. Strike out the offending passages and—" He broke off, aware of a flabbiness in his choice of language, the whine of surrender in his voice.

"You approved the play."

It sounded like an accusation to him. "That is hardly the point."

"You saw it, you said it was fine, a beautiful performance."

"We are discussing the moral standards of the community, not esthetics. Blasphemy is not acceptable on this campus. Obscenity is not acceptable. Attacks on the common standards of behavior will not be tolerated. If you won't do what is in order, I will."

"The drama department is my responsibility," said Kate.

"Only so far as you dispatch that responsibility and understand it properly."

She filled her lungs with air. "I won't do it. Don't you see, I can't."

"I see that you are a stubborn and willful woman with a lack of concern for the good and welfare of the school and the students. Very well, don't say you weren't warned."

"What do you mean?" Her fear rose steeply and she had to struggle against the impulse to surrender, to plead for forgiveness. She was tired of fighting, of trying so hard. "What are you saying to me?"

"Your future is at stake here."

"Are *you* threatening me, Dr. Moody?"

The tiny eyes were like blue ball-bearings, polished to a high hard gloss. "Tonight, immediately after this evening's performance of the play, the Moral Arts Council will convene in the theater . . ."

"Tonight? What is this Moral Arts Council?"

"Certain interested citizens, a cross-section of the community. A representative sampling. Each one with a profound concern for the moral and spiritual well-being of the town, the county, the college."

"A trial?"

"An inquiry."

"What are the charges?"

"Not a trial, I told you." He wanted her to understand, to accept his version of the matter. It was important to him and yet he knew he was going to fail as he had failed in so many essential details of his life.

"What if I don't attend?"

"That would be a mistake, a mark against you. Please be there, I advise you to be there. The council will discuss what has transpired, the influence this situation has on your students, the damage done to the school population as a whole."

"Damage?"

"If any."

"And if I'm not present?"

"With you or without you, makes no difference. This is all your own doing."

She stood up. "I don't have a chance."

"Nothing's been decided. If you defy the Council, it will further erode your already deteriorating position. Will you be attending?"

She left without answering. He felt that he'd suffered a profound personal defeat, as yet unspecified.


Presenting herself for ultimate acceptance and approval. No different than going to an audition. Not much to lose; only everything.

They were waiting for her on stage. As if about to embark on a learned literary discussion of the play they had just witnessed.

Student stagehands had set up a library table and chairs as soon as the theater was empty. Upstage a single work light cast long, spooky shadows. The members of the Moral Arts Council took their places and the stagehands withdrew. When they were seated, Kate made her entrance, all eyes turned her way. She walked proudly down the central aisle, emerging dramatically out of the darkness and into the harsh glare of the work light, a well-staged entrance. B. J. Moody, at the head of the table, rose to greet her, a man of impeccable good manners.

She took her seat in a series of carefully controlled movements, ending with hands folded in her lap, presenting a quizzical smile to the people at table. At last she came to Moody. "Do sit, Dr. Moody. Needn't stand on formality, need we?"

He flushed, he frowned, he sat. It was, she acknowledged, a small and inconsequential victory.

"You know everybody, of course?" Moody said.

She didn't.

He made introductions.

Professor Harley Moss, Chairman of the Department of Theology. Lean, funereal, avoiding her glance.

Lucas Mark Anderson, President and Chief Operating Officer of Sweetjuice, Inc., a subsidiary of Gault Enterprises. Sweetjuice marketed concentrate made from oranges out of the Gault groves.

Charles F. Jayne, senior partner in one of the state's most prestigous law firms, legal representative for Gault Enterprises.

And Mrs. Joelle Peden, member of the King of Heaven School Board, member of the Planning and Zoning Board, mother of Lonnie and Warren, operator of an exterminating business, native to King of Heaven. She contemplated Kate with resolve and distance, eyes inflated by gold-rimmed glasses, eyes that revealed nothing.

"And Reverend Seely," Moody concluded.

"I'm not actually a member of the Council, Miss Fellows," he said. His smile was disarming. His voice was soothing.

She measured him warily.

"Reverend Seely's interests," Moody said, with all the pedagogical sincerity he could muster, "go far beyond the pulpit."

"God," Seely said, "is concerned with all human endeavors. Can a man do less?"

Kate glanced at Charles Jayne. "Shouldn't I have a lawyer?" she said. Her confidence was fading.

Moody seemed surprised. "This is not a legal proceeding. What we have here is simply an investigative panel, interested citizens. . . ."

Charles Jayne cleared his throat. "No cause to be concerned about me, Miss Fellows. I'm here in my capacity as a member of the Council, not as a lawyer. All we are striving to do is get to the heart of the matter. Sort out the complexities and resolve the problem at hand to everyone's satisfaction, with a minimum of danger. . . ."

"I feel I'm being put on trial."

Seely flashed a clench of perfect white teeth. "In a trial—Charles will correct me if I'm mistaken—charges would be brought. A jury convened. Due process insured. No, no, this is no trial. Merely an inquiry."

"Let's proceed to what matters," Anderson said. "The point is to put an end to this business. There you have it, plain talk about a simple problem. This disgraceful play—I was embarrassed for the ladies present—it is offending people left and right. You listen to me, Kate. Just eliminate the dirty parts and let us all get back to living our lives."

"Dirty parts?" she said.

"Clean up your act, lady, and that's that."

"*Long Day's Journey Into Night*, Mr. Anderson, is a work of personal art created by one of America's great playwrights, perhaps its greatest. It will live long after all of us are gone, certainly it will survive this inquisition. It is not a dirty play."

"Inquisition is a harsh word," Seely said.

"You mean to tell us it's not about sex?" Mrs. Peden said, voice harsh and sharp as a razor.

"No more than the Song of Solomon is about sex."

"No!" Seely said. He stood up. "I cannot stand by, and permit this blatant attack on Holy Scripture. No equation between the inerrant Word of God and the immoral pornography of a secular literary pretender can be permitted. Enough, I say."

"I am the one being attacked," Kate said quietly.

Moody felt impelled to speak, to make his presence felt among this imposing group. "This is a Christian college, Miss Fellows." There. That would help.

"In a Christian community," Seely added. "In a Christian nation."

Moody slumped back in his chair. No matter how hard he tried, he seemed to be losing more ground. "Let's all try to remember that," he said to no one in particular.

Kate searched her mind for an adequate response, seeking to place herself on firm ground. "I would only remind everyone that we live in a democratic country and that no church of particular religion is a part of the government. The Constitution—"

Mrs. Peden, eyes aglitter, leaned forward. "What are you, some kind of an atheist?"

"Are my religious beliefs on trial?"

"Answer the question."

Professor Moss drummed on the table top. "Ordinary good sense informs us that one cannot separate one's beliefs, one's experience, one's entire conditioning from what one says and does at a given moment, Miss Fellows. I have examined Mr. O'Neill's play and I, too, am offended by its language, its disregard for the prohibition against the taking of the Lord's name in vain. Present here is a subtle but insidious attack on the primacy of our Lord in Heaven and the vitality and importance of the human family here on earth."

"Address yourself to that," Seely said toughly. His jaw

squared off, eyes blazed. He took command.

"O'Neill referred to *Long Day's Journey* as a play of old sorrow," Kate said. It no longer mattered. Minds were made up, positions frozen; this stage, this theater, which she had labored so hard to make into a vibrant arena of sensitivity and exploration and truth had become a platform for desecration and destruction. The inquiry was a device programmed to bring about a desired end, all the while presenting a reasonable public face. She wanted to laugh, she wanted to cry. "These people," she went on slowly, "were his ghosts, this play his way of exorcising his past. This is an unflinching portrayal of one man's life, his anguish, an act of magnificent courage. It was written, in O'Neill's words, in 'tears and love,' an act of faith in love that permitted him to face his death at last."

"You have not answered Mrs. Peden's question," Seely said accusingly.

"Answer," Mrs. Peden said harshly.

Kate's head came around. "Both of us are women," she said. She offered it as something special, an emotional and experiential tie. "Whatever our differences, there is so much we have in common. Why do you hate me?"

Mrs. Peden blinked and rejected the offering. "We have nothing in common, nothing. I'm a decent woman, a mother, a Christian. We are not alike, not alike at all."

"Are you an atheist?" Seely bore in, teeth displayed in an awful grin.

Kate fixed on Mrs. Peden. "The play is an act of contrition," she said quietly. "A lovely love letter by O'Neill to his family. A plea for recognition of the damages done him as a young man by those closest to him, a family torn apart by its differences and unable to give love freely or wholly. Don't you see, it's his way of forgiving them all for what was done to him?"

"Forgiving!" The word snapped out of Seely with whiplike force. "Hardly that. What we have here is an act of revenge. A public mutilation of father and mother, public denigration of the family itself. A castigation of the living institution most revered in God's house. Absent is all human sentiment. Nowhere is there recognition that Our Lord is present in all men and all families are living evidence of His presence in each and every home. Love! Oh, no. Only degradation and meanness and loathing . . ."

"O'Neill was responding to a moral imperative. . . ."

"He distorted truth. He does no honor to his father and his mother." Seely held one big fist aloft, a quivering threat. "All morality is absent in this play."

"Do you deny that the Tyrones were a thin disguise for the O'Neills?" Lucas Anderson said.

"No. Neither did O'Neill. Can't you see? He was concerned with the collapse of human relationships. He *cared,* about people. He was *concerned*. He would be concerned if he were alive today. Everywhere we see facades reflecting empty values. Symbols, little arrows, that point the way to disaster and to failure. We've become anesthetized to honest emotion, to each other. We exist on our separate plots and planes, fragmented, apart from each other, out of touch. Nobody listens, nobody understands, nobody cares."

"No!" Mrs. Peden said. Her voice was brittle with triumph. "In King of Heaven, we know our neighbors and respect and honor them. Here folks live right. Think right. Do right."

"Praise God," Seely said.

"All this is beside the point," Professor Moss said. "What we have here is a play about used-up people who have nothing to teach the rest of us."

"It's about loneliness and loss, about ruptured relationships, about fathers and mothers and children who can't manage to communicate with language," said Kate.

"Failures," Anderson said. "America is about successful people."

"Amen to that," Seely said. "There is lewdness abroad and it must be terminated. Crime is rampant. Hostile behavior everywhere. The work ethic has come under attack. Cities fall apart and politicians line their pockets.

"America has ceased to live according to righteous and proven principles. Rejected time-tested standards. We ignore the truth at peril to our immortal spirits. We are a people big at heart with keen vision and courage.

"God gave us memory so that we could have roses in winter and youth in the winter of our lives. And so that we would

remember always that Christ Jesus died on the Cross for us
and our sins . . ."

He glared at Kate Fellows, startled by the intensity of his
own reactions. This woman, this Jezebel, this painted creature
with her tempting figure and taunting mouth, was a danger to
everything good and holy, to everything God intended man to
become. And in that fractured moment he understood his mission in all its frightening totality—to make war directly against
such creatures, the enemies of God. To accuse them. To expose
them by name and by crime. To bring them down with sword
and with sorcery. This then was the true purpose of the Tenth
Crusade. Here was the Infidel, unrepentant, arrogant, seduc-
tive. A roadblock on the road to the Lord. He would not be
stopped.

"You," he said. His voice trembled with righteous fury.
"You are the personification of evil. You shall be destroyed. . . ."

They sat silently around the table, Kate Fellows long gone.
They sat without looking at each other. They waited as if for
Divine inspiration.

"Well?" Mrs. Peden said with characteristic annoyance over
the delay.

"We must do something," Anderson said.

"What choice do we have?" Professor Moss said. "The
woman is guilty and defiant."

"Fire her," Mrs. Peden demanded harshly.

"There is a contract," Moody said. "A legal contract."

"Is it legally binding, Charles?" Anderson said.

The lawyer fingered his tie. "Naturally, I read the contract
prior to coming here this evening. As matters now stand, there
are no valid legal grounds for dismissing Miss Fellows."

"Ridiculous!" Mrs. Peden said.

"Buy it up," Anderson, always businesslike, said.

"Get rid of her!" Mrs. Peden insisted.

"That could bring a great deal of unwanted publicity down
on the college," Moody said. "If she should sue . . ."

"She would probably win," Charles Jayne said. "An out-
of-court settlement would be my advice, though even that might
be costly."

"She must go!"

"What can we do?" Moses said.

"Close the play," Seely said.

"What? She's chairman of the department. We've always maintained autonomy and—"

"Close it," Seely said again.

"I'll consider—"

"Do it."

"I could, I suppose."

"Do it."

"And that woman," Mrs. Peden said. "Fire her, send her away. Today, this minute, right now."

"Not so fast," Seely said. "We made every effort to help her. She refused to cooperate. She refused our help. Let her pay the price. Let her learn a lesson. God's work will be done."

"Praise God."

# CHAPTER
## 20

MARTHA WAS ASLEEP, Seely was grateful. No point any more in denying how much she bored him, a burden to him for all the years of their marriage. Every gesture, every word, her every thought, was predictable. He found himself completing her sentences in his mind, anticipating her responses to every situation; if only she would disappear. Go away. Die.

In the quiet of his rectory office, he turned his attention to more important matters. The Tenth Crusade.

He began rereading the plan of operation he had worked out. He saw it as the product of a thorough intelligence, of a brain creative and daring, the effort of a man dedicated and devoted to a singular cause. Here and there it needed refinement, expansion, a slight change of direction. He concentrated hard; after all, he wanted everything to be right. Perfect.

The unexpected ring of the telephone startled him and he snatched it up. "Reverend Seely here. . . ."

"I have to see you."

"Do you know what time it is? Callin' at this hour this way. What are you thinkin'!"

"It's important."

He set himself. "There is no way. I'm sorry I can't help you."

"We must talk."

"You have my last word—it is ended."

"At the usual place." The firmness of her voice surprised him, made him uneasy. "In exactly one hour," she said.

"No," he said.

"Either I talk to you or I talk to your wife."

"You can't threaten me. I will not be intimidated."

"One hour," she said again, and hung up.

He stared at the phone as if it were the cause of his trouble and considered his options. Not many. Damn girl left him no room to maneuver. He went up to the bedroom. His wife still slept peacefully. She always slept peacefully. Sleeping was the major accomplishment of her otherwise unremarkable life. He made up his mind to see Jody. One last time. He would make the severe consequences of any further intrusion on his existence plain to her. The decision made, he felt much better.

They met in the parking lot of the Triple X Motel. Ordinarily she was anxious to greet him, presenting her soft young mouth for his kiss. Ordinarily he had to hold her off, caution her against public displays, against the risk of anyone's recognizing them. Not tonight.

Tonight she remained slumped behind the wheel, chin down. He went over to the car and said her name. She gazed up at him without speaking, her eyes rimmed with crimson and puffy and she wore no makeup. She was so young, so pretty. He set himself against her, against being weak. He had so much to lose.

"What is it, Jody?"

"Don't be angry with me, please."

"Let's sit in my car, it's more comfortable."

"Can't we get us a room?" she said, when they were settled.

"That's not a good idea."

"Always before you were so all-fired anxious to get me onto my back and do me. Did all of a sudden I get ugly?"

"It's over between us. I told you that. Now what's got you so riled up?"

She came around to face him and then, with a small, smothered exhalation, launched herself at him, arms holding tight, forcing him backwards against the car door.

"Oh, Dorr, I've missed you so much! Can't get you off'n my mind. The wild notions that come into my head. The things I remember. The things I do to myself. . . ."

He pushed her away and set himself against the weakness of his own flesh.

"That's enough, Jody. Don't you talk that way. Or think that way. It's wrong, you hear? That's the voice of Satan in your mouth."

"Oh, Dorr, I need you so much. What have I done to hurt you? Whatever it is, I'll make it up to you, I promise I will."

He was pleased. What a beautiful child she was. Wild, an uncivilized little animal, vibrant with unfulfilled appetites. More than two years of her had kept him stirred up and ready, but no more. He had more important things on his mind. He was movin' on. No longer could he afford Jody Joiner. Perhaps later on, when the Crusade was well established, his situation secure, his reputation firmly fixed in place and unblemished, perhaps then he would permit someone else into his life. Someone equally beautiful and anxious to please. Someone a little more mature, a little less demanding. Someone able to accept the limitations of his new existence, willing to take her proper place in it and not make waves. But that was later. For now, Martha would have to suffice.

"Have I treated you badly, Dorr? I must have, else why would it all go so bad for me? I was angry with you for a while, real angry. But not anymore. I tried to understand what was goin' down and I have, I honest and truly have, Dorr. After all, I'm just a kid still and you're a grown man, a preacher, a married man with responsibilities and obligations and all that stuff. I do understand, I do. It all came to me at once when I saw you on the television."

"You saw that?"

"You were so handsome in that white suit."

"A nice touch, white. The color of purity and fidelity, of Heaven and faith. Of course, it was just a regional telecast. But it's the beginning. The mail response has been excellent. Our share of the audience reached thirty-nine percent, and that's goin' head to head with Merv Griffin in a number of markets. Next time, we'll do better, God willin'."

"Oh, you will. I know you will."

"They've invited me back. Twice a week from now on, Sunday mornin' service from Independence Baptist and Thursday evening. I've decided to use the high school auditorium, dress the student chorus all in white behind me. Lots of singin' and stompin', turn it into an old-time revival meetin', for white folks, of course. My associate's been auditionin' soloists. A young man and a young woman, with the right look to 'em. Clean-cut, handsome to look at, the kind of young people you'd want your children to be."

"Not like me, you mean?"

He squared his jaw and his spirit against her. "Jody, my ministry on earth is at hand. The Lord has summoned me to do His work and I have discovered the means by which to do it. There will be no time, no energy, no interest in anything beyond that. You must understand."

It was as if she hadn't heard. "I liked you much better than Dr. Taggart or Reverend Falwell or like that, Dorr. You have a sort of—well, sexy holiness, if you know what I mean." Her hand came to rest on his thigh and he stiffened as she reached for him.

He pulled away. "I told you, Jody, no more. All that was sinful and corrupt between us, it is behind me. I have spoken to the Lord and accepted His guidance, His wisdom, He has put me back on the righteous road and from here on henceforth there shall be no detours for Dorr Seely. Praise God."

She shifted closer to him. "Nobody's touched me since you, Dorr. Except for my own self." She giggled. "But I was thinkin' about you all the times I did it so I guess I have been true to you all along."

"You mustn't talk to me this way."

"Oh, I admit it, there have been those who tried. Mostly young fellas, some boys from out at the College. But except for a little kissin' and messin' around, I didn't let them do anything, Dorr. Not one blessed thing."

"Except for Warren Peden?" he said with surprising intensity.

"You heard about that?"

"Poor Joelle Peden, a good woman. Decent and God-fearin', raised him and Lonnie without a father to help. And now Warren's gone bad on her. Lord be praised for makin' Lonnie into the fine son he is."

"I'm not all that certain it was Warren."

"What do you mean?"

"Well, I never did see the face of whoever did me thataway. Truth is it was a mess..."

"A mess?"

"He roughed me up and kept on callin' me names and me wigglin' and squirmin' and him gettin' off on my belly..."

"Are you sayin' you weren't raped?"

"Oh, I was raped, all right. But the poor fool was too worked up to stay inside of me till it was over. He came all over me, got me all slimy...."

"The deputies arrested Warren."

"Could've been him."

"You sound as if you're sorry for him."

"Well. Must be somethin' the matter with a boy who goes around doin' girls thataway."

"You enjoyed it, didn't you?"

"Course not, Dorr. You know better'n that."

"I can hear it in your voice. Wished he had stayed inside've you, don't you? Wished he'd filled up your belly 'stead of splashin' all over you. How'd it feel, him rubbin' his old machine up against you thataway? Make you nice and hot and gooey? Make you wish you could have it like that a lot more?"

"Wasn't that way at all. I was scared of him and I hated him."

"But no more. You think on it a lot, do you? Do yourself and all the while thinkin' on Warren rubbin' up against you."

"That's just not so."

"Maybe that's what you need, all of you, bein' forced, told what to do, forced to do it."

"No!"

"Here!" He opened his pants. "Look at this!"

"Not like this, Dorr."

"This is what you came after, take it."

"No, I want to talk."

"Put your mouth around it, the way you want to. The way you wanted to do Warren's..."

"No."

"Take it. Do like I say. For the last time...."

His hand was hard, fingers digging into her scalp as he forced her forward. "Go on, do it, do it the way you do, the way you did to a hundred other men, take me in and—"

She bit down hard.

He bellowed in pain and jerked away.

"Bitch!" he shouted. "Evil bitch! What have you done to me?"

"Just nicked you a little."

"I'm bleedin'."

"Don't look so serious to me."

"You shouldn't've done that."

"Just tryin' to get your attention."

"I got a mind to slam you aside the head a few times."

"Just try it, and I'll raise a ruckus folks'll hear back in King of Heaven."

He adjusted himself, placing his wounded penis tenderly back in its cotton pouch, zipping up his trousers. He switched on the ignition. "Go on, you get out've here. And don't you ever call me again."

"One more thing before you go, Dorr."

"Don't want to hear anything you got to say."

"I am goin' to have your baby...."

"It's your decision to talk."

"But you should attend it, the way you went to the way you wanted to draw area."

# CHAPTER
## 21

GOFORTH BRACED HIMSELF against a seething discontent. Inez was the cause. After booking Warren Peden, he'd gone back to see her. She refused to admit him, saying she wanted to be alone, sent him packing into the night, to sleep restlessly in his own bed.

A bad night. He dreamed in fragments, always of women. Each different, each an aspect of Inez. Until the last: Kate Fellows. Stripped bare, red hair flowing across graceful shoulders, womanly breasts high and thrusting defiantly; he knelt before her, paying homage to her beauty, to what he could never have, to all that he had given up.

And woke in a sweat, afraid of what was happening to him, without understanding, yearning for the vital parts of his being he had surrendered over the years, aching to be a whole man once again. His own man. He tried to sleep again without success, brain leapfrogging along the uneven jungle paths of his past and future. Once he dressed himself and made it as far as his car, vowing to force Inez to see him. To make her understand that he occupied a place in her life that nothing could alter. Out of some veiled place in his unconscious came a warning; leave her be. Give her time to adjust to his cop's way of doing things. In the daylight, after a good night's rest, she would understand better that he *had* to bring her into his work, that he knew what he was doing. That it was all right.

He had his first cup of coffee at five in the morning. By eight o'clock he'd had four more. Hungry and irritable, his eyes shadowed and narrow, he drove downtown to Francine's Diner. He ate three fried eggs and sausage patties and a double portion of toast and had two more cups of coffee. He lit a cigarette and left, faint cramps lining his stomach. Had he eaten too fast? Or was the job getting to him; tension was always a part of it, tension and fear, although he'd never openly acknowledged either to anyone.

He walked across Courthouse Square along the crushed shell path past the statue of Robert E. Lee to the sheriff's station. He made his way to the cells at the rear. Except for a vagrant sleeping it off, all cells were empty. He went back to the desk and Jimmy Ray Wilson, a large, fleshy man waiting for the dayshift to relieve him.

"Where's the prisoner, Jimmy Ray?" His voice came up low and slow from the diaphragm, a rough rumble edged with threat.

Wilson was not a man who dealt easily with conflict or criticism. All his life he'd tried to be a tough guy but alongside men like Duke Venable or Billy Goforth he failed to measure up, and he knew it.

"Bailed out," he said. "Somethin' wrong, Billy?"

"When?"

"About an hour ago."

"Shit, piss and corruption," Goforth muttered. He barged into Duke Venable's office without knocking. The sheriff accepted the intrusion casually. But the tiny eyes grew smaller under folds of crinkled skin. "Mornin', Billy."

"He's out."

"Young Peden? Yes, he's out. Sam MacAlmon set bail for him."

"In the middle of the night?"

"Judge MacAlmon took pity on the boy, bein' so young and all. Justice tempered by mercy, you might say."

"What in hell's happenin', Duke?"

"Peden's entitled to bail, like anybody else."

"He's a rapist."

"Innocent till proven guilty, it's the law of the land."

"How much bail?"

"Ten thousand."

"Damn, might as well turn him loose."

"His momma's a solid citizen, Billy. The boy ain't gonna cut 'n' run, if that's what's worryin' you."

"Who is representin' him?"

"Charles Jayne."

"He's Gault's man."

"Most every lawyer worth his salt is, wouldn't you say?"

"He ain't goin' to come to trial, is he, Duke?"

"Now, Billy, simmer down. You did some good police work. No more young ladies are goin' to be molested in King of Heaven. Time takes care of these things, time lets folks forget. Let it go at that."

"He raped those women, beat them, robbed them."

"Billy, I got to tell you straight out, the case against Warren ain't too strong."

"I caught him—what in hell are you sayin' to me, Duke?"

"Onliest witness you got is some colored gal and you know how much ice that's goin' to cut in court. Exactly none is how much."

"Benjamin and I both saw it go down. We were right there."

"Charlie Jayne is claimin' entrapment."

The low-grade pain returned to Goforth's stomach. "So he walks?"

"Oh, there'll be a trial."

"A reduction of charges, maybe a hearin', a slap on the wrist is all."

"No sense sendin' a boy away that never done any other bad thing we know of, is there? Lonnie gave me his word, he'll keep the boy clean from now on. Let matters take their natural course."

"I want that boy sent over."

Venable clasped his hands across his middle. "There ain't no witnesses to testify against him. No white gal's able to make a positive identification. And that queer fella, he denies ever bein' here, says nothin' ever happened at all."

Goforth let the words out deliberately. "There's Inez Macklin."

"Ease back a mite, Billy. Whatever's goin' on between you and that little colored gal's your affair. Onliest thing is, keep it thataway. Don't let it get into your work."

"So you know about that?"

"It's my business to know about everythin' in the county. One day it'll be your business to know, remember that."

Goforth couldn't let go. "I can go out there and make first-class busts from dawn to dusk and never repeat myself, Duke. Close down Miss Ivy's for one. Take Lonnie in for runnin' illegal whiskey into the county. Pull in all the folks peddlin' liquor by the glass in all those back rooms and out at the Field Club. Clamp down on every load of stolen fruit passes out of the groves, charge the foreman who false weight shipments. I could turn this county on its ear."

Venable pulled at his nose. "It's our job to keep the peace, let's do that."

"Bring Warren back in."

"Boy, you listen to me. Soon you are goin' to be movin' in behind this desk. Things look a lot different from this chair. You'll like the job. Lots of benefits. Not county benefits, but the fringes that come your way. A man gets to my stage of livin' and he thinks about things like pensions and ownin' some land somewhere nice, a nice little house to retire to, enough money so he and his won't go hungry. No sense spoilin' it for yourself, not when you're this close. You got a lock on the future, boy, leave what you can't change anyway alone. Leave it lay."

"I don't know if I can do that, Duke."

Venable's voice grew hard. "Well, you better find out soon. You just better. . . ."

Inez mocked him. "Give it up, Deputy."

"Dammit, girl, don't call me *that*."

"Yassuh, Mistuh Billy." She did an exaggerated shuffle. "Anythin' you says, Mistuh Billy, suh."

His laugh was mirthless and the weathered face tightened and grew bony and hard again. "I can't let them do this."

"You can't stop 'em."

"I'm a peace officer, I have a job to do."

"Haven't you learned yet there's no law around here, unless it works for the folks at the top of the heap?"

"What's Warren got to do with them up on The Hill?"

"You said it yourself. Lonnie does a job for the sheriff and Warren's Lonnie's brother. Clear as day, it doesn't give me any trouble. So let it go."

"I can't do that. If I do my job right then everybody else—Duke, the court—they'll have to do their part."

"Fool! They're doin' you, can't you see that?"

"I can deal with anything they hand out."

"Oh, yes, you can! Hard-rock Deputy Goforth. Lean mean Billy Goforth, toughest dude in the county. Look at yourself, man, *they* have done what they wanted done. It's all over now. There's not a blessed thing anybody can do anymore. You said so yourself—all your witnesses are gone or won't talk or didn't see anything, smell anything, feel anything. Nobody saw who did it, nobody can identify your man."

"Except you."

"Except me. Oh, that's just fine. One black school teacher goin' up against Duke Venable and who knows who else! Man, we are a losin' team, and you better believe it."

He felt the hot ball of rage move up into his throat choking him, making him afraid and the fear sending him out toward the far edge of control. "Listen to me," he said. He drew out each word. "I am goin' to do this thing, I will talk to the Joiner girl. She will come around."

"Why you doin' this?"

The question startled him. "It's my job."

"To hell with the job! Can't you see for lookin', they are goin' to break you?"

He stared at her and saw the muscles pull together in her face, the deep dark shining with emotion. Anger? Hatred? Pity? How little he knew her. What did she want of him? What devilish force had brought them together? He blew stale air and allowed tension to drain out of his body.

"All right, I'm doin' it for you."

"No."

"He raped you, he beat you."

"Not for me."

"Not for the job, not for you. What else is left? Why am I goin' through this garbage?"

"'Cause it's your life, and if it don't work the way it's supposed to then your whole life is wasted. Shot to hell, all the years bein' deputy, doin' *right*, enforcin' the law. But it was never the law. Only the people in power you were workin' for. They chose the laws they wanted enforced and those they didn't. Now you are beginnin' to get in the way. They'll come down on you, Billy. They'll hurt you bad."

He looked at her as if seeking more, some acceptable explanation, some finite answer to questions he had yet to think of. She looked back, giving nothing, waiting for him now.

He reached for her hand. "I love you. I want to spend every night of my life with you from now on."

She pulled away. "Don't say that to me. What we do is what we want to do. You pleasure me and I pleasure you, that's all there is to that. Comin' here in broad daylight this way. White deputy, black girl. Smarten up, else they goin' to burn a cross on your front lawn yet."

"It's got nothin' to do with color."

"It's got everythin' to do with color. If I was white, and willin' to testify, fine-boy Warren would be a dead duck and we both know it."

"That's got nothin' to do with you and me, that part of it."

"Now you're just jivin'."

"I mean it. We'll go away, you and me, any place you like. Nobody has to know who we are, what we are."

"You mean, I can pass as white?"

"I'll get a divorce, we'll get married. Nobody has to know."

"I'll know."

"Damn, girl, what difference does it make?"

"If you don't understand, I can't help you."

"We'll talk about it tonight, I'll come back tonight."

"Forget it, Deputy."

"You think I'm givin' up on you, I ain't givin' up on you."

"Goodbye, Deputy."

"Tonight," he said before leaving. She didn't shut the door of the small house until he was back in the squad car and rolling away.


Kate Fellows was alone in her office in the Theater Arts Building when Goforth unexpectedly appeared. Hat in hand, he blocked off the doorway, lean and angular, giving off a sense of muscularity held in check. She invited him to come in and sit.

He remained standing. "Don't mean to bother you—"

"It's all right." He struck her as different than most of the men she'd known. All of them had a certain pale softness to them, inner flaws made manifest in the flesh. Billy Goforth appeared to be a man able to take care of himself, no matter the circumstance.

"I'm lookin' for Jody," he said.

"Is something wrong?"

"Just a few questions."

"What happened to her, it's hard for a young girl to go through."

"Nobody's got a right," Gorforth said in that slow, thoughtful way of his, thinking about Inez. "Folks are entitled to do as they want to with their own bodies."

She located Jody's class schedule in her files. "Jody's not in the building right now. Try the English Department, Comp. Lit."

"What?"

The puzzled expression on his face made her laugh. "Comparative Literature."

He nodded, turned to go. He swung back. "If you don't mind my askin', you okay, Miss Fellows?"

"I'm fine," she said automatically. "Why do you ask?"

"You look a mite troubled is all. . . . Glad to hear it."

"You know, don't you?" Tension and anger mingled in her, none of it directed at the deputy.

"Folks talk. Not many secrets stay that way for long in King of Heaven."

She exhaled, her limbs heavy and tingling. "I seem to have stepped on some toes."

"That can make folks testy in these parts."

She measured him. "I imagine you've bruised a few toes in your time."

He thought about that. "Can't say as I have, not in recent memory, anyways. Seems like I've always been mighty careful where to put my feet."

"Somehow you don't strike me as the careful sort. I figured you to be someone who takes risks."

"Funny," he said, before he left her. "I'd've said the same, only it ain't so. Not a bit of it. . . ."


Lonnie Peden, big of shoulder and broad of back, hunched over a cup of coffee at the counter in Francine's Diner. Goforth ignored him, taking a place near the cash register. Francine brought him a menu.

"What can I get you, Deputy?"

He was beginning to dislike that title. "Been tryin' to locate Jody. She around?"

"Goes to classes days."

"I tried out at the school."

Francine shrugged and opened the menu.

"This is police business, Francine."

"Has my girl done some kind of crime? She accused of anything wrong?"

At the edge of his vision, Goforth saw Lonnie coming his way. "She's an eyewitness, Francine, a victim. Assault, rape, attempted rape, robbery . . . Warren's been charged with just about everything short of murder."

Lonnie, at Goforth's right shoulder, swore. "Back off the boy, Billy. Leave him be."

"I'd sure like to talk to Jody, Francine."

"Police have talked her out, asked every question there is. She's got nothin' more to say."

"Warren's innocent," Lonnie said loudly. "They turned him loose."

"Out on bail ain't exactly free and clear." Goforth swung around on his stool, looking up into Lonnie's battered face.

"Where'd the bail money come from, Lonnie? That whiskey money?"

"You accusin' me of anything?"

Goforth rose slowly, arms hanging stiffly away from his sides. Those reptilian eyes were lifeless and still, and lips barely moved when he spoke. "One more time out with a load, boy, and you're busted."

Lonnie rolled his thick shoulders. "Day you bust me, I'll whip your ass."

"Now's as good a time as any," Goforth said in a low, clear voice. He looked at Lonnie without moving and Lonnie looked back. Then he blinked twice and took a step away. Eyes holding on Lonnie, Goforth spoke to Francine. "About Warren," he said. "I want to talk to Jody."

"My girl ain't gonna testify to none of it, and that's all there is to it. She swore to me nothin' actually happened, nothin' real bad, that is, and even if it did she didn't *see* nothin' to tell about."

Goforth filed it all away in the archives of his mind for future reference. He struggled to find a neat framework within which to exist, possibly to prosper. But reality refused to conform. Strong emotions hammered at him, and it took all his strength and willpower to walk out of the diner.

# CHAPTER
## 22

AT HIGH NOON with the temperatures soaring into the low nineties, Papa James, at rest in a copper casket lined with real silk, was lowered into the family graveyard that could be seen from the big house on The Hill. In addition to the immediate family, attorney Charles Jayne was present, Duke Venable, a half-dozen top executives of Gault Enterprises and a dozen deputies to serve as pallbearers and keep the curious and the morbid away. Dorr Seely recited the Lord's Prayer and said a few complimentary words about the dear, recently departed, now eternally at peace in the lap of the Lord.

Mr. Nolan led them all back to the house as soon as the first shovelful of dirt was dumped on Papa James. A brunch of eggs, scrambled or fried, hotcakes, sausage links, bacon or breakfast steaks, home fries, grits and hot and cold cereal, was served on the glass-topped iron tables on the back veranda by efficient and silent black men in dark pants and white jackets.

At about that same time, respects were paid to Papa James throughout the county; in the groves and the fields, the factories

and the offices, the concentrate ,plant and the sawmill. One
minute of silence, as decreed by Mr. Nolan, marked by the
tolling of every church bell in the county. Up on The Hill, the
sound was muted and mystical, rather pleasant. In the center
of town, however, the din caused dogs to howl in anguish and
a number of people complained of pain inside their ears, and
headaches.

The formalities concluded, Mr. Nolan withdrew to the
study—now all his—and spoke privately with each of the
invited mourners in turn. He wanted every man to understand
that Gault authority and power had been transferred in its en-
tirety to him. He made clear in which direction Gault interests
lay. Wesley was last on his list.

Mr. Nolan watched his son slouch into the bright, warm
room, place himself carelessly into a chair and heave his long
legs up to the desk, crossed at the ankles. Wesley grinned at
his father.

"Nice funeral," he drawled. "Got Papa James planted quick
and easy, the reins of power in your hands at last, Daddy."

"Yours is a rare talent, Wesley, the ability to be insolent
and charmin' both at the very same time."

"The armaments of survival, Daddy, for a lesser Gault, that
is."

"I'm reassured to discover that you still consider yourself
to be a member of the family, that is indeed a relief. The lone
remainin' Gault after myself, I might remind you."

"You've never let me forget."

"Nor shall I. From this moment forward, you would be wise
to remember that the quality and the style of your life depend
to a great extent on my decisions and my generosity."

Wesley's feet came off the desk. He straightened in the
chair. "Meanin' what?"

"Meanin' that you have been coddled and spoiled and permitted to believe you can do and say anythin' you want to do
because you are a Gault, and there is a great deal of truth in
that. Up to a point. That point has now been exceeded."

"What are you gettin' at, Daddy?"

"Gettin' at Papa James' will, which will be read on Saturday
afternoon next by Mr. Charles Jayne in the livin' room in this
house at precisely eleven in the mornin'. You will be there?"

"Wouldn't miss it for anythin', Daddy." Wesley placed his hands on the arms of the chair, gathering his weight under him, about to make a rapid exit. His father's next words put that notion out of his head.

"Let me disabuse you of any ideas of sudden wealth and power, Wesley. Nothin' could be further from the truth. A great part of all this—" He waved a thick arm in an awkward, indicative gesture. "All this will undoubtedly be yours one day. But Papa James and I agreed—oh, yes, we discussed your prospects quite thoroughly before a final draft of the will was put together and approved and signed by him and the appropriate witnesses."

"Get to the point, Daddy."

"The impatience of youth. Very well, then—Papa James left you a great deal of money makin' you an extremely wealthy young man. . . ."

"Papa James was thoughtful and generous."

"He was selfish and tight-fisted and squeezed every dime he ever came across and made me do the same. In death as in life, he gave nothin' away for free. There's one or two provisos in the will you ought to be acquainted with. . . ."

"Oh?"

"For example, you receive a predetermined amount every year from now until your fortieth birthday. Enough to keep you from goin' hungry, my boy, not enough to pay for your several pleasures and perversions. . . ."

"He can't do that!"

"He can, he did, and it is my function to see that his wishes are carried out. This I shall do."

"I'll get a lawyer."

"Fat lot of good that'll do. In addition to Charlie Jayne, six hotshot lawyers were in on the drawin' of the will. No loopholes. . . ."

"Damn."

"Exactly. Permit me to interpret for you—it means, and this too is spelled out in the will, you *must* be gainfully employed in order to receive the bequest. Gainfully employed by Gault Enterprises in a capacity of *my* choosin' and in a manner to *my* satisfaction."

"That's slavery."

"Indentured labor is a term more to my likin'. So that's the way it's goin' to be, boy. Or else. . . ."

"No court will . . ."

"There's more. Move out of Tokeneke County—without my written permission—and you forfeit all bequests made. That is automatic, irrevocable, final. Control of your principal remains within the executor's hands."

"And I don't have to ask who that is."

Mr. Nolan responded cheerfully. "You are lookin' straight at him, boy." The gross round face drew together, the tiny eyes withdrawing into folds of fat, the plump lips smacking decisively. "Wise up, Wesley. Once a Gault, always a Gault. Time you started actin' like one. Pay attention to business, at home and at the office. Set an example for the folks out there and prepare yourself for the day when you take over as head of this family. Continuity, tradition, concern for the way things have always been done around here, these are what count. Folks in the county depend on the folks on The Hill. We supply the goods of their lives, jobs, money, the simpler pleasures. We are the keepers of their existences, the source of everything good. Protectors of their institutions and beliefs. Defenders of their rights. We have a debt to them and don't you ever forget it. Folks depend on us Gaults, Wesley. They depend on you."

Wesley, face pale and tight, body poised as if to fight or flee, jabbed one long finger at his father.

"I could tell you to stick it, then what?"

Mr. Nolan squinted narrowly at his son. "Then, by God, you'll pay the piper. Until then, you will dance to my tune. . . ."

# CHAPTER
## 23
---

"...I SAY TO you people—turn away from *sin*. Put your backs to *un*godliness.

"I warn you against sin and inequity and ungodliness. Walk in the Light of the Lord. They that believe in Him and live godly lives in Christ Jesus, Our Savior, shall be rewarded in Heaven and in this life as well.

"Oh, yes. Godliness in man is its own happiness. Its own joys. It brings its own *material* and spiritual rewards. Live Godly lives, walk in the path of the angels and you shall reap life everlasting and remember that in matters of sin God is the final judge and a harsh judge He can be.

"Say Amen to the truth of the Word of the Lord.

"You ask why do some men acquire great wealth and great authority and great prestige and great status and great political power? Well, listen to me. It is because they live Godly lives. Yes, indeed. The righteous are *rewarded*. Search your soul— are you a sinner? You know you are. Have you sinned today? Yesterday? Last night? You know you have. In body or in mind. Have you taken the Word of God and smashed it on the rocks of greed or lust or deception? You have, you know you have. Live in the shining light of Our Lord Christ Jesus and see what changes occur in your daily existence. All things shall come to him who finds shelter under the Divine light.

"The Holy Book says, '. . . God so loved the world He gave His only begotten Son. Who so ever believeth in Him should not perish but have everlasting life.' Everlasting life. There it is! Cause and effect. Profit and loss. Winners and losers. Plain as day.

"Praise God.

"Let me give you an example. Take some of those lowdown misfit politicians over in Tallahassee or up in Washington, D.C. A bunch of more worthless good-for-nothings you will never find. Bureaucrats getting fat off the honest labor of decent folks down here. Telling us how to think. How to act. Saying what we should do and when we should do it. Tell us how fast to drive our automobiles, they do. And what to eat and what's supposed to be bad for us. I say you know what's good and what's bad for you, better'n any shifty-eyed bureaucrat with his nose up in the air and his backside plastered down on a soft cushion all day long. They tell us where our kids should go to school and with whom and how they should get there. They tell us we have to lock God, the one true and Old God, out of our schools. They tell us God is dead and patriotism is old-fashioned.

"I say to you . . . you listen to me, now! I say to you, God is alive and angry as a swarm of honey bees around a bear. And I tell you I am a patriot, once and for all time, and I know millions more of ordinary Americans who salute the flag and sing the National Anthem with pride and believe in our United States of America.

"You take taxes. Bureaucrats claim they tax us evenly and fairly. Well, I'll tell you. If'n I wasn't so *mad* about taxes I'd have to laugh. You know what the ancient Greek philosopher said? He said that, 'When there is an income tax, the just man will pay *more* and the unjust *less* on the same amount of income.' Plato said that and by all that's holy ain't a man or woman within sound of my voice can dispute it. Nosirree.

"How about this—maybe it's time the good people, the

righteous people of our great and noble land banded together and launched a crusade to reclaim what is rightfully ours. Our tax money. Our government. Our judicial system. Our schools . . .

"I talk to you here in the Independent Baptist Church on Rhapsody Drive in King of Heaven, Florida, my voice going out over the radio waves to millions more of you good people and millions more able to see my face and the faces of the good and pure young folks of the King of Heaven Heavenly Choir behind me on the television. And I hope and I pray that your radio receivers and your television sets were constructed in honest American factories by efficient and dedicated American workers just like yourselves, Amen. And to you all I say, we have been taken advantage of.

"I am speaking to *you!* So pay attention. Getting mad, are you? Well, all right. So . . . am . . . I! Nowhere. Nowhere in that great and good Book does it say that man and the beasts are one and the same, descended from the same ancestors. Go on, show me where it says that! You can't, nobody can. Not you, not some biology teacher, not some evolutionist, not that dead old man Darwin, himself. No way.

"God created man in the image of Himself, in the image of God He created him, male and female He created them.

"That's it. Not a word about men developing from the beasts, from apes, from monkeys or any other lower order of life.

"They don't want you to know the truth. The truth of God's holy word in Scripture. They want to turn your children's minds to baser thoughts and ways of doing things. They want to impose wild and speculative theories on you as an insidious replacement for the one, the only, the everlasting truth which is the Word of God.

"Enough, I say.

"An end to it.

"And so I bring to you our very own crusade to fight the infidel in the halls of government and the academy and the political parties. I bring to you The Tenth Crusade, a blessed movement of true believers in our Lord God and His only begotten son, Christ Jesus, Amen.

"Join up! Enlist now in the greatest adventure known to man. Get on God's side. Those of you here in the Independent Baptist Church will be given application blanks on your way out after this morning's service. Those of you out there in radio and television land, write us in care of the Independent Baptist Church for an application fee. Charter members as Knights of the Tenth Crusade are only ten dollars for men and five dollars for women and children over the age of ten. By mail you will receive your membership card and a beautiful silver and enamel membership pin to wear on your lapel or sweater to show the world that you stand firmly with Our Lord.

"In keeping with this, we've been getting lots of mail asking for transcriptions of our Crusader sermons and it's just about impossible to fill all the requests. So here's what we've done. We've brought in some very excellent people to record these sermons on records and on cassette tapes. A series of eight tapes or three long-playing records are available in limited amounts for only thirty-five dollars a set. So you just send your check or money order along with your name and address and a note saying Crusader Sermon tape or record and we'll get it to you right off.

"Also, we have prepared a pamphlet you will enjoy receiving and studying in order to prepare yourself for the conflict ahead. It will tell you what the Founding Fathers truly intended for our country and how the secret forces of evil have tried to steal the land from us and subvert the American Dream. Just send along your check or money order for five dollars and we'll get it to you right off.

"Until next time, friends, may the Good Lord love you, keep you, and bless you and reveal to you Christ's great purpose for your life. Now listen to the sweet voices of our King of Heaven Heavenly Choir singing a special selection of fine old hymns. . . .

"Praise God.

"Amen."

B. J. Moody clapped Seely on the shoulder. "Stroke of genius, that business about evolution. That's always been a bone in the throat of a lot of Christians. Evolution versus creation. The written word versus scientific theory. Make it one of the planks of the crusade, Dorr."

Seely was pleased and he said so. "Just popped into my head out there."

Seely examined the other man; more and more he felt uncertain about Moody's commitment to the crusade, to Scripture, to God Himself. He had begun to suspect the other man of being an opportunist, quick to exploit every chance that came along, but none too reliable over the long pull. He would bear watching in the weeks and months ahead.

"Praise God," Seely said. A chill wrenched his spine. Was he so much different from Moody? Was he more the Believer, more the true Christian; was he closer to God in his life than B. J. in his? Only one answer came; every day Seely's doubts were dropping away, all questions being answered, all weaknesses of belief shored up for the oncoming struggle. Never, he assured himself, had his faith been stronger. Never had he thrown himself as much on God's mercy and trusted His judgment in all matters. As for B. J., as vital as he had become in this holy war they were launching, he had better remain subordinate to God's will, and to Seely's authority and leadership. "Have you spoken again to Mr. Nolan, B. J.?"

"This morning, we had breakfast together."

"And?"

"I explained our thinking about a Political Action Committee. He pointed out that ever since Watergate there have been campaign spending limits imposed on candidates and parties. I told him what we had in mind, that PAC can spend all the money it wants, as long as it is not allied with any single party or candidate."

"What was his reaction to that?" said Seely.

"Positive. The man came up with a hit list of politicians in and out of the state. His list is remarkably coincidental with our own."

"Well, good. What about additional funding?"

"He'll come up with some money. But of course we'll have to raise more elsewhere. He promised to put me in touch with sympathetic people all over the country. I explained that we were talking about direct mail and concentrated television advertising, that it would cost a lot. He likes the idea of isolating our political enemies and defeating them. The man sees politics as a demolition derby."

"Search and destroy," said Seely.

"Exactly."

"Then we go all out. Next election we make our mark. A couple of big wins and we'll be on our way."

"There's just one thing."

"What's that?"

"Mr. Nolan wants to put his own man in the United States Senate," said Moody.

"That makes sense to me."

"Wait till you hear who he's pushing."

"Who?"

"His son," said Moody.

Seely leaned back, hands forming a steeple. "There's a great deal in the boy's background that will have to be overcome. Cleaned up. Polished. Can it be done?"

"I think so."

Seely sighed. "Wesley's not the only one got a problem. . . ."

"Something you want to tell me, Dorr?"

Seely saw no way out. There was no one else to turn to. "There is something," he said. "That young lady I mentioned to you . . ."

"Jody Joiner?"

"The one and the same. A little something has come up. . . ."

# CHAPTER
## 24

THE PHONE CALLS kept coming. To her office, this time a man, harsh, insistent, condemnatory, washing over her in a by-now familiar cold spray. Her emotions went spinning backwards to when she was a little girl, troubled, lonely, sensing rejection wherever she went. Forced to attend a teacher's college in order to satisfy her father's demand that she learn something practical, something that would enable her to support herself. Make a living in the uncaring world that confronted her.

"Damned slut," said another voice on the phone, full of loathing and disapproval. "You won't get away with it, corrupting our fine young men. To take their cocks in your rotten mouth, to take away their manhood. You're warned, give it up. Get out! Leave town! Leave the state! Right now! Today! Before sunset. Don't say you haven't been warned."

She trembled and wept for a long time after each call. Her brain tipped and tilted and her limbs grew weak and she was afraid she might be sick. Her lungs ached for more oxygen than she could bring and she repeatedly asked herself what she had done to be punished this way.

The phone rang. She refused to respond. It kept ringing. Slowly she lifted it up. "Here it is, honey. Bang, bang, there goes Kate. Smack between the boobs, honey."

She screamed and dropped the phone and snatched it up again. She dialed the wrong number and started all over again. A voice came on, Mae-Mae; she had called Wesley's home by mistake. She tried once more, this time got through to him.

"You aren't supposed to call me here."

She flinched. "I'm in trouble."

"I can't talk now."

"I must see you, right away."

"That's impossible. I'm in the middle of—"

She began to cry.

"What is it?" he said, with considerable concern. "Are you hurt?"

"I'm so afraid."

"What's happened? Do you need a doctor?"

"Please. . . ."

He hesitated only a little. "All right. In half an hour. The beach okay?"

"Please hurry."

At one end of the curve of Silver Sands, some adolescent boys playing touch football, girlfriends watching. Scattered along the sand, sunbathers. Kate took off her shoes and stood at the edge of the water, the damp sand cool underfoot. Wesley came up behind her.

She walked and he followed. "What is it that couldn't wait, Kate? You dragged me out of the middle of a very important meeting."

She went faster, trying not to hear his words. "You sounded out of control," he said.

She spun around, told him about her last talk with Dr. Moody, about the phone calls. "If I'm losing control, I have a right to." She didn't believe that for a moment; she lacked strength, will, courage. Weakness prevailed. She shivered.

"Do you think you should call the police?" he said.

"Do you?"

He made no answer and she understood that he was incapable of supplying what she needed. What exactly did she need? What complex underground requirements had propelled her to this point of her life, had deprived her of so much that most people wanted and acquired, left her apart and ultimately alone? What had she won in its stead?

"We buried my grandfather," Wesley said without warning.

"I know. I'm sorry."

"He was ninety-four years old."

"Did you love him very much?"

"He was a vicious old man and he should have let go twenty years ago. He drifted in and out of senility. He was useless most of the time but he still wielded power over everything, everyone. All he talked about were the women he had when he was younger and diet supplements and natural laxatives. I hated him."

"And now?"

"Now? Now there's my father, ruler of it all. Ruler of us all. He's different from Papa James, smoother, more sophisticated, tuned in on how things are done nowadays. But no less ruthless, no less greedy and power-mad. I don't know what to do."

"What about?" she said reflexively. She felt isolated and vulnerable, more alone than at any time in her life.

"About my future, of course. About my own place in the world."

She glanced over at him. There was a petulant cast to his mouth she'd never before noticed, giving him the look of a sullen little boy. Not sure what to say, she said nothing. Where the beach narrowed and bent out into the Gulf, a slender young woman lay on her stomach, her bra removed. Her back was smoothly brown, strong. Kate remembered when she had looked that way, devoid of excess flesh, free of the marks of time and age. She mourned briefly for her lost youth.

"That girl," Wesley said.

"She's lovely."

"The beach patrol finds her like that, she'll be fined. This is Tokeneke County. . . ."

A low moan broke out of her and she increased her pace. "I am so afraid."

"Settle it, then."

"Give in, you mean?"

"A lot of fussin' over nothin'."

"I can't do it."

"Go along with Moody and those phone calls will stop."

"You think he's behind them?"

"Moody!" He laughed aloud. "No way. But word gets out. Gives the local crazies a chance to get in on the action."

"They frighten me."

"You frighten them."

"That's absurd. Why would anyone be afraid of me?"

"You're different. Educated, beautiful, sophisticated. You've been places, done things, felt things they will never know. They're stuck here. And you—one day you'll leave. They hate you for that, for being an outsider and different, a mirror that reveals their own inadequacy and the futility of their lives. You're a threat to a number of folks in these parts."

"You, too, Wesley?"

He grinned. "In a way. When I'm with you, I am forced to scale myself upwards, be better than I've been before, measure up to all those great guys you've known out there in the big wide world. Be the best Wesley Gault I can be and believe me that is hard to do." Another laugh that ended in a nervous little sputter when she did not respond.

She faced him. There was a careless, slack set to his features she'd never before noticed. A man prettier than he had a right to be but without resolution or determination, as if some malformation of character had left his face with an undertone of flabbiness.

"I'm not the threat. It's this place, it's your family, Wesley, it's you."

"Oh, come on!"

"I mean it. All you Gaults, and your hired hands, locked in to the status quo. So set against anything outside the county. At war with change or growth or a new idea. Keep Tokeneke the way it is and always has been. What a pathetic way to live. So hopeless. So defensive. So frightened."

"I'm not that way."

"You will be, when your turn at running things comes along."

"I'm gettin' out, you'll see."

"When?"

"When?"

"Yes. Go home, Wesley, pack a bag. Tell Mae-Mae you're up to here with her child's games, her whining and complaining. Tell her, and tell your father you're leaving. Tell him to pack in this tight little private world of his. Tell him to stuff his money and his hill. Tell him you're running off with Kate Fellows, fifteen years older than you are, a woman damaged by time and by all the mistakes she's made. Tell him we're going to dance down the yellow brick road like two damned fools. Go ahead, Wesley, tell him all that."

"And do what?"

"Something marvelous. Make love in a graveyard. Go skinny-dipping. Read Proust out loud and the Russian novelists. Be poor. Get old. Live. Die. What else is there to do?"

"You surprise me, you truly do."

She looked out at the Gulf. She disliked knowing that the soft blue water ended somewhere beyond the horizon, ran smack into the restrictions of another land mass and the people who existed on it. She wanted life to be pure and lovely and go on forever. What a fine, futile fantasy. . . .

"Sometimes I surprise me, too, Wesley."

"You're acting like a child. Life isn't like that and you know it."

When she answered, it was tenderly. "You never surprise me, Wesley, and that is a sad thing to learn about someone you're supposed to love." She started back toward the car.

"Kate!" She turned back and waited. "What are you going to do now, Kate?"

A surge of relief lifted a heavy burden from her. At once she was glad that he was unable to run off with her, glad that she didn't have to run off with him, glad that they were not bound forever to each other. She understood at last that she wasn't cut out to play the role of mother to a grown man. Her smile was comfortable and cheerful. "I don't know," she replied.

"I'm talkin' about the play."

"I don't know."

"They'll come down hard on you."

"What are you going to do, Wesley?"

"About what?"

"About your life?"

"Don't be angry with me. You have no right to be. I didn't get you into this mess, it's all your own doin'. Just give in, it's still not too late. Tell Moody you'll do it his way."

"You're right, Wesley," she said finally. "You didn't get me into any of this and it's not up to you to get me out."

# CHAPTER
## 25

FRANCINE KNOCKED GENTLY and when there was no response she knocked again. She opened the door and entered Jody's room. Her daughter lay on her bed in the darkness staring up at the ceiling.

"I knocked," Francine said.

"Momma, I don't want to talk to anybody."

"You feelin' poorly?"

"I'm all right."

She touched the girl's brow. "No fever. What's botherin' you?"

"I said I'm all right. I'm all right."

"I been your momma for eighteen years, reckon I can tell when you're all right and when you're not."

"Just tired is all."

"You had your supper? I'll fetch you some food, if you want."

"No thanks."

"Look, I'm on my way out. I'll call it off, stay home and

we can talk. We ain't had nearly enough girl-talk, you and me."

"No, you go. I'll be okay."

"It messes me up seein' you like this. It's this damn rotten business with Warren Peden."

"Momma, I got some thinkin' to do is all."

"Well. You need somebody to talk to or a shoulder to cry on your momma is here. You understand?"

Jody looked away and after a beat Francine left.

The Gulf Fishing and Boating Club was behind the marina, part of Enos Gay's boatyard. Signs announcing that soft drinks only were served and dancing was prohibited were prominently displayed. A juke box played soft rock music and three couples were dancing at the far end of the bar. Name-brand liquor could be bought by the bottle at three times normal prices, wrapped and sealed in brown paper bags. Mixers went for a dollar a bottle, plus a clean glass and a bowl full of ice. Enos also served half-pound burgers, choice of chili, cheese or bacon, and French Fries. Lonnie, waiting in a booth, greeted her with a wide grin. She avoided his kiss and slid into the seat opposite him.

She appraised him as if for the first time. Big, handsome, rugged; the kind of man she had dreamed about as a girl. A genuine American hero in whose glory she would bask and from whom all good things would flow her way.

"You look good enough to eat," he said.

Her roiled emotions made it difficult to think clearly. And Lonnie made it worse; a powerful, vital force that swept out of the center of him making her weak and aware of ancient cravings, of old fears, of childhood never fully dealt with or put away.

"I don't think I want to see you again, Lonnie."

A terrible hurt washed up into his eyes to be replaced swiftly by a red rage. For one long breathless moment, she believed he was going to hit her. Then the anger subsided and was replaced by confusion and tenderness.

"Don't fool with me like that, Francine. It ain't funny, it just ain't."

"I'm sorry, I didn't plan it. But I know it's right. I can't go on with you, Lonnie."

"You found somebody else?"

"It's not that."

"I can understand another man. If it's that, I can fight that. You met another man, right?"

"There's no other man."

"What then? Dammit, Francine!" He struggled to contain his emotions. "Listen, it's never been easy for me. Nothin' came easy. . . ."

"The football, you had it all, Lonnie. The money, the cheerin', the women. Back in high school, college, the professionals, it all came your way."

He shook his head and rubbed his mouth. "It was never the way it seemed. I mean—it ain't easy for me to say this to you—I was always scared, Francine. . . ."

"You?"

"EveryGodhelpmegame. Never let up, not one time."

"You was the toughest boy ever at King of Heaven High."

"Thing is, I never let on. Never dared let folks know. When I got most scared I'd put my head down and keep bullin' on ahead. The guys used to slap my fanny and say how ballsy I was, but I was as scared as a man could be and nobody knew."

"Why? Why do it then? Why keep playin'?"

The question surprised him. "What else was I goin' to do? Kill cockroaches for Momma for the rest of my life?"

She had no answer to give.

"Don't put me aside, Francine."

"There's all the women you want out there."

"I went that route. Football freaks, the lot o' them. Never had to come through for them, never had to be anythin' but a football hero to them. Made 'em feel like they was scorin' touchdowns and gettin' on TV and all. Made 'em feel good to be with this year's hero. When I busted my knee up the first time—man, nobody came around when I was up in the hospital bed hurtin' somethin' fierce and not knowin' if I'd ever play ball again or not. Nobody came by, not the other players, not the coaches, none of the freaks. They just found themselves another fool could run with a football. Ah, Francine, whatever it is is wrong we can fix it. We got somethin' fine goin' on between us, let's hold on to it. Don't throw me away, Francine. Don't do that."

"It's not only you."

"What then?"

"It's me, and Jody, what happened with Warren."

A protective shade drew down over his eyes. "Warren ain't been convicted of a thing. Jody can't say for sure it was Warren, you told me so yourself."

"I keep thinkin' it is him, Lonnie. I can't help it. That other girl, that Inez Macklin. Goforth says Warren did her, jumped her, just like he did Jody and—"

"No, dammit! You ain't gonna take the word of some cheap nigger over my brother's. You ain't gonna blame me for all this mess! You ain't—"

She touched his hand and he fell silent. "Don't you see, it doesn't matter, whether Warren was the one or not. She and me, we've never been real tight the way a mother and child's supposed to be. Sometimes she looks at me like I was some stranger off'n the street. But I am her natural momma and if there is any way for me to help my girl I want to do it. There's all that pain in her, my only child. Every time she walks downtown now folks stop and watch her like it was her done some terrible wrong thing. But she ain't, she ain't."

"It's got nothin' to do with you 'n' me."

"Can't you see, man? Got everything to do with you 'n' me. Jody's my baby and when she hurts, I hurt for her. Can you understand that?"

"Francine, there's so much feeling in me for you, more than I ever had before for anybody."

She felt her resolve slipping and stood against it. "I feel for you, Lonnie, but I can't get what happened to Jody out of my head and that brings me 'round to Warren again."

"Damn!" he said. "Damn it!"

"You can't turn you back on your brother any more'n I can on Jody."

"I thought we would get married," he said softly. "Make our own family, make a good life."

"Oh, Lordy. I am sorely tempted, yes I am. But I ain't goin' to give in." She stood up. "Take care of yourself, Lonnie."

"Don't do this to me," he said to her retreating back. "Don't do this to me. . . ."

* * *

Dorr Seely visited Duke Venable in his office. They shook hands and made small talk. "I hear good things about this crusade of yours, Reverend. You sure got a way on the television. Look like some kind of a movie actor, you do. Remember Randolph Scott? Fine rugged man, fine actor. Remind me of Randolph Scott, you do. And you sure do come on somethin' fierce."

"The Tenth Crusade is attracting a great deal of national attention," said Seely. "I been checking out like-minded folks with a view toward putting together a Christian Coalition for the advancement of our mutual political and spiritual goals, if you follow my meaning."

"Not sure that I do."

"What we're aiming at, Duke, is to use the ballot box against the godless humans that have infected this country, to turn America and Americans back to Christ Jesus and a righteous way of living."

"Sounds good to me."

"We are all sinners."

"Can't argue with that."

"Jesus loves every one of us," said Seely.

"I'll say amen to that."

"Glad to see we are in accord, Duke." Seely smiled a humorless little smile and inspected the other man gravely. "Folks say in King of Heaven when there's a problem, go see Duke Venable."

All Venable's senses were alerted. Any favors asked for strengthened his hand. Any favor granted made him more secure. He decided to let Seely know the extent of his power and his influence, to make clear that no secrets existed from Duke Venable.

"You referrin' to those little meets of your'n out at the Triple X Mo-tel?" He waited.

Seely hardly flinched. "You're good, Duke, very good."

"I try my best, Dorr. Folks do enjoy tellin' me things. Now about this problem?"

"The girl is pregnant."

"Any possiblity of making a case for it being the result of that rape?"

"Not very likely from what I'm told by the doctors."

"Damn fool thing for you to do. Been messin' around with that girl for more'n two years. Only fifteen years old back then, that's all she was. Should've been scared off back then for your own good. Okay. You want an abortion arranged?"

"The girl refused flat out."

"You asked?"

"I did. Cussed me out something outrageous, she did. Offered to set her up with a stand-in husband and that really set her off. Heaved her school books at my head. She means to have the child."

"In this town? A bastard kid, that ain't goin' to sit well with folks."

"She means to name me as the father."

"That would certainly stir the kettle up. Not a very good idea."

"I told her so."

"What about leavin' town, settlin' elsewhere?"

"By the time I mentioned that she was wailing and howling so much she didn't hear me at all."

"So you came to me?"

"To the man who solves problems."

"You want me to take over from here?"

"I would certainly appreciate it and so would the man up on The Hill. He's behind our crusade one hundred and fifty percent, you know."

"I'll handle it."

Seely rose. "Appreciate it, Sheriff."

"Don't you want to know how?"

"I guess not."

Venable chuckled behind his fat lips. "Didn't think you would. Of course, you owe me, Dorr."

"Whatever you want, whenever you want," said Seely. "Just say the word."

"Depend on it, Dorr. I will. . . .

Lonnie Peden sat alone halfway up the bleacher seats along the third baseline of the county baseball field out on Mill Pond Road. Frustrated and bitter, he refused to accept as final Francine's decision. He swore aloud and slammed a fist into his other hand. His feelings for Francine ran strong and deep. He had exposed himself to her as he had to no other woman, revealing his weaknesses, his fears.

And it had worked against him. He tried to remember if any other woman had ever rejected him; not one single time. For a while, he considered going back to her, trying again, forcing her to see what a mistake she was making.

He rejected that notion. No way he would put himself on the line again, let her mock him, make him look bad. He had offered her her last best chance, let her suffer the consequences.

He stood up and looked at his watch. Dammittohell, where was the man? He had planned on making another run tonight, pick up a load of Canadian whiskey. 'Course, it could wait a night or so. His private storehouse was pretty well filled up and there was no all-fired rush to get more.

Behind the bleachers, a car drew up, and heavy footsteps came his way. He sat back down and lit a cigarette, elbows on the bench behind him. He blew smoke at the high black speckled sky, making a mighty effort to appear laid back, under no stress.

Duke Venable came into sight. He located Lonnie, and came on. Slow moving, he managed to look bigger in the night, more menacing than behind his desk.

"Evenin', Sheriff."

"Evenin', Lonnie." Breathing hard from the climb up the risers, Venable lowered himself to a bench a few feet away. "Nice night, ain't it?"

"Yes, it is." Lonnie felt constrained to be polite and cautious around the sheriff, careful to defer to the big man's moods and desires. From Duke's office flowed a good many of the rewards available to people like himself and he had no wish to undercut his position.

"Sorry to keep you waitin'. Business."

"No sweat, Sheriff."

"Been workin' on those folks tried to hijack you, Lonnie. The truck was stole and that boy you bought your liquor from seems to have disappeared."

"Don't amount to much anymore, I guess."

"Does to me. Can't tolerate outsiders movin' into my territory, stealin' my goods, roughin' up my help. How's it look

I let it slide? Bad is how, real bad. Nosirree, I'll find those people and squash 'em flat, make 'em know it. And I got to tell you, boy. I do not take kindly to you free lancin' thataway. I'd be obliged you keep from doin' it even a itty-bitty little bit from now on."

"It won't happen again, Sheriff."

"Better not."

Lonnie straightened up and flipped his cigarette away. There was an edge to the sheriff's voice he didn't like. He wondered again, this time with considerable trepidation, why he'd been called here.

"Anythin' you want, Duke, you just say the word."

Venable looked at him out of those squinty eyes and Lonnie felt suddenly afraid and insignificant, made smaller in every way under that intense scrutiny.

"I am goin' to tell you about a certain situation that exists with a certain individual who is very important to King of Heaven, very important to me. This fella, well, he had an itch for a certain young lady and started off playin' games with her in motel rooms and the like. . . ."

Lonnie laughed. This was familiar ground and his confidence came rushing back. "Man, I know the feelin'. Ain't nothin' like a taste of sweet young pussy to clear the pipes."

Venable was not amused. "Point is, this young woman went and got herself in a family way."

"No problem, Duke. I can carry her up to Atlanta and get her cleaned out good and proper and legal. No sweat."

"Sure you can and so can just about anybody else cares to do it. Only the lady ain't havin' none of it. No abortion. Insists on havin' the baby. . . ."

"Well—"

"This certain individual is married."

"She means to make trouble?"

"I'd say so. Big trouble. There is no way she can be allowed to do that, Lonnie. No way."

"How do you aim to stop her?"

Venable brought his eyes back to Lonnie and Lonnie felt sweat break across his shoulder, trickle down the hollow of his back. He shuddered and grew cold.

"What would you suggest, Lonnie?"

"Me?"

"Best thing for us all would be if the girl just up and left town."

"Will she do that?"

Venable went on without pause. "Young girls leave small towns every day. Never cause a ripple. Never missed. No fuss. No bother. They go, they disappear, never heard of again. Gone without a trace. Ain't that so, boy?"

A churning emptiness came into Lonnie's belly and his mind raced wildly. "What are you askin' me to do, Duke?"

" 'Anythin' you want, Duke, you just say the word.' That is what *you* said, Lonnie. That is what *you* meant, ain't it?"

"Well. Yes."

"And you, a man of your word, are beholden to me in a number of ways. Which brings your brother to mind. . . ."

"Warren?"

"A lot of folks are mighty uneasy about him bein' out on bail, about him maybe gettin' the charges reduced, gettin' off too light. You ever consider that, Lonnie?"

"He's just a baby, Sheriff."

"Not so babyish he can't work over ladies and men alike. Not so babyish he can't rape 'em and rob 'em. I'd say your baby brother presents a clear and present danger to the community, like they say. Warren may have to take a long, hard fall for his crimes."

"That'd just about wipe out my momma, Sheriff."

"Livin' is a matter of choices, boy. Lesser of the evils every time. Don't you agree? Sure, you do. You're smart, you been around, you won some and you lost some. Big football hero like you, you know all about adaptin', makin' the best of things. If you can't go through 'em you go aroun' 'em, ain't that a fact, Lonnie?"

Lonnie found it difficult to talk. "I . . . can't . . ."

Venable started to get up. "You know anything about hard time? That baby brother of your'n, pretty as he is, he'd be fresh meat to all that rough trade in the slammer." The big man's laughter was harsh and lifeless. "Those boys will ream him out in every hole he's got, sure as pigs eat shit they will. See you aroun', Lonnie."

"Hold on. . . ."

"You got somethin' to say to me?"

"I never killed anybody."

"Killin'? I ever say that word to you? No, I did not. Don't say that word to me."

Venable shoved himself up to his feet, grunting at the effort. "Boy, maybe I made a mistake takin' you into my confidence about the problems of a certain highly placed individual here in King of Heaven. Maybe I overrated you. Maybe I figured you for more of a man than you are."

"I'm as much man as I have to be," Lonnie said quickly.

"Whatever you say. That hijackin', your bad attitude about things, maybe we just ought to roll up our little arrangement and call it quits. . . ."

"No, please."

"You'll find some way to make a livin'. There's lots of things an ex-jock like you can do, ain't that so, boy?"

"If I go along, where would I—?"

"Far away from here is where. A smart boy would get aholt of a power boat and go out into the Gulf with his passenger, maybe for a hundred miles or more. Some place deep and solitary. Or back in some swamp down south of here, far south. Ain't for me to dictate how a man spends his time, where he wants to take a holiday."

"If I do . . . Warren . . ."

"Like they say, one hand washes the other."

"And what about after, when you retire, Duke?"

"Nothin' changes. One good man follows another. Life goes accordin' to plan, everythin' smooth and easy, friendly arrangements that are good for folks, good for the county, you can depend on me," Venable ended with a thin smile.

Lonnie braced himself. "All right, I'll do it."

"Well, good," Venable said drily.

"Who? Who is it?"

Venable told him with a certain amount of derisive satisfaction in his voice.

# CHAPTER
## 26
---

THE HOUSE WAS gloomy and still when Francine came home. She brewed a pot of tea and carried it on a tray to her room where she undressed and ran a tub. She needed time to unwind, to examine the conflicting thoughts and emotions she was experiencing.

A small sound caught her attention and she donned a robe and went out into the hallway that separated her room from the rest of the modest house. There it was again. She went to Jody's room, opened the door, and saw her daughter curled up on her bed sobbing. She touched the girl and Jody jerked away to the far side of the bed.

Francine brought a box of tissues out of the bathroom but Jody refused them with one quick shake of her head. She sat up snuffling, face streaked and her eyes swollen.

"There's nothin' wrong with cryin'," she said in defiance.

"Nope, nothin'." Francine felt the distance between them as never before, mother and daughter connected by a great deal of feeling and mutual need, and eighteen years of living together. Yet separated by differences of temperament and experience and the times in which each of them had been young. "Can't we talk, Jody?"

"We never talked," Jody said. "Not about anything that mattered, Momma."

"Is that true?"

Jody nodded vigorously.

Francine considered; she'd been mother and father to the girl, cook and breadwinner, and at the same time trying to squeeze out a dollop of pleasure for herself here and there. "I'm sorry," she said.

"What's troublin' me isn't your fault."

"Something happen at school?"

Jody stared at her mother as if she were an incomprehensible alien. She reached for a tissue.

"Is it about that night on the beach?"

"I won't ever forget it, I won't ever stop hatin' that boy, but I can live with it."

"I ain't goin' to see Lonnie anymore, I told him so."

"Because of Warren? I can't say for sure it was Warren. Because of what happened to me?"

Francine moved as if to embrace Jody, then checked herself, stiffened in place. She longed to weep with the girl over their separate failures and pain, the disappointments of their lives; she could not. She shook her head as if to clear it. "Guess it was for myself only," she said, the words echoing inside her head as if it were the voice of her own mother, harsh and flat, condemnatory. "Time is what does you dirt," she said sadly. "Creeps up on you and turns you middle-aged and on the other side of life before you even known it's happenin' to you. How'd it happen? How'd I get here so quick? Where'd the best part of my life go to? There you are—one day a young girl loaded up with dreams and hopes and all at once turned into a grown woman with a daughter who is a woman, too. Where did all the time go?"

A faint smile lifted the corners of her mouth, the full upper lip pushing forward in a vain attempt to conceal her teeth. "Lonnie and me—hell and damnation, no way that was goin' to turn into a good thing. Too much keepin' us apart as it is, too many gaps that can't be bridged over. Aw, shoot, things work out for the best mostly. Ain't that right, Jody?"

A smoldering anger fixed Jody's eyes in a resentful glare, stiffened the clean young lines of her face. "Oh, Momma, you just don't understand."

"I'm tryin', honey. I'm honesttoGod tryin'. Only there's a big difference between tryin' and gettin' it done. I always wanted to be different than my momma was, smarter about makin' money and work and such. Doesn't seem I am, though. She made a botch of her marriage and so did I. She lived with hurt and regret every day of her life, flittin' from one man to the next one, and so have I. She wanted more for me than she could give, I see that now, same as I want more and better for you, honey."

Jody straightened up, braced for attack, defiant. "Does that mean I have to pay the price, for you and me both?"

"I don't know what you're sayin' to me."

"I," Jody said in a low, intense voice, "am goin' to have a baby...."

Francine rose slowly, all joints locked, a weakness in her middle. Then a wave of dizziness hit her and she sat back down, her movements awkward as if controlled by an inept puppeteer. "No," she bit off, head shaking from side to side. "No, dammit, no. No."

"I don't like it any better than you do."

"I built a place for myself in this town. A pretty good business. A decent life. Now this. I ain't goin' to let you spoil it for me, young lady. I just ain't going to let you do that. Not now, not after all this time, not after all the hard times. No, no, no..."

The phone kept ringing and Kate confronted it stubbornly, refusing to respond. The more it rang the more her resolve softened. Finally she picked it up. It was her mother.

"How are you, Katherine?"

Why this call?

What occasion had Kate failed to remember and properly commemorate? What lapse of good taste and daughterly concern had she displayed? Where had she gone wrong again?

"I was going to call *you*," she said, throwing up the lie as her initial defense.

"How are you, dear?" her mother said again.

"How are *you*?"

"Well enough, all things considered."

The tide of guilt began to flow. "Is something wrong? Are you ill?"

"As good as can be expected."

"Do you need something? Some money? I might be able to send you a few extra dollars this month."

"You do whatever you think best, dear. You always do. At least, I hope you do."

What did she mean by that? Kate scanned the littered landscape of her recent past for evidence of her apparent fall from maternal grace. "Mother, I don't know what you mean."

"Please, Katherine. Must you take that snippy tone of voice with me? After all, I am your mother."

"Sorry, I didn't mean—"

"You always were a rather curt child. Getting you to obey the rules of good manners was a difficult task for your father and me, God bless his soul."

"Mother, what is it?"

"Your father was a marvelous man. Clean and decent in mind and body. Not once, not one single time in all the years of our marriage did he use bad language. The man was a saint. Never an obscenity, and certainly he never blasphemed. A fine man, upstanding, a credit to us all. He lived and he died in the service of Christ Jesus. But you, Kate, leaving home the way you did, you gave your father and me a great deal of grief. You always gave more grief than joy, but that's all right. We understood. It was your life. Going to New York, becoming an actress, never having a family . . ."

Kate experienced a quick thrust backward into impotence and frustration, made infantile and dependent.

"Mother, what has upset you? Why are you scolding me?"

"I never scold. That has never been my mode of expression. Though I confess, I am troubled by your behavior."

"My behavior?"

"Coyness at your age doesn't become you, Katherine. Cute

and coy and devious, pretense; these have always been your ways. I am talking about that nasty, filthy play of yours."

Kate's knees gave way and she came down heavily on the edge of her bed. This woman she had known all her life. The woman living in Corpus Christi, hundreds of miles away and even farther in experience and understanding and perception of life. This woman of eighty who survived with fraudulent memories of a world that was as she had wanted it to be, of an America that had existed only in myth and in legend, a woman garbed in sourness and petulance and rancor.

"Who have you been talking to, Mother?"

"Makes no never-mind. In the name of everything that's holy you have got to strike the offending language out of that play. Folks are up in arms over what you're doing, even out here in Corpus they are. Ministers giving sermons, editorials in the newspapers. They are saying you are contributing to the downfall of our youth."

She felt despair and giddiness. Pain and disbelief pricked at her. She opened her mouth to speak and no words came out. None could meet the challenge. None would do at all.

"I just can not believe that a woman raised as fundamentally sound and moral as you were raised could go wrong. But clearly Satan has worked his wiles on you. Oh, Katherine, I am ashamed, and afraid for your immortal spirit. Kick and scratch the way your daddy would've done, girl. Fight back against the Powers of Darkness, girl. Do the bidding of the One True God and climb back up on the straight and narrow and—"

"*Mother!*" She screamed it out.

"No need to shout." Said with calm indignation. And a great deal of hurt. "After all, I am your mother."

"Who called you?"

"Didn't say anyone called."

"Tell me."

"I will do nothing of the kind. Listen to me, girl. Do the right thing. Make that play a proper vehicle for the ears of young Christians. Fulfill your obligations as a God-fearing, church-going Christian teacher."

"I haven't been to church in more than twenty years."

"It shames me to hear you admit it."

"I don't believe, I haven't believed. . . ."

"Don't say such things. Wipe evil out of your life, Katherine, the way your father in Heaven wants you to do. Listen to your conscience and the voice of your father speaking to you. Listen to me, dear. Cleanse your heart and do right. Empty your mind of filth. Bare your soul to Christ Jesus and be redeemed. Come back to your beginnings and be saved. . . ."

"Oh, Mother."

"You have always been a disappointment to me, Katherine. As a child you were rebellious, troublesome, obstinate. You defied me and you opposed your father. You painted your face and gave us cause to regret having delivered you into the world. All your strange ideas, your wild notions, your unacceptable language. You *embarrassed* us. A minister's daughter acting the way you did. Going off to New York, becoming an actress, doing God alone knows what! You disappointed your father. He died disappointed and sick at heart. I always hoped time would make you wiser and more agreeable, softer and easier to love. I was wrong. You are no less demanding and willful and arrogant. No less selfish than you were as a child. Oh, you are a continuing burden to me, the Cross I will carry to my grave. . . ."

The phone went dead. A muddy flood of emotion transfixed her, left her without energy or comprehension. Her hand trembled as she dropped the phone back into its cradle.

It rang almost at once. She stared at it in trepidation, mesmerized by the power and the poison it was capable of transmitting. She raised it to her ear tentatively, and a thin voice said her name.

"Kate? You there, Kate? Listen to me. We are gonna get you, sugar, ride you out of town on a rail. Shove a burnin' branch up your filth hole. Teach you once and for all what blaspheming our Lord gets you. Time's run out for you. We are comin' to get you right now. *Right now!*"

She fled the apartment, desperate to escape the hatred that came at her from every point of the compass. She came panting up to her car and blinked in disbelief. There it stood: the tires flat, all four of them, slashed with a sharp instrument. And on the hood in shining red paint were two words: COMMIE CUNT.

# CHAPTER
## 27

IT WAS LATE on a Sunday afternoon when they came together in Mr. Nolan's office in the otherwise deserted Gault Office Building at the end of Frontage Street. Outside the sun had begun its descent into the Gulf, dispatching long, graceful shadows over King of Heaven. On the bandstand in Courthouse Square, the American Legion Brass Band was playing a medley of George M. Cohan tunes, a Sunday ritual all year long, plus the Fourth of July, Labor Day and on every Presidential Election Day. The pounding of the bass drum penetrated into Mr. Nolan's office, jangled his already frazzled nerves.

"I ain't goin' to have it!" he insisted in a rising voice, as if trying to drown out the band. I just ain't goin' to have it!"

"But Mr. Nolan, the transaction's been completed." The County Executive was slender and precise in a gray suit and a complexion that matched. He swiveled his eyes over to Duke Venable who looked past him, on to Wesley Gault, with a faintly supercilious expression on his handsome face, and finally back to Mr. Nolan. "What can I do about it?"

Mr. Nolan clicked his teeth, causing Wesley to remember

Papa James. He vowed that he would never allow himself to become fat and ugly, or old and feeble and weak in the head. It occurred to him that he was enjoying the County Executive's distress and decided to add to it.

"There's the Planning and Zoning Board," he said.

The County Executive turned a shade grayer. His eyes were washed out, without color or definition, the look of fog coming in off the Gulf, the look of imminent death. "But the Board approved the sale of Wing Farms to Henderson Development. There was no lawful means of blocking the sale."

"Change the law," Wesley suggested.

Mr. Nolan beamed at his son. "That's the way. Ain't no point in having a P and Z that can't do what has to be done. You heard Wesley, change the law."

"But how?" The County Executive couldn't clear the mist out of his ordinarily competent brain. It slowed the electrical impulses, clogged the pockets of knowledge, deadened his normal response time. He began to stutter.

"Bet you've got a way, Wesley," Duke Venable prompted. He was enjoying himself hugely, his presence a gesture, the majesty of the law in all it monumental and terrifying physical proportions.

"Matter of fact, I have," Wesley said. He took pleasure in the unusual attention he was getting.

"Well," Mr. Nolan said with considerable impatience. "Let's have it, boy."

"That's multiple dwelling zoning out there past The Bottoms. Only place in the county is. Goes against the entire history and tradition and philosophy of Tokeneke. Means more services to more people with a diminishment of tax revenues. . . ."

"There you are," Mr. Nolan said.

"You're goin' strong," Venable said.

The County Executive remained silent.

Wesley went on. "Put a hold on the filing of the subdivision. Call the P and Z into emergency session. Today. Tonight. Get the Health Department to condemn the preliminary building plans."

"On what grounds?"

"Inadequate sewers. Faulty drainage. Shortfall of social and other public services. Insufficient water pressure would create fire hazards. No roads. No public utilities. The tax structure must be examined and—"

"They'll sue. They'll go to court."

"And rezone the entire property."

"What the hell you talkin' about, boy?"

"Ten-acre zoning, Daddy. Only ones can afford ten-acre divisions work for Gault Enterprises. White and right, Daddy."

Mr. Nolan rubbed his big belly. "White and right, the way to go. Y'all heard the boy, get on it. Now. At once. Immediately."

"But—"

"Buts ain't worth diddly to me. Not gonna have niggers and white trash movin' into this side of the river, hear. Not gonna have nothin' in the county go against my wishes. . . ."

"The Federal Government is involved. There are subsidies and tax abatements and—"

"There you are. Well, I won't have none of it. Not the Feds, not unions, not Civil Rights not Human Rights nor Rights of Women and Gay Rights and all the rest of that horse manure. You sure about what you're sayin', Wesley?"

"Worth a try, ain't it?"

"Hell, yes, it is. Do it, Mr. County Executive. Do it or get off the job. Am I making myself clear?"

"I'll get on it right away, sir."

"You do that. Too much backin' and fillin' goin' on around here. Trouble is Papa James was old and stuck on those vitamins and laxatives of his 'stead of tendin' to business. Well, those days are over. We lost our clout up at the capital in Tallahassee and in Washington, D. C. Gonna put that right again. You, Wesley, maybe you are right and you don't belong in the business. Maybe you ought to get out of King of Heaven. What would you say to Washington, D. C.? What would you say to the Senate of the United States?"

Wesley was unable to respond.

Mr. Nolan chuckled and shifted his great bulk around. "Well, you consider that, my boy. And consider this—how is it goin' to look for a Senator of the United States of America to be mixed up with some spoiled actress from New York City? You give it your best thinkin' and when you have figured it all out you come back to me and say what it is you'd like to do. You hear me, boy?"

Wesley, overwhelmed by what he'd just been offered, and not trusting himself to speak, nodded once. It was enough.

She said, "I'm sorry."

"It's not your fault."

But it was, she wanted to insist. A woman's function was to cater to a man, to please him, to transform herself into the loving creature he desired and needed. How long since such thoughts had occupied her mind? Not since those early days in New York, days when she had come to sense and to understand her value as a human being, and as a woman. A value never given her by her parents or her life with them on the evangelical trail. She experienced a rush of resentment toward Wesley, toward everyone and everything that had moved her backwards toward her timorous past.

"This is the first time," he said.

The first time they had been unable to complete what they had begun. Her resentment increased, turned swiftly to indifference. Go away, she commanded silently; his presence forced her to confront her shortcomings. She needed to be by herself.

"At my age," he said, "that's a real shocker."

And what about my age, she asked in the privacy of her mind. A middle-aged woman thickening through the waist, with wrinkles and breasts that had begun to sag.

"It doesn't bother me," he said. "It's always been good between us, best I've ever had."

"You haven't been hurt enough," she said without feeling.

"We're all damaged goods."

"Goods?" she said. Objects was what he meant. Pieces of animated flesh designed to provide him with comfort and pleasure.

"I love you anyway," he said.

"Despite my failure to bring you to climax? How romantic you are, Wesley, still untouched by this outrageous existence of ours."

"Why outrageous?"

"We have upset the delicate balance of this good and sensitive community, haven't you noticed?"

"You're being too sensitive."

"Am I? Threatening phone calls, a trial by the Lord High Inquisitor and his college of secular cardinals, my livelihood in jeopardy."

"Your imagination is runnin' wild."

"Is it? Did I tell you that dear Dr. Moody has canceled my play? Ask yourself why I am in this bed slavering over your cute little cock when I am supposed to be at the theater. Do you think I have retired from life in order to be eternally in your sexual thrall? Well, think again, mister. The Indians are on the warpath and I am General Custer...."

He sat up and lit a cigarette. "Why so stiff-necked?"

"Because I can't make myself surrender to these know-nothings. I don't want to. I can't do it and live with myself. How about *that?* A stand on principle at my age and from someone who's never stood for anything. Up to now I've been a moral straw-in-the-wind." A biting laugh seeped out of her.

"Under the circumstances, you can't blame Moody for closing the play."

"That's just it, I do blame him."

"You should have fought him, then."

She looked at him in disbelief. "I argued my position. I pointed out the issues involved: art for art's sake, freedom of speech, freedom of individual conscience, academic freedom, one or two other freedoms that escape me at the moment."

"It did no good?"

"No good at all. Dr. Moody closed the case with a most telling argument. I quote him in full—'I have never been accepted by the people who control this county, and now I'm a knight in shining armor riding out front in their crusade. I like the attention. I want the rewards that are sure to come my way. I intend to keep it that way.'"

"What's he talking about? What crusade?"

"The Tenth Crusade. Dorr Seely's high-minded legions dragooned into battling for truth and justice among the heathen, namely people like me. Good old Seely, he and his boys are going to nail us bad guys up on the cross and it begins to look like I'm victim number one."

"You're bein' overly dramatic, I fear."

"I am in serious trouble, Wesley."

"Tell me how to help."

"It helps if you laugh," she said, "but not at all funny. It's too late to help. They need a scapegoat and I'm it. I wasn't smart enough to realize what was going on earlier. They want me to stand firm. That way they can turn it into a political and moral circus. Next they'll fire me."

"They can't do that."

"Oh, they'll find a way. I'll insist that my contract holds and they'll come down on me with all the finesse of a rampaging bull elephant."

He looked at her as if looking at a stranger.

"There was an editorial in the school newspaper today. No mention of me by name. But no mistaking who they had in mind. Twice in the last few days I've been jostled and groped on campus. My fanny squeezed, my boobs pinched. The first time it happened, I just stood there not believing it and do you know what this exemplary Christian youth did? He laughed, and kept stroking my ass. The second time, I cried. That got rid of him, all right. Men can handle insult or anger, but never tears. Tears diminish their manhood in some strange, wet way. Isn't that odd?"

"The bastards. . . ."

"The best and the brightest America has to offer, to coin a phrase. The product of a true Christian education in cracker-land. One of the best young persons in King of Heaven, as Dr. Moody might so elegantly put it."

"I won't stand for it," Wesley said, beginning to dress himself.

"My hero. . . ."

"I mean it."

"Of course you do. What will you do?"

"I'll talk to my father. He'll know what to do. He'll stop it. You'll be all right, you'll see."

"Oh, Wesley, all right is what I'm never going to be, not any more. And neither will you. . . ."

# CHAPTER
## 28

"NOBODY ASKED YOU here, Deputy."

"You hung up the telephone when I called."

"Seems like you didn't get the message."

"I ain't about to turn my back on you."

"Ain't you that's doin' the turnin', it's me."

She went through the small living room into the bedroom and he went after her. On the bed, a partially packed suitcase. It all came back to him out of some zone of his mind where Charlene would always exist; and in some unfocused way Charlene and Inez dissolved into one, brought into alignment by his shifting needs, and the simmering corner of possiblity where his dreams were stored. Done once, done twice.

"You can't leave," he said.

"There's nothin' but trouble for me here."

"There's your job."

"I gave it up."

"And me?"

"You, too, Deputy. I gave up on you, too."

"Women give up easily on me."

She looked up at him, pain holding her features in place. "Not so easily, Deputy. It wasn't long with us but it was intense and, you got to admit, full of happenings."

He answered her grin with one of his own, rueful and quick, and took a step toward her.

She held up one hand. "Uh-uh. You are a handsome devil, but no. No, thanks."

"You'll be comin' back?"

"That business out at the lake, that was just the tip of it. There's too much between us, holdin' us apart. A lot of stuff that went down before we ever met each other, before either of us were born. No, I ain't comin' back."

"We can change the ways things are. We'll get married, go to New York, California if you like. Where nobody knows us, start all over again."

"Weddin' bells and kids, all of it?"

He ignored the sarcasm. "All of it."

"A nice house with a green lawn in a quiet suburb?"

"If that's what you want." His desperation mounted; to lose her now would leave him depleted, desperate and lonely in a way he had never before been lonely. Lonely and afraid of what he might become and how he might act. She was, he wanted to tell her, his last chance to hold on to the man he'd always imagined himself to be.

She looked at him for a long time and somewhere behind her eyes something moved and was altered profoundly and he held out some hope that she would change her mind. "It's what I want all right."

"Without you," he said, unable to stop himself, "there's no case. You're the only witness we've got."

She laughed, laughed at him, and the steely glint of resolve came flowing back into those dark eyes, set in place with the permanence of concrete.

"The ultimate cop's argument. Can't be sure what's got you most hot, me or bustin' Warren. Well, that's all right. I can live with that, if you can."

"Don't let that little bastard get away with it. Don't do that."

"Just you watch me."

"Why?"

"Okay, I'll spell it out. Because I am scared is why. Because I have had my belly full up with this business, and with you, too. Because the man came around and said there was two ways for me to leave town—hard or easy. Hard was to wake up with a load of buckshot in the back of the head some dark night. Easy was the bus out of town. He had an envelope with bus fare in it. Five thousand dollars' worth."

"You took the money?"

"My momma didn't raise no fool."

"Who was it?"

"Let it go, Billy. Oh, damn, for a while back there I made believe we was goin' to pull it off, you and me. Get on real good for a very long time, all the way, even. And do that boy for what he did to me and the others. But it ain't to be.

"They put the dogs on us, Billy. Rough, tough, playin' for real. Take the money or die, the man said to me. Take the money or die. Don't get down on me for takin' it."

"No," he said, the rough voice heavy with resignation and a spreading sense of loss. "No blame attached. Who was it?"

"Let it lay. I don't want harm comin' to you."

"I have to know."

"They'll cut you down, Billy, waste all your goodness."

"Who?"

"You ain't goin' to thank me, you know."

He waited patiently.

"The sheriff," she said finally.

"In person?"

"Big as life. Said it was his last important job for the county. Now what do you think he meant by that?"

"Man is just playin' out the string. Job gets to be a habit and you keep on doin' things the way you've always done 'em." He went to the door. "Maybe you'll change your mind, stay on."

She shook her head. "It's a hard life, ain't it?" she said in that quiet, almost absent way she had.

Under the roguish mustache, his smile was wistful and without hope. "You take care of yourself, hear."

"You the same...."

                                    \*   \*   \*

Goforth found Duke Venable drinking beer and eating pretz-
els and watching "The Ten Commandments" on the television
in his living room. Mrs. Venable, a modestly turned out woman
in her late middle years, offered him refreshments, inquired
about his health, and politely withdrew.

"You seen this picture?" Venable said. He washed a half-
chewed pretzel down with some beer.

"We got to talk, Duke."

"First-rate movin' picture. The Mr. DeMille, he surely did
get his Bible pictures right. Take a seat and next commercial
I'll fill you in on what's happened so far. First part tonight,
continuation tomorrow, eight o'clock. Come over, you want,
we'll watch 'er together. The missus doesn't cotton much to
the television."

"I don't like what's happenin', Duke."

"Hold on, now. This is a good part."

Goforth hit the off button and Charlton Heston faded from
view.

"Hey, now, what you wanna do that for? Put it back on."

"Now, Duke, let's talk now."

The magpie eyes glittered. Venable took a long swallow of
beer and belched. "This goin' take very long?"

"The case against Warren Peden, it's come unravelled."

"From where I sit, it's come undone. I'd say, there ain't
hardly a case at all against the boy."

"I caught him in the act. Witnesses."

"What witnesses is that? Only witness was that nigger gal—
what's her name? I hear she's leavin' town."

"I saw her not ten minutes ago."

Venable frowned and checked his watch. "Should be across
the county line inside of an hour, I'd say."

"You bought her off."

"She tell you that?"

"Five thousand dollars, and a strong threat."

"Not so strong as you might like to think. And there weren't
much hagglin', either. Just laid out the facts of life and she
understood right off. That's one smart nigger gal—what's her
name?"

"There's still Benjamin."

"Ah, Bill, you are beginnin' to disappoint me. I figured you was smarter than that. Benjamin put in his papers, he's retired, at full pension, too. Didn't he tell you, wasn't entitled to much over one half but I talked to this one and did a little deal and got him a full pension. Good ol' boy, Benjamin. Won't have a worry in the world for the rest of his life."

"Scare 'em off and buy 'em off."

"Bein' sheriff has some awesome responsiblities. Main thing is gettin' the job done right. You'll see, you're next up."

"Am I?"

Venable's voice turned flat and chilly. "Long as you keep your nose out of stuff that ain't your business."

"And if I don't?"

"Billy, ever since you worked for Miss Ivy, I've admired the way you do things. From the start you were a good deputy for me. Best I ever had, truth be told. Why spoil it all now? Why put your butt in a sling just when you are about to get your hands onto everythin' you ever wanted?"

"Whose money was it, Duke? The money you gave to Inez?"

"Boy, you are crowdin' into areas that don't concern you a bit."

"Wasn't you put up that kind of money."

Venable shrugged and looked longingly at the television.

"Who wanted Warren to go free?"

"Let's say it was a family matter, that satisfy you?"

"The money came down from The Hill, didn't it?"

"Hit that starter button on the television before you leave, Deputy."

"Why? What can the Pedens do for you? Or for the folks on The Hill?"

"Seems to me I might've made a mistake. Seems to me you ain't near as smart as I figured you to be. Seems to me bein' sheriff may be too much job for you to handle in your present state of mind."

"Tell me about Lonnie. He beholden to you now? None of this smells right to me and I intend to dig into it."

"You are makin' me miss my program. Makin' me damned unhappy."

"There's somethin' else goin' on and I want to know what it is."

"And you will, when the time comes. Now turn the television back on on your way out. Do that little thing for me, hear...."

# CHAPTER
## 29
---

THE FOLLOWING MORNING all Goforth's questions were answered. Summoned to Duke Venable's private office, he found the big man preoccupied and efficiently remote.

"This here's a warrant," he started out. "For a lady name of Kate Fellows."

"The one out at the college?"

"One and the same. Bring her in."

"What's she done?"

"Corrupting the morals of a minor is what. Seduced one of our pure and innocent young locals, carryin' on with the boy, forcin' him to do all that dirty and perverted stuff they do up in New York City, New York."

"Who is the boy?"

"Imagine it, a grown-up woman teacher doin' a boy that-away. Don't seem possible."

Goforth's hand tightened on the warrant. "Who is the boy?"

"Can't depend on nobody any more. Our institutions are collapsin' aroun' us. Ain't nothin' holdin'. Ain't nothin' worth believin' in, is there?"

"Who?" Goforth said in a strained voice.

A mocking grin turned the corners of Venable's small mouth. "It's all there in that paper. Name of Warren Peden." He sat back in his chair and looked steadily at Goforth. "Coincidence, ain't it? That's how it is sometimes. Hardly can tell the good guys from the bad guys these days."

"That's it?"

Venable's expression hardened.

"Bring her in."

"I know about Fellows and young Wesley. Okay, they're after her up on The Hill but this is the only way to do it?"

"Seems so."

"You're the one doin' it, Duke."

"You got this all wrong, Billy. Woman's been messin' aroun' with a underage juvenile. Got to protect our youth. If we ain't willin' to protect our young ain't hardly a righteous people. Ain't that a fact?"

"Man, this smells bad."

Venable squinted slightly. "Do it. Do it by the book. Go out to the campus and serve her, read her her rights, put the cuffs on her, bring her in."

"Cuff her! This ain't no dangerous criminal. There's no need to make her look bad. I can telephone the lady, tell her to come on down by herself. . . ."

"Do it, dammit! Do it my way. Do it now."

"Yes, sir."

He phoned her from a both in Pinky's Ice Cream and Confectionary Parlor on the east side of Courthouse Square. He told her about the warrant.

"I don't want to cause you any embarrassment, Miss Fellows."

"You're going to arrest me?"

"Yes, ma'am. I'll be parked behind the gym building on campus in fifteen minutes. You want to meet me and we'll drive off together. Not likely anybody's goin' to see or care thataway."

"Fifteen minutes," she said, as if trying to make sense out of his words.

"Is that enough time for you?"

"Oh, yes, plenty of time." She thanked him for being so kind before she hung up.

By the time they reached the sheriff's station, she had lapsed into a silent depression, afloat in a thick mist that excluded all sights and sounds. Goforth got her booked and seated on a bench in view of the deputy at the desk. Then he went into the sheriff's office.

"She's outside," he said without expression.

"She give you any trouble?"

"No, no trouble. Woman doesn't know what's happenin' to her."

"You booked her?"

"Yes."

"And put her in back?"

Goforth tried to order his thoughts. "You mean to lock her up?"

Venable contemplated his deputy for a breath or two out of those little eyes. "You are startin' to worry me, boy. 'Course lock her up. She's charged with a criminal act, ain't she?"

"I don't like this, Duke."

"Since when you got to like it? Do what I tell you to do. Lock her up."

Goforth rolled his head as if to loosen the great muscles reaching up the back of his neck. He started to speak, thought better of it. His shoulders slumped and he left without a word.

Outside he motioned for Kate to follow him and led her into the cell block. "I got to lock you up." When she made no response, he reminded her she was entitled by law to a phone call. She said nothing.

"Do you want to call anybody?"

"Who would I call?"

"Your lawyer."

"I don't have a lawyer."

"You'll need one. There must be somebody who can help."

"Maybe," she said at last.

He took her to a telephone and watched her dial with a trembling hand. "Wesley," he heard her say, and now it began to fall into place for him: Wesley Gault, Kate Fellows, Warren

Peden, so much was happening so fast. Like an earthworm under attack, King of Heaven was curling up in a defensive position, taking care of its own. Or at least that part of itself it was concerned with.

"I need your help, Wesley. Oh, Wesley, they've arrested me, they've put me in jail. Help me, Wesley, please help me. . . ." And for the first time since she left home more than twenty years ago, she began to cry.

A deputy she had never seen before escorted her to Duke Venable's office. Her eyes were dry now but her makeup was streaked and she felt she had left behind the region of real events and slid unwittingly, out of control, into the shimmering zone of possiblities. All strength and courage had been voided and she stood before the sheriff with shoulders slumped and eyes downcast.

"Is this the woman?" Venable said brusquely.

A stenographer, seated against the wall, made ready to inscribe whatever was said.

"Hold up your face," Venable commanded.

Her chin rose slowly, a monumental effort.

"Half turn to the right."

She almost stumbled, almost fell.

"Is this the woman?"

"Yes. Yes, that's her, all right."

"We require a positive identification."

"I guess I'd know her, wouldn't I?" There was a leer in the answer.

"What?" Kate managed to get out. Her eyes came round to the tall youth facing her. "Who are you?"

"Ah, Kate, you know me, all right. You know all there is to know about me."

"Shame," came another voice, beyond her line of sight. "Shame, shame, shame."

Kate's eyes skittered over to a middle-aged woman with pinched features. Vaguely familiar, but where from? Her eyes snapped back into place.

"I knew you were bad," the woman said, "but I had no idea you did the handiwork of Satan himself. Shame, shame."

"Who are these people?" she said to no one in particular.

"This is Joelle Peden, Kate," Venable said.

Kate remembered; the Moral Arts Council.

"And for the record—this is Warren Peden, Mrs. Peden's youngest boy."

"My baby!" Mrs. Peden wailed. "Not even sixteen years old. And spoiled forever!"

"What am I accused of?"

"You want it spelled out for you, lady?"

"I never saw this boy before. . . ."

"Liar!" Mrs. Peden said. Her voice spat out the word. "God will punish you in the everlastin' fires of hell."

"Warren?" Venable said.

"Oh, she's the one. She's the one and we've been doin' things for a long time now. She said it would be okay, said it would be fun and make me feel good, made me do things to her I never even knew about before. When I told her it was leavin' me bad feelin's, when I said I wanted to stop she said she'd tell on me, get me into trouble. Old as she was, I was truly scared."

"Why are you doing this to me?" she said to Warren.

"I've got to tell the truth at last, Kate."

"I never saw you before. You know I've never seen you before."

"Aw, gosh, Kate. I know you're upset and all, but that ain't no reason to lie about it. What's done is done and I was hopin' we could still be friends, after all we been to each other."

"I don't know you."

"Aw, Kate—"

"Don't you dare call me Kate. Don't you dare call me Kate. Don't you dare . . ." Her chest began to heave and she gasped noisily for air.

"This boy bein' under the legal age of consent, Miss Fellows," Venable said formally. "You are hereby charged that you performed with him and caused him to perform indecent and perverted sexual acts in contravention of state laws and local codes. Specifically that you did cause him to commit sexual intercourse with you on numerous occasions and in numerous places and did cause him further to commit sodomy

and to perform other as yet unspecified indecent acts of a sexual
manner in places public and private still to be identified
and—"

"Noooo!" She sank to the floor, body in spasm, moaning
and in pain.

"Carry her on back to her cell," Venable said.

"You'll get yours!" Mrs. Peden shouted after her. "You'll
get yours!"

Darkness drifted across King of Heaven and closed in on
the Gulf by the time Wesley came to see her. Without anything
being said, she understood that he had waited for the protective
covering of night before visiting her at the jail. His caution,
his concern for himself, brought home to her as nothing else
had how tenuous her own position was.

They brought her to the interrogation room, a sober green
chamber without windows. It smelled stale and was too warm
and a sense of impending disaster made her anxious and afraid
once more.

"What've you done?" he said, in greeting.

She stared at him as if seeing him for the first time. That
delicate, sensuous mouth now turned weak and tremulous. Those
warm, liquid eyes were unsteady, unable to hold her own. His
fingers plucked at each other and his voice was nasal and thin.

"I haven't done anything, Wesley."

"The charges?"

"I never laid eyes on the boy before."

"They say you seduced him."

She rummaged around the back chambers of her mind, coming upon a vagrant thought. "They are trying to get rid of me."

"Ridiculous. This is some kind of a mistake. What you need
is a lawyer."

"They are using me as a scapegoat, someone to blame."

"Blame? Blame for what? You didn't have anythin' to do
with that boy, did you?"

"I am beginning to see things clearly now," she said. "First
a low-level attempt to get me to change a few lines in the play,
a few words. Then the pressure built up. Charges are made, a
trial conducted to lend a certain insane legitimacy to it all.
Word leaks out that I am corrupting my students and the phone

calls begin, verbal attacks, my car.... And eventually this contrived crime I'm supposed to have committed to certify to what an evil woman I am."

"But you haven't done anything wrong."

"Wrong?" she said again. "No, I don't think so."

"You're not sure?" Alarm flared in him.

"I'm sure."

He was relieved. "You can tell me the truth, you know. You can trust me. I'll understand."

"Your family wants to be rid of me, Wesley. I'm a threat to them, to your marriage, to everyone in this town."

"It's not too late. I'll get a lawyer."

"I don't think so."

"What will you do?"

"The best I can, thank you."

"Anything you want, I'll do for you, Kate. You know that, don't you?"

Her voluptuous mouth turned; without warmth, without hope, hardly a smile. "You can go now, Wesley."

"I want to help." He kept remembering that last conversation with his father—Washington, D. C., the Senate, an exciting future—and put a tight rein on his words. "You just tell me what to do."

"Goodbye, Wesley."


B. J. Moody was disappointed in Kate. "I always held you in high esteem," he told her. "I always believed you were too smart to do anything this sordid. I am disappointed in you, Kate."

They brought him to her cell and they faced each other through the bars. "It's all my fault..." she said. Her voice was lifeless.

"You made your own bed."

"I've had enough," she said.

"I would imagine so."

"I must get out of here."

"You're accused of a very serious crime."

"The charges can be dropped...."

"In return for what?"

"I won't see Wesley Gault again."

"I wonder if anyone cares anymore."

"I'll resign my job at the college."

"You have a contract. . . ."

"I won't hold you to it."

"I don't know. There's the question of the play."

"Oh, yes, the play. I'll say it was all my doing, the play staged in contradiction to your orders."

"You would sign a confession?"

"Sign a confession! Yes, I confess. Everything. Have it typed up and I'll sign it."

"I have always been fond of you, Kate. I'd like to help you, if I can. . . ."

"I'll leave town at once, never come back."

"Perhaps I can talk to some people. . . ."

"The right people?"

"I'll do my best for you."

"Right away, Dr. Moody? Please—"

"There are some phone calls to make, the paperwork taken care of. Perhaps in the morning." He gave her his best smile, part encouragement, part self-satisfaction that he had accomplished what he'd come for. "What will you do now, Kate? Go back to your acting?"

She stared blankly through the bars of the cell as if seeking an answer that never came. In that extended moment she felt only loathing for what she had allowed herself to become, for what she was doing to herself. Nothing else seemed to matter.

A deputy ushered Francine into the cell, then slammed the door shut and strode away. "You didn't have to come," Kate said.

Francine shrugged. "We didn't know each other for very long, or very well. But I decided that there was somethin' between us. That we were friends."

"I appreciate that." Kate indicated the bunk hanging from the wall. "Place isn't decorated the way I'd like, but please sit down."

Francine wrinkled her nose. "I just didn't believe it when they told me you was locked up."

"I'm glad you came. You are my friend."

"I telephoned the school, which is how I found out about

them bustin' you. I got to tell you, I just don't believe it, what they say you did."

"I didn't do anything wrong, but it doesn't seem to matter. A lot of people need a scapegoat and I am it. I guess I've had my run in King of Heaven and now it's finished. In a way it's all my fault, I haven't been very intelligent about the way I've handled my life here. Truth is, I never have been as smart as I might've been."

"Me the same, I reckon. Maybe that's the trouble, none of us is smart enough to deal with the world. You told your family about this?"

Kate shuddered and turned away. "There's only my mother and it would kill her if she found out. No," she quickly amended, with a short bitter laugh. "No, it would only confirm her low opinion of me. It would prove she and my father were always right about me, about how bad I've been, how rebellious and inadequate. My mother and I, we've always existed in two separate realities."

"Oh, Lordy. What is it with mothers and daughters, all that scrappin' and not gettin' on? Times I look at my Jody and the most awful ideas come into my head, like she is my enemy. She's my very own flesh and blood but that don't stop me from wantin' to hurt her. Punish her. What for? What's gone wrong with my own life ain't never been her doin'."

"What's happened to her, it's difficult for everybody concerned."

"Yes, but that's not the whole of it. Fool girl's gone and got herself pregnant."

Kate felt empty suddenly, not able to consider someone else's problems, not wanting to let go of her own anguish, her own fright. She shook her head and raised her chin. "I don't know what to say."

"Not much to say." Francine looked sidelong at her, unsure of how to proceed. "It's why I really came, I got nobody else to talk to."

Kate breathed out. "What are friends for?" she said ruefully. She held Francine's hand. "I don't know if I can help."

"You got a load of troubles all your own."

"Let's talk about Jody."

"Oh, I done a dumb thing. When she told me, about the

baby, I come down on her. Hard. Like it was too much for me, like my own life was comin' round a second time and there was no way I could tolerate goin' through it again. Damn fool girl. No different than I was. Foolin' around when I was fourteen, fifteen years old, thinkin' I was all grown and in control. Until I got caught, caught just like Jody. My momma cussed me out and said it was me got myself into it and it was me had to get myself out. No different than how I talked to Jody."

"What did you do?"

"Back then? What I had to. Found me a colored lady lived out in the country and she did me...."

"An abortion?"

"These days it don't have more meanin' to some girls than gettin' their teeth fixed. It wasn't that way for me. Sometimes I think about that baby all grown up and alive today and I get sick with longin' and teary-eyed. Tremblin' all over. That's why the second time it happened I had the baby...."

"Jody?"

Francine jerked her head in assent.

"But you married her father, so it all turned out okay."

"No. He was a sweet and lovin' boy and used to make me weak in the knees when I was with him. But the damn fool got hisself killed."

"Oh, I am sorry."

"On his way home after spendin' the evenin' with me. One of those slow, easy evenin's full of good stuff. I told him about the baby and he said he was goin' to marry me and we'd have lots of kids together. Then he went and drove hisself right off the road doin' seventy miles an hour into a big ol' tree and that was that. It took considerable gettin' used to, that did."

"That's hard."

"Hard is what life is all about, I reckon. Gettin' hurt and waitin' for the pain to go away so's you can get hurt some more. And now I put my back to my own baby, give her pain. And here I am burdenin' you down with my troubles...."

"What about the boy, Jody's friend?"

"No boy, that one. He's a full-grown man...."

"Will he marry her?"

"He's got a wife of his own. Hypocritical ol' fool, preachin' against the sins of the world and all the time doin' my girl in motels and off in The Bottoms and in the back seat of his car. . . ."

Kate froze in place, trying not to remember herself with Wesley, trying not to feel diminished and used.

"I'd sure like to tell the whole of King of Heaven," Francine was saying. "Let everybody know that Dorr Seely is seducin' young girls and cheatin' on his wife and—"

"*Reverend* Seely!"

"The same."

A vagrant thought fluttered through Kate's mind. "Has this been going on for a long time?"

"More'n two years. Jody was only fifteen the first time she went down with him."

"A preacher," Kate said automatically.

Francine, misunderstanding, spoke with revulsion. "No different than other men, just as raunchy and dirty-minded and set on gettin' their own way."

Kate said slowly, "My father was a preacher. . . ."

"No harm intended," Francine said quickly. "Ain't all the same."

"Always going on about how people should live, preaching love and forgiveness and kindliness and never once, not one single time, did he ever put his arms around me," said Kate. "All those years, and no affection. Not a word to indicate that he loved me or even liked me. Not once did he admire anything I ever did, not once did he tell me that I had done well in school or elsewhere, that I had made him proud. Just what he found wrong with me. And there was so much of that. To him I was inconsiderate. Selfish. Demanding. All wrong . . ."

"And your momma let it happen?"

"My mother was—is—a silly woman and she went along with my father all the way. To this day, she can manipulate me, make me feel incomplete, guilty, less than I know I am. Dammit, why do we do this to our children? And to ourselves?" She twisted around to face Francine. "Don't do it to Jody. Don't turn away from her. Otherwise you'll regret it for the rest of your life."

"Looks like we got a lot in common, you and me."

"Looks like it," said Kate.

Neither of them spoke for a long time, then Francine stood up. "What about you, what's goin' to happen to you?"

Kate filled her lungs with air. "They've offered me a way out, the easy way."

"You goin' to take it?" said Francine.

"I was." Kate smiled a small, sad smile. "Now I don't know. There's so much to think about—what the choices are, what I can deal with . . ."

Goforth came later that night. Eyes motionless, glazed, glinting in the poor light of the cell, the crumpled face grave behind the roguish mustache, watching as if he expected something of her.

"Why?" she said at last. "Can you tell me why they are doing this to me?"

"You happen to be handy is all. What we have here is King of Heaven raisin' its uglier head, and it requires a suitable target."

"And I happened to be convenient."

"Couldn't've worked out better, the way things was."

"But I'm innocent. . . ."

He brushed at the mustache with one knuckled finger. "Of the charges, sure. But neither of us is completely innocent. Both of us got stuff to hide, stuff they can root out and hold against us. Only difference is, I am wearin' this badge and you got very little over on your side."

"They want me to sign a confession."

"That'd ease matters some. . . ."

"They said they'd let me go."

He shook his head. "Not that easy. The way I hear it, first there's your confession. Then they mean to set you up in front of the whole town, out front of the courthouse. They figure to have a good-sized crowd show up to let Reverend Seely do a number on you. Regular show, it looks like. Loudspeakers, TV cameras, the like. You bein' an actress and all, they mean to do a first-rate spectacular special in your honor. . . ."

"But why?"

"Because Seely needs it for that Crusade of his, because

the Gaults need it to make sure everybody knows they still hold the strong hand, and Duke Venable needs it to make sure he has a smooth and secure retirement."

"Isn't there something I can do?"

"No," he said softly, on his way out. "But might be there's somethin' I can do. . . ."

Francine sat in the kitchen of her house, smoking and sipping a Dr. Pepper that had gone flat, trying not to think or to feel, struggling to contain the spreading fear that left her uncertain and unfocused. When she heard the car drive up ouside, she crushed out her cigarette, lit another one and went into the living room. Moments later Jody appeared.

They looked at each other, and Jody said, "Momma, I am leavin'."

"Leavin'?"

"Goin' away from this town. I been doin' a lot of hard thinkin' and for a while back there I wondered if I wouldn't be better off dead, doin' myself and the baby."

"No!" Francine took a step in Jody's direction and the girl backed away, one hand raised protectively. "Don't ever think such things."

"For a while it seemed it was the only choice I had, the way things are. Then I figured I had a better choice, to go off where nobody knows me and have my baby and raise her properly. Oh, I know it's goin' to be hard, but I can do it. I want this baby, I want her to grow up knowin' her momma and knowin' that her momma always wanted her and loves her and—"

"Yes," Francine said. "Yes."

"You believe it's the right decision?"

"What about your career?"

Jody grinned and ducked her head, a girlish gesture, a reminder to Francine of how young her daughter was. "Oh, Momma, ain't goin' to be a career, I reckon I know that now. Guess I've always *suspected* as much. I'm pretty enough, but it don't go much beyond. I mean, I ain't *special*. . . ."

"I think you're special."

"In looks, I mean. And I ain't got much more'n a smidgen of talent, just enough to get by in a backwater like King of

Heaven but hardly enough to make a ripple in a big pond like Broadway. Anyway, no law says a girl's got to be an actress, or whatever, unless she truly wants to. Ain't that a fact, Momma?"

"There's plenty of time for you to think about a *career*, Jody. First things first. There's this baby of yours to take care of. You want this child. . . ."

"Oh, Momma, I do! I do!"

"Then you are goin' to have it. *We* are goin' to have it. I want to help, if you'll have me."

"You mean it?"

"It ain't easy, havin' a child and raisin' it without a father. But it sure does help if you got a grandma nearby willin' to lend a helpin' hand. If you let me, Jody, we'll give the poor little sucker a really righteous welcome into the world, give him a hell of a run at havin' a fine life. . . ."

"Oh, Momma!"

Francine opened her arms and Jody came to her.

"Momma, are you sure?"

"As sure as I've ever been about anything. Now why don't I make us a pot of coffee and we can start makin' plans. Seems to me, there's a whole lot for us to talk about, you and me, one hell of a lot. . . ."

# CHAPTER
## 30

WESLEY WENT HOME. And found Mae-Mae curled up in the big chair with the rolled arms and huge daisies splashed over a bright yellow fabric. She was eating peanuts and drinking Coke over ice, and watching television.

"Hey, Wesley." She never took her eyes away from the screen. She chewed a peanut and drank, dribbling Coke down her chin. She wiped it away with the back of her hand.

"Kate's in jail."

"Well, good," she said. "Dallas," she said, indicating the television. "Honey, I do believe ole J. R.'s about to get what's comin' to him at last."

He watched her watching the television and the slow realization came that Mae-Mae was imbued with many of the qualities he required of a wife. She was perky and pretty, her tastes were simple—even simple-minded—and made small demands on him for attention or understanding.

For the most part, Mae-Mae was merely present, a body and a persona to be ignored most of the time and catered to only on rare occasions. In return, Mae-Mae delivered wifely services as best she could.

The program played out to its conclusion and Mae-Mae switched the set off with a contented sigh. It took so little to please her, Wesley noted. "I certainly do love that show. Have a nice evenin', sugar?"

"Kate Fellows is in jail," he said again.

She looked at him steadily. "I do not believe I care to discuss that awful woman in my very own livin' room, if you don't mind."

"People resent her. She's too sophisticated for them, too experienced, too beautiful."

"What she is is positively evil, that's what she is. Evil."

"Mae-Mae, there are times when you talk like an absolute idiot."

"Don't you call me names, Wesley Gault. I am your wife and to be respected as such. Maybe I am not as clever as some folks, but I have feelings and you have wounded me gravely. Gravely," she repeated, enjoying the sound of the word. "I have made every effort to be a good and faithful wife to you, Wesley Gault, there is no denyin' it. I have tried my best."

"There is no point in arguin'."

He lapsed into a deep silence caused, she assured herself, by his sincere regret and remorse. After all, he had treated her badly for a long time and at last it had been made known to him and he was racked by guilt and a profound desire for atonement. Mae-Mae had never been one to nurse a grudge. Forgive and forget, was her motto. She was overcome by good feelings for her husband and she sat next to him on the sofa. "You always were the best-lookin' boy in the county, Wesley."

He stared straight ahead.

"You should never have allowed yourself to be involved with that sort of a woman. She was bound to betray you."

"I can't believe it," said Wesley.

"You're good, Wesley, and you want to believe the best of people. That woman blinded you to the right road. She was so shrewd, a schemin', plottin' female determined to snatch you away from me and your family."

In so many ways, Kate Fellows had excited and pleased him. She utilized her mind and body with imagination and variety, she was experienced, adventurous, willing to tempt the unknown, to risk new experiences. In the bedroom and out of it, she provided a continuity of satisfaction and pleasure no other woman had offered him. Add to that an underground hint of danger, and ever-present recklessness, a willingness to go one step beyond anything he himself would dare.

Wesley had never fully understood her, was constantly challenged by her in unspoken ways, made afraid by qualities in her he neither possessed nor understood. But his time with her had been wonderful and now it was over. Over? Oh, yes, over. Ended. Terminated. For Kate's sake and for his own. For the salvation of his immortal soul and for the sake of his marriage and his future.

Not that Mae-Mae would ever grow into the woman Kate was. But then Wesley knew that he was not now and never would be man enough to live out his life beside Kate Fellows. She demanded too much, from him, from herself, from life in general. More than he could give, more than he dared to give.

Time to return to the fold. To reclaim his marriage, to abide by the rules and traditions as set forth by Papa James and by Mr. Nolan, by the generations of Gaults who had lived and died up on The Hill. Time to follow in their footsteps and prepare for the day he would take over as head of the family. That was his destiny. That and Mae-Mae.

"I never perceived Kate as evil," he said.

"Of course not, innocent as you are. Women are instinctively attuned to the wicked peregrinations of other females. First time I laid eyes on her, I knew all there was to know. The way she moved her hips when she walked. That garish hair of hers. Those cold green eyes. Sendin' out invitations to poor, helpless men, promisin' secret delights that no decent woman would ever perform."

"Is that the way she is?" Exactly the way, he told himself. And he had known it all along. Enjoyed it, too. But now it was over. Once again he was a Gault, a man of purpose and ambition, able and willing to accept his place in the family, in King of Heaven, in the world.

He thought about Kate, how it was to be with her. Her mind ranged freely in time, touching so many areas, always curious, always surprising, always exciting. He had begun to believe she was too much for him. Too much and too old, the years between them marking more than just time used up. There were fundamental differences, he knew that now. And all that talk of marriage—what madness! Fantasies and illusions; Gault men did not marry women older than themselves, women past the childbearing years, women who were worldly, women who were controversial.

His eyes came round to Mae-Mae. "Daddy's talkin' again about me goin' into politics."

She massaged his chest, slowly opening the buttons of his shirt. "You'd make an ideal public servant." She stroked his stomach, explored his navel.

"Daddy's right, of course. The family needs closer ties up in Washington, D. C. In the Senate of the United States, for example. I believe I might make a first-rate senator."

"You'd be ideal."

"Life could be good, part of the year here, part up north."

"Who knows how far you might go? There's always the White House."

He watched her hands unbuckle his belt, working the zipper of his trousers down. "You'd like bein' wife to the President?"

"I would love it." She brought his penis into view, kissed the swollen pink tip. "Imagine, sugar, me doin' you this way in old Mr. Lincoln's bed." She giggled, eyes rolling up to him. "Anythin', Wesley, anythin' at all, long as you are nice to me."

"Do it," he said thickly.

"I want to have a baby, Wesley."

"Do it."

"A man in public life should have a family."

She had a point. Two children, perhaps—a boy and a girl. Enough to keep her busy, out of his hair.

"All in good time."

"You mean it, sugar?"

"I said it, didn't I? Now do me with your mouth."

"I'm not sure I know how."

"Just think on it. If you had a toy like that, how would you like it done?"

She kissed his penis again and it leaped in response. "Did I hurt you, sugar?"

"Take it in your mouth."

"You won't—"

"What?"

"You know."

"Say it."

"Do it, when I have it in there?"

"Come in your mouth, you mean?"

She made a face. "Uh-huh."

"You can trust me. This time."

"This time?"

"You are goin' to practice until you learn to like it."

"Will I ever. . . ?"

"Like it, you mean?"

"Uh-huh."

"You will."

"And the other?" she asked.

"What about it?"

"You will make me pregnant? All successful politicians are family men. It's what Mr. Nolan wants, it's what Papa James wanted for us."

"Is that right?"

"He used to put his hand on my little titties and give 'em a squeeze and say for me to have sons to suck 'em and make 'em bigger."

"Papa James did that?"

"He sure did."

"And what did you do for him?"

"Why whatever do you mean? Oh, Wesley, what a filthy mind you have!"

A vision of Kate hovering over him came to mind, the sweet, delicate touch of her lips, her tongue, the loving way her hands had aroused his body.

"We'll be so happy, Wesley. We'll divide our time between King of Heaven and Washington. I can make sure you have everythin' you want in your life: a lovin' wife, beautiful children, a fine and suitable home. And after you retire from politics and we come back to King of Heaven to live out the twilight years of our lives we'll have our family and our county and our memories. Oh, sugar, it's goin' to be so good. I can hardly wait. . . ."

"Do it," he said roughly.

"For a little while. Until you're worked up enough to give me a baby. You will try, won't you, Wesley?"

"We'll see. . . ." He watched her narrowly. Her lips were cool and firm, the biting edges of those perfectly matched white teeth scraping against him, eyes clenched to exclude all unwelcome sights, barely breathing lest she inhale the sweaty male scent of him. She was, he reminded himself, everything he didn't want a woman to be and he deserved to live with her for all the days that remained of his life.

# CHAPTER
## 31

HE PERSISTED AND finally she agreed to meet him. He offered to come by the house but she didn't think that was such a good idea.

"Some place where there's people," she said.

"You don't trust me," he said, aware of a deep weariness to the point of not caring if he lived or died. Such ideas were foreign to him, and frightening. Always life had been something to pursue energetically, to live out, to let happen. What had changed, he wondered.

"I can't afford to trust you, Lonnie. Spivey's Drug Store, in ten minutes. You can buy me a soda."

That would put them too close to the sheriff's station, too close to the center of life in King of Heaven, too likely to be seen and recognized. "Make it the Cozy Nook, we can have a drink."

"I'll need a little time."

"Half-hour okay?"

"I'll be there."

The Cozy Nook was a key club half a mile beyond the marina. Rumor said Duke Venable owned the place, but no one seemed to know for sure. Lonnie had been a member, key and all, since he'd begun supplying the place with good booze at a good price. He was waiting in a booth against the back wall when Francine arrived.

She came his way with that free and easy stride, hair worn loose and swinging down across her shoulders, breasts bobbing under her blouse and making him remember how it was to be with her, to love her. He longed to hold her again, to put his hands all over her and hear the little animal sounds she made when aroused.

He rose to greet her but she avoided his kiss and slid into the seat opposite him. "I haven't got much time, Lonnie. What's on your mind?"

"Could be I just wanted to see you."

She frowned and he noticed that she was wearing no makeup. She seemed softer, more approachable, and somehow more desirable than before.

"You look awful good to me, Francine."

"Lonnie, you said you had somethin' to talk about with me?"

A waitress took their drink orders: bourbon and water for Lonnie, a Coke for Francine.

"I can't get you outa my mind," he said.

"Don't tell me that, don't talk about your feelin's or mine. That's all over, between us."

"Why's it have to be? It can be worked out, whatever's in the way. Try hard enough, everythin' can be worked out. I believe that."

"I don't."

"Listen. The minute you showed up here I just knew there was no way I was goin' to let you get outa my life. No way, Francine. No matter what I have to do."

"This ain't no football game. It ain't up to you."

"Listen to me," he said. He swore silently not to get angry, not to let her get away.

The waitress brought their drinks; he waited until she went away.

"I am crazy about you, Francine."

"You been crazy about lots of women before and will again. What did you want to talk to me about, Lonnie?"

"I want us to get married."

The words startled her and she looked into his eyes and saw the fright that was in him, the still adolescent fear of the unknown, and something more. As if he had holed up somewhere inside himself and most of his essential systems no longer functioned. He spoke of love and marriage and being together as if it was a game plan to be plotted out on a blackboard under the careful scrutiny of coaches and teammates who would help him work out his destiny.

"We could make it, Francine, find some happiness together."

"Happiness? I long ago stopped thinkin' about happiness. I don't know what it is. Some time I've gotten exactly what I told myself I wanted and—I wondered, what was it? What was that all about? Mostly something I didn't really need and didn't do me much good at all." She raised her eyes to his. "I am leavin' King of Heaven," she ended quietly.

"Goin' away?" He slurred the words as if trying to bridge an abyss. "For how long?"

"Once and for all. I've put the diner up for sale and I'm on my way."

"But why?"

Tell him or not? She wanted to do the right thing. By Jody, by herself, by Lonnie. But the rights or the wrongs seemed irreconcilable, one against the other. And suddenly right and wrong didn't matter a damn and she knew that the only important thing was *feelings*.

"Jody's goin' to have a baby," she said.

He answered without thinking. "I know."

A swift sadness faded onto her face as if she had peered down the road behind her and at the uncharted course ahead and seeing past and future had terrified her and destroyed all hope.

"You know?" Part question, part accusation, part despair and defeat.

There was no holding back. No dissembling or concealment. No lies to cover the jumble of emotion that spooked him and dragged him down. No way to keep the terrible truth from her.

"They're after Jody."

She recoiled and went pale, quickly took hold of herself. "What are you sayin' to me, Lonnie?"

"You're right to leave. Take the girl and get out of here. Soon, right away, tonight."

"Who is after my baby?"

"She refused to get an abortion," he said flatly. "She refused to cooperate with them. The man asked for help. He got it. They put a contract on Jody. . . ."

"A contract?"

"To waste her," he said. He saw the look of disbelief on her face. "Kill her, dammit! Don't you understand, this is for real. It ain't no game."

It took a while for her to digest it. Then, "It's you, isn't it, Lonnie? You're the one supposed to do my little girl? It's you, ain't it?"

He nodded. "I done a lot in my time I don't want to think about. I blacked out on a whole lifetime of awful behavior, Francine. But no more. There's no way I can do somethin' so terrible to anybody. I just couldn't do it.

"Oh, sure, I've busted up my share of barrooms and beat up on guys and done a lot of wrong things to women, but no more. This thing's been tearin' me up, Francine, turnin' me into some kind of a weird monster. How'd I get here? How'd I become this way? I never aimed to hurt nobody or destroy nothin'. I just started out wantin' to have some fun, get somewhere in my life, make somethin' special outa myself. Man, I surely have made an ungodly mess of things, haven't I?" When she didn't answer, he looked away. "I'll go back to your house with you. Help you pack and see you out of town, out of the county. Nobody's goin' to trouble you while I'm aroun'."

"Why are you doin' this?"

"I told you—I truly do care for you."

She looked steadily at him. "I believe you do and I feel likewise for you, Lonnie. Only it won't change anything."

"The thing is to get you out, safe and sound. You and Jody. Where will you go?"

"That doesn't matter."

"Don't blame you for not sayin'. Just gettin' there is enough. You ready to get started?"

"Doin' this for me and Jody, will you be all right, Lonnie?"

"I can take care of myself."

"You do that, hear. You take good care of yourself."

"You the same."

"Yes. Well. Better get started, I suppose."

"I suppose so."

# CHAPTER
## 32

"THIS IS A special place to me," Goforth said, and took a pull on the beer in his hand.

Next to him on the narrow porch of the small frame house, Benjamin rocked and looked out into the dark. "And to me."

"For the most part, the people are good."

"Good enough, bad enough sometimes. Same as most places, same as always," said Benjamin.

"The thing is, sittin' here this way listenin' to the insects—there is a powerful presence to it. Hear the way they fade in and out, the brittle noises they make."

"What brings you way out here to Northtown, Billy, late as it is?"

"All the years I know'd you, Benjamin. Time to time, we worked together, took a meal together, drank coffee and smoked a cigarette together."

"Mostly out on some country road, in the dark of night, Billy. Mostly like that."

"Guess so. I enjoyed fishin' with you those times, Benjamin."

"Same for me."

"Man like me don't feel right talkin' to just anybody, never did. Seems like you and me could've done a little more with each other, spent a little more time with each other. Wouldn't you say so, Benjamin?"

"Black and white, Billy. Don't pay to press your luck too much in these parts, maybe nowhere else, either."

Goforth pulled steadily on the beer. "Went by her house before I came. Inez is gone, you know, she's gone."

"Oh, she's gone, all right."

"You figure she'll be comin' back, Benjamin?"

"Hard to figure what a human person is likely to do."

"But if you was sayin'?"

"If I was sayin', I'd say she won't be back."

"That's the way I make it out to be. I keep tryin' to put it all together, exactly what happened between Inez and me. I keep waitin' for some lightnin' to strike, some incomplete memory to fall into place and make the puzzle whole."

"I've had my share of incomplete memories," said Benjamin. "Like one of them movie shows you think is so good. You go back a second time and if it was truly as good as you thought you keep bein' surprised by stuff you never even noticed first time 'round. 'Course, sometimes they're not nearly as good."

"If Inez could've found it in her heart to stay we might've worked it out."

"You know better."

"I would've taken care of her."

"You know better'n that, too."

"What happened, Benjamin?"

"It ain't what *happened*, it's what you are, you and her. Too different, too far apart, too much inclined toward different kinds of lives. She wasn't much of a school teacher, in case you didn't know. No better'n I was bein' a deputy."

A vague annoyance took hold of Goforth. He was tired of catering to Benjamin's softness, that playful reluctance to shoulder his own burdens, to take on his own obligations. A set of harsh words came alive in his mouth; he bit them back. "You did your best, Benjamin."

"Just gettin' by. Man grows old and alone, gettin' by is all he can muster up strength enough to do. I disappointed you, Billy. I know it and it distresses me. You come here to give me what-for over not backin' you up with the Peden boy, you go on and do it. I won't like it much but I'll understand. Ah, shoot, Billy. I disappointed myself one hell of a lot more."

Even in the dark, Goforth could see how much Benjamin had aged, the years etched deeply into that leathery black face. A heavy slump in the once strong shoulders. "It's over now," he said, almost to himself. "Not one of us comes out of the job smellin' of French perfume, I'd say."

"I sure wanted to be a good deputy, Billy. Same as Inez wanted to be a good teacher."

When Goforth failed to answer, they sat and listened to the night creatures going about their lives, and drank beer and smoked. "You know where she went, don't you, Benjamin?"

"Said I wouldn't let on. Said wild horses couldn't drag it out of me. Said I wouldn't say, 'specially to you, Billy."

"Never?"

"Not unless she lets me know different first, and that ain't likely. Stop thinkin' about her, man. Flush her out of your system. What you had with that gal is all you are goin' to get."

"Damn," Billy said.

"Double-damn, but there it is."

"It all turns to shit in the end."

"Seems so."

"What's a man to do?"

"What he's made for, as good as he can. The rules they put down out there, just like the walls of a prison. Onliest thing is to find your own rules and live up to 'em so's the work and the rest of your life let you feel good about yourself."

"That's it?"

"That's it."

"Benjamin, boy and man, I've lived and worked in this town. But I ain't got a single friend. Nobody I'm tight with, nobody to say all the things I've got locked inside to, nobody to cry with."

"I know," Benjamin crooned, "I know."

Goforth rested his chin on his fist and his elbow on the arm of the chair he was sitting in, and stared at length into the darkness, as if seeing farther ahead in time than he had ever before been able to see. After a while he shrugged himself back to the present, and to what he had to do.

"They was sayin' about you, Benjamin, sayin' you handed in your papers."

"Time for this old man to retire."

"Retire to where?" said Goforth.

"To right here, is where. This little house. Not much, I admit it, but I hold it dear and it's paid off. I believe I'd be contented to die in this house."

"I own my house."

"That's good."

"I'm not so sure. My wife never liked it much. I never listened to her, never paid much attention to what she wanted. Just bought the place and stuck her out there in the woods. Now she's gone off and I got the house all by my lonesome. That's all it is to me, a house. Not my home. King of Heaven, just a place I happen to work."

"Bein' a peace officer, that matters to you."

"When I was a boy I'd study the deputies struttin' around town their hats squared off on their heads, pieces ridin' high on their big belts, boots polished. Man, they were *heroes*. When I see some boy lookin' at me that way I get all puffed up and proud of myself. Only lately I been wonderin'. Is it me or just the uniform and the gun and the hat. Maybe I'm no different than anybody else doin' a job, earnin' a paycheck, waitin' to take his pension."

"Nobody's ever that sure about hisself, is they? Got to hang in and believe you are doin' right. What is it you come around for, Billy? What is it you expect to find here?"

"Duke Venable's retirin' the end of the year."

"I heard."

"Says the sheriff's star is mine, if I want it."

"Somethin' changed your thinkin'?" said Benjamin.

"All kinds of changes goin' on inside my head, Benjamin." The small room seemed even smaller. He addressed Benjamin. "No way a man can be sheriff and stay straight."

"You just find that out?"

"Is that what I want?" said Goforth. "To be a cop makin' deals, pussyfootin' around the law, breakin' the law, keepin' the appearance of doin' the job when all I'd be doin' is coverin' up?"

"And gettin' rich."

"You think I can handle bein' sheriff?"

"When I was young I was loaded up with ideas and dreams," said Benjamin. "Oh, those dreams, all polished up like they were precious and real. But there was never the breath of life in 'em. Lived inside those dreams for a long time, I did. Tried to turn myself into someone I never was meant to be, just imagined my own self up. But a time came when I had to recognize the truth, man. Made me awful sad to see what other folks saw when they looked at me. You know what I am sayin' to you?"

"I'm thinkin' it's over now." Clouds of anguish swept around the inside of Goforth's skull and muffled voices hammered at him, a lost army of friends, lovers, enemies. "That I ought to begin from the beginning, Benjamin. Make Billy Goforth up all over again."

"Got anythin' particular in mind?"

"Studied the law a long time ago. Thought I'd maybe take another shot at it. Become a lawyer."

"And turn the world over into some pure and perfect?"

"Maybe just my own small part of the world, just enough to keep folks riled up and a touch more honest than they would be otherwise. Hell, Benjamin, no harm in tryin' to make it pure and perfect. Never get there, I know that, but no harm in tryin'."

"Where you goin' to go to? After you become a genuine lawyer, I mean."

"Back here."

"And work for Mr. Nolan and them up on The Hill?"

"Not likely. Maybe raise a little hell here in town, kick up a ruckus now and again."

"Lawyers get rich and sassy and eat well."

Goforth laughed, not much amused. "All these years, Benjamin, I been goin' inside my head, haunted by my ghosts, collectin' my secrets, tryin' to understand what it's all about. The deeper I go, the smaller I get. Know what I always wanted to be, Benjamin? A hero is what. Don't that make you laugh?"

Benjamin frowned. "Best a man can hope for is to love his own self a bit and love somebody a little bit more, and give it all his best shot."

"You mean the poets are right, after all? That love does conquer all?" Goforth finished his beer and stood up, extended his hand.

Benjamin took it. "Maybe," the old man said in a flat voice. "Maybe, if you can love enough. . . ."

# CHAPTER
## 33

DUKE VENABLE GREETED Goforth with a scowl. The big fleshy hands curled into fists, the tiny eyes drew down to menacing slits, his pendulous underlip stiffened with annoyance.

"I am a busy man this mornin', Billy."

"It's about Kate Fellows."

"That is no business of your'n. The lady's done wrong and she's goin' to pay for it."

Venable hawked his throat clear but his voice remained hoarse. "You get on out of here and do whatever it is you supposed to be doin', Billy."

Goforth set his booted feet solidly. "No way I will let it happen, Duke."

Venable blinked as if struck. His breathing grew louder, a quick harsh intake. "You are beginnin' to get on my nerves," he said.

Goforth met Duke's gaze for a long time, until the big man shifted uncomfortably around in his chair.

"I told you I was busy, boy."

"I am about to pin that lard ass of yours to the wall, Duke."

Venable brought his huge hands down flat on the desktop. "Boy, you are askin' for all kinds of trouble."

"When it comes to law enforcement, you are useless, Duke. Two pounds of shit squeezed into a one-pound bag. You are rotten from the core out to the skin, always have been. I am here to wipe you up, to wipe you out. From now on, I call the shots, you hear me?"

"What the hell are you talkin' about?"

"Kate Fellows, for one."

"The lady is none of your affair."

"The hell you say. Dorr Seely's settin' up a loudspeaker system out front of the courthouse. Seems to me he's makin' Miss Fellows too damned much of his business."

"Stay clear of this, Billy. It don't concern you none. What is it, boy? You been gettin' some of that fancy nooky and it sticks in your craw that the lady ain't available anymore? I can understand that. Only it is over for her in this town, and don't you forget it."

Goforth leaned forward, fingertips resting lightly on the sheriff's desk, the far-seeing eyes polished and hard. "Duke, inside all that blubber, you got no real heart. You're a tough man among the pygmies. But you never went up against anybody like me, Duke. You know it, you lack the balls to take me on."

"Boy...!"

Goforth slammed his hand down hard on the desk and the sheriff jerked back as if struck. Goforth's teeth came into view; it was not a smile.

"Make one move, Duke, and I'll bust you up bad. If it comes to it, I'll blow you away."

Venable paled. His breathing turned harsh and sweat broke on his brow. "What in God's name are you after?"

"I want the woman."

"Kate Fellows? She's guilty as charged. Guilty and confessed to it."

"She's confessed to nothin'. I just came from her cell. I listened to her tell Mr. B. J. Moody what he could do with his

confession and when she was finished I escorted the good Dr.
Moody out the back entrance. . . ."

"You had no right . . ."

"So you see, Duke, no confession. Seems like the lady's
got a lot more belly than you give her credit for. She's goin'
to fight the lot of you."

"Fight! Shoot, man. Fight with what? She stands accused
and caught, witnesses and all. I have to, I'll take her to trial."

"She'll fight, and I'll help her. But there ain't goin' to be
a trial. The lady is innocent. . . ."

"The Peden boy will testify. . . ."

"No he won't. I paid that boy a visit. There's almost as
much water in his blood as there is in yours, Duke. No, no
trial. No witnesses. No testimony. Nothin' ever happened, the
boy is lyin' and you talked him into lyin'. That's a prosecutable
offense, Duke."

"Talk don't cut it. You ain't scarin' me none."

"The hell you say. You got no place to stand, Duke. Your
entire history is testimony to your duplicitous nature and the
corruption of the department by you."

"Watch your mouth, boy." It was said weakly, more out of
habit than conviction.

"It's ended, Duke. Over for you. I am goin' to spell it all
out so you know what you're dealin' with. Let's start with
Miss Ivy's place. You been takin' your piece of that action
from the start. In cash and in time with those girls of hers. To
hear Miss Ivy tell it, you get first turn on every new girl she
hires."

"That," Venable said huskily, "is a goddam lie and . . ."

"There's more, Duke. Bootleggin', for example. These days
Lonnie Peden is your carrier and it was Clyde Sims before him
and Ed Jack McKinnon before him. You provide the suppliers
and the outlets. Those after-hours clubs of yours. . . ."

"You can't prove a bit of it."

"You aim to put your future in Lonnie Peden's hands? Or
some of the others? I don't think so. And there's the oranges.
Gault oranges. Every box illegally picked and delivered for
shipment and run across the Gulf . . ."

"That's just blowin' smoke. . . ."

"Darryl Haynes and Mike Ray, the foremen out at the groves. Neither one of 'em is prepared to face hard time, Duke. They talked to me, they'll talk to anyone else pressures them. I got tape recordings and signed statements. Seems like some of those folks got the idea I was doin' an official investigation. . . ."

"You bastard, I'll—"

"Back off, Duke. We got even more important stuff to discuss. Warren Peden, to name one. Warren's been doin' rape and mayhem on the women around here and you turned him loose."

"No proof."

"The hell there ain't. Benjamin and me, we caught him in the act."

"Entrapment."

"Bullcrap, Duke. He jumped the Macklin girl."

"Ain't nobody goin' to take some nigger gal's word against a white boy. Anyway she's gone."

"Bought off by you, with money from The Hill."

"Who says? I ain't—"

"She *told* me, Duke. And it wouldn't be hard to track her down, bring her back."

Venable spread his hands, the fat face pale losing definition. "Now see here, Billy, why on God's earth would I want to go to all this trouble for Warren Peden? He don't mean diddly to me."

"Because he's Lonnie's brother and Lonnie belongs to you. You got to protect your own. Second, it gives you a perfect case against Kate Fellows. . . ."

"The woman corrupted the morals of a minor."

"Beautiful, the rapist as a victim, and you think you can make it stick."

Venable came halfway out of his chair. "Sure as hell can, if you get off my case, Billy."

"Warren's lyin'."

"Why should he?"

"Cause he's been told to, payment for gettin' out of the rape charges. And just like that you're servin' two masters—gettin' rid of Kate Fellows for Mr. Nolan. . . ."

"Why—?"

"Which brings us round to that pissant, Wesley. He was shackin' up with Kate Fellows and that put Mr. Nolan's nose out of joint. He wanted Wesley home with Mae-Mae makin' Gault babies and at the same time Reverend Seely gets a warm body to nail up on the cross of that Tenth Crusade of his'n. Very neat, and everybody's happy. Except Kate Fellows, and me."

"You can't prove a bit of it."

"Try this on, then—Jody Joiner."

Venable flinched. "Francine's daughter, that one?"

"The very one, Duke. She's goin' to have a baby, Duke. And guess who the daddy is? The very same Reverend Dorr C. P. Seely."

"I don't believe you."

"Now if I was to go out front, appropriate Seely's microphone for a while, tell the folks what's goin' on—that'd end Seely's hold on Kate Fellows, wouldn't it?"

"You ain't goin' to do that, are you, Billy?"

"It's in my head to do it. And afterwards, to call up the F.B.I. office up in Jacksonville, tell those Federal boys how Miss Fellow's civil rights have been violated, how the law is bein' twisted and misused by the sheriff here in King of Heaven. If I was to do that, Duke . . . well, with me testifyin' against you, you might just end up in a Federal jail cell."

"You're bluffin'."

"Am I? Duke, you got a lot to lose, and a lot to hide. There's that nice house of your'n up-county. Way overpriced for a man in your salary range. . . ."

"A man's entitled to his home."

"And that place of your'n down in Longboat Key—and the condos you own over on Padre Island. There's the shoppin' center in New Orleans and the retirement home in Lakeland, the rental units in Miami." Venable seemed to sink in on himself, head descending between those mountainous shoulders. "You got yourself a little ol' powerboat, you once told me. Only what you didn't say is that it is more like a yacht and cost nearly half a million dollars. Now I would not enjoy havin' to justify that kind of expenditure on a county sheriff's salary.

"Then there's that collection of antique cars in a warehouse down in Tampa—includin' a white Silver Cloud Rolls-Royce convertible with red leather hides. Folks tell me they made only about fifty of them babies and you own one in mint condition, which is very nice for you. You also got a little fleet of private cars all your own includin' two Buick wagons loaded for bear and a shiny new pickup."

"You been doin' a lot of snoopin'."

"I have never been the cop I might've been, Duke, but I ain't so dumb either. All these years, I been makin' notes to myself. I got names, dates, places. I got witnesses who ain't able to resist pressure.

"You're a confident man, Duke, doin' your own thing for a very long time without any questions. You're set in your ways and that builds up into a kind of arrogance and arrogant men always make mistakes. That's why crooks get caught, Duke. Isn't that what you used to tell me when I was startin' out? The bad guys always find a way to blow it, no matter how smart they are, no matter how careful. You left a wide trail, Duke, your mark is everywhere. Won't be hard for Internal Revenue to pick up that trail, find out exactly how much income tax you ain't paid. . . ."

Venable's breathing grew harsher, quicker, the round face mottled, the tiny eyes sunk back in among folds of fat. "I could have you killed. . . ."

"You can try, Duke," Goforth said, voice tinged with regret.

Time passed with neither man speaking, then Venable shifted his position in the chair, ponderous, burdened by his massive body, resigned.

"What exactly do you want, Billy?"

Goforth experienced no flush of victory, no joy, no great satisfaction. Only the anger remained, sharply focused, controlled, adding to his strength and his purpose. He regulated his breathing, forcing the tension out of his limbs. Only then, in a voice low and slow and charged with threat, did he provide an answer.

# CHAPTER
## 34

REVEREND DORR C. P. SEELY stood on the courthouse steps with upraised arm pointing steadfastly to the sky. Some in the crowd watching perceived in him the same immutable majesty as the burnished Robert E. Lee setting so proudly astride a bronze Traveler on the near edge of the square.

To Seely's right, a uniformed member of the Pioneers for Christ held aloft a huge cross made of balsa wood. Below Seely, a ring of photographers and television camera crews and reporters fanned out as if in obeisance, recording his every word and deed on tape and on paper for eventual dissemination to the faithful and to the wicked.

Said Seely in a thunderous voice to the crowd, "Why are we here?" He allowed no time for an answer. "We are gathered in an act of Christian charity and mercy, though our anger and disgust are profound and mighty.

"Let the wicked be on notice—Dorr Seely carries God's precious words to the faithful and to those who would be redeemed, those who can still be saved. To our enemies, the

Tenth Crusade will trample them into the dust. We shall show
no weakness, no compassion to those who oppose God's Divine
Will.

"Praise God."

"Praise God," they responded.

From behind the corner of the courthouse, Billy Goforth
and Kate Fellows appeared. They moved without haste, looking
straight ahead, making their way around the outer rim of the
crowd.

Seely raised one arm, tracking them as they went, as if
inviting them to join him. Until the realization broke that Goforth had no intention of delivering the woman into his hands.
Surprise was transformed into dark frustration and anger. The
hand was transformed into a fist, lifted high above his head.

"Listen to me!" he cried out. "I am sent like Jonah to protest
against evil. Like Jeremiah, I am commanded to root out, to
pull down, to destroy and to build and to plant.

"I stand against wickedness and evil. Against the unbeliev-
ers who dare work their anti-Christian wiles in the dark corners
of the world. I shall pull evil down, I shall stamp it into the
dust, I shall destroy it wherever it does its filthy work. Say
Amen."

"Amen," droned the crowd.

On the far reaches of the assemblage, Goforth and Kate
proceeded along the rim of the square toward the shopping
district, advancing under the great canopy of shade trees. All
eyes were turned their way, a dismayed murmur rising on the
thick morning air.

"Praise God!" Seely shouted to the sky. "For I am a prophet.
I am bold. I am strong. I will put it to you straight out. Look
at this fist: big enough to punch out Satan, I tell you. God has
blessed me with a body big enough and powerful enough to
conquer Satan. And a heart courageous enough to keep on
fightin' until victory is ours. And God's."

"I tell you, Dorr Seely's on the prowl. The Tenth Crusade
is on the march. Bang, bang. There go the bad guys, and you
better believe it."

Goforth and Kate kept walking. Seely's amplified voice,
mingling with the cawing of gulls circling overhead, caught
up.

"That female, that idolator, that adulteress, that pathetic creature of sin and mendaciousness has done evil. God forgive her. We forgive her in His name. She is weak and will one day comprehend the wrongness and destruction caused by her disgusting ways. . . ."

Kate stopped walking and turned to face Dorr Seely.

He flung a quivering finger in her direction. "She must be *punished*!"

"Keep on goin'," Goforth said, for her ears only.

She shook off his hand and moved forward, the crowd giving way before her. Seely, watching her come, glowed with anticipatory excitement.

"The Lord has delivered the Evil One into our hands!" he cried.

She kept advancing. Goforth trailed after her, alert to any threat.

At the foot of the platform, three steps brought Kate up alongside Dorr Seely. The unyielding expression of hatred and rage in her eyes surprised him and all color drained out of his face. He took a single step backward, caught himself and raised his hand as if to smite her. Before he could say a word, she spoke in a voice firm and laced with revulsion.

"What a hypocrite you are. A lying beast. Scum. Twisting the truth for your own selfish ends without consideration for who you might hurt, for the lives you might spoil. If there is indeed an anti-Christ, then he talks in your voice."

"Woman! You have lain with an innocent boy. . . ."

She swung her right hand with surprising force, catching him across the face. He staggered backwards, confused and abruptly afraid. "You disgust me," she bit off, words floating out to the crowd. "You disgust all decent people. You mock the word of God and betray the sacrifice of Jesus in your every action. Shame, shame, shame. . . ." Then she was gone, retracing her steps and passing through the crowd again, a crowd watchful and sullen, uncertain of how to respond. Goforth, at her shoulder, led her away from Courthouse Square, away from the oppressive silence, away from the staring empty eyes.

It took a minute for Dorr Seely to regain his composure, to work his way back to the microphone. He ached to charge in pursuit, to smash the woman and her protector into the ground, to deliver severe punishment for their transgressions against the Lord and the law. Against himself.

"Praise God," he said instead. "Praise God," he said in rolling sepulchral tones, and wondered what had gone wrong.

And the crowd answered him: "Praise God...."

Goforth stopped on the sidewalk outside the Trailways stop and faced Kate. "Well, it's all over. Just go on inside and buy yourself a ticket to wherever it is you're goin'."

She looked up into his crumpled face. "I owe you a great deal."

"Just doin' my job."

"Beyond the call of duty, as they say. You're a special man, Deputy."

He breathed out. "No different from you. Both of us are out of place in King of Heaven, it seems."

"A couple of misfits."

"Ain't that a fact. Tidyin' things up. Puttin' our pasts behind us, in a manner of speakin'."

"I still can't get used to the idea that I'm leaving this way. For a long time I figured teaching at Gault Christian, living in King of Heaven, that it was a lifetime contract."

"Appears to me as if nothin' is forever, Miss Fellows. You thought about where you're goin' to?"

"New York, at least for a while. I left some essential part of myself there and I need to find it again."

"You want to get back to actin', I reckon." His pale eyes searched her face.

"I'm not so sure anymore. Back in your jail, I had time to think. Maybe I'll write a play—try to, anyway. It's something I've carried around inside me for a very long time and never had nerve enough to try. Maybe now I do. Maybe now I can lay my ghosts to rest and become the woman I want to be." A quicksilver grin lit up her face, and as swiftly disappeared. "What about you, Deputy?"

"Me? Same as you—go on. Been playin' with the idea of finishin' up law school, doin' what I always wanted to do, be on the side of the law."

"That sounds good."

"If you ever need a lawyer..."

"I'll call you." She held out her hand and he took it. "You ever come up to the wicked city, you look me up."

"I might do just that. Good luck to you."

"And to you, deputy."

He watched her inside the bus station, skirt flaring around her strong legs, waited until she was out of sight. Then he turned back to the courthouse, to the sheriff's station, to talk to Duke Venable one last time. Walking faster, he took off his badge as he went.

# PAUL THEROUX

**"... will successfully startle you ... shock you ... impress you ... but never, never bore you!"***